THE
TRUTHSAYER'S
APPRENTICE

BOOK ONE OF THE LOREGIVER SERIES

DEBORAH CHRISTIAN

TOR®

A Tom Doherty Associates Book
New York

THE TRUTHSAYER'S APPRENTICE

Edited by Steven de las Heras

Design by Jane Adele Regina

Tor® is a registered trademark of Tom Doherty Associates, LLC.

ISBN 0-312-87269-0

First Edition: December 1999

Printed in the United States of America

This book was written during a very difficult time in my life. I dedicate it to those special persons who helped me get this project done and keep a vague semblance of sanity while doing so. My special thanks go to:

My late brother, Don Miller, who was extraordinarily proud of my writing. His final gift to me was a legacy that helped buy me writing time in which to complete this book.

Saphyre, for transformational alchemy and helping to keep me on track.

Amanda Burton, Susan Peacher, Jo and Ian, and Karen Hutchinson for helping to turn angst into creative energy.

My editor, Steve de las Heras, for forbearance and support above and beyond the call of duty.

My agent, Chris Lotts, for giving me some clues.

ACKNOWLEDGMENTS

Three role-playing gamers first breathed life into essential characters in this story. I thank Tina Estrada, Rich Bush, and Mike Wykes for the seed of inspiration that they planted, and offer a tip of the hat to the U.S. Bureau of Mines office in Reno, Nevada, for bringing us all together many years ago.

I am grateful to the World Design E-mail discussion list and its participants for inspiration and being a useful sounding board from time to time. I participate in that forum only fitfully, but it has provided a wealth of perspective and background information useful for serious world building, both for role-playing game purposes and for works of fiction inspired by same, such as this book is. For more info see: http://rider.wharton.upenn. edu/~loren/world-design.charter.html

A special thank-you goes to the authors who agreed to look at this manuscript on short notice. Your help was invaluable and much appreciated.

And as always, thanks to my lifelong cheering squad, my mother, Helen Christian.

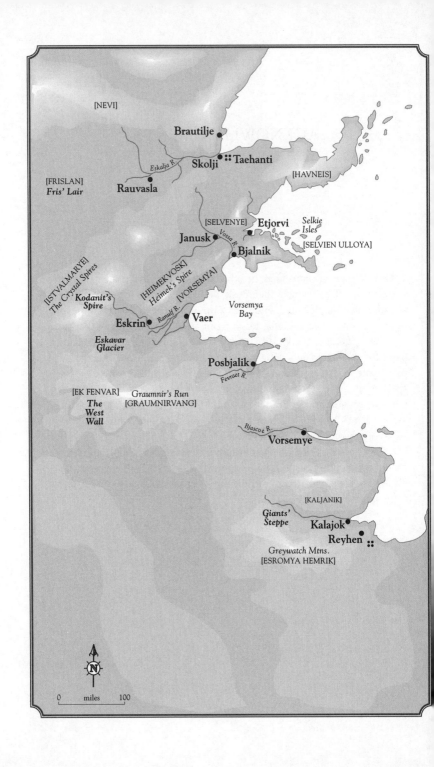

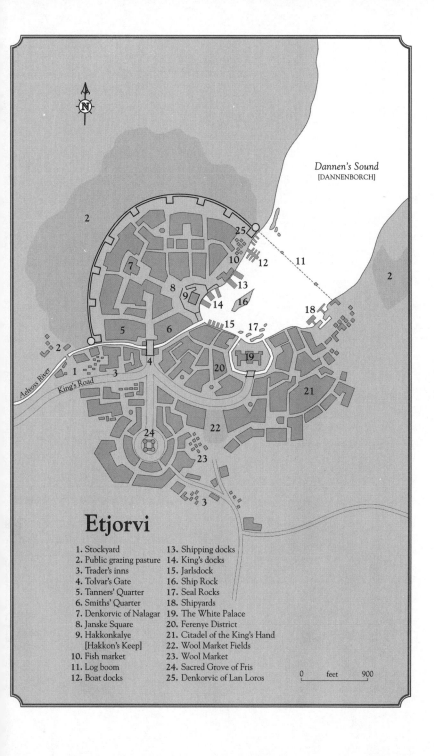

Dannen's Sound
[DANNENBORCH]

Etjorvi

1. Stockyard
2. Public grazing pasture
3. Trader's inns
4. Tolvar's Gate
5. Tanners' Quarter
6. Smiths' Quarter
7. Denkorvic of Nalagar
8. Janske Square
9. Hakkonkalye
   [Hakkon's Keep]
10. Fish market
11. Log boom
12. Boat docks
13. Shipping docks
14. King's docks
15. Jarlsdock
16. Ship Rock
17. Seal Rocks
18. Shipyards
19. The White Palace
20. Ferenye District
21. Citadel of the King's Hand
22. Wool Market Fields
23. Wool Market
24. Sacred Grove of Fris
25. Denkorvic of Lan Loros

0   feet   900

THE
TRUTHSAYER'S
APPRENTICE

CHAPTER 1

A BITING WIND fresh off the Spires caught the Truthsayer's apprentice where he huddled in the cavern mouth, awaiting his master's summons. Dalin wrapped his bearskin robe tighter against the wind and tucked his buckskin-covered legs closer to his chest. The numbness of ears and nose he had long since learned to ignore. As he stared out at the vista of snow-crusted rocky barrens before him, fine stinging ice crystals abraded his cheek on an errant blast of wind. He squinted eyes shut against the barrage and began to hum the Song of Waiting, rocking back and forth on his heels to the rhythm of the wordless chant.

Deeper inside the cave, down a twisting passage that cut the wind and channeled Dalin's chant to listening ears, the Truthsayer sat upon his dais before a fragrant fire. With a flick of the wrist the old man cast pine twigs and aromatic barks upon the coals for a third time, and a renewed swirl of smoke rose to wreath him in vision-bearing vapor. But the pictures he strove to see would not come: vague shapes and ominous glimpses played in the mystical smoke, diffused too easily by the breeze from the outside passage. What should have been clear forms were muddled images he struggled vainly to see. Granmar Truthsayer cursed and kicked out at the coals before him, scattering them beyond the stone firebed and across the cavern floor, then glared at the outside passage.

"Boy!" he shouted. "Come here!"

It was not the entranced or happy summons of the noble mystic that Dalin expected to hear. It roused him rudely from his patient chant and drove him stumbling on frost-numbed feet into the Truthsayer's cavern.

"Master?" he inquired, falling to his knees and bowing just short of the scattered coals.

Granmar turned a scowling eye on the youth cowed before him, son of his sister's son, his apprentice in lieu of the boy he had never taken time to father. Yet it was needful to carry on the tradition, was it not? There had never *not* been a Truthsayer, in all those long years since Kodanit first came from the skies, delivered by the gods to divine truth from lie among the Ice Tribes of Tura-kem.

Or perhaps that time was coming to an end, and the uncertainty of it fueled Granmar's anger anew. "I saw nothing!" the old man growled at Dalin. "Did you bring twigs from virgin trees, never used before for man's purposes?"

"Yes, Master!" Dalin nodded his head sharply.

"Are you certain?" Granmar demanded in an angry shout.

Dalin dared to look up from the floor. "Of course, Master. As you told me. I asked the trees first."

"And did they offer themselves—"

"—freely? Yes, Truthsayer. As you ordered."

Granmar glared at the youth sourly. "The barks? You got them from the red cedar? And the blackthorn?"

"Only the best pith, taken where no hurt would be done the tree."

Temper left the old man's face, and he slumped sitting onto the stone dais. He poked at the glimmering coals with the toe of his elkskin boot and heaved a sigh. Crossing wrinkled hands in his lap, his brows drew together and eyes almost closed as he contemplated the useless scrying fire before him.

Dalin watched his master as the Truthsayer studied the coals. Granmar's white hair strayed in scraggly clumps, his greasy black bearskin tunic barely visible behind the folds of the robe of office that he wore. The old man sat encompassed by the odd, square-cut robe many sizes too large for a man to wear, a sturdy work of red and white stripes and intricate patterning in brilliantly colored geometric designs. Dalin recalled Granmar's tale that the robe had once belonged to the frost giants of a far land; now it was the Truthsayer's cloak of office. Divination was never done without it.

For what that was worth. "I see nothing," the Truthsayer muttered, to himself and Dalin. "Yet still the dreams come, and the foreboding grows." He turned bright green eyes on his apprentice, the gaze of an elderly eagle awaiting a misstep from its prey. "Are you ready to begin your journey, then?"

Dalin swallowed. He had not thought it would come to this, so soon. Apprenticed to the Truthsayer, his granduncle, for little more than three years, Dalin had come to the Crystal Spires as honored offering among an escort of kinfolk and highland warriors. They had not trusted him, a boy of twelve, to find his own way over glacier and barrens to the home of the fabled Truthsayer, and though in fancy Dalin had made that trip many times, in reality he wondered a little if he truly could have managed on his own. To have his first snow-lion kill behind him was one thing; to path-find through wilderness, another.

Granmar did not ask if Dalin would, or could, find his way back through barrens and glacier. He demanded that his apprentice go, and that was an end of it.

"Don't forget the waybread," Granmar told him unthinkingly, launching once again into his rote list of cautions and reminders. "The rawhide rope I gave you already, did I not? . . . Hmm." The old man shrugged off the Truthsayer's robe and began to fold it, its brightly colored weave somehow untarnished by time and the touch of many hands. "And I told you how to find the freehold at the foot of Eskavar glacier. It's longer around, but safest down. Avoid the Ranulf—the river makes the ice run rotten; you'll fall in a crevasse and never be seen again . . ."

Granmar continued his litany of travel precautions. Dalin nodded and grunted assent without listening as he picked up and stored the barks and colored, powdered stones the Truthsayer had arrayed for scrying. He didn't think of the way down the mountain and didn't think of Granduncle's many-times-repeated instructions; the time to worry about that would be when he did it—he, Dalin, a hunter's son from Nevi Freehold, ice-tribesman in name but not proven yet, like his father, his older brothers, his kin. Not trusted to come here on his own, and never trusted by Granmar to leave, not once, not for provisions or trade goods, or to trap snow hares any farther away than the tree line at the edge of the lower Spires.

". . . remember, don't you?"

"Master?"

"Foolish boy!" Granmar clenched a fist, waved it in his direction. "You remember why you're going, don't you? What you have to do for me, yes?"

He ducked his head hastily. That was one thing he daren't ignore, when Granduncle spoke of it. "Of course, Truthsayer." Dalin used the title of respect. "I'll fetch the runemaster."

"Hmmph." Granmar turned back to his robe of office, lifted it in his arms to carry into the inner caverns and the chest where it was stored. "You do that. Fetch the runemaster. We'll see why that travel rune no longer works for me. And a few other things."

Dalin nodded agreement and went about his chores as the seer left the chamber. It was unsettling, indeed, that the travel rune had suddenly ceased its magic. How long it had been that way the Truthsayer did not know, although when Granmar had tried to use it a seven-day ago, to answer a dream-call from the King in Etjorvi, the rune had remained but lifeless marks in stone in one of the inner chambers. After it was invoked, there was no flare of magic, no transposition in space—just silence and a look of surprise on the Truthsayer's face that would have been comical had the implications not been so dire. For without the travel rune, both seer and apprentice were virtually stranded in the Crystal Spires, isolated from the world by the same rugged, treacherous terrain that kept curiosity seekers far distant.

Supplies were already running low, and in the course of this month the summer warmth of the lowlands, though not obvious in the glacial peaks, would rot the ice and loosen the snow and make travel through the Spires more hazardous than any other time of year. If provisions were to be fetched—or a runemaster summoned to fix the travel rune—the time to do so was now, before a journey posed more hazard than it did benefit. Granmar, hobbled by age, could not go. Dalin was committed to the trek that lay before him.

CHAPTER 2

Next morning the Truthsayer's apprentice departed, with a final recital of cautions resounding in his ears. He paused a last time at the foot of the trail to the seer's cave and waved his walking stick at Granmar, watching stolidly from the cavern mouth. Then Dalin turned, warm in his bearskins and leathers, and trotted down the well-worn path toward the base of the Middle Spire.

The apprentice knew this part of the trail well, at least. It led to the tree line and rocky slopes where he spent much time gathering obscure plants and talking with trees, as Granmar had taught him. The path was clear and open. Dalin descended it in less than an hour and stopped to look back up at the Spires, the bold basalt and frozen obsidian peaks that had sheltered him during his time with the Truthsayer of Tura-kem. Although a bit reluctant to be completely on his own in unknown woods, Dalin felt no hesitation at leaving what had been his only home for the last three years. *This little adventure came just in time,* he thought. *I've wanted to go farther afield, and now I can. Granduncle has no choice but to let me.*

The failure of the travel rune was none of his work, though more than once he had thanked the gods that it had ceased to function. Granmar was certain it portended something ill. Dalin was not so sure of that. So far it had worked to his benefit.

The youth resettled his pack on his shoulder, turned back to the woods—and froze where he stood. To the northeast, through spindly lodgepole pine stunted by altitude, he glimpsed the movement of dark figures. Men or creatures, whatever they were, should not be here unannounced by bird or tree, and so far Dalin had heard no warning of intruder or welcome visitor from the woods around him.

Dodging nimbly through the trees to get a better look, the Truthsayer's apprentice paused at the edge of the woods. The figures were men, certainly, emerging from the tree line and already following the lesser-used trail to the Middle Spire. There were five of them, lowlanders in thick fur cloaks and felted trousers, bows slung on backs and heads hidden in hoods that sheltered them from the icy blasts from the heights. They moved rapidly and with purpose, studying the crags ahead of them, clearly intent on their destination.

Dalin thought to hail them, then bit the words back. Why had the trees not whispered of their coming? He set his hand on the trunk of a scragglepine, the stunted spruce relative that dwelled with the lodgepole, and felt no murmur of plant consciousness. This was wrong! Dalin went next to a lodgepole, then to another. The woods were unnaturally silent, stifled as if they slept in the deepest winter freeze.

He turned a suspicious look on the strangers—no, intruders—clambering the steeper trail that led to Granmar's cave. Without the travel rune, the Truthsayer had no quick escape should these people wish him ill—and the unnatural silence of the wood boded nothing but. And there had been the old man's dreams, of late. . . .

I must return, Dalin thought. But how?

The youth studied the path. The one he had come down, the easier descent, was long and circuitous, skirting the foot of the Middle Spire in easy loops. The intruders took the trail that mountain goats used, the steep and scrambly bits hindering them little as they made their surefooted way up it. Though they dressed like lowlanders, it was clear that they had mountain experience. But for Dalin there was no shorter way he could take to beat them, except for straight up the cutting, flaky sides of the Spire. Even if he could manage that route, they would surely see him.

Dalin cursed, dropped his pack beneath a tree, and shed his bearskin cloak. Turning to retrace his steps, he sprinted back up the switchback path, feet pounding over the trail he had so easily descended just minutes before. Unencumbered by robe and pack, he made far better time than on an ordinary ascent—yet he judged where the others must be, out of sight around the curve of the spire, and he spurred himself to new speed. Breath began to burn in his lungs as he ran up and up—and slowed, inevitably, as the footing became looser scree and the slope grew steeper.

This was the last part, the slowest part, before he would round the Spire's skirt and come once again within sight of the cave. Dalin dug in with the end of his walking stick, poling himself uphill with a shove, then another. He came in view of the cave just as the last bit of a stranger's furred cloak disappeared inside.

Dalin halted, undecided, sucking great breaths in through open mouth.

He welcomed the freezing wind off the peak, a cooling blast to ease his over-heated body—but in the moments of his indecision the cool turned to biting cold, and he began to shiver on the trail. Five strangers, come unbidden, the silence in the woods—everything about this cried out Danger!—and Dalin wanted to help Granmar yet didn't see how he could. What could he do against five men, a boy unarmed but for his staff and sling and snares? Still, he couldn't stand out here and let Granduncle be hurt or threatened. The Truthsayer had plenty of tales of people who had come demanding knowl-edge or magic the seers were unable to give and how they had been magi-cally thwarted and driven away. Then again—if the travel rune didn't work, what else didn't work?

Dalin had gathered himself and started upslope when the unthinkable happened. Two men appeared again at the lip of the cave, Granmar caught between them. The old man struggled and called out imprecations; unheed-ing, the hooded strangers hauled back in unison and pushed forward at once. Their hands flew open, and Granmar, cast over the edge, plummeted down the slope of scree and obsidian, striking stone and tumbling out of control down the skirt of the Spire. As the Truthsayer fell to his death on splintered crags far below, the wind carried cruel laughter to Dalin's ears. The men turned and went back inside the seer's cave.

Transfixed by horror, the young apprentice crouched behind a rock, not daring to advance, unwilling to retreat. He waited with stiffening muscles until the men came out of the cave again, this time bearing the chest that held the Truthsayer's robe. Cautious of their burden, they chose the longer route down, and Dalin, barely able to move his cold-clutched limbs, slith-ered out of sight behind boulders dangerously downslope of the path. Un-heeding of cuts razor-sharp obsidian sliced in his hands, he stayed there, carefully balanced with a deadly fall at his back, as killers walked by single-file on the path.

"Easy pickings, hey, Joro?" One carrying the chest called to the man who led them.

"Almost too easy," agreed the man, bundled in his cloak of green wool.

A yellow-bearded fellow snorted in the rear. "Surprise visits are the best, I think."

No Turakemi thieves, these: the men spoke in the short, clipped accents of Nimm across the great bay, a tone Dalin had heard imitated by storytellers back home. They laughed and walked on past down the trail. Before they were too long gone, Dalin collected himself from his hiding place and, suck-ing at the cuts on his palms, followed them down the mountain.

CHAPTER 3

Nᴜᴍʙᴇᴅ ʙʏ ᴡʜᴀᴛ he had just witnessed, Dalin followed the strangers by reflex alone, falling instinctively into the rhythms of the stalk. Using all the caution he would were he tracking a mountain lion, the youth followed neither closely nor too far behind. He trailed the murderous thieves down the flank of the Spire and into the shelter of the high alpine woods. He darted aside to recover his cloak and pack, then followed them into the lodgepole pine. The sparse trees offered so little cover that Dalin adopted the pose his father called Bear Cub Scurries. The scuttling crouch blended into terrain and saved the young woodsman from the need to throw himself to the ground the few times the yellow-bearded man in the rear glanced behind.

When Dalin saw Granmar falling in his mind's eye, he felt tears start to well up. He brushed them from his lids and smothered his sorrow with rage against the murderers he followed. He kept his attention on the trail, then, so as not to be distracted by thoughts and emotions. *Just watch where you tread,* he told himself, *and see there, mind you step on the gravel so it doesn't crunch. Mark their path by that crushed lichen on the rocks underfoot. . . .*

They're easy to follow. They don't expect pursuit, that's clear. They make no attempt to hide their path.

What would he do when he caught up with them? That thought he put from his mind. Maybe nothing, now. Yet. First, see where they're going. Learn who they are. Maybe they would head for Eskavar, too. No freehold was close to the Spires. The trails down out of the peaks were few and led near only a couple of settlements. It shouldn't be hard to tell where they were headed once they were under way.

That line of thought was optimistic enough, it seemed to Dalin—and almost enough to get him killed, for thinking it, he scuttled in the rolling, ground-hugging Bear Cub gait around a small, rocky hillock and right into a horse's head, impaled and stinking on a wooden pole driven into the ground.

Dalin gave a strangled yelp and staggered backward, gagging. Then, realizing the noise he had made, he dashed farther back into the woods and cast himself to the dirt behind a scraggle-pine. Just in time, too: the murmur of men's voices greeted his ear as two figures came to investigate from beyond the stake and its gruesome burden.

It was Yellow-beard, the rear guard, and the one they'd called Joro. Skirting the noisome carcass, they moved cautiously into the trees, eyes scanning the ground and searching between pines for sign of an intruder. Dalin lay motionless and knew that his bearskin cloak would be visible to Joro as soon as that man walked forward another few paces.

The Truthsayer's apprentice closed his eyes and held his breath, not daring to duck his head or change the angle of any limb. Instead, he reached out with his second sense to the tree against whose sturdy root he lay and let himself go as quickly as ever he had, blending his thoughts and consciousness with those of the tree, pulling its plantlike energies to him. His thoughts stilled, his heartbeat slowed, as a stoic gentleness fell over him, the patience to probe the cracks of rocks slowly, to explore thin soils and catch the sunlight of summer upon needle and twig, a sturdy sapling growing next its parent—

The work of illusion was done in time, the Tarn magic that let one blend into natural surroundings undetectably. Joro walked past a pine and its sapling offshoot and continued for a few feet more.

"I don't see anything," the man ventured. "Sounded like a fox bark to me."

"This high up?" Yellow-beard replied.

Joro shrugged. "There's nothing here. Come on, Aral. The skenjis keeps us safe. We've more important things to do."

His companion shrugged; not seeing anything out of the ordinary, the pair turned and walked back around the outcropping to their camp.

"The skenjis keeps us safe. . . . The words echoed in Dalin's head as he lay cloaked in illusion, maintaining rapport with the tree longer than was necessary. He took the time to think about what he had just heard. So that was the revolting talisman he had confronted so unexpectedly. He had heard of a skenjis but never seen one before: a powerful magic token set to wish ill and cast bad luck upon a hated enemy. He raised his head from where it was cradled on his arm and peered past the tree trunk to the decaying horse's head. Yes, there, on the stake that held it up: runes of defeat and ill will, to Dalin's eyes subtly aglow with the baleful red-orange light of magic fueled by

hatred. The horse's head gazed sightlessly upslope, looking toward the Middle Spire that was the Truthsayer's home. Was this why Granmar's magic had failed? Dalin thought it likely. It was foreign ignorance that assumed the token also lent protection: any Turakemi knew it did not. A skenjis offered only bane and grim fate for the enemy it was created for.

His blood ran cold to think someone hated the Truthsayer enough to death-wish him. He let the tree-seeming slip from his form and crept softly forward once more. With a sign of warding for the evil thing that he skirted, Dalin climbed the rocky outcrop that flanked the foreigners' camp. Bracing himself carefully near the top, he peered over lichen-speckled granite to spy upon the camp below.

It was a cold camp, concealed in a hollow, obviously the place they had spent the night and from whence they'd marshaled their attack on the Truthsayer. On the far side of the clearing, the raiders prepared to leave. One portly man with wavy brown hair and a slender one in a gray-green cloak saddled riding horses beneath the spare-needled branches of black lodgepole. Aral Yellow-beard and a woman struggled to secure the unwieldy stolen chest atop the goods on a pack mule. The youth frowned as he watched. A woman? With her hood up, he had not glimpsed her face before, not realized her gender. With her face revealed, there seemed something odd about her. Her hair, so lightly tow-colored as to appear white, was caught back in a long braid that hung to her waist. There was a strange slant and curve to her eyes, and the tips of her ears looked almost pointed. Suddenly it registered what he was seeing, and Dalin's eyes widened in surprise. This must be one of elvish blood! Winter tales about the ice-elves of the great northern glaciers sprang to mind. This intruder could not be one of those, for her hair was not silver and her height lesser than what Turakemi elves should be. Still, an elf . . .

Disturbing, that a woman of whatever race should involve herself with a brutal venture like this. It said much—or little—of the men who would let her join them.

Then his eye was drawn by Joro, crossing the clearing to talk with another man who sat below and to the left of Dalin's perch. The seated one was Turakemi, no doubt, for his blond braid and long mustaches marked him a native, and the red beadwork on his tunic suggested the highland tribes of the Havneis. As the man gestured in conversation, his sheepskin cloak fell away from his arm, revealing a blue-and-black tattooed pattern across the back of his right hand. Dalin knew with a certainty that this must be the runemaster who had set up the cursed skenjis, who had focused ill wish and evil on the Truthsayer.

Was he a renegade, then? What runemaster would work in foreign pay, to death-wish for worldly gain? Dalin shook his head: such a thing didn't seem possible. Was it a man, then, who had reason to hate Granmar personally? Many times men were angered by the Truthsayer's verdicts, for the truth did not always favor petitioners in their petty schemes, and Granmar, like his predecessors, often sat at the right hand of the Selkie King in Etjorvi, dispensing justice. An act of revenge? Of theft? The thieves securing the carved cedar chest were taking away the robe of office of the Truthsayer—and without it, Dalin suspected, it might not be possible to *know* the truth in that unerring way that made the seer adviser to kings. And now, there was no more Truthsayer. Just a partly trained apprentice, who was watching his future being stolen away.

Dalin swallowed as the thought struck home. He knew in that moment that it was not enough to follow these thieves and murderers—if he could, they mounted and he on foot. He must also retrieve what was rightfully his. *And how am I to do that? As easily bring them to justice—then I can claim the Robe as my own. But I am one, they are six . . .*

And the less he knew about them, the less effective he would be against them. *"Know your quarry,"* his father had often said. Time, then, to find out more about this quarry. Dalin climbed back down the rock, moving silently as only a Nevi hunter could, and crept within earshot behind a boulder at the edge of their camp.

It was the runemaster he heard speaking first, a gravelly baritone without the odd foreign accents of the intruders. ". . . no need for such haste," he was saying. "Bide awhile, and let me see the robe. I'll tell you if you have the right one."

An undisguised snort was his answer. "It was the only one there. It fits the description. You'll see it when we return you to Etjorvi, as we agreed, and not before."

"Nevertheless, there might be—"

"Might be some other reason you want to delay on this forsaken mountainside? Why, Hanno? We have what we came for. We're leaving, now. There's nothing to be gained by staying here any longer."

Amulets clinked as the runemaster shook his head. "I've sensed something . . . some magic astir in the woods. I don't know if it's safe to travel. Let me scry."

"Kaylis has done that for us already, and she reports no hazard."

"Nimmian spell-casting." Hanno spat on the ground. "I speak of a nature force, a quality in the heart-throb of tree and stone. Not something your citified magic would detect."

Anger gathered in the runemaster's voice, and Dalin could well understand why: no one spoke to a runemaster in this way. To interrupt, to deny his advice. The Truthsayer's apprentice wondered what kind of barbarians these Nimmians were, to treat a runemaster so lightly.

"That's as may be," Joro said, ignoring the danger signs. "If you want to return to court and advise your king once more, you'd best prepare to leave here. Your work is done. Ours is just beginning. We have a ship to meet, and you have to get us there."

Silence greeted the man's statement. He rose to his feet, dusted off his russet trousers, and rejoined his companions without a further word.

Dalin flattened himself to the ground as the raider chief walked away, and Hanno began a low-pitched muttering of self-complaint. The words were too low to make out, and Dalin cautiously eased back from his listening post and moved a ways into the woods.

There was danger here. The stirring the runemaster had sensed in the woods could well have been the Tarn magic that had sheltered the apprentice from enemy eyes. If Hanno scried him out in spite of Joro's command, Dalin would be caught as surely as if he had walked right into their midst. The safest concealment for him now, then, would be a natural one. Upslope a short distance was ground broken by boulders the size of a shepherd's lean-to. Moving into their midst, Dalin still had the barest glimpse of packhorses in the clearing. It was sufficient for now. The Truthsayer's apprentice settled down to watch and think.

Immediately his thoughts went back to that brief phrase from Joro: *"If you want to return to court and advise your king once more . . ."* That put him in mind of several tales Granmar had told over the years: of corrupt judges and self-serving advisers, their machinations revealed by the Truthsayer working at the King's request. The wrongdoer suffered shame, loss of office, and sometimes criminal punishment. Those incidents were rare, of course, for as long as the Selkie Kings had sat on the throne of Tura-kem a Truthsayer also stood ready to advise, reconcile differences, and point out falsehood and deceit. With such a ready safeguard against deception, few of the day-to-day advisers at court tried it. Those who dared were exceptionally clever and ambitious, or very stupid.

Hanno did not appear to be stupid. Could he have been one of the clever ones, caught out in duplicity of some sort by the Truthsayer's magical insights? If Hanno hoped to advise the King once more, it couldn't have been too disastrous a thing that drove him from court. A mere suspicion could suffice. Dalin frowned, searching memory for any mention Granmar might have made of one pushed from court though not caught in blatant wrongdoing—for then it would be impossible to return to King Hammankarl's inner circle at all. But it was fruitless. Dalin could recall nothing that might relate to a disaffected runemaster. Maybe Hanno was someone Granmar had dealt with before he'd taken an apprentice. The youth shook his head and wished for some scrying skill of his own.

He looked back toward the clearing and sat up in surprise. The riding horses had already left, and he caught only the flick of the last pack mule's tail as it followed behind. Dalin gritted his teeth and cursed himself for woolgathering at a time like this. It seemed Granmar's old complaint was justified. Swallowing past the lump in his throat, the youth slipped out of his rocky nest and edged past the clearing. Hanno was gone as well, and the jingle of bridle and bit clearly heralded which way the party traveled through the woods.

There were no regular trails though this part of the woods, just tracks made by deer and reindeer, and it was one such that the strangers followed now. Staying many yards upslope and to the rear of them, Dalin followed the party from a safe distance. The youth knew that his passage was not as silent as it would be were he to follow on the animal path itself, for paralleling their course he was forced to step through beds of ancient pine needles and scramble over patches of treacherous small boulders. Yet any small sounds he made would be obscured by the louder noise of the raiders' own travel: the creaking of harness leather, the thunk of hoof against rock, the snap of twig and needle underfoot.

Trusting to his woods experience, Dalin pursued as closely as he thought wise. The strangers kept their mounts to a walk, and as long as they did so, a comfortable pace kept them just in sight through the trees. The raiders did not leave the path, and though Yellow-beard dropped back now and then to survey the trail behind them, he failed each time to spot Dalin, blending motionless into the soil and black tree trunks in his dark fur cloak.

It was all the more stunning, then, when the runemaster appeared without warning, materializing from thin air at the edge of a gully not twenty feet ahead of Dalin. Hanno laughed at the startlement on the youth's face and tossed a stone almost leisurely at his feet. It was not an ordinary stone, he saw too late: the bit of rock flipped end over end, revealing a yellow rune inscribed and stained on its surface. Dalin had time enough to gather himself in alarm before the rune stone hit the ground before him and a brilliant sunbright flash of light exploded around him.

Blinded by the light and smitten by a supernatural force that deadened his hearing, Dalin was thrown back hard against the ground. With the wind knocked out of him, he lay stunned by the blast and the impact, unable to fight off hands that rolled him onto his face as he struggled to draw air into paralyzed lungs. Cruelly and efficiently his arms were bound with leather thongs. A foot rolled him roughly onto his back as he gasped for breath.

Someone knelt beside him—the runemaster, Dalin knew. He could feel a hand on his chest, pinning him to the ground. A voice murmured a question he couldn't make out, seeming distant although coming from the man next to him. Dalin opened his eyes and saw only a white haze that held no suggestion of form. The haze hurt, and he clenched lids shut again as tears welled up with the pain.

The voice came again, more distinct this time as the ringing lessened in his ears.

"Who are you?" Hanno demanded faintly.

Dalin shook his head in angry defiance and suddenly felt a knife blade sharp against his throat.

"Let me put this another way." The runemaster spoke patiently, as if from a great depth. "Answer my questions, or I have no reason not to kill you where you lie. Will you talk?"

Carefully, Dalin nodded. Jagged rocks pressed painfully into his arms and back, made worse as Hanno shoved against his laboring chest. The runemaster didn't shift his weight or move the knife from where it touched the young man's throat.

"Good. Who are you?"

"Dalin of Nevi."

"That tells me nothing, Dalin of Nevi. Why are you following us?"

Several responses played in Dalin's mind, then the picture of Granmar falling to his death intruded again, and he could not measure his words or his answer. "You killed my master!" he blurted, then clenched his jaw, regretting what he had revealed with that one statement.

"Ah, ha!" The blade caressed his throat less closely, and Hanno was silent for a moment. Then he questioned his captive again. "You are what? Servant to Granmar?"

Was the question meant to trick? Or did Hanno truly not know that Granmar had an apprentice? Not many did, except for Nevi villagers. If word had not traveled to the Havneis, whence Hanno appeared to come, then it could be he was truly ignorant.

I've seen how ready they were to kill the Truthsayer. Surely they would be as ready to kill his apprentice.

Those considerations took only a moment. "Yes, his servant," lied the Truthsayer's apprentice. "I saw him falling. . . ."

He could feel the runemaster shrug, take a noncommittal tone. "An unfortunate accident. Not planned, I assure you. And what did you hope to accomplish by following us, Dalin Serf?"

Dalin swallowed back anger. Obviously he was no serf, a bondsman sentenced to servitude until some debt, civil or criminal, was worked off. He did not wear the iron collar of the serf, and bore his clan signs in the beadwork of his leather tunic, something no serf was permitted to do. The runemaster was insulting beyond belief, but Dalin was playing for his life here. He ignored the remark and answered the question.

"I couldn't stay with the Truthsayer. We've little food here. I was sent to fetch some. You were going downmountain, the same way I need to go. It was chance."

"Tsk, tsk. You are not a convincing liar. You needn't follow us in order to go downmountain." The knife left his throat as Hanno rifled through the small pack Dalin carried. The runemaster considered for a bit. "Hmm. Perhaps I am mistaken. You are ready for a little journey, are you not? Snares. Tinder. Waybread. Well, no matter."

He closed the flap of the pack and removed his hand from the youth's chest. "Let me tell you something, Dalin Serf. Your master was a lying, conniving bastard and deserved his death. You, I don't care about. Now, if my friends knew you were here, they'd probably slit your throat for the fun of it. Still . . . you're a countryman, of a sort, and they aren't. I care only that you not follow us, and you're not going to."

Hanno rose to his feet and regarded the bound figure before him. "The Sunburst rune I greeted you with: its effects were noticed only by you. The others continue down the trail and leave me to my scouting. Your vision will return. Probably. I'm not sure when. That depends on you. Meanwhile, you won't need this." He stooped and pulled Dalin's knife from his belt and threw it far away on the mountain slope, into a field of treacherous scree. Small rocks slid loose and bounded down the mountain, a cascade too faint for Dalin's damaged ears to perceive.

"I'm leaving you here like this. I suggest you don't try to walk or stumble too far—you know the slope is dangerous, and if you lose your footing, there's no telling what rock you'll bash your brains out against. Am I right?" He prodded Dalin's jaw with a toe until the youth nodded agreement. "It's not freedom, exactly; then again, it's not death, either. Yet, anyway. If the gods smile on you, no wolf will find you, and eventually you may work your way back to Kodnanit's Spire. I'd guess there's a knife there or something else you can free yourself with. Now, I bid you farewell. If you follow again, my friends will have your head."

Hanno walked away, his footsteps fading too rapidly in the muffled distance. Dalin strained his arms against the bonds then, only to hear a last word from the runemaster. "I wouldn't try that. You're tied with a Geffian knot. It grows tighter with struggles. I've seen a man lose circulation and his hands get the green-rot that way."

Dalin ceased his efforts and lay still, panting as he broke out in a cold nervous sweat.

"Enjoy the day," Hanno wished him. It seemed he heard the taunting laughter long after the runemaster had returned to the trail.

CHAPTER 4

THE TRUTHSAYER'S APPRENTICE lay on the rough ground, arms pinned beneath him, elbows bound close together. His shoulders were beginning to cramp with the unwonted strain. He cracked his eyes open, and vague shadows swam out of the blinding white haze around him—treetops, perhaps—but the pain forced him to close his tearing lids again before anything came into focus.

Blind, bound, out of reach of help—Dalin squelched the panic that threatened to rise up inside and concentrated instead on calming his too-rapid breathing. *You can do it,* he told himself. *"The first step to self-control is control of the breath." Father and Granmar both told me that, though I didn't see the point of it when I was young. Without the right breathing, an arrow won't fly true, and shape-illusions won't form. All right. Without the right breathing, I won't get out of this.*

It was working, then, long practice taking over. He filled his lungs slowly and deeply, held the air for a count of three, expelled it as slowly, and forced the last of it from his lips like coin measured from a purse. Again. Again. Gradually the nervous panic subsided, his cramping shoulders eased a little, and he could think more clearly than in the fright-driven moments just past.

With newfound confidence, Dalin sat up, heaving himself forward so his body no longer lay atop his tightly bound arms. Dizziness swept over him and for a moment it was hard to keep his balance—he was sitting cross-slope, and the weight of his torso leaned unexpectedly to the right and downhill. He slid a leg hastily to that side to brace himself, scrapping buckskin through gravel, and wrenched a muscle in his back as he kept himself upright by brute force. A picture of himself off-balance and tumbling blindly downhill flashed through his mind. He put the image out of his head and quieted his pounding heart with more steady breathing.

He swung himself about so his legs pointed downhill and his leather-booted heels dug into the rocky soil for purchase. It would be easier to keep his balance when he stood. *But before I stand, where will I go?* He tried to recall the terrain he had just passed through, and parts of it came back to him with great clarity: broken boulders that could catch a foot and break an ankle if he lost his balance; a knee-high snag that could trip him in midstep and dump him headfirst into jagged deadwood branches; flakes and pebbles of rock, massing into a field of scree slick as ice and ready to pitch him off the mountain in the same wise as Granmar.

They were all obstacles a sighted and woodswise man could pass with little or no difficulty. Obstacles that could kill a blind man without arms for balance and senses to find the subtle path home.

Dalin remained sitting. *I have two choices. I sit here until my eyesight returns, and hope no wolf or mountain lion finds me if I have to wait through the night. Or I walk home blind—and I don't think I can make that.*

And if your sight doesn't return, he argued with himself, *then you are hungrier and weaker and near-frozen if you wait overnight. And then you still have to find your way home blind. . . .*

The youth sat, undecided. Neither alternative was appealing. And in either case he remained bound. Already the feeling was gone from his hands and lower arms. Now, *that* was something to be immediately concerned about. If he could free himself, it would pass the time until his sight returned; if not, at least he would have tried and known it not possible. It was easier to contemplate a stumbling trek back to the Spire when he knew there was no other choice.

How can I do this? Dalin frowned in concentration. His best dagger was tossed away like an old bone by the runemaster, his walking stick—dropped somewhere nearby—offered no help, and the meager items in his pack even less. Perhaps a jagged stone could cut the thongs. . . . He shook his head angrily as he discarded that idea. Already he had waited too long. His hands and fingers were so deadened he could no longer feel them and had no hope of holding or identifying a rough-edged rock.

He would have slumped, if his restraints had permitted it. Dalin sat on the mountainside, only a kind of mental quietude holding despair at bay. The freezing winds from the heights infiltrated his tunic where his bulky fur cloak gaped open. Sweat turned icy where it chilled on his chest and ribs. A boulder fell crashing from one of the spires, bringing smaller pebbles and a clatter of rocks leaping in its wake. Dalin tensed automatically, feeling hairs rise on his neck in an atavistic sharpening of senses. The rockfall passed harmlessly to the north, far to his left. No cause for concern, this time.

Yet the longer he remained here, the more rockfalls would pepper the slopes. The weather would turn freezing at night. Wild creatures would roam the mountainside. "I can't just sit here!" Dalin berated himself out loud. *I have to do something. But what?*

Schemes and manic wishes passed through his mind, each rapidly discarded. He couldn't fly; he couldn't snap his bonds; Granmar wouldn't come back to rescue him. Dalin realized coldly that if he could not help himself, no one else would. He was likely to die right there on the slopes of the Truthsayer's Spire from exposure or accident—

He kicked himself for envisioning any such thing. "Remove that thread from the loom of fate," he chanted three times aloud, banishing the thought from his mind and the listening multiverse. Then he focused solely on his dilemma.

First free your arms. What can cut these ties? No knife. No rock. Have flint in tinderbox, can't hold it. . . . Need something sharp.

He reviewed his small knowledge of magic, enchantments and dweomers learned from the Truthsayer. Nothing there to manifest a blade. No way to free bindings. Only spells to blend with rock and tree, to talk with small creatures—

Small creatures. Like birds and mice. Even up here, in the rocky heights, mice lived, burrowed amongst the needle pack and tree roots, the sometimes-prey of hawks and forest wolves. A mouse summoning he could do, had done, many times before, though only to carry messages to and from Granmar as a learning exercise. To persuade it to nibble on the thongs that captured his arms—was that possible?

I'll make it possible, Dalin promised himself as he lay down again, this time on his side, so that a bespelled mouse might reach his bonds. Once again the breathing exercise, now intended to put himself into the spellchanter's trance, and a mumbling, wordless hum began to come from his mouth. Small sounds, like mice: a chitter, a crunching of nut, the luring murmur of burrowmates. . . . The magic twined itself into a summoning thread, blended with the downslope skirls of wind, wove between the trunks of trees along the deer path, and sought out a single mouse, just leaving its needle-shadowed burrow tens of yards from where Dalin lay on the rocky slope.

The Truthsayer's apprentice had no way of knowing when his call was heard. In the way of small summonings he could only continue until it was answered, or until he grew tired, or until the magic wore itself out and danced on the wind no more. So he mumbled and chittered and chanted bits of earth-song on the mountainside, and slowly, with many deviations from a straight path, one curious mouse came to investigate what called so irresistibly from uphill.

Dalin first knew his summoning was answered when an inquiring chit-ter from the rocks before him echoed a chirp of his own. In surprise he forced open his eyes, gummy and crusted shut from tearing. The world was returning in shades of brown and gray and hazy blue, though he still could not distinguish the small figure before him. He rested his eyes again and con-tinued the spellchant without thinking, that one habit becoming, for the time, all his universe, but now he smiled. Even if he could not see the mouse, he knew it was there.

Dalin wove a new thought then, this one of gnawings and tastings and furtive explorations. In a moment, small, many-toed feet scrambled up his wind-chapped cheek, stood tickling his ear as tiny teeth explored his hair, then slipped down his arm between cloak and back.

For a time, then, nothing. His arms were too numb, his shoulders too cramped, to feel what the mouse might be doing. Dalin continued to urge the small fellow on, twisting the purpose of the spell to turn the mouse into a chewer of leather thongs instead of a bearer of messages. For that was the heart of this spell, really: to bring a message-bearer, to give it a sentence or three, and send it to seek the message's recipient, within an hour's walk or flight. Hardly of help to Dalin now, but the spell itself planted urges and thoughts into a small creature's brain and let its mission be shaped by the spellcaster. The youth was in unexplored territory, attempting free-form magic of his own design. Granmar had never sanctioned that, would never hear of it. "That's for later," he'd shake his head, "much later. You're not ready." So Dalin had no guidelines, no knowledge. Just intuition, and his sense of the mouse, curious, hungry, searching . . .

After a time, the magic did exhaust itself, and the last note of a long hum died in Dalin's raspy throat. The youth guessed an hour or two had passed. In the timeless state of continuous spellchanting it was impossible to know for sure. During that time, with all his will he had urged the little creature to free him, to bite through the thongs that held him tight. If it was going to work, it had worked by now—but the young man lay stiff and cold on the rocks and could not tell if he was free or not.

He gave a tentative tug with his arms, unable to feel whether his muscles were too numb to respond or whether he was still tied. He swung his shoul-der forward then, to see if his arm would follow—and rolled over on to his face, out of balance. Two lead weights where his arms should be told him that he remained bound as snugly as before.

His face pressed into the pebbly grit beneath him. Dalin squeezed his eyelids tighter shut against tears that came anyway.

CHAPTER 5

THE MOUSE WAS gray and black, perfectly camouflaged to hide among the stone and twig in its mountain home. That camouflage served it well, for it was nearly invisible as it made its way with hops and short dashing sprints between rocks and tree roots, stopping now and then with thumping heart as it darted quick looks about for threatening movements.

None seen, it continued on its way, a meandering path from cover to cover, always down the mountain flank. The small creature was driven in a way it had never felt before and would never feel again. It wanted—no, *needed*—to find a giant, like the one with strange smells and tastes sprawled upon the slope above.

Every rodent instinct the creature possessed warned it to give up its quest, to return to its burrow, yet something stronger drove it on. An urge like the mating urge, like the nesting instinct. A feeling so confusing that the little beast stopped at times, shaking with warring impulses, to catch its breath beside a shadowing stone. And then it would lead off again, always downslope, instead of toward the security of its now-distant nest.

An unheard humming drew it, like murmuring burrowmates, like the crunching of pine nuts, a promise of comfort and solace if only it could find one of the giants. For in spite of Dalin's best efforts to alter the spell, the magic sought a target, a recipient for the message he had unwittingly planted in the mouse's head.

Driven by the spell, the creature might have expired on the mountainside, worn out by its impossible trek. But the Truthsayer's apprentice had an urgent need, and his song of desperation resonated in bone and stone until the entire flank of Kodanit's Spire sang with it.

On the next rocky spindle-peak to the east, Hanno Runemaster paused in his scouting. He hearkened to the wind, then shrugged dismissively.

There was no throb of earth-magic, no pulse of wind-song to threaten him. He led the Nimmians on their way.

On the slope where he lay, Dalin felt his heartache drain into the rocky soil beneath him. Exhausted, he fell into a mindless doze, in which a refrain of the summoning song was crooned back to him by the cradling earth.

And an hour downslope, on the crest of the last ridge that skirted the Spire, an elf paused, sharp ears cocked to the wind. No spellsinger he, yet sensitive in the ways of nature, he felt a thrumming underfoot—an odd vibration that transcended the normal slow pace of the mountain's heart. Arandel looked at the ice-cloaked Spire overhead and wondered what he heard. Sensing no threat in it, he continued to pick his path, moving, as the spell would have it, directly toward the mouse that blindly sought him out.

It was a time before they met, midafternoon. The mouse, as drained as Dalin, halted its progress an hour's mouse-walk from where the youth lay. A long trek for its kind, indeed, that lived from stone to tree root, with short jaunt to pine branch in between. Unable to go forward, unwilling to go back, it rested and nibbled on old seeds, scavenged beneath a scraggle-pine's spreading limbs.

Arandel continued uphill, avoiding scree fields, skirting black granite outcroppings where ice and snow clung belligerently into this alpine summer season—though it felt more like early spring, by the elf's standards. He missed the woods of his homeland, that now would have the sharp scent of sun-warmed sap and sturdy new needle growth greening every branch—

Put that out of your mind, briyu, he lectured himself. *You have much to accomplish before you dare see Caerlian again.* And he turned his feet upslope once more, marking the best way for his comrades to follow.

In calf-high boots of thick, scuffed brown leather, he picked a careful path between crumbling rock and slippery pebble-strewn inclines. Such boots were sturdy enough for broken terrain, though not the elf's first choice for exploration: he preferred to feel the ground beneath his feet, and would have worn the soft leather *linaes* of Caerlian, had he come away from home with any. But he had not, and so it was that, when a gray-and-black mouse leaped atop his foot, Arandel felt nothing and continued his uphill trek, eyes searching out a path many yards ahead.

Unnoticed, the mouse scrambled up leather trouser leg and over belt, clung mightily to a fold of leather tunic when a rock rolled out from beneath the elf's foot, and struggled finally to a perch atop a shoulder cloaked in thick gray wool. Still the giant lurched up the hillside, unheeding.

The mouse spoke.

Elvish instincts, for once, served for naught. Arandel started and stared at his right shoulder. Reflexively a hand rose to ward against the unexpected, then halted in midswipe as he realized it was only a mouse. Or not "only" a mouse. The creature spoke again.

"Chew thongs," it repeated, and returned the elf's stare with a bold black eye.

"Chew thongs?" Arandel echoed incredulously.

A third time it recited its message. "Chew thongs." It pulled a nut from its cheek pouch, cracked and nibbled the snack, much-needed refreshment after a long journey. It swallowed. "Chew bindings," it added, almost an afterthought.

Its message delivered, the mouse turned and began to scamper down the length of Arandel's arm.

"Wait a bit there, little fellow!" The elf's hand darted out, snagged the mouse just before it could leap to the ground. The fluffy gray body froze in his hand as fear of danger overwhelmed it. The mouse went limp, as if it had died.

"Oh, no. I know that trick, my friend," Arandel said in a soft voice. He brought the creature closer to his face, regarded its pose of death, and eased his grasp a little. "Can you say anything else?" he asked the small figure. "Do you have a name?"

Silence and studied limpness greeted his inquiry.

"I suppose you're just a messenger, then, is that right?" Arandel regarded the mouse, then looked thoughtfully around the rocky mountainside. He knew of animal messengers, commonly used by certain elves in the forests of his distant home. Though for one to seek him out in this barren wasteland, where no one should expect to find the elf or his companions . . .

"What's amiss, little one? Hm?" He loosened his grip entirely, stroked the limp, gently breathing little body with one finger. "Show me who sent you, will you? There's a good fellow." He set the mouse down on a nearby rock, stepped back a pace, then squatted near the ground so he would present no threatening bulk to the creature. He waited in that patient, unmoving manner that Caerlian forest guardians learned and watched the mouse.

After a time, the gray-furred body stirred to life and, sensing no threat, followed its instinct: to escape from this place where the giant had grabbed it, to flee back to the safety of its nest. With the message delivered, magical imperative faded, and the mouse sprang off across the slope, darting from cover to cover as it retraced its path back home.

Arandel grinned to himself as the rodent dashed away. *Now, here's a challenge,* he thought, and keeping his sharp eyes fixed on the small animal, he followed a short distance behind, moving as silently and rapidly as only an elf can across the treacherous ground. And though he thought he lost his quarry once, he followed his hunter's intuition and guessed which route of cover it would follow. Instinct proved him right. He trailed at the mouse's now-tired pace for more than an hour and only lost the creature one last and final time when it burrowed into the needle pack beneath a scattering of lodgepole pine.

There Arandel stopped and surveyed his surroundings. A deer trail, recently traveled, it seemed; a gully; a boulder-strewn slope—and there on the slope, an unmoving form. "Thank you, my friend," the elf murmured to the needle pack, and started uphill toward the fur-cloaked body lying there.

CHAPTER 6

Arandel's touch was unexpected and his foreign accent even more so. Dalin stiffened as he recognized the same Nimmian dialect used by the murderers he had trailed. As his rescuer's face swam into near-focus, he spotted the pointed ears and slanted eyes of an elf.

Dalin's eyes widened in sudden recognition. Sloe-eyed and slender, with graceful, languid movements . . . this was like a fireside tale come to life, and he could not help but stare at what could only be an elf that tended him.

"No need to so frowning be," Arandel told him. "I bite you not." The elf cut his bonds as Dalin considered his words.

With his singsong lilt and twisted grammar, it seemed that Nimmian was not the stranger's native tongue. *Of course not, fool,* Dalin chided himself. *He must speak Elvish, and Nimmian is a learned tongue. And not too well learned at that.*

"Who are you?" the youth asked as the stranger helped him sit up against the protest of misused muscles.

His rescuer paused and made a half-bow from his kneeling position. "Arandel na'Toreneth e Mithlond," he introduced himself, "Silverleaf and warden of Caerlian." Then he began to massage one of Dalin's arms that hung limply by his side.

Silverleaf, Caerlian . . . strange names, those, unknown to the Turakemi youth. He squinted at a gleam of silver that held a gray woolen cloak upon the elf's shoulder and made out a brooch in the shape of a large silver leaf of odd design.

"And where is Caerlian? Not in Tura-kem, I think?"

"Not here, no. In Nimm, across the Sea of Lan Loros." Arandel dropped one arm and took the other as Dalin tensed anew. The elf paused and looked him in the face, brilliant green-eyed gaze meeting brown. "You of Nimmians know? The raiders?"

Dalin held his breath, ready to fight or flee. Who was this stranger? Why did he suddenly talk about raids? If he intended harm, why had he cut Dalin free?

"What do you know of raids?" he asked brusquely.

The elf shrugged. "I have see how they do, the men of Nimm." He continued his ministrations, dipping salve out of a small horn container and smearing it gently on the near-bloody chaff marks on the youth's wrists. "I am thinking men like the great contest, yes? Nimm raids here, Tura-kem raids there."

He set Dalin's hand down, and the youth rubbed his forearms against the agonizing sensation of returning circulation. "We be not of that folk," Arandel went on. "We be *calianestu,*" he said, as if that explained everything. "Offer us no harm, and we offer you none, too."

He clearly meant this to reassure, but Dalin was less reassured than ever. In his three years on Kodanit's Spire, the Truthsayer had received no visitors, except for tribesmen bearing offerings and live beasts for midsummer sacrifice and once a lowland jarl come to petition for a divination. Now, in the space of less than a day, foreign brigands had turned Dalin's world upside down, and then another outlander happened along to help. It was beyond comprehension, unless the hands of the gods were manipulating his fate. The youth shuddered at the thought.

"How did you happen to find me?" Dalin questioned his rescuer. "And what are you doing here?"

"You sent a mouse. It finds me, I find you." Arandel smiled at the look of surprise on the human's face. "As for why are we here . . ." He grew more serious. "We are visiting the Truthsayer."

Dalin's vision was better, though not yet perfect. He studied the Silverleaf's face, trying to discern hidden meaning, and failed. "Who is 'we'?"

Arandel motioned downslope. "My companions. I scout ahead for the way."

"Why do you seek the Truthsayer? You don't look like an ordinary petitioner."

Again the elf shrugged. "We are not. But needing to speak with him, we must find him first. Truthsayer is for months not in Etjorvi, so journey here we must."

No, the Truthsayer had not been in Etjorvi for months. Still, he had a successor now, of a sort. The youth had not been anointed nor dedicated nor suffered through a vision-seeking. Yet in other ways he knew much that only the Truthsayer had known. And with Granmar gone, who remained to wear the Robe? *Only me,* Dalin thought, although to claim the office was bold . . . maybe overbold. But who else was there to carry on?

He cleared his throat. "I'm the Truthsayer," he volunteered, keeping a quaver from his voice.

Gravel crunched as Arandel shifted his weight back on his heels. A strange look passed his face that Dalin was not able to catch—disbelief? Amusement? Then the elf spoke again.

"Truthsayer we know is old man, Granmar Keljornik. You are he?"

The cold wind off the Spire's snow field blew a rattle of ice crystals along the slope where they sat. The grit stung Dalin's eyes and perhaps accounted for sudden moisture there.

"I was his apprentice," he admitted. "Granmar is dead. I'm Truthsayer now."

"Dead?" Consternation rang in Arandel's voice. "What is happen here? Explain."

The Silverleaf listened attentively while the young man related the events of that morning, interrupting with only a few questions about the strangers the youth had observed. When he was done with his tale, Arandel rose to his feet. "You are feeling like walking now, I think, yes? We must join others and of this tell them."

"I don't know. . . ." Dalin hung back, reluctant to travel off with this stranger, well-intentioned though he seemed. "I need to find my knife and have to go back—"

"Your knife together we can find. And what waits at home for you? No, no, you come along. This is more important than you are knowing."

Dalin hesitated, and Arandel spoke sternly.

"You are wanting the Robe back?"

"Well, yes. . . ."

"You are wanting justice for death of Truthsayer?"

"Yes."

"Then you have help. Now, come with."

No further resistance seemed possible. Arandel found Dalin's good staghorn knife at the bottom of the scree field. The Truthsayer's apprentice followed mutely where the elf led with quiet assurance.

CHAPTER 7

THEIR PATH LED to lower ground, beyond the Skirt of Grace, the last ridge bordering the Spire, and into the valley fold on the other side. It was not much of a valley, just an indentation framed by two ridge crests and covered with a thicker concentration of scraggle-pine than most folds at the Spire's base. There, woodsmoke tickled the apprentice's nostrils as he entered a twilight-shadowed hollow. Arandel led Dalin to a modest campfire almost hidden behind boulders. His guide pushed him down to sit atop a log placed for the purpose beside the flames.

"What stray this be?" complained a gruff voice with the most outrageous accent Dalin had ever heard, misspoken Nimmian—close cousin to the Turakemi dialect—and grammar fractured far worse than the elf's. He strained to make sense of the foreigner's speech and discerned a squat form in the shadows beyond the firelight. The voice spoke from just near shoulder-height, with a resonance that suggested great girth of chest. "You have our Truthsayer found, perchance?"

Arandel replied as other figures drew near. "A mouse-messenger led me to this one, trussed on mountainside like a hog on market-day. Leave him there I could not, human though he is."

A feminine form was the first to step close and inspect him—not a human, but a female elf. Ears and eyes and lilting speech were the same as Arandel's, although her mastery of Dalin's dialect was better. "So, who are you, boy?" she asked curiously.

He wanted to ignore the question and found himself staring rudely instead. From knowing of elves only as the subject of winter-night's tales, here he was suddenly surrounded by them. Like the one he'd seen earlier today, this one's hair was long, blonde like Arandel's, and worn tied loosely back. She wore a white shirt and blue-dyed leather jacket, with mannish leather trousers and tall black thigh-high boots he did not expect to see upon a woman. She regarded him out of bright green eyes that sparkled with pinpoints of reflected firelight.

She smelled of herbs and horse sweat, and ignoring her did not make her retreat. Her slender hand reached out, turned his chin to look at his profile. He pulled his head out of her grasp as she smiled, and a voice spoke from behind him.

"He's not a curiosity, Nalia. Leave him be."

She stood upright, frowned petulantly, and addressed Dalin. "I *do* find you a curiosity, young human. Come talk with me later."

She left the circle of firelight as a dwarf hove into view on the other side. Nearly as broad as he was tall, the stocky fellow glowered at Dalin from behind bushy eyebrows and a thrice-braided beard. Behind him stood another elf, one like Arandel in build, but brown of hair and quiet of demeanor. The two stood silently as another companion took a seat on a neighboring log.

This was the one who had spoken to Nalia, and at first, from his great height alone, Dalin was not sure if he was an elf or a giant of a man. His ears were concealed behind a fringe of longish blonde-brown hair, but his eyes were unmistakably slanted and his accent identical to those of his friends.

"Forgive our rudeness," he said. The voice was a mellow tenor, his bearing regal and self-assured. Even seated he towered over Dalin, for he was taller than any man the youth had ever seen. Taller maybe than the ice-elves of legend. "We did not expect a visitor. I am Thengel na De'reth, Guardian of the Silverthorn, a protector of the Grove of Caerlian." Thengel offered a halfbow, white-shirted arm crossing chest, then rested hand on a slender blackhilted dagger at his belt. "Here, my comrade, Hagar Gemsinger, of the Nunori Mountains."

The dwarf crossed arms upon his chest and nodded his head.

"Behind him, Belec, Eil'Fin Keeper of the Path, one of Onderye's Chosen."

Onderye's Chosen . . . that meant nothing to Dalin, but he nodded politely as the brown-haired elf in worn leathers bowed at the introduction.

"Nalia Mithlond you have met, cousin to Arandel. And Arandel Silverleaf, forest warden, you know already."

Dalin glanced to the side and saw his rescuer watching him lazily.

"We bid you welcome," Thengel spoke formally. "And you are . . . ?"

"Dalin Truthsayer," the apprentice volunteered, suppressing a qualm as he claimed title he wasn't sure was rightly his. He was even less sure as he saw Thengel's eyes narrow and a frown crease the elf's brow.

Before he could be questioned, Arandel offered a summary of Dalin's news, of the raiders and Granmar's murder and the theft of the Truthsayer's robe. Then Thengel turned to the youth and asked him pointed questions: of the style of the strangers' clothes and if they bore embroidered markings, of the kinds of weapons they carried and other minutia that Dalin had barely noticed at the time.

No matter that the elves seemed helpful, the young man was at first reluctant to answer. Yet it helped having someone to talk with about the tragedy, and Dalin soon found himself sharing every detail he could remember.

"They could being who?" the dwarf suddenly demanded in his garbled speech.

It took the apprentice a moment to realize the question was directed at him. "Excuse me?"

The dwarf growled low in his throat, then switched to the Trade tongue, a patois shared by most folk who ever dealt with merchants from the Koribee Empire. Dalin's eyebrows rose: he hadn't spoken Trade since the last time bartering furs with his father in Rauvasla, but it was a language he'd known since birth.

"Do you have any idea who these people could be?" Hagar rendered his question more fluently than before.

"No, I don't," Dalin answered in the same patois. "If they're from Nimm, why would they know or care about the Truthsayer? The runemaster, though—he said Granmar was a scoundrel and deserved to die. He must be known. He's going back to court after the others meet a ship. . . ."

The elves fell into Trade as well and spoke it better than they had Dalin's own tongue. "So they scurry back to Nimm," Arandel remarked. "Then it is clear where we must go next."

"But—," Dalin started to speak.

"Not go. Follow," Belec added. "You say they've left a broad-enough trail. Else we may not catch the thieves before they take ship."

"But—" The youth opened his mouth again.

"Then we leave before first light," Thengel said. "Belec, you still have the lightstone?"

The brown-haired elf nodded.

"Then you can light our way until sunrise, and we can pick up the trail then."

"We leave this manling here?" the dwarf asked, as if Dalin were a piece of baggage.

"Yes. When we near the coast—"

"You will not leave me here!" Dalin shouted and sprang to his feet.

Spontaneous plans fell silent and every eye turned to him. He pursued his advantage.

"You're going to follow these killers?" He jabbed a finger at Thengel.
The tall elf nodded.

"And you think to catch up with them and recover the Robe?"

A guarded look fell over Thengel's face, and he nodded again.

"And did you plan to bring it back here to me when you have it again?"

The accusation hung in the air. Thengel neither nodded nor declined
but kept a steady gaze on Dalin's face. The youth clenched his fists in anger.

"You have no right!" he exclaimed. "You want to steal from those who
stole, not for Granmar's sake, but to keep the robe for yourselves, don't you?"

A dangerous gleam came into the dwarf's eye. Dalin continued, unheeding.

"I say again, you have no right. I am the Truthsayer now, and that robe is
my inheritance." He added in a flash of inspiration, "And I am the only one
who can use it. If you don't take me with you, you will have a useless scrap
of cloth on your hands, and nothing more."

Silence reigned around the campfire while elves looked thoughtful and
the dwarf growled again.

"Hagar," Thengel murmured cautioningly.

Nalia spoke from beyond the circle of firelight. "He would recognize the
Nimmians," she suggested. "We have only the runemaster to follow, otherwise."

A moment later, Thengel nodded in decision.

"Please, sit down, my young friend. No need to glower so. We do not in-
tend to bereave you of your . . . inheritance. You wish to come with us? You
may do so."

"Folly!" snorted the dwarf.

"I think not, Hagar," the tall elf said. "Nalia's right. Dalin knows those
who killed his mentor."

"And I know how to use the Robe," Dalin boasted, not at all certain he
could effect anything with the robe of office that Granmar had never permitted him to touch. Yet he hoped these strangers believed him, or it seemed he
could very well wind up trussed upon the mountainside one more time.

"That could be helpful," Arandel conceded. "Let's see what happens."

And if I get the Robe and still can't truth-see, what then? Dalin asked himself,
then hurriedly put that thought out of mind. *First, find the Nimmians. Then
worry about the Robe.*

"Well then, young Truthsayer," said Thengel. "You are one of us. Be welcome at our fire."

For the time being, thought Dalin cautiously. *For the time being.*

CHAPTER 8

DALIN ROSE BEFORE dawn, his breath hanging like moon-silvered frost in the air before him. The elves and dwarf broke camp quickly, silently, with the practiced movements of a group long days on the road together. "Stand clear," Hagar grumbled as they worked around him, making bedrolls of their sleeping furs, collecting the water pot and cooking gear. Dalin stumbled aside and sat in pitch-darkness beneath pine boughs. How they could see enough to go about these chores was beyond him. The thin crescent moon was nearly hidden below the far western peaks, its feeble light barely bright enough to strike a gleam of frost from stone or twig.

He pulled an oatcake from his pack and munched it as he waited. The cakes had been baked the night before by Arandel—the elf's contribution to the morning march in place of a breakfast they would not spare the time for. Dalin chewed while he squinted his eyes, straining to make out the activity around the burned-out campfire. Suddenly branches rustled as a form hunched low before him, stooping to kneel nearby.

Dalin was wondering how this one could find him in his dark roost when the figure spoke.

"Do you ride?" Thengel asked.

"Ride? Horses, you mean?"

"Yes."

Forgetting the darkness for a moment, the youth shook his head. Thengel replied as if he'd seen the gesture. "You'll have to learn, then. But we haven't a horse to spare right now. You'll ride with Nalia. She has the best mount, besides my own, and she's a better rider than the others. Come."

The elf led Dalin from beneath the tree. Horses had been tethered near, and they were brought now into the campsite by Nalia and Arandel. The young moon had fallen out of sight behind the mountains, and now not even outlines were visible. Dalin could not see the horses, just smell them and hear their drowsy stampings. It was even more baffling how the elves got bedrolls and gear secured on the packhorse, nary a fumble or curse in the darkness, their movements as assured as ever. There was a creak of saddle leathers as people mounted around him. Thengel's hand was upon his shoulder then, steering his dark-blinded footsteps closer to one horse. An arm reached down to grasp his own—Nalia's hand, a strong, sure clasp on his forearm.

"Put your foot here, then swing your leg up." Thengel guided Dalin's booted foot into the stirrup, then Nalia pulled and the tall elf helped him settle onto the saddle pad behind her.

Groping in the dark, uncertain of his seating, Dalin nearly overbalanced and started to slip to the other side. Impulsively he grabbed at the rider, the only stable thing nearby, and his arm slipped around her waist to hold himself in place. He settled himself and blushed mightily, realizing how he held the stranger. He snatched his arm away, and clear laughter rang like a bell from the elf's throat. "You'd best hold tight, manling," she chided, "unless you wish to fall."

Glad they could not see his face—or could they?—Dalin kept his arms to himself and tried to keep his balance by holding on to the meager cantle of her saddle.

Thengel spoke again, his voice coming shoulder-high in the darkness. "I've your walking stick," he said. "We'll strap it on the pack load until you need it."

"Thanks," mumbled Dalin. Flustered by these dark-bound preparations, he'd forgotten his stick. *Stop woolgathering,* he told himself, and heard Granmar's voice in the words. He bit his cheek so the pain would take his mind off that loss, before he could embarrass himself again.

"Here," someone murmured, and a sudden light flared in the clearing— a bright, unwavering glow that made Dalin blink and look away. The campsite was illuminated with noon-bright sunlight, its source a black pouch held in Belec's hand. The tie had been loosened, and light flooded from the opening like sun piercing black storm clouds. The elf sat atop a tall, sturdy chestnut with long-haired fetlocks. He leaned down to hand the pouch to Arandel, who fussed with the thing, twisting the cloth, setting it just so, until the lightstone trapped within shone its brilliance through only a small hole in the opening. Nodding in satisfaction at the limited and easily darkened light, the Silverleaf swung nimbly into the saddle of his long-maned black, then turned to address the group.

"We can catch their trail by skirting the spire flank. By sunup their tracks should be in sight."

"Lead, then," said Thengel from atop a large gray, Hagar mounted double behind him.

Arandel nodded and turned his horse's head upslope. "*Fa*, Daile," he murmured, urging the black with his heels.

Nalia nudged her dapple to follow after. Dalin lurched as the horse stepped out and grabbed with both arms for the elf's slender waist. Her laughter rang out again and the youth gritted his teeth, but kept his grip—muscles flexed in haunches beneath him, the ground was uneven, the slope immediate, and if he let go, he knew he'd plummet to the ground like a rock. Belec came after, leading the packhorse, and Thengel brought up the rear. So they moved out in the freezing high mountain morning, the sky gone black as the woods around them, the lightstone their only fleeting guidance through the tangle of pines and rocky ridge folds.

They struck the trail as Arandel had predicted, in early daylight, the gray of the mountainside just coming distinct from brush and tree trunk. The Silverleaf gestured for a halt and leaped lightly to the ground. Then he ducked between the trees and ran uphill, out of the spruce toward the thinner lodgepole growth above. After a time he returned, nodding to Thengel, certain this was the path he sought.

"I'll scout ahead," Arandel said. "Keep on this trail until I return. It's clear enough to follow." He waved a hand in farewell and trotted out of sight.

Dalin looked downslope and saw, as the others must, that this was a reindeer track. It was also the trail he'd once used on his first approach to the Spires and a likely route for any strangers to take who came this way.

But the elves he traveled with had not approached from this trail, he reflected. They had cut straight across country, as if they were sneaking up on the Truthsayer from an unexpected direction. That thought sat unpleasantly with the youth, and he frowned at his companions, newly visible in the light of dawn.

If they noted his suspicious looks, they gave no sign. Thengel moved to the front of the group and led the way down the track. The others followed after.

CHAPTER 9

A DAY'S JOURNEY away, a different fellowship also made progress through the gray light of dawn.

The party of Nimmians crossed icy rivulets and skirted gullies along the northern flank of Eskavar glacier, descending toward the wooded valley below. There, beyond a lazy bend of the Ranulf, the ancient walls of Eskrin Freehold hunkered. Yet some hours' journey distant, the smoke of cook fires cloaked the small settlement in a hazy pall, the merest smudge to the travelers' eyes.

Hanno Runemaster turned in his saddle enough to gesture at the sight, as if his outland companions could not see the obvious in this country not their own. Joro acknowledged Hanno's condescension with the merest sneer. The runemaster turned haughtily away and continued to lead downtrail.

The byplay was not lost on the others. Aral Yellowbeard frowned at the unheeding guide. He made a sour face then, his challenge gone unanswered, and spoke over his shoulder to the companion riding behind him. "So, Oathkeeper," he asked, "have we at least satisfied this part of our vow? I'll be glad to leave this untrusty land behind."

Berin Oathkeeper rode stiffly in chain and plate, the green-and-white surcoat of his priestly calling plain to see beneath his cloak of tawny mountain lion fur. He shrugged off the warrior's question. "It's of no matter when we leave or how much we accomplish along the way. We're oath-bound until the very end, Aral."

Yellowbeard lowered his brows, but Joro spoke up before he could retort. "What's wrong?" he asked, lightly mocking. "Want to be rid of your vow so soon?" A teasing light came to the man's eyes, and the burly warrior scowled back at him.

"I'm content to be oath-sworn in the service of our lord," Aral grumbled. "I only want to know the limits of this geas."

"The limits?" Joro arched his eyebrows. "The limit is when we have all three parts of the Panoply in the hands of the Duke of Nimm. And not before."

"I know that much," Yellowbeard said testily. "I mean, why doesn't anything feel different, now that we have the Tapestry?"

Berin tugged at a long mustache, luxuriant growth above the short-trimmed curly beard he wore. "Accomplishing portions of our mission has no effect on the greater oath. Only when all is achieved will you feel anything different. Unless you try to step aside from this quest, of course."

"I won't, priest."

Berin studied him thoughtfully. "I don't suppose you will. That's not what I meant to imply."

"What did you mean, then?"

"Simply this: if you want to test the strength of your oath, turn and ride away with some other intention in your heart. Think of a journey to Koribee and ride south—and see how far you get. Vikkar Tornor watches you and watches your actions. You'll know the god's displeasure soon enough."

"Any would, who defied a Great Oath," Kaylis spoke up sharply from the rear. Slender Rudic just in front of her shook his head. "Don't test it, Aral. Unless you doubt our Oathkeeper's binding magic."

Aral shook his head and rode silently.

"No need for any of us to test anything," Joro said. "We've our work to do, and we're doing it, that's all. The only place we need journey to right now is Nimm-on-Witholl. Look you—Hanno," he called to the runemaster, riding slightly in the lead. "How long yet 'til we make the ships?"

"Tesvi Cove," the runemaster said curtly. "A day after our stop tonight."

"There, you see?" Joro enthused to the air and anyone who would listen. "We'll have the Tapestry back home soon enough. I trust we'll all feel something different then. The gratitude of the Duke, mayhap, and full purses to measure it with, as well." He laughed aloud at the prospect, pleased at the sound of his own voice, his high spirits joined in by some, but not by Aral. And not by Hanno, who heard the chatter at his back with a look of cold calculation on his face.

CHAPTER 10

Arandel knelt between fir tree and cedar and prodded at horse droppings. He frowned unhappily downslope. "Eastward they wend, taking the easiest trail down."

"Are we closer?" Thengel asked.

The Silverleaf shook his head. "I'd say they draw ahead. Mostly their path is clear to see, but follow it we must, lest we lose them for all the turns and windings they take."

"Time we lost, in the crags," grumbled Hagar.

Arandel squinted against the wind off the peaks. "And more time we'll lose again, for every rocky basin they cross, every streambed they follow." He turned his green gaze on Thengel. "Follow we can, but catch up with them . . . I'm not so sure. We're a day's travel behind."

Thengel's brows drew together. "If we only knew where they were headed . . . ," he muttered.

Dalin heard those words and started. Intent on the pursuit, he hadn't thought ahead to the end of this trail. Neither had the elves, but they must not know what he did. There was only one settlement the Nimmians could be headed for, the one where a trader's track began, which gave the swiftest route to the coast, and ships. . . .

"Eskrin," he blurted. "They must be headed there."

All eyes turned to Dalin; even Nalia peered over a wool-cloaked shoulder at him.

"You know where they are going?" Thengel asked, his voice sharp.

"I, um . . ." Dalin swallowed, uneasy at the sudden attention. "I'm not certain. I think so. This way lies Eskavar glacier, and the freehold below it. It's the closest settlement east of the Spires on a route to the sea." Those

Spires were tall peaks now high above them and nearly lost from sight behind looming wooded ridges.

The tall Guardian of the Thorn studied Dalin with troubled eyes. "You've seen our progress and heard our talk. Half a day of careful tracking and slow travel lies behind us—and just now you think to tell us where our quarry has gone?"

It was true; all morning he'd listened to their talk, the stoic silence when the trail was lost, the small congratulations when it was struck again, the worried speculation that the gap between them was not closing. And that talk all in Trade, the patois that had become their common tongue—a courtesy, he was certain, so that he and the dwarf would not be left out of conversation.

And like some witless babe, he'd journied silently along, concentrating on keeping his balance on horse-rump, fighting off unease when he must hold on to Nalia, content to let the woods-wise elves do his work for him.

"I, uh, didn't think, until now, where they must end up," he offered weakly.

Arandel rose from the trail and faced Dalin. "Do you know how to get there? To this glacier and freehold?"

"I had directions from the Truth—from Granmar. Much like the way we've come so far."

Thengel spoke to the Silverleaf. "If we know where to go and head straight there, how soon will we catch them?"

Arandel shook his head. "Without the need for tracking, we'll be hours faster. But still hours behind."

Dalin heard that unhappily. He remembered what else Granmar had warned him of and bit his lip. It wasn't a wise recommendation, but now, so far behind—*and my own fault for that*—it might be the only way. . . .

"There's a shorter way to Eskrin," he volunteered, then squirmed beneath Thengel's unblinking gaze. "Much faster. But dangerous."

"Well?"

"Um. . . . The Nimmians skirt the ice fields, here along the northern flank of the glacier. We could cut over to Eskavar and follow the Ranulf down from the heights. But the ice is rotten this time of year."

"How long a journey, that way?" asked Arandel.

"A half-day. Maybe more." He raised and dropped his shoulders. "I'm not certain. I was warned away from that route."

"A half-day," Thengel repeated. "Or days, perhaps, if accident befalls us on the ice. Do you know glacier travel, Dalin?"

The young man licked his lips and gave his answer. "Yes."

"Good," the Guardian of the Thorn replied. "We have no glaciers in Caerlian. You can guide us."

The elves nodded as if it made perfect sense; Hagar directed a bushy-eyebrowed frown at Dalin, as if to warn, *You'd better not be lying. . . .*

Arandel remounted, and the riders all looked to the Truthsayer's apprentice.

"Please." Thengel gestured at the wooded slope with one broad hand. "Lead the way."

CHAPTER 11

Hanno led the party through the ancient stone walls of Eskrin. The two lazing gate guards were youths who moved livelier once they recognized the runemaster who had passed through a mere ten-day before. They bowed runemaster and escort through the creaking wooden gate and into their steading.

Eskrin was a freehold steading, something between a large farmstead and small village, in the style of most upcountry steadings with workshops and houses enclosed within fortified walls. In Nimm a similar style prevailed, of freehold fenced round with wooden palisades; in older Tura-kem, where kin-war and god-war and war against creatures from over-ice had occupied centuries, walls of lasting stone were the rule and the requirement. Eskrin huddled within its ramparts of outsize gray river boulders, its houses and workshops snugly built of smaller rocks and local timbers. There was no proper inn there, but Torvin's long hall guested all comers. A few more mouths to feed were small price to pay for new faces and news and sometimes goods to trade.

Torvin's men took the reins of riding and pack animals in the foreyard of the hall. They led the beasts away, including the horse with a wooden chest among its pack goods. Aral looked after as if inclined to follow. "Our things will be safe," Hanno reprimanded him in an undertone. "It's not done, to scratch and peck about your baggage like a broody hen."

Yellowbeard scowled at that, and Kaylis opened her mouth to protest. "Guests are treated differently here than in your land," Hanno said pointedly, then turned his back on the glares that greeted his remark.

The runemaster was made welcome at the fire, his companions given smiles and bowls of hot porridge. A loaf of barley bread was shared out and ale poured. When Torvin heard of his distinguished guest, he came back into the hall he had left some while before. The freeholder poured mead into the runemaster's drinking horn, then sat with them at the long table and talked of minor things while the visitors broke their fast.

Hanno smiled beneath his long mustaches, secretly pleased that the Nimmians occupied the lower benches; to avoid drawing attention to themselves, they played the role of his escort and kept silent and subservient in the presence of others. A runemaster was an honored-enough guest that most eyes and ears would stay on Hanno, not his companions—just as well, for the centuries of bad blood that lay between Tura-kem and Nimm assured that these outlanders would not have a warm welcome once their origin was clearly noted. They depended on Hanno while traveling in Tura-kem, for his guidance, his magic, the cover he lent them on the road. It chafed them no end, and he smiled again at the strained silence that spiced their dining.

The runemaster spared them nary a glance, making it clear that they were not of enough note to be included in conversation. Torvin accepted those subtle cues and spoke with Hanno as if they were the only two in the hall.

"Your journey was satisfactory, I hope?" the grizzled freeholder asked, his face alight with good humor. It would not do to press a runemaster with rude questions, but local curiosity would not be denied.

He had asked more directly when Hanno had first passed this way. Torvin had guessed at his goal of visiting the Truthsayer straight out—for why else would a master of magic journey to this desolate place and venture through alpine wilderness into the crumbling heights of the Spires? The only thing worth seeing there was the seer and adviser to kings who lived in remote isolation. Hanno had smiled and evaded those questions, leaving all to understand that his business was his own. But all knew it must be with the Truthsayer.

Now it was time to play a role. Later, when he was in Etjorvi and powerful once again in the King's court, questions would arise about the absence of the Truthsayer and his possible fate. Hanno's journey here would surely come to light, sooner or later. All the way down from the Spires, he had turned this moment over and over in his head, rehearsed what to say, what word to offer. The outright murder of the Truthsayer had not been a part of his plans, and now he must weave it into his own dealings as best he could. Best to forestall suspicions now, however he might.

"My trip was for naught," he grumbled unhappily. "The Truthsayer wasn't there."

The freehold chief looked surprised. "Surely he would be back soon?"

Hanno lifted his shoulders and drained his drinking horn. Torvin filled it up again. "How to know? We waited a week, still no sign of him. He could be with the King a month or more at a time, and that's longer than I can wait."

"Ah." Torvin refilled his own horn. "His boy couldn't tell you when he'd be back then?"

The Nimmians paused in their eating, a falter that only Hanno noticed. The boy. "What boy?" he asked innocently.

"Boy's gone, too?" Torvin raised bushy brows. "Well, then I'd guess the Truthsayer is off for a longer time."

"He has a servant, then?" the runemaster fished for more information.

"Nay." Torvin smiled. "No servant. The Truthsayer's apprentice, he is. Been there three years, now."

Hanno felt a sudden knot in his stomach. He forced himself to smile, to chat with the freeholder, but his thoughts were elsewhere. The boy, an apprentice. He had been lied to neatly by that one. And the youth, still alive, perhaps.

I don't need someone around who knows what happened to Granmar. I should have slit his throat when I had him in front of me. Damn.

He cursed himself for his softheartedness and felt the worried energies from the Nimmians. He hadn't mentioned the boy, and now they must be wondering if the youth had seen their theft and plundering. As he indeed had.

Hanno turned talk to other matters, of the slow thaw this year, of the road to Vaer, and Tesvi Cove beyond it, and refused more drink, anxious for the meal to conclude. Eventually it did. Torvin saw his visitors to the gate, where the runemaster gladly waved farewell. He led his party down the road, aware of eyes watching from Eskrin walls and the tension of the Nimmians who rode behind him.

The trader's track ran from the freehold gate, skirting the boulder-choked Ranulf, finally dipping down to the Vaer trail and the way to Tesvi Cove. The silence lasted until the path bent around a forested slope and hid them from watching eyes. Then Joro spurred his horse forward and cut in front of the runemaster.

"What in the Icy Hells was that all about?" he demanded. "The Truthsayer has an apprentice? And you didn't tell us?"

Hanno reined up with a tug of his tattoo-covered hand. "I didn't know," he spat at the leader of the outlanders. "No more than you did. We didn't see anyone besides the old man, did we?"

"Not seeing doesn't mean we weren't seen," Rudic said dryly.

Hanno wheeled around. "And so, if you were? You'll be gone soon enough. If one boy cries a sad story, who will come after you? *I'm* the one who'll be endangered by a tale-teller, not you."

Aral looked to Berin; Kaylis narrowed her almond-shaped eyes. Joro turned his horse aside from the runemaster's path. "True enough," he conceded. "Hopefully this apprentice saw nothing after all." His acquiescence rang insincerely in Hanno's ears. "Let's go on."

Hanno set his mount into a trot, pulling ahead of the others, glad to move them to their ships as soon as possible. Then he, too, would take ship, bound for Etjorvi and the return to power he had so carefully planned for.

There was no room in those schemes for a youth who had seen him associated with thieves and murderers. Maybe the boy had perished, fallen to his death or ravaged by wolves in the night.

Hanno hoped so, for he knew if he ever saw Dalin of Nevi again he would have to kill him.

CHAPTER 12

Eskavar appeared to be a harmless field of snow filling the gaps between the mountain's bones. Upslope, a sheer and naked black rock face marked the eastern escarpment that supported the Crystal Spires. The glacier extended downslope from that point on, like pudding poured into a mold—contained by mountain ridges, narrow in places, broad in others. Before Eskavar dipped sharply in a slanted plunge toward the lowlands, the glacier flowed around three upthrust crags like the knucklebones of an ice-submerged earth-giant.

Dalin studied the vista from a northern ridge that flanked the snow-crusted ice. Thengel and the others hung back as he walked from vantage to vantage, sizing up the glacier and the best routes of travel in the noontime light. Then he hunkered in the snow, insulated by his bearskin cloak, and crouched, elbows on knees, chin on interlocked fingers, and stared and stared at the ice fields before him.

Moments grew into long minutes, and still Dalin did not stir. Hagar took an impulsive step toward the Truthsayer's apprentice, but a touch from Arandel held him back. "Let him study it out as he needs to," the Silverleaf urged quietly. The dwarf scowled, but settled down to wait with the others as their guide surveyed the terrain.

Arandel's words carried to Dalin. His back was to the party and he winced to himself, his expression safely hidden from their observation.

"*Study it out,*" he repeated to himself. *Hard to study when I've never set foot on a glacier before. . . .*

Not that he had lied, exactly: Thengel had asked if he knew glacier travel, and the answer he had given was true. He knew from many tales told by his father and uncles and cousins. Knew well the story of Uncle Segrim, the man and a season's fortune in furs lost to a crevasse on his homecoming from a trapping expedition. Knew the stories of the goddess Elsta, icy sibling to fertile Ardruna, sleeping atop Heimek, Father of Earth and Winter, sliding the long, hard length of him in her languid way, trying to crush him beneath her, now succeeding, now failing. And sometimes settling for human men instead, small warm bits of flesh to suck into her hungry spaces, taking their warmth into herself as she extinguished their bothersome lives. . . .

None of which prepared Dalin for crossing Eskavar glacier. *Which of those folds in the snow was a pressure ridge?* he wondered. *And which the concealing crust of snow dusted over a crevasse, ready to yawn open to the first step upon it? Which route would bear the weight of horses, as well as men . . . ?* There was no way to tell by looking.

Think, Dalin, think, he scolded himself. *You know what you know, and it's far more than these lowlanders who've never seen a glacier before. What will you do to get them down Eskavar?*

For a moment he considered turning around, telling Thengel that in fact, no, he could not see them across the glacier. Now that they had come farther out of their way, navigating ice-locked ridges unthawed by summer's warmth, penetrating the mountain folds that had caused the Nimmians to take the longer, circuitous way down to Eskrin—

No, that did not seem a wise confession to make, if it was not needful. Dalin knew that ignorance was deadly upon the bosom of the ice—but in that regard, he was the least ignorant of any of his companions. If only he could apply what he had absorbed by warm fire pits on late winter nights. . . .

The words of the hunters of Nevi Freehold came back to him now. *"Travel slowly; caution and respect for the Ice Mother are your friends. Probe each step with your walking stick before you trust it to your feet. Avoid the long sags in the surface, for those mark the open mouths of crevasses, lightly covered by snow. Avoid the kenniki, the isolated outcrops of rock surrounded by ice flow, for crevasses always form around the base of such interruptions. Study the route from the side from a height, if possible: certain obstacles can only be spotted from such a perspective. . . ."*

As he was doing now, and his vigilance already rewarded. Below the kenniki, a long line like a bloodless knife slash marred most of the width of Eskavar's surface. Surely it was a large crevasse, marking the place where the glacier dipped suddenly downslope and tore itself away from the upper ice fields. It was easiest spotted from this height; once noted, it was simpler to avoid when crossing the ice.

As he got the lay of the snow and ice before him, Dalin's confidence returned. It was a straightforward process, after all, and not so very different from river-walking in the winter: being careful of one's footing, probing ahead when the ground was in doubt. As for the inevitable crevasses, they could jump across the smaller ones and skirt the large ones. There was no reason they could not get down the glacier in fine order. They did not need to travel to its farthest end, after all, where it fed the Ranulf and Avar Rivers, where crevasses splintered the glacier until the ice broke into bergs and cliff-edged chunks. They need only travel until even with the end of Heimek-kvosk, or Heimek's Spine, that range that concealed the resting place of Heimek, Lord of Mountains and Father of Earth and Winter. That was a line of peaks Dalin saw clear in his mind's eye, the legacy of Granmar's nighttime ramblings with charcoal on stone. For one traveling land he had never walked, the Truthsayer's apprentice had a clear picture in his head, at least, of where he was and where he was going.

I think, he amended to himself.

Dalin decided to head for the part of Eskavar that lay between the ken-niki and the stony ridge that was his vantage point. A careful trek between ridge and crevasse should carry the party past the point of obvious danger and into the more stable regions below. Of course Granmar had warned that the season's thaw would cause ice to rot. . . . Well. Nothing for it now. They must travel on the ice, and he would lead the way.

He stood, gripped his walking staff firmly, and inclined his head downs-lope. His companions followed on foot, horses on leads as they traversed the ridge down to Eskavar glacier.

Dalin halted the party at the edge of the ice. Even in the high overcast of this sun-subdued day, light poured across the glacier and threw it sharply back into the eyes of the travelers. He bit his lip. It was long since he had been in such a vast snowfield, and he was grateful it was not brighter. Snow blindness would not help their quest in the least. Soon enough, he hoped, they would be back in the gentler light of the woods. . . .

The snow atop the glacier was old, thawed, frozen, and thawed again, 'til now it was a damp, icy crust before them. The young man's feet crunched through the top layer and sank into rough ice crystals below, neither snow nor ice but somewhere in between. Sturdy enough, he thought, to carry the weight of others behind him and yet not be the impediment that completely slick ice, slush, or packing snow would be. He turned to wave the party on and grinned triumphantly at them: this was a sure route; he could feel it. Then he faced ahead, downslope, and probing with his walking stick, began to pick out the path his companions should follow.

Hagar watched his progress with a half-curled lip and a brow furrowed as if in pain.

"Well?" Thengel asked the dwarf, knowing a comment was inevitable.

"He like a snow-git prances does," Hagar complained in Elvish to drive his earnestness home. "He floating will over a hole that a dwarf swallow could."

Thengel translated that for a moment, then raised his eyebrow and replied pointedly in the Trade patois they spoke most fluently in common. "You're afraid you're going to drop through ice that holds his weight, is that it?"

Hagar spat. "No fear. I am making my own trail, I be thinking." The squat warrior stepped out in the wake of Nalia and Belec.

"Don't stray far," Thengel cautioned him. "We're staying with our guide, Hagar. For now, anyway."

The dwarf paused, shot a glower at Thengel. "Do not be forgetting who calls the icelands of Schoinevrik home."

He had a point. Grumbles trailed behind the bearded warrior as he followed in Dalin's direction, picking his own path to one side with a heavy tread and a pause, a stomp and a pause. . . .

Thengel watched the progress of the two, one light-stepping and cautious, the other poised at any moment to leap clear should a bold stomp cause a sudden shift beneath his feet. The elf shook his head and, taking Turon's reins, trailed along in a direction that split the difference between the two.

Dalin's careful advance brought the party even with the kenniki, but far to one side of those gnarled, ice-bound stones. The glacier lay in folds and ripples around their base, treacherous sloughs raying out along the ice far from that point of interruption. These, too, Dalin skirted, testing the ground ahead with his walking stick—and drawing himself up short when one firm thrust kept going. Ice did not pack beneath the tip of his pine staff. Instead, the stick punched into the empty air that heralded a crevasse. He yanked it back out again at an angle, disturbing the snow crust as he did so. One jab, another—and frozen snow broke into clumps, tumbled suddenly out of sight into the depths of the glacier below.

Dalin's heart beat faster. This was exactly what the fireside tales had warned him of. He hastily threw up his left hand; the elves halted as the youth studied the hazard before him.

A small dark hole gaped in the crusty snow. It didn't look like much of a problem . . . but that was, no doubt, not the extent of the cavity that yawned unseen before him. Wielding his staff, Dalin tested the ground around the hole and soon discovered the limits of the crevasse. It was a double arm's length wide, but long, stretching away to left and right beyond the many yards Dalin walked to gauge its distance. Compared to the massive thing it could be, though, it seemed like something they could easily leap, to span the gap.

"Wait here," he said over his shoulder to his companions. Standing back from the edge, Dalin dropped his pack and bearskin cloak. Tightening his grip on his staff, he set his feet, took a breath—and dashed for the pitfall before him.

Short of the edge, he stretched his stride into a leap. He flew across the concealed maw of the crevasse, but his balance was off, and he realized as he touched ground that he should have tossed his walking stick across ahead of him, not run with it in his hand. A thought too late to help him keep his feet, for he stumbled as he struck ground, foot punching hard through the crust of snow, his momentum pitching him forward to the icy surface.

Abrasive crystals filled his mouth and the front of his tunic. He lay still for one heartbeat, then another, waiting to see if the ground beneath him was solid or might shift and give way as the snow across the crevasse had. It held.

Dalin came to his feet, brushing snow from his chest, and turned to grin at his companions. "See? It's safe. Let me make sure there's room for your horses; then you can jump over."

He balanced his staff in two hands and prepared to face ahead once more. He began to turn—and the ground fell from beneath his feet.

One moment, Dalin beheld white ice field and gray-white overcast that was the sky and the black mountain flanks to east and west. The next, his stomach lurched and a shower of snow and ice cascaded down around his head. Then his arms were near wrenched from their sockets, wrists burning with sudden fire and sharp-strained tendons protesting as he hung in the air, legs flailing. His hands were locked in a death grip on the pine sapling that had saved him, one end jammed into a wall of the crevasse with the force of his sudden descent, the other resting at an angle on the far lip of the hole that had swallowed him.

Ice showered down from the edge, over his head, into his eyes. . . . He sputtered and spit out chilling debris. Elsta's cold breath surrounded him. *Like your uncle,* he could feel her thoughts, *I will gladly have you, too.* . . .

"No!" A panicked shout rose from his chest; he gulped in fast, labored breaths. Where were the elves? He'd dropped from sight before their very eyes; surely they were coming to help him. He had only to hold on. Hold on with wrists afire. His feet flailed reflexively at empty air, seeking purchase, failing to find it . . . and his body's torque twisted the slightly flexing sapling in his hands, bowing under his full body's weight.

Another cascade of ice fell in a flurry down about his head and shoulders, and the staff sank a handspan deeper into the glacier's wall. . . . *And what if that chunk gives way? Where do I plummet then?*

Dalin fought the panic that rose in his breast and threatened to make him thrash and scream for help. For any sudden movement here could be deadly; he knew it as he knew his name.

Through sheer effort of will, he forced himself to be still. No kicking out to seek purchase for his feet; no fretful tensing of his biceps; no flexing of his wrists, were they capable of moving anyway . . . but they were not, no, they hurt too much. And no sooner was his attention full on them than Dalin realized his fingers were cramped for his very life, and his wrenched joints seemed barely able to hold his weight—and yes, just there—his grip had started to slip.

He gritted his teeth mightily and his nostrils flared with the effort not to struggle, not to cry out or add to any movement that might hasten the slipping of the staff or the loosening of his grip.

Where are they? He mentally summoned his companions with the intensity of desperation. *If they want a way down this mountain, now's the time to lend me a hand.*

On the glacier above, Thengel had taken in Dalin's broad grin, his widening eyes as the ground gaped at his feet. The rangy elf sprang forward in response before the others realized what had happened. Hagar let loose a string of curses and dashed in short-legged stride after Thengel while the others trailed behind.

One long-legged spring carried Thengel over the first crevasse, and a pace or two more took him to the edge of the second. Lacking a staff to probe the ground, he pulled his long sword, stabbing hastily ahead of himself, hoping to flank the hole that had swallowed Dalin. The elf's hurried explorations proved sufficient, not so much because they were thorough as because the hole that had captured the Truthsayer's apprentice was a small one, one meager abyss compared to the glacier's myriad.

By time Hagar cleared the first obstacle, Thengel was already sprawled near the icy lip of the crevasse, peering over the edge to see if the youth still lived. A white-knuckled grip on a bowing sapling staff and a snow-dusted visage greeted him.

"I'm glad you are still with us," he said.

"Not for long," Dalin gritted. The pain in his wrists was unbearable now, a burning like the slash of a knife running from thumbs through wrist, forearm, and elbow to shoulders.

Take your mind off it, he chided himself. *If you notice, it only gets worse. . . .*

"Put a stick along the lip of the crevasse," he grunted, "and a line over it. Else rope bites in too deep. Knocks snow loose. Can't climb back up over edge."

That much, at least, he knew from Nevi kinfolk.

Moments later Thengel's sheathed long sword lay parallel to the mouth of the crevasse, and disembodied voices came to Dalin's ears. "I will anchor the rope," came a gruff voice he recognized as the dwarf. Then an incomprehensible string of elvish, a rapid exchange between Nalia and Thengel that seemed to go on entirely too long.

With a sinking feeling, Dalin realized his left little finger was slipping off the staff in spite of his best efforts to hang there. The minute shift in position brought a drizzle of snow down from the edge where his walking stick shifted slightly.

"Hurry!" he bit out thin-lipped. His eyes scanned the frozen walls nearby, hoping for a foothold but seeing none. He felt Elsta's chill expectation like a palpable thing waiting to snatch him from below.

Something twisted then in the corner of his vision and he stopped himself from starting with an effort. Voices had ceased above and with relief he recognized what uncoiled beside him: two ropes, snaking down into the crevasse that threatened to be his doom. Then a black-booted foot appeared, and legs followed—the foot sought out a stirrup tied into one line and braced itself there. Handspan by rapid handspan, Nalia was lowered into the icy trap an arm's length away from Dalin.

"You?" He was amazed these elves would risk a woman in this treacherous place. "You're in danger!" he blurted.

Nalia looked at him with mild amusement on her face. "Far less than you." She gestured overhead with her chin, a brief look up, then back to Dalin. "I can leave, manling, worth saving though you seem."

"I—you. . . . No. Never mind." Dalin swallowed. He blinked mightily, clearing his eyes of ice crystals, and glanced below. What seemed black from the surface was translucent blue and gray-white here beneath the glacier. Textured walls of ice on either side of him refracted light the length and breadth of the Ice Mother's body. . . . She who embraced warm man-flesh, hungry for warmth the Earth Father denied her.

He felt his grip loosening more and sucked in a sharp breath. He squeezed his eyes shut, concentrating on putting all his strength into his fast-weakening hands, and when he felt Nalia's light touch at the side of his ribs, his only thought was that her least nudge would dislodge him from his precarious grip and send him to his death.

"Don't—," he began.

"*Fashe,*" she said softly, and something wound swiftly about him, holding his chest in a close and binding embrace. Startled, his eyes flicked open and down, and he stared in amazement at the rope that coiled snugly about his chest.

Dalin knew of magic, but this was no rune working or scrying fire. He gave a yip of surprise, and the sudden exhalation was enough to undo him. The minute movement of his body strained hands and wrists beyond the point of recovery. One hand lost its grip on his staff, fingers sliding reluctantly down and free of the wood. The other hand, unable to take his weight, slipped free as well . . . and Dalin began to fall.

But not far. Before he could even yell in surprise, the rope around his chest jerked him up short only a few feet lower in the crevasse. Before his nose, Nalia's fast-darting hand snatched the walking stick out of the air as it tumbled free of the frozen walls.

Dalin twisted slowly in midair at the end of the rope. Reflex had put his heart in his throat; now, awareness of his reprieve washed over him and registered in his stomach. He returned Nalia's smile as best he could, a new feeling quirking his expression into an uneasy grimace.

"Can we get out of here now?" he asked. "I think I'm going to be sick."

CHAPTER 13

Dalin sat pale-faced and exhausted at the edge of the impromptu camp that Arandel had set up on the ice. His failure to lead his companions safely and his own brush with disaster sat in his stomach like a stone. He shrank from Belec when the elf knelt nearby and only surrendered his hands to the priest's touch when Thengel spoke sternly to him. The warmth that flowed from the elf's hands into his own was a surprise. It eased pain and stiffness away until his hands and arms felt as fit as ever.

"You're a healer?" he asked.

Belec nodded. "Pathkeeper. We keep Onderye's people safe and well, when we can."

"I'm not one of Onderye's people."

"No." Belec smiled. "But you need healing, and that is a care-taking that is not hoarded."

Dalin heard that in silence. Nor was his way-finding an aid that was hoarded, and back home he knew he could have led any number of travelers across the taige and hills of Nevi hunting grounds. Except for the glaciers, beyond his kenning.

"Can you lead us, Hagar?" Thengel asked the dwarf at the far side of the camp, yet not so distant that their voices did not carry. Dalin closed his ears to Hagar's reply, his heart sinking at the loss of face he had suffered by mishap, at the way these people were stranded now atop Eskavar because of his haste. The dwarf might know ice lands, but that was not the same as a glacier, the most powerful manifestation of the Ice Mother's body. . . .

Why had he been so careless, in that moment? Why should glacier travel seem so far beyond his kenning? It felt like it should not be beyond his skill to read and travel. That analogy came to him again, that it was not so different from walking river ice. So he lacked the learned skills that many ice travelers had. . . .

But those were not the only abilities he had.

Dalin thought of how he talked with trees, to discover which one wished to surrender its bark to be tinder in a scrying fire. It was the same kind of listening he was aware of doing with the ice-bound streams near Kodanit's Spire: asking if the frozen water cared to bear his weight, not merely trusting blindly to his sure tread and probing staff. And yet what had he done, upon the surface of Eskavar? Gone through the motions that imitated what he had heard tell of . . . but without his sensibilities engaged.

And with them? How would Eskavar respond to him then?

Not that his companions would trust him to lead them again. He heard Arandel mention rope and plan with Hagar how to tie the party together. A safe technique, yes, but not really necessary for the ice-wise and canny. . . . Dalin's grandfather had been that way, so attuned to the elements and the voices of the gods that he walked glaciers and ice-storms and swam freezing torrents as safely as Granmar once hiked among the Crystal Spires.

Why can I not do the same?

Perhaps he could. In fact, he had never tried, really. Not with conscious intent.

He sat wrapped in his warm bearskin and closed his eyes, retreating from the conversations that passed him by. When he did Tarn magic, when he blended shape with root and stone, he fell into rapport with his surroundings and in the doing, *knew* how a tree grew or how a rock lodged in the ground. What could he learn of the glacier, did he do the same here? His breathing steadied and he sent his senses down, not into the ground but into the body of Eskavar beneath him.

It was not a small icy stream, of course, but a great, deep, thick river of ice, moving imponderably slowly as it crept in minute increments down the mountainside to the rivers and sea beyond. It had a rugged surface, like land split with ravines; sun-softened snow lay upon the top with the harder layers below. And deep within the glacier's heart, Elsta's cold grip locked air and interstices and bodies of ice into an intricate frozen matrix, more solid than not, but riddled with the Ice Mother's killing breath. . . .

Dalin's breathing grew rhythmic, his heartbeat slowing as the tarn-trance took him over. He felt the boundary between self and environment blur, in that familiar way that let him blend into trees and countryside. But this time he sought to understand what was around him, not merely to look like one with it. He felt the expanse of ice stretching around him, the party of elves and dwarf and horses a small blot atop a vast field, his senses running along the surface like sensitive fingers over a face. Crevasses like wrinkles there, and an energy beneath it all, slow, cold, deep . . . the depths of water, without the haste of the liquid. . . .

A humming came to him, not a chant, but a crooning that echoed what he felt below him, around him. A cool, passionless song, a resonance with power stored until it broke loose in the sudden flex of ice on a warm day, the splintering off of an iceberg, the gaping of a chasm. . . .

Dalin came to his feet. The ground beneath him felt different. Firmer. He took a few steps and sensed that same quality to the ground where he stood. Reassured, he took a few more.

There, to his left, was a place he did not care to tread. No crevasse, but a pock in the surface of Eskavar, a longish slough that could trap a foot or twist an ankle. Dalin opened his eyes, half-lidded, and looked. The snow crust glittered in the sun of early afternoon, no hint at what lay beneath its surface. Except for the shallow longish sag, which suggested unevenness below.

But I know what is there. He looked to the east, then towards Eskrin. *And what is along this way?* he wondered, and began to walk in that direction.

Nalia was the first to see him go, treading surefooted but looking like one half-asleep. At first she thought him seeking a place to relieve himself. He did not stop but kept going. "Manling!" she called, but Dalin paid her no mind. The others stared. "He's off." She pointed and began to follow after.

"Hey!" Hagar called after. "Stop! That's a—"

A crevasse the dwarf had spotted while Dalin lay desultory after his rescue. It was not visible from the youth's line of approach—but before Hagar could say more, Dalin turned on his heel and skirted the line of the chasm unerringly. Without aid of walking stick. Without seeing the marks farther along where Hagar had probed the edge.

Hagar's eyebrows crept up his forehead as he watched Dalin's progress.

Nalia took the reins of her horse and struck out in Dalin's footsteps. No one moved to follow, but all watched his bearskin-clad figure move in an erratic line, zigging here, going forward, then sharply left or right—but the longer the elves observed, the farther away Dalin progressed without mishap, and Nalia right behind him.

Hagar and Thengel exchanged surprised looks. Arandel shrugged. "It looks like he has found a way after all."

"It's not safe," said Hagar.

"It's fast," said the ranger. "And he's avoiding the hazards we've already scouted out." He shrugged again. "I'm following after."

One by one the outlanders trailed behind Dalin, not willing to follow too closely, not daring to interrupt his progress or distract him from his peculiar focus. South and eastward he wended, often straight ahead, more often making progress by traversing the glacier back and forth at apparently random intervals. Hagar, snorting in irritation, stopped at one such juncture to test the ice ahead and promptly shook snow loose from an abyss that gaped wide enough to swallow horses.

"Hm," mused Thengel, who set out once more in the rear of the procession. Pausing only to point out tracks to Hagar—footprints in a soft patch of snow, not belonging to any of the elves, but neither were they mannish. Nearly like a bear paw, yet narrower and with toes close together. They looked sharply in Dalin's direction, but the youth was far ahead of the trailing elves, and his back was to them as well. "Hm," the elf breathed again, then followed once more behind the rest.

A half hour passed successfully, then an hour with no mishaps—only the ever-wending, random-seeming path that Dalin followed pressing on, farther down the glacier and closer to the eastern edge. Until finally he came to a halting point, on a line with a stony ridge that was the outlier of rugged tree-clad peaks.

Dalin turned back to his companions, his eyes sleepier than ever. He stuck out one arm, pointed due east.

"Leave Estla here," he said to Nalia, the closest one in earshot. His voice was an unrecognizable croak in his throat. "Come to the Ranulf; follow him downstream. There's Eskrin, not far."

His eyes showed white as they rolled up in his head, and Dalin collapsed in the snow.

CHAPTER 14

"I'M GOING TO commission the best bow that Siuvan makes," Rudic Greycloak proclaimed happily. "Seasoned yew, laminated with horn and a fine layer of greatoak for flexible strength. Inlaid. Perfectly balanced. Strung with griffon sinews impervious to rain. Mm. Sweet." He bunched his fingers and pressed them to his lips in a kiss. "Bespelled for distance and accuracy, naturally."

It was nearly evening as they descended the heights from Eskrin, following the trail that forded the upper Ranulf and cut south along the Avar River. Talk had turned to the rewards they would receive for their mission accomplished and how each would spend them. But Rudic was the only bowman here; the others were not dedicated archers and listened to him with merely polite interest as he described his dream weapon.

Their lack of enthusiasm was not lost on him. Unconsciously he adjusted his black velvet cap upon his brow, its red and blue feathered cockade symbol of his mastery of the bow. "The Beruithwë elves are the best bowyers in all of Nimm," he asserted defensively. "All of Tren and Darrim, too. And my kinsmen. A Siuvan bow is worth a dowry in Telerìan."

He spoke of the greatest elvish settlement in their homeland, the stronghold of the *derenestu* nobility allied with the human clans of Nimm. To which Aral sniffed dismissively, "That's not what we value in Clan Terbal lands."

Joro interrupted the bristling half-blood before he could make a sharp retort. "They haven't seen you win the Chief's Keg at Regnorheim, Rudic, or compete at the Duke's Ascendance Day games, as I have. Some people have yet to cultivate an appreciation of an archer's talents."

The pair exchanged knowing smiles. The others on this expedition were hand-picked by Galan Vikkarnor, warchief and nephew of Arn, the Duke of Nimm. The sole exception was Rudic, Joro's own choice—a man with the clean-shaven youthful face and sharp eyes of the elven-blooded, one whose affable demeanor lulled those around him into thinking him harmless and entertaining. Rudic's public face had served them both well over the years. Joro and his associates in the Nightrunner's League saw many ways, yet, in which to use the half-elf's talents. The rest of this oath-bound party would come to appreciate that in time as well, Joro had no doubt.

"What will you be doing with your share of our bounty?" he asked Aral, turning the conversation away from contention and back to the realms of happy planning. He listened as Yellowbeard spoke of building a steading in Clan Terbal territory, his reasoning not hard to divine: founding a freehold of his own was the necessary first step to becoming an independent power within his clan.

Hanno Runemaster listened also, his back to the party as he rode in their lead, their words carrying easily to his ears. He kept his opinions to himself, but the sneer upon his face would have stopped the conversation cold.

Let them dream, he thought. *Soon enough they'll be bereft of the Robe, and their lives along with it.*

Though the Nimmians called their booty a tapestry, Hanno thought of it only as the fabled Robe of Truth, the ancient garment that had cloaked Truthsayers in hallowed vision as they served the Kings of Tura-kem for generations. Not that Hanno aspired to be a Truthsayer—why be mere adviser to kings when there was real authority to be wielded as Riedskana, the High Councillor at the court of Hammankarl II? Old Freggi, the former Councillor, had died recently, and the office was not yet filled by another. Only a runemaster could hold that post, and who did Hammankarl need now but someone not involved in court intrigues, not allied with any faction, with a history of good service—albeit some years agone? . . . Without a Truthsayer to oppose him or reveal his machinations, there was but one realistic choice for the office, and that was Hanno of Havneis, the runemaster once distinguished and since retiring.

Yet I'll come out of retirement to help you now, Hammankarl. Hanno smiled grimly to himself. *Indeed I will.*

With the added bonus of the Truthsayer's robe, his power and influence would be unquestioned at the court of the Selkie King. It remained only to wrest the Robe from these interlopers. Their path had paralleled his own long enough, and their outland arrogance wore sore upon his nerves. As if they had a right to the Robe. The runemaster scowled. No matter these fragments he had gleaned from their barely guarded conversations: they believed the cloak of seers to be a weaving desired by the Duke of Nimm. It would serve some purpose, they fancied, in ending conflict that embroiled their homeland in strife.

Hanno chuckled out loud. Let the Nimmians perish by the sword and battle-axe. What matter to Tura-kem? Those far-distant cousins had long ago defied the gods and slain their kin, following false prophets and renegade deities across the Sea of Lan Loros—a long good riddance, and welcome to whatever ill fate chose to claim them. They could stay out of their abandoned ancestral home and keep their thievish ways to themselves.

His hand strayed to the elkskin pouch at his belt and felt the largest lump within, an oft-used stone embued with runic magic. There was more than one way to rid himself of this foreign nuisance at his back. They had unwittingly secured for him the silence of Granmar, who could have thwarted his bid for power, and brought into his grasp the powerful icon of the advisers of kings. Now it was time to see the Nimmians swept from the playing table. Then on to Etjorvi, and his future.

CHAPTER 15

THE TURBULENT, BOULDER-STREWN Ranulf was unnavigable for its length and treacherous to ford even in the midst of summer. The trader's path followed the easier route down the broader, gentler Avar, which was also fed by the ice waters of Eskavar but wound through southern foothills and into the fertile valleys of the jarldom of Vaer.

Vorsemya Bay was broad and good for fishing, but its steep and rocky shores offered few natural harbors. Vaer was one such, once a mere fishing village, grown slowly into the seat of the Vorsemya jarls. It had become a center of boat-building and a shipping port for charcoal and copper, a town of modest prosperity and population.

Most trade in the region moved on the King's Road along the coast. The Nimmians approached Vaer by means of a little-used trail out of an even less-visited hinterland. The upper Avar was devoid of farmsteads. During the day, wiry mountain goats bounded over the riverside crags, bleating their irritation at the intruders in their grazing grounds. Now, at twilight, reindeer left the sheltering woods to graze in meadows along the river valley. Hanno pointed to one grove where pine and scattered birch flanked the Avar. There would be firewood and needles to sleep on and enough trees to obscure the smoke and light of their fire—not a necessity now, perhaps, but a habit of cautious travel.

"There." The runemaster pointed. "A good place for camp."

Joro agreed, and soon the travelers had settled in for the night. Making dinner on a brace of grouse Rudic had shot during the day, the party ate and laughed and bickered casually. Hanno excused himself from their festivities, making his own small cook fire a stone's long throw distant where he could sit away from the chatter of the Nimmians. By now they were used to his holding aloof from their company, but Joro still gave him a wondering look as he picked up a bird for his dinner. "You're welcome to eat with us," he said reflexively.

Hanno shrugged. "I need to meditate," he said, "away from distraction. It's best if I'm by myself. You understand."

Joro did not, exactly, but he knew priests like Berin often did the same and was not surprised that this local mystic felt a similar need. "As you wish." He nodded agreeably.

Hanno walked to his small fire with nary a look back. He sat facing the Nimmians so he could be aware of what they were up to, should anyone come to disturb him. He need not have bothered; except for the guard they posted in the woods near the trail, the party of outlanders amused themselves jovially around their own fire and showed no interest in the runemaster. Assured of his privacy, Hanno untied the pouch from his belt and pulled out the large stone wrapped in charcoal-smudged deerhide. He tumbled the rock into the palm of his hand and regarded it by the light of his fire.

The stone was a river rock, or had been when he had found it years ago. It was round, flat on one side, domed on the other; it filled the palm of his hand, fingers curling comfortably around its edge. It was a dark green, seeming black in the firelight, and charred black on the bottom from resting in the ashes of countless fires. The domed side was marred with a line carved into the stone, starting in the center and spiraling out in a long curve that circled around itself again and again. Or did it start at the outside and spiral in? Hanno could never remember how he had carved it, for that working had taken place in a trance, as vision from the god Koram imbued him with transcendent knowledge of the moment and the wisdom to create that rune.

No matter. He knew how to use the Gateway rune, and that was what he had before him now.

He cooked his dinner and ate it and later, before his fire burned down, he set the Gateway stone in the embers before him. To onlookers it would seem as if he merely poked in the coals. And so he did: the fire burning modestly upon its bed of embers, he prodded the runestone into the ashes, spiral side up. . . .

A flurry of sparks wafted into the air; then the fire settled down once more. Hanno set aside the stick that he had nudged it with. He sat cross-legged, staring into the glowing coals, letting the heat battle the cold night air flowing south and east off the far upland glacier. A glance at the Nimmians assured him that they were making for their bedrolls. His attention returned to the embers and the rune that began to glow there.

A spiral, it was, symbol of eternity, of no beginning and no end; a vortex to open a path, a gateway that would take him where he wanted his Sight to see. Embers flickered and glowed and lulled his senses; the Gateway spiral lit with a radiance of its own and pulled Hanno's eyes down, down into its depths, and off somewhere beyond.

Whether it was vision or waking dream the runemaster experienced in this state he never knew, but again, as many times before, his visual focus became soft as he began to *see* on another plane. There was a runemaster in Vaer, of course, adviser to the Jarl of Vaer. He did not remember the man's name, but knew his face from a conclave a decade ago . . . bent-nosed, thin-lipped, a stoic fellow with a ferocious temper once provoked. . . .

The spiral opened a field of vision for him, and there he saw a white-bearded man—it was the one he sought, older and ailing now, it seemed, but still the runemaster of Vaer. He sat late in his lord's hall, drinking, but not as deeply as he had that decade agone; he seemed thinner, stooped, a man in the twilight of his healthful years. He set his drinking horn down, and Hanno noted the age marks and heavy blue veins that marred the back of his hand, distracting from the time-blurred tattoos of vocation the man wore there.

Ah, well. Bragla claims us all. As long as he can hear my dream-seeking, I'll have no problem.

There were ways and ways for a runemaster to seek one out across a distance. It was possible to project a seeming, but that would be visible to others in the hall, and there was no need to advertise his presence in that way. Better would be to wait until this runemaster was asleep and talk to him in a lucid dream. The man—what *was* his name? Ah. Sigurd, it came back to him. Sigurd could surely hear him in dream-time. And he would know a visitation for what it was, not mistake it for an ordinary dream. So then. To craft the warning and find the time when he slept . . .

Hanno's patience paid off an hour later. When Sigurd's eyes closed in distant Vaer, the runemaster's own body slipped into a doze by the side of his low-burning fire. In dream-time, Sigurd's body was youthful, younger than the man Hanno had met years before. In that dream he was at a feast, a woman to one side, a young boy to the other, his arm around each.

Hanno sat on the tabletop before him, clearing away trenchers and food with a thought. "I bring you warning," he said. "And a request for aid."

The style of his braid, his tattoos, the amulets around his neck all identified him as runemaster, and those items stayed intact in this dream state. Sigurd saw, and responded as years of training dictated he must. The woman and boy faded from his side, though the banquet table remained. "What word?" the Vorsemya runemaster asked.

"I travel with raiders from Nimm."

Sigurd's expression darkened. The coasts of Tura-kem were harried by Nimmian longships; every steading man was ready to guard against and fight the interlopers at a moment's notice. Any man on the coast would be happy to see them dead, and that was the reaction Hanno had counted on.

He spat in punctuation of his words. "My only purpose for being with them is to bring them to a swift end. I suspected them of thievery and murderous intent, and now I know it is so. I ask your help to destroy them."

"What can I do?" Sigurd asked without hesitation.

"We are on the Avar, nearing Vaer tomorrow. They think to travel incognito." Hanno quirked a bitter smile. "I think it would be better if they had a special welcome. . . ."

Sigurd nodded agreement. The two runemasters talked late into the night, until finally Hanno let his lucid dream drift naturally into sleep, and he dozed heavily by the burned-out ashes of his fire.

CHAPTER 16

Dalin's ribs ached and he felt nauseous: the result of riding belly-down over Nalia's saddle for miles and miles. Belec was the first by his side when he collapsed, but when the priest assured the others that the only thing wrong with Dalin was exhaustion, Arandel and Hagar had been quick to wrestle the youth onto horseback and bind him there like so much cargo. "We are still behind our quarry, yes?" the ranger commented. "Then haste still matters. Our pathfinder can rest in Eskrin."

And so in unconscious discomfort the youth had traversed miles of mountainous woodland in oblivion, until he groaned back to waking on the last ridge outside Eskrin. The travelers paused then, and Thengel helped the young man to his feet—snatching his tunic quickly to hold him upright as the blood rushed from his head and he threatened to topple right over.

"I want to know how you did that," Thengel said.

"Feel dizzy?" Dalin looked blood-drained.

"No. Got us across the glacier. But later, when you're up to it. For now. . . ." Thengel nodded downhill, to the stone-walled stronghold before them. Twilight shadows were stretching over the valley and cloaking the settlement in dusk. "Eskrin. We'll have dinner and ask about the Nimmians."

Dalin shook his head. "Let me ask. They'll talk to me."

Thengel cocked his head. "And not to me, you are saying?"

Dalin shrugged. "You're not from here. They'll wonder why you pry into their affairs."

"Mm. Give it a try, Truthsayer. We'll see what you can learn."

Dalin stopped short. "Don't call me that. Not yet." He hesitated. "They'll think that's Granmar. I need to find a way. . . . I mean, to tell them. . . ."

Thengel ignored the youth's stumbling. "I understand," he said softly. "We'll leave it to you to say."

They set off to Eskrin.

FOR THE SECOND time that day, Torvin had visitors come to guest at his long hall. This party was stranger than the last: a boy, native to Tura-kem but not local, in company with people clearly outland in face and manner. One loomed taller than any man the steading chief had ever met—he had to bend his head to pass through the outsize door of the great hall. And thin he was, and would have seemed frail did he not move with a warrior's sure confidence. . . .

Torvin brought his eyes back to the boy before him, the fuzz of a first mustache sparse gold on his upper lip. He regarded him kindly, encouraging the shy youth who stumbled nervously introducing himself and his friends. Odd names they had, and pretentious titles that he paid little heed to, but for the youth himself.

"Dalin of Nevi. Nevi is far, but your name I have heard."

"No doubt, sir," Dalin said. "I am the Truthsayer's apprentice. Or was."

Recognition came over Torvin's face, followed quickly by curiosity. "Was? Have you left his service, then?"

The question took the boy strange, and were it not unmanful, Torvin thought he would have cried. Knew it, when he heard Dalin's words choked through a strained throat. "The Truthsayer is dead. Murdered by outlanders."

The freeholder sat bolt upright. "What?"

"I saw it myself. Men from Nimm. They threw Granmar to his death and stole the Robe." He gestured to his companions. "We are on their trail to retrieve it and bring them to justice."

The strangers with Dalin exchanged looks among themselves, but did not contradict what the youth had to say.

Torvin stirred uneasily. "Hanno Runemaster dined here with companions, midday. He said the Truthsayer was not to be found. How long ago did this happen?"

Dalin's brow furrowed. "A runemaster traveled with the murderers. He helped them seek out Kodanit's Spire and left me to die on the mountainside. He's one of them."

"Left you . . . ?" Torvin's jaw dropped. "Did he harm the Truthsayer?" he asked incredulously.

Dalin paused before answering. "No. Not directly. But he death-wished Granmar with a skenjis. I saw the workings upon it."

Sudden anger colored Torvin's face bright red. He pushed himself back from the table. "And I sheltered this treachery under my own roof?" It was unthinkable for a runemaster to be involved in such a crime, but that thought warred with the chieftain's memories of old gossip, of a runemaster whom Granmar had pressed to leave the King's court years agone. . . .

If Dalin's story was true, he had been taken in and taken advantage of. "Describe the men you saw."

The youth complied, and Torvin's heart sank. There was no mistaking the boy's description of the strangers who had broken their fast at his table. He cast a suspicious eye at the new group of strangers, also outlanders, who peopled his hall now. "And these? How do I know they are trustworthy?"

Dalin drew himself up. "That is not for you to judge. I tell you they are my friends and have saved my life. They are helping me to find these murderers."

"Who I guested here today. Pfaw!" Torvin spat among the rushes and slammed a fist onto his tabletop. Then paused, a last doubt in his mind. "But a runemaster . . . ! Boy, can you be certain of what you saw? Your accusation is not something to be made lightly."

The youth spoke with calm certainty. "I was the Truthsayer's apprentice, and after Granmar's death, his heir. I know what I saw, and I speak the truth. Will you help us?"

Torvin held eyes with the young man for a long while. He saw honesty there and he saw conviction. And he saw grief.

It was that last that convinced him. He heard true, from the youth who would be Truthsayer. He had unwittingly aided murderers and a runemaster who, if Dalin's story was correct, had done the unthinkable in bringing about the Truthsayer's destruction. He nodded decisively.

"Yes, you have our aid." He came to his feet. "They are on their way to Tesvi Cove, north of Vaer, but traveling through that town first. Hanno inquired of the route down the Avar."

"How far ahead of us?" the tall stranger asked.

"A half-day's travel, perhaps more."

"If we leave now, and ride fast—"

"If they've left the trail for any reason you'll miss them. No. You cannot catch them for certain if you follow behind. But you can beat them to Tesvi Cove if you go there directly."

"How so?" asked Dalin. "The only road—"

"Is the trail down the Avar, yes. But there are other ways. Along the Ranulf, and cutting over to the coast."

"I thought the Ranulf impassable?"

Torvin was impressed. The boy had good knowledge of the countryside, for one who had lived laired in the Spires with the reclusive Truthsayer.

"True, for the most part. But we know ways."

"You'll show us?"

For answer he turned to a clansman at his side. "Get Efric and Sembra and their men. We leave before first light." He turned back to the youth and his companions. "I'll take you to Tesvi myself. No murderers and thieves use my hospitality falsely. And if you're right about the runemaster—that is someone you'll need help taking to Jarl Gruithe."

"Jarl?" asked Dalin.

"Of Vaer. He would hear the trial of a man of such rank, not the Justiciar." It was clear from the boy's expression he had never thought that far ahead. "He'll have to stand trial, you know. So will the others. Unless they fight us and we must kill them." Torvin smiled meaningfully.

Dalin looked a little shaken at the thought.

"It might be necessary, boy," Torvin added more gently. "Besides. They're Nimmians, you say."

The youth nodded.

"Well then. We aren't obligated to give them a trial, now are we? If they don't come as bidden . . . they won't need to come at all."

CHAPTER 17

ARAL WAS IN better spirits this morning than he had been in many a long day. Rudic was on guard, Joro at the riverside fetching water. Berin tended the horses. Kaylis was alone nearby, feeding the breakfast fire in the chill twilight of dawn.

The firelight caught her form just so, her soft doeskin leathers clinging enticingly to her body, their bleached whiteness warmed to golden yellow by the flames. Aral was taken in that moment by her alien beauty, the suggestion of smoldering sensuality behind her cold elvish exterior. He saw it in her eyes, or thought he did, when she thought herself unobserved.

No matter that she held rank in the exclusive Collegium Magisterium—she was not of the human clans of Nimm, and the ways of elves were different, more hedonistic, less constrained by propriety than the men and women of his homeland. Or so was Aral's understanding of the elves, with whom he seldom mingled, and that was sufficient to inform his attitude towards Kaylis Rutherin. Never one for finesse, he took even less care to edit his words with this female than he would have with a human woman. He had not been with a woman in weeks. He would be frank.

"I want you." He said it bluntly, a statement and a proposition in one.

His words carried, but she showed no immediate sign of hearing them. She finished building up the fire, set down the stick she used to arrange the wood . . . then turned leisurely in his direction.

Firelight caught her high cheekbones, her almond eyes, struck yellow highlights into her long near-white mane of tow-colored hair. Her imperious face studied him, and to his gratification, no sneer or snarl of rejection flew his way. Instead, she sized him up appraisingly, eyes running from head to toe and lingeringly back up again. Then a slight smile quirked her lips, and she turned back to the fire.

How unreachably beautiful she looked in that moment—enough to forestall the words that clamored at his lips, that would press her for a response. She had given no reply, and yet, she had answered him, he thought. Bemused, Aral gathered up his bedroll. Here was something new to tantalize himself with, to break the monotony of long days on the road. He smiled at the prospect of taking her one day, perhaps soon, and her willing for the sport. And the anticipation that would build between now and then. . . .

Though he should have been rear guard on their march, it was for that reason that he pulled up instead to ride alongside the elvish woman. His forays at small talk were larded with innuendo. She did not take his attentions amiss, it seemed to him, although she responded with neither warmth nor offense, as a human wench would have. He was figuring out how his comments struck her—amused her? Titillated her?—impossible to tell with that regal expression that sat so naturally upon her face, a veil to her true emotions. . . .

And so Aral Yellowbeard was not the first target of opportunity to be picked off from the rear when they rode into ambush. It was Berin, lagging behind at the slower pace of the packhorses he led.

Ffffft. An arrow cut the air in flight, pierced his cloak of mountain lion fur, and shoved the priest forward over the cantle of his saddle with the force of its impact. A second took him in the left arm just above the bicep. As a cleric more at home in the halls of Tornor's temple than on the trail, his riding seat was never so secure in the best of times. Berin gave a cry and tumbled groundward from his horse.

The sound of the first shaft was enough to alert Rudic's fine-tuned ears and archer's reflexes. "Take cover!" he cried, spurring his mount into the trees beside the trail.

Joro started and dropped his reins, fumbled toward the broadsword at his belt. Aral cursed and wheeled his bay while Kaylis pulled up her horse and sat motionless, fair game for the arrows trained upon the party.

Hanno looked over his shoulder, feigning consternation in keeping with his role as innocent leader of the party. A stirring in the brush he had just passed marked where more Vaer archers loosed into the chaos behind him. He reined his horse half about as Sigurd stepped onto the path, cocking his arm back. A stone flew from his fist into the close-packed Nimmians milling a short sprint's distance away. End over end tumbled the rune stone, glinting like a chip of glacier ice in the sun. It fell to the ground not far from Kaylis, and an eyeblink later a freezing blast burst upon the trail, a fierce explosion of air and ice and hell's own frost.

Hanno squinted against the fury of the ice-rune. Whoever was not slain outright by the archer's first attack had surely succumbed to this death-dealing squall of unnatural cold. He began to smile in triumph—until his brain registered that what transpired before him did not match the image he had born in mind's eye all day long.

Joro had not fumbled for his sword after all. His hands crossed to opposite sides of his belt, emerged from beneath his cloak with glinting blades in hand—throwing daggers that flew swift as thought from his fingers, one to left and one to right, before Sigurd had stepped full upon the path. The archers closest to Hanno gave strangled outcries; bows loosed arrows askew into brush and tree trunk as the men fell, clutching their throats.

Rudic's charge into the trees had trampled one ambusher underhoof, set another to scrambling for his life. Before the second could dodge far enough away, the mounted archer had pulled his bow from its saddle case and strung it against his thigh. His red-and-blue-fletched shaft buried itself in his assailant's back just before Rudic's feet touched the ground in a springing dismount. A second arrow and a third left the half-elf's bow, seeking enemy archers who were concealed from the trail, but not from among the flanking trees.

Aral's hide-covered shield was already upon his arm, the leather concealing the markings that would otherwise proclaim his Nimmian origin to all onlookers. An arrow pierced his thigh as he wheeled his horse about, but his sturdy five-link chain mail hauberk kept the wound shallow. He gritted his teeth and snatched a throwing ax from his belt. It split the chest of a swordsman who left concealment too soon by the side of the road. Without lingering to see the ax fly home, he spurred the short distance to where Berin lay in the dirt and pine needles of the trail.

The warrior leaped to the ground, staggering upon his wounded leg. Ignoring the sword at his own belt, he pulled Berin's blade from its sheath as white-feathered arrows thudded into his deftly held shield. The borrowed broadsword blazed in his hand, mirroring the heraldry concealed upon his buckler—for there beneath the leather cover was depicted Vikkar Tornor's golden blade of truth, bold upon a white stripe on a green field, symbol of the ruling Clan Terbal of Nimm.

Berin's oathblade, Redeemer, was as much kin to that holy symbol as temple artifice and prayer could make it, entrusted to the priest to further the mission of Tornor's pledglings. The thrice-blessed sword shone with the brilliance of summer's sun, and Aral's heart grew bold as he felt its power in his grip. With a mighty cry, he charged the two enemy swordsmen who had stepped upon the backtrail nearby.

It was exactly at that moment that Sigurd's ice-rune exploded with freezing wrath. The gusting wind battered friend and foe alike. Aral was at the edge of its range, guarded by Redeemer's power, and charged on raging into the enemy. Rudic, sheltered by trees, hunkered beneath the sudden onslaught of hellish cold, cursed as he realized his fingers were near frostbitten. Cursed again when his bowstring snapped as he pulled it taut. Then he laughed, realizing the same must have happened to all bowmen round about and now he was safe from the unpredictable attack of missile fire. The master archer drew his long sword and darted through ice-coated underbrush toward the closest enemy he had spotted.

Joro was shoved nearly out of his saddle by the icy blast, his horse staggering on the trail toward Hanno. The Nimmian leader shivered uncontrollably and locked eyes with the runemaster in a startled moment of assessment. Berin stirred feebly upon the path, frosted with the same icy glaze that suddenly coated path and horse and people close to the blast.

Except for Kaylis, motionless at the heart of the storm, untouched by its blizzard fury.

Like a queen of ice at home in her element she sat, light-haired, white-garbed, atop her Turakemi mare the color of golden cream, woman and mount unscathed by the killing frost. No arrows had touched her; Hanno saw shafts on the ground nearby, as if dropped from a hand, and knew they should have transfixed her long before coming to rest on the earth. Her lips were pinched with the merest hint of disdain, and her amber eyes narrowed as she fixed Sigurd with her attention. Her right hand lifted, the only movement in the center of the ice-striken path. Silver rings sparkled on little finger and thumb, and one slender forefinger pointed to the runemaster of Vaer.

"*Neneile,*" she breathed.

The word carried like a whisper through the air over a frozen lake. It traveled with preternatural clarity to Hanno's ears, and the ears of its target, and something else came in its wake, a surge of power not visible, but speeding with the same swift surety as the arrows so lately loosed upon the foreigners. That something found Sigurd and choked a gurgle from his throat. Hanno tore his eyes from the elvish woman long enough to glance toward his compatriot—and then stare in openmouthed horror.

Sigurd had staggered back one half-step as if pushed in the chest by a strong man. Something had touched him there, indeed, but no man it was. That something frosted his tunic, breathed hoar-ice across his chest, a hellish chill that spread a frozen icing over torso, up shoulders, neck, down arms and legs: man and clothing alike freezing through, slowly at first, then with gathering speed. Sigurd stumbled, reached one hand stiffly toward opposite forearm in disbelief before his fingers became unmoving claws, his nails turned blue with the killing cold of Elsta's breath, pervading him from within.

In the space of a few heartbeats, the man glazed over like the victim of a snowstorm, found frozen days later in the drifts between byre and cottage hearth. The life left him long before his balance did. He teetered like an axed tree, overbalanced, and toppled to the ground. He hit with a thud that spoke of meat long frozen in the depths of winter.

Hanno groaned involuntarily. Brush crackled as ambushers retreated, and the runemaster realized he had not been the only witness to this terrible demonstration of power. No wonder the Vaer men fled. He would have fled in that moment, too, if he did not fear more that wrath behind his back, seeking him out upon the trail for his treachery.

A double-dealing he must be quick to disavow.

"Th-thank you," he managed to get out. "You saved my life."

Silence greeted him. Kaylis perhaps had not heard, but Joro had, and the Nimmian stared blandly at the runemaster who had ridden past the jaws of the trap that had closed upon his party.

Hanno jerked his head toward the ice-logged corpse of the Vaer runemaster. "They would have tried me, for being your guide. And then beheaded me."

Joro pulled his horse around in a tight circle, scouting the nearby woods with a glance, verifying what his senses already told him—that they were alone, their enemies gone. He halted his circuit, shrugging his shoulders, and thawing sheet ice dropped from his cloak and his horse's flanks.

"Since when do runemasters lead warriors into the empty woods, Hanno? Why attack us, if they did not know we are Nimmian?" Joro rode close, leaned over his saddle horn towards the older man. "How did they know we are here?"

Hanno's expression was worried and quizzical at once. "That I would like to know, as well. If you have been recognized as outlanders, then I am in trouble along with you."

Joro frowned and opened his mouth, but Aral's shout interrupted whatever he might have said. "Here!" he called. "A prisoner, and answers to be had!"

He dragged a man by the scruff of the neck—a man who could no longer walk, hamstrung from behind by one crippling slash of the oathblade Aral bore. The Turakemi was pale and trembling, shock or fright—or both—taking their toll upon a man who would never walk again, if he survived beyond the warrior's gentle questioning.

Rudic had slipped back through the woods and was the first to tend to the priest, facedown in the trail. Kaylis had joined him as Aral dragged his living booty past Berin Oathkeeper and dumped the prisoner on the ice-blasted ground. Joro nudged the runemaster ahead of him, escorting the man back into their midst.

"How is Berin?" he called over to Rudic.

"He'll live," the half-elf replied, tapping on the cleric's back for emphasis. Berin groaned. "Half-plate over the shoulders and upper back," the archer observed. "Punctured by that arrow, but the wound is shallow and the armor repairable. This one will hurt, though." He pointed to the man's arm above the bicep.

"I expect he can heal it, with Tornor's help," Joro said dryly. "Just make sure the shaft is out and the bleeding stopped."

"I should scout around," Rudic said, looking doubtful. "If they return, we're easy targets again—"

"They aren't returning," Kaylis said in a distant voice. "I'm watching the area."

Hanno studied the woman's face. Indeed, she looked distracted, focused elsewhere, and now and then cocked her head to the side as if listening to a voice only she could hear. He shuddered.

Never had he suspected that here was a Nimmian witch in their midst. Or was that elvish sorcery that she practiced, immunity to cold and a deadly dealing of the Ice Mother's breath . . . ? No matter; it was horrible and powerful, far more so than he had been prepared for. And the rest of them, also more skilled and battle-ready than he had believed them to be.

He vowed he would not underestimate these outlanders again. . . .

"Then I believe you have some news we'd like to hear," Joro said, prodding the Turakemi who sprawled bleeding at Aral's feet. "If you hope to live, you'll talk to us."

The man saw Joro with glassy eyes. Hanno could see he was in shock; the Nimmians realized it as well. "Let's patch him up a bit first, Aral," Joro said. "It would be a shame for him to leave our company unexpectedly."

Yellowbeard scowled. "He's not going anywhere," he began to protest, and then realized how Joro must have meant that. The warrior's frown deepened, but he sheathed Redeemer at his belt, setting his own ordinary broadsword aside, then knelt by his captive and began to tend his wounds.

Joro turned a jovial smile on Hanno. "Dismount, I beg of you. I think this is a fine place to make camp for a while. Now that we have a guest to entertain and gossip to hear."

The runemaster scowled at Joro's invitation. Could the man not speak straightforwardly? His false lightheartedness irritated Hanno, who would as soon have slit throats and growled terse orders, had these been his people to command. But this was not the time to seem uncooperative. He grunted acquiesence and climbed down from the saddle.

Aral Yellowbeard's treatment was rough but efficient. A tourniquet on each leg stopped the bleeding that threatened to drain their prisoner of life. Blood stained the ground beneath him, though, and ice tinged pink where he lay. Aral gave the man to drink of a vial, a healing draft the warrior carried against just such need himself. Color returned to the Vaer swordsman's face, and Hanno chewed his lip thoughtfully. What had Sigurd told these men he'd led to waylay the Nimmians?

Yellowbeard knelt by the prisoner's side, pulled the knife from his belt, and set the point beneath the man's chin. "Now, you bastard," he said in quiet tones. "We are going to have a little talk. How did you know we were in these woods.?"

The Vaer man was no youth. He was a warrior of middle years, no doubt seasoned in battle, at least in coastal skirmishes against raiders. Frightened, clearly, but stubborn as well. He scowled at his captor and licked his lips, but otherwise offered no word. Hanno could feel the man calculating his chances. Saw the glance he shot his way, an indecipherable expression at seeing a runemaster standing behind his interrogator.

Aral saw that look and expression, too. "What?" he asked with a prod of the knife. "Surprised to see our friend? Now why would that be?"

Still no response from the prisoner. Aral curled a bearded lip and reached down, grabbing one of the prisoner's hands in his own. The motion was followed by his knife blade. A moment later the prisoner screamed and snatched his hand to his chest, cradling it with the other. The Nimmian flicked something bloody to the side of the trail and turned back, grinning, to his captive. "Let me ask you this again," he began.

Hanno shut his eyes before he turned his face away. His feet took him away from the interrogation, but he was unheeding of that distancing; he wished only that he could close his ears to the prisoner's entreaties and shrieks without seeming weak before the Nimmians. For it would not do to seem vulnerable before such savage interlopers. He gritted his teeth and thought of the battlefields of his youth, of the cries of injured men and the pleas for mercy from the horribly dying wounded.

His eyes flicked open. The prisoner was babbling now, answering everything Aral asked. His name; where he was from; who led them. Did he know that Hanno had visited Sigurd in dream-time? Could he betray the runemaster's treachery? Very likely so. Hanno did not dare wait to find out, but how to silence the suffering man without giving himself away? Overt magic would not serve. . . .

The skenjis that had death-wished Granmar was far away, but the rune magic that powered it was a collection of symbols still vibrantly malevolent in Hanno's mind. The wounded man, tortured now to near-incoherence by Aral, was already weak, near shock; his body close enough to dying, if it went untended. Mayhap something subtle would serve to tip those scales, but he had little time. Already the man talked about Sigurd, runemaster of Vaer, and how he rose that very morning with the words of a dream on his lips. . . .

Hanno squatted on his haunches to the side of the trail. He dandled his hand close to the ground, the tip of his finger among dirt and pebbles, aimlessly to the onlooking eye.

Not so to the runemaster. There the rippling lines of water, the dotted peaks of corroding stone or sand: the pictogram for weakness, for the draining or loss of strength and power. One of the many symbols that had adorned the skenjis, that ill-wishing totem. Now the rune for weakness came to life on the grounded surface beneath his feet, a surface that connected to the Turakemi prisoner, a man weak and bleeding, in great pain, who lay screaming his lungs out. . . .

And in moments, his life. Hanno watched with his second sight as the dirt-scribed rune glowed a baleful orange, an angry color that seeped along the trail toward the warrior like water seeking its lowest level on the ground. A groan of pain squeezed from the man's lungs, his tortured hands dropped listlessly to the ground at his sigh, and a great breath rattled from his throat.

The runemaster kept a smile from his lips with effort. The prisoner had expired without breathing Hanno's name.

Aral cursed the corpse before him, rose to his feet, and kicked the dead man vengefully.

"Tsk," Joro admonished him. "We have enough information, do we not?"

"I could have gotten more," Yellowbeard fumed.

"Then next time you should question more gently, especially when they are ailing." Joro's disapproval was evident. "But we've learned what's important, have we not?"

"They're alert to our presence," Aral snarled. "We daren't go on through Vaer. We'll have to move cross-country, head straight north, and then cut east to Tesvi Cove."

Joro turned to Hanno. "Can you show us the way?"

The runemaster came to his feet, took a step that shuffled his foot across the rune scratched into the dirt of the trail. "Yes," he replied.

"Good." The leader of the Nimmians studied Berin, sitting up braced against Kaylis, as Rudic finished bandaging his arm. "Are you fit to travel, Oathkeeper?"

"I will be," Berin said in a strained voice. "Give me time, yet, to pray for healing. I'll be better soon enough."

"Very well. Leave that carrion," Joro said to Aral, "and let us collect ourselves. As soon as Berin can sit saddle again, we head north."

CHAPTER 18

No rooster yet crowed when Torvin gathered his kinsmen at Eskrin's broad wooden gate. Some few carried torches, flames dancing in the cold breeze off the frozen heights. The firelight fell starkly upon the rugged features of woodsmen and hunters, their leather leggings laced up over sturdy homespun trousers, their faces clean-shaven but for the long mustaches favored by the men of Tura-kem. They wore bows slung a-back and hand axes at their hips; some held spears as well. All stood ready to travel swift and light into the wooded country that flanked the Ranulf.

Torvin's eyes flickered over the mounts of the strangers, four-legged hindrances that would keep them away from boulder-strewn river course or the shortcuts traversable only on foot. He gestured for the gate to be unbarred. His kinsman Efric, a grim, stocky hunter from the upland woods, led the way through the steading's gate.

They went down gravel-strewn pathways well worn by cattle, across a broad grazing meadow to the riverside. There, as the eastern sky began to lighten, they turned onto a trail that skirted the glacier-fed watercourse. They heard the Ranulf before they saw it: a noisy, raucous tumble of chattering white water and boulder-strewn riverbed, the rush of ice water tumbling through its crowded, swift-flowing channel and resounding far into the trees. In sight of the foam-topped water they took a trail that headed south and east through pine woods and long-frond cedar.

Not far from Eskrin the river ran quieter, broadening along a bar into an expanse of swift but shallow water. The track came close to the water's edge. "The ford." Torvin pointed. "Beyond is the Avar trail. We'll keep on, though." And the party passed the route that Hanno Runemaster had followed earlier, continuing along the river's course. Daybreak saw them hiking around the end of a wooden ridge, sticking to the north bank of the river as it curved eastward, gouging its way through mountainous folds and into the densely wooded country beyond.

"Back and forth he cuts," Torvin said of the river. "Following ravines, plunging over a scarp or two . . . picking up force as he plunges to the lowlands."

"Where can we cross?" Thengel asked.

"Not until we are far to the north and east from here. When the Ranulf reaches the lowland valleys of the Vorsemya farmlands, there is Finskili, Sembra's home steading."

"How far?" Dalin asked.

Torvin shrugged. "We'll be there by sundown, perhaps. Or later." He glanced at the horses as he spoke.

"Then why did we not cross at the Avar ford," Thengel asked, "when it would already put us across the river?"

Torvin shook his head. "We would have to follow the Avar river seaward, and that does not put us ahead of our quarry." He gestured along the trail. "This way is long about, but speedier still than our alternatives. Sembra knows the river crossing."

His words had a tone of finality, and the others let the conversation lapse. Dalin looked for the man whose name was invoked, but failed to see him on the wooded path they followed. Already he was far ahead with his kinsmen, leading the way for the others, within hailing distance but not easy sight amid the tree-lined, wending trail. Dalin had a vision of being trapped in deep trackless woods for entirely too long. "I hope he's right," he said, half to himself. "We must get to Tesvi Cove before those men can take ship."

Torvin looked back over his shoulder at the youth. "That is my ambition as well, Dalin of Nevi." He glanced to the horses, hand-led along the rough trail, then back to the Truthsayer's apprentice. "We will do our very best."

The Eskrin chief faced ahead and moved out with lengthened stride. Dalin frowned at Torvin's back. Already the man's words sounded less certain than what he had declared in outrage and bold conviction the night before. He wondered how swiftly they would really travel, how soon they would reach their goal. A day from here to Finskili, another day beyond to Tesvi. . . .

Preoccupied by calculations of time and travel, Dalin and his friends fell silent and followed their Turakemi guides ever on along the turbulent Ranulf.

BRIGHT SUNLIGHT STREAMED through high needled branches and lent uncommon warmth to air that had frosted before dawn. Dalin's heavy bearskin cloak draped Thengel's saddle; others shed their cloaks and extraneous gear as well, leaving it for the horses to carry along this strenuous upslope path. Sembra had led them a detour from the river's edge, cutting along the flank of a steep northern ridge to avoid the boulder field beside the river.

Footing was precarious here, each step sliding downslope through slick needle pack, halted only by the soft loam and rough rocks beneath. Dalin picked his way along as cautiously as his friends, not wanting to twist an ankle or slip and crack his head on the broad fir trunks downslope.

Their escort made no halt for breakfast, nor breaks along the way. Bread and cheese were taken from pouches and eaten on the trail. At one such mid-morning interval, one woodsman fell back along the way, offered a large ale-skin to Dalin.

The man was near Dalin's own age, but old enough to wear a full mustache. He had the look of Efric's kin, broad, muscular shoulders and a heavy, creased brow. "Here." He offered the drink with a strange duck of his head: a gesture half-subservient or, perhaps, reverent. He watched as Dalin took two long swigs, then held out his hand for the return of the skin. He looked surprised when Dalin turned to Thengel instead.

"Drink?"

The tall elf wrapped long fingers around the aleskin, nodded his thanks, drank, and passed it back along the line of his companions. The young woodsman looked disconcerted. He did not demand the skin back but was quick to snatch it from Hagar's fingers when it was passed forward again. The man shot a cryptic look at Dalin, then trotted ahead to resume his place in the order of march.

"What's wrong with him?" Thengel mused.

"Human sense of hospitality," Arandel muttered under his breath.

The jibe bothered Dalin and he spoke reflexively. "He's reluctant to mingle with you, that's all," he said over his shoulder.

"Why should that be?" Thengel was sincerely surprised. "We but follow their lead, have offered no offense."

Dalin shrugged. It was evident that their escort gave the elves and dwarf a wide berth, and intuitively he understood why. To Dalin their guides offered a stilted deference, no doubt because they honored him as Truthsayer's apprentice. But these outland folk—what to make of them?

He had to admit that if these people had come to guest at his family's steading in distant Nevi he, too, would have been standoffish until he knew better what sort of folk they might be. Hagar was of an ilk known to the clansmen of Tura-kem: tales of dwarves traveled by hearsay, and the miners and craftsmen of the Greywatch Mountains to the south had a reputation that journied even to the flanks of Eskavar glacier. Besides his own proud declaration of race, Hagar's squat frame could be mistaken for nothing else but stone-kin and creation of Heimek, Earth Father.

But of elves the Turakemi knew and saw little. The only knowledge in common men's heads were the winter tales of a folk that hunted scant-clad among the glaciers of the Great Ice to the north, who wielded magic fit to rival the gods and stole human children for adoption or sacrifice; none knew for sure. Merchants spoke of elves as well, but who could believe even the most mundane story told by a Koribi trader?

Dalin looked again to Thengel and saw the elf regarding him questioningly. "They don't know you, yet," he tried to reassure the outlander. "They'll stand aloof until they do."

"You are right, young Dalin," the elf said softly. "We have met this attitude before among your countrymen. I suppose we shall have to prove ourselves wherever we journey here."

"Wherever they haven't heard of us, you mean," Hagar grumbled.

"Heard of you?" Dalin asked.

"We are known in some small parts of your land already," Thengel said dryly. "We have been honored by the Jarl of Kalajok, for one."

"And dined with King Hammankarl in Etjorvi," added the dwarf.

Dalin half-turned to stare, near tripped over his own feet on the treacherous pathway. He did not know of the jarl they referred to, but the rank spoke for itself, and to be guested at the King's own table . . . ! His face lit with a hundred questions. "How—?"

Thengel forstalled the onslaught with a raised hand. "A tale for later, for a warm inn and much wine by a fireside."

Self-important foreign titles were one thing; acquaintance with the King of Tura-kem quite another. "If you are so well-connected," Dalin blurted, "why did you not say anything to Torvin?"

Thengel pursed his lips. It was for Nalia to chime in with her throaty laugh. "We're not here to curry favor with backwoods freeholders. Let them scorn us; we have recognition aplenty where it truly matters."

Dalin was forced to face ahead and tend his footing. "Is that why you came seeking Granmar?" he blurted out. "Because of your connections?"

He regretted it as soon as he said it, for it seemed a prying thing to ask— and yet something in his words struck a chord with Thengel, for the tall warrior looked faintly surprised and then guarded.

"Not why," said the Guardian of the Thorn. "How. Friends at the King's court told us how to find the Truthsayer. But we found you, instead."

The King's court. They knew the Selkie King, had been to Etjorvi—a journey Granmar had always promised him, but not lived long enough to effect. Dalin studied the path ahead earnestly, blinking away sudden moisture from his eyes. His mind replayed the Truthsayer's death, the struggle at the lip of the cave, his master's shriek as he plunged down Kodanit's Spire. . . .

Only later did Dalin recall that Thengel did not mention why they had sought Granmar. By then, the moment for discussing it had passed.

CHAPTER 19

Hanno struck off to the north across country, taking a route that ran the length of wooded valleys, past scattered farmsteads and fortified holdings but avoided settlements clustered in valley floors. The Nimmians threaded a labyrinth of pathways: deer trail connecting to fox run connecting to mountain goat track, feeding into reindeer trail, all along ridge flank or wooded crest. Hanno kept a Way rune clenched in his left fist and followed the pathways as if he had marked them out himself. North they traveled, sometimes diverted, sometimes switching back, but always, in the end, to the north. Never too close to human habitation, nor treading ground too difficult for their horses to cover.

When the runemaster struck off to lead the march, Aral returned to his neglected position as rear guard. He reined up briefly next to Berin, the priest white-faced but sitting saddle once again.

"I took this in need," the warrior declared, laying hand on the blessed broadsword at his side. Aral's ordinary weapon rode now where he had placed it in Berin's sheath.

The priest regarded Aral, tugged thoughtfully on his mustache. "If you had been anyone else . . . if you were not a follower of Vikkar Tornor and were not dedicated to his cause . . . you could never have touched that sword. You would have been struck dead, or close enough to it. Did you know that?"

Aral's eyebrows rose and he looked down involuntarily. The large, square-cut tourmaline set in the pommel of the sword caught the sun brilliantly, marked the sword as oathblade and holy weapon.

"It can be wielded only by one of the faithful, in the name of the demigod himself. Anyone else who tries will die."

Aral licked his lips, his only betrayal that the priest's news was unnerving.

"And now you want to keep Redeemer, to use it should need arise."

Yellowbeard nodded.

Berin looked away, into the forested distance, then shrugged. "They gave it to me to aid our quest. You are better with a sword than I; there is no question about that. This blade does not speak more strongly to a priest than to one of the faithful."

He stretched out an arm, touched the sword's pommel with one finger. The tourmaline glowed a brilliant green, shining with internal sunlight. "Just remember. It serves only the faithful. Let your trust in Vikkar Tornor falter not, Aral son of Teril, nor turn aside from your vows, nor alter your heart. Or it will become anathema to your touch, just as surely as if you were a nonbeliever or an enemy of our ethos. Do you understand me?"

Aral looked up, met the man's eyes. He swallowed. Here did not speak scholarly Berin, inexperienced comrade in a fight. Here spoke the Oathkeeper, the cleric with god-given power to ensure that he and his companions remained obedient to their sworn word. Surely Vikkar Tornor's voice expressed through this man, for the words he spoke gave the warrior a chill. Aral sketched the empty-handed sword salute that punctuated prayers and vows made in the name of the demigod of oaths and truth and unshakable fidelity. Satisfied, Berin released him with a nod. "Wear it well. But if I need it back, Aral, no argument."

The son of the house of Terbal opened his mouth, then thought better and shut it again. Acknowledging Berin's wishes with a nod of his head, he wheeled his horse around and rode back to his guard position, Redeemer at his side.

Even with the aid of a Way rune, the going was much slower than if they had ridden openly on the coast road. Twilight saw the Nimmians encamped on a thickly wooded ridge, concealing their fire from the eyes of habitation in the valley below. Hours of tedious travel had changed Aral's eager vigilance into sour disaffection. The warrior chafed because they were not yet in sight of the coast, not yet at their goal.

"You think he's led us right?" he growled an aside to Joro.

"He says he has."

"Ask me, we're wandering aimlessly all over these ridges. Nightfall and still no ship harbor made."

"It took longer, these off-road ways," Joro said, but he turned to the runemaster laying out his bedding. "How much farther?" he asked.

"Midmorning," Hanno assured him, "we'll reach the cove."

Joro turned back to Aral. "There you have it, then. In the morning."

"Better be so," the warrior grumbled. "Or I'll find it myself and dispense with the guide."

"That's not your decision," Joro replied curtly.

Aral spat pointedly. "You're letting him lead us on."

"If we're in Tesvi tomorrow, you have no complaint. If we're not—it's my problem to deal with. Not yours."

"You'd better deal with it then, Duke's man, before my patience runs out."

"Here, now. What's that supposed to mean?"

"Just what it said." Aral pushed past Joro. He joined Kaylis by the fireside as if nothing were amiss. Joro studied the belligerent warrior through slitted eyes, then nodded once to himself and slipped away into the dark.

RUDIC STOOD TRAILSIDE halfway up the ridge, a position that let him pace and remain observant while Joro held forth from his perch on a lichen-covered log.

"Posturing is one thing," he said, "if that's all he does. But he's not the type to leave it there. He's looking for ground to challenge me on."

"Of course he is," Rudic agreed from some yards away. His back was to his leader, but his sharp ears were attentive to the conversation. "He's been at it since we left Nimm-on-Witholl."

"He's making me angry," Joro said softly. "I don't like it when I get angry."

That earned a look over Rudic's shoulder. "I don't like it when you get angry, either." The archer strode back down the deer trail, talking as he moved. "He heard Duke Arn name you leader of this expedition. Why does he defy that? He has his orders, same as the rest of us."

Joro cocked his head and considered for a minute. "You recall when the Duke brought us together in the Seresloi Chamber?"

"Yes."

"He said of us, 'Here are men who have performed special tasks for me many times.'"

"So?"

"He implied it by his conversation, but he never named the Nightrunner's League."

"Ah. You're right."

"So to begin with, our surly warlord's nephew does not seem to realize he deals with assassins and spies and the secret executors of the Duke's will."

"Berin and Kaylis seem to read between the lines well enough."

"I would say they are deeper thinkers than our impetuous friend. And more circumspect, or they would have said a friendly word by now. He probably takes us for adventurers and opportunists."

"Both true," Rudic chuckled.

Joro grinned in response. "But not commanding of respect, you must admit. And he is convinced he's more deserving of command than I. He's been leading Clan Terbal troops all over the Bernauer hills fighting the rebel clans, you know. He *knows* he's an experienced leader and is cocksure of himself. He's seen nothing of what I can do and hasn't heard a single rumor or bit of reputation about me."

Rudic laughed. "Of course not. Since when do Nightrunners lend their exploits to tavern tales?"

"Exactly. If we ever did we'd be babbling League secrets and then some other poor Runner would have to put an end to the storytelling. Not a pleasant way to conclude an evening."

"I dare say." Rudic leaned into the darkness beneath pine branches and vanished from sight, the Tarn magic of his concealing gray cloak blending flawlessly into the night and shadows.

His voice carried softly down the trail. "So how are you going to handle him?"

Joro blew a long breath through his lips. "I need to take him down a notch in a way that leaves a lasting impression. Trouble is, I can think of a hundred ways to humble him, but he'd resent every one of them."

Rudic's voice smiled. "Sometimes you're too tricksy for your own good. There is one way you can humble him that he won't resent."

"Oh? What's that?"

The archer appeared out of the darkness at Joro's elbow. The Nightrunner's hand was halfway to his throwing blade Eyebiter before he overrode the reflex. The cloaked man leaned over, spoke a few quiet words into his friend's ear.

Joro threw his head back and laughed. Not loudly, lest it carry. But heartily.

WOODSMOKE FROM THE dinner fires at Finskili scented the night air on the banks of the Ranulf. Soon Dalin's party came in sight of the settlement, the light of dwelling and cook fires seeping over the high stone walls before them. Barking dogs greeted Sembra's call at the gate, followed by the shouts of kinsmen and the portal groaning wide to permit the woodsmen entry.

"Come." Torvin clapped Dalin on the shoulder. "Dinner awaits, and a good rest."

The Eskrin headsman trailed his kinsmen toward the open gateway, but Dalin's footsteps slowed. Thengel sat horse unmoving, as did the other elves. With one mind, the companions held their mounts steady, made no motion to enter the steading. Thengel turned halfway about in his saddle, listening to the susurrus of the Ranulf at his back, a bowshot distant to the west.

"What?" the Truthsayer's apprentice questioned the hesitant figure, but it was Arandel who answered.

"If we leave at first light, it is yet near a half-day to Tesvi Cove. My journey-sense says, the ones we seek arrive there more swiftly than we."

"How can you know?" Dalin asked.

"We traveled that country," said Nalia, "on our way to Etjorvi. It is not the lengthy road you might think."

"Journey-sense tells me what is where," Arandel explained. "I know it, even from afar. If the Nimmians are not in Tesvi by now, they will be in the morning. It is not a long trail for them."

A sudden sense of urgency came over Dalin; he glanced back to the open gate of Finskili, undecided. Torvin turned back to see what delayed them.

Thengel spoke down from the great height of his horse, his mellow voice making a pronouncement in casual tones. "We shall cross the Ranulf tonight."

Torvin laughed, a rude snort. "Not possible."

"We must. If we travel only at first light, we will miss our quarry at Tesvi."

"It's not possible, I tell you. No one crosses the Ranulf at night. It's too dangerous when it's dark. It's risky enough in daylight."

"Then I would propose," Belec said, "that we use daylight now and be on our way."

A flood of sunlight illuminated the clearing before Finskili and brought Torvin's protest sputtering to a halt. Belec held the lightstone unveiled in the palm of his hand, and the light of noon banished night for a stone's throw all around.

"Is that sufficient light to see by?" Thengel asked dryly.

"Yes," Torvin spoke slowly, "We should be able to see well enough," he admitted. "Let us refresh ourselves and rest for a while. We can leave when the moon is high."

Belec covered the stone, extinguishing its brilliance in the concealment of wrappings and a snug leather pouch. Dalin followed the headman into Finskili. The elves came after.

A FEW STRIDENT frogs sang their night songs by the river's edge. A wash of sunlight startled them into silence, and for a moment the only sound at the riverbank was the chatter of the Ranulf. Then horse hooves crunched on gravel as men rode onto the rock-covered bar that protruded into the water.

Belec sat his mount fetlock-high in the water, the lightstone gripped firmly between thumb and two fingers and held aloft, the better to illuminate the width of the river. A broad scattering of head-sized boulders broke the waters upstream of the ford; a rippling, white-tossed sheet of shallow rapids interrupted the water's flow until it slowed and pooled broadly across gravel bars.

Torvin and his kinsmen had taken to horseback for this last leg of their journey. "If you wish to make speed," he conceded, "then we all must ride," and with that the stables of Finskili were emptied to mount the woodsmen. The party gathered now at the lip of the river, Sembra at the fore between Belec and Thengel.

"The channel is deepest just past midriver," Sembra pointed out. "There we must swim. A man afoot risks being swept far downriver at that point. A bowshot downstream rapids begin again, hence the danger. But horses do better. The current will push us a ways, but keep on for the far shore and you should be fine." He gestured to the edge of the daylit area before them. "Your horse will find purchase on the gravel bars there soon enough."

"How far out is it safe to sit a horse?" Thengel asked.

"As far out as you can withstand the current. Near the end of this bar." Sembra pointed with his chin to the submerged spit of land beneath their feet. "Belly-high on a horse, I'd say."

"Take up position there, Belec," Thengel directed his companion. "We'll have most light farthest across the water that way. Come over with the last of Sembra's folk."

"Before you do that," the Finskili man said, "you might want to strip off. We'll all be soaked before we're across. Unless you want to ride wet for the rest of the night, that is, or carry wet clothes with you."

Thengel saw the wisdom in that advice. He and his companions joined the woodsmen ashore as they removed boots, leggings, and trousers and wrapped garments in cloaks for the river crossing. Dalin dismounted from behind Nalia and followed suit. As he folded his leathers into his bearskin cloak and tied the bundle tight, he looked up at the woman, sitting fully clothed upon her horse, a half-smile upon her lips.

Dalin had seen naked women in sweat houses and baths, but he knew that women away from kin-hearth were more body-shy than ever they would be around family. "Come stand behind me," he offered. "They won't see you. And you can leave your tunic on for the crossing."

Amusement danced across her face. "Thank you," she said. "But I prefer not."

Dalin's eyebrows rose. "You'll be drenched. And your boots will be ruined." He glanced to her fine thigh-high boots, supple black leather polished fastidiously as ever, banishing all trace of the last day's hard foot travel. When did she ever have time for that boot care? He never saw her tend to them, but clearly she took pride in their appearance.

"I'll dry off soon enough," she said. "Just you see you don't lose your grip midstream. I don't want to have to fish you out of the rapids."

Dalin frowned. He could swim, a little, but not enough to best rapids. He was glad to have a horse to cling to across this waterway, but he did not think his own ability to sit the horse would be the problem on this crossing. He shook his head at her foolishness. Better dry than wet and freezing in the after-midnight chill. Well. If needed, he would share his bearskin with her, to warm her as they rode. . . .

When everyone but Nalia was ready, Belec took up position in the river, stepping Nowës out to the end of the gravel spit. Cold mountain water chilled his legs, dashing high up his thigh on the upstream side. The black-stockinged chestnut hunched his back against the cold and wet but stood against the jostle of the water.

Sembra led the way across, walking the gravel bar until the water came chest-high on his mount, and then, between one step and another, the horse was swimming. Water lightened the man who stuck to the animal's back, leaning forward, crooning encouragements to the beast that carried him into the deepest part of the river. Then the current caught them, a giant hand pushing them downstream. The horse swam on, drifting downriver, but soon found footing on the opposite shore and clambered to dry land.

The other men of Finskili were used to this ford. Three followed close behind Sembra, and then the elves joined the procession of bodies crossing the water. Thengel, whose gray Caerlian charger forged slowly but steadily though the watercourse, Hagar clinging tensely to the saddle, the elf half-swimming alongside his horse. Close behind, two more Finskili men, in case he should need assistance. Then Nalia nudged Frelin with her heels, and the dapple gray carried her and Dalin into the cold rushing waters of the Ranulf.

The horse stepped off the gravel bar and lurched into the water, striking out for the far shore. As Thengel had done, Nalia drifted off her mount, half-clinging, half-swimming on the downstream side, leaving Dalin to clutch the saddle as the horse swam across with him. He was aware of men following behind—and then had mind only for the elemental thrust of water that grabbed him and Frelin and pushed them both forcefully downstream. For a time it seemed the horse treaded water frantically but stayed in one place as the far bank moved past of its own accord. Nalia urged her mount on, one hand fast in his mane—then Frelin had his legs under him once more, and the woman slipped back into the saddle as the trio emerged from the river. Up the shallow bank they went to firm ground.

Dalin dismounted at her command, and in a moment she stood beside him, her waterlogged garments clinging and streaming a pool of water around her feet.

"Safe and sound," she said.

"Your clothes."

Nalia looked at her bedraggled self and back at Dalin. Holding his eyes, she smiled and put her hands in the air palms up, shoulder-high. "*Caesca ye ni,*" she said, with a peculiar twist of each wrist and a downward flourish of her hands.

Water vanished from her person from head to toe, sucked downward and seemingly into the ground at her feet. Where water had collected only moments before only a damp spot remained. She stood as dry as she had started out on the far side of the Ranulf.

Dalin's jaw dropped, and Nalia smiled in self-satisfaction.

And then they were plunged into darkness.

The loss of light and a startled cry from the river whirled them about. The river glowed bright, lit from within by what could only be the submerged lightstone. Belec was off his horse, and though his mount swam steadfastly for the shore, the Keeper of the Path had lost his way completely. He bobbed in the river, head barely above water as the current shoved him toward the rapids downstream. His figure was clear to see, lit eerily from beneath by the magical light. His arms flailed; then his head disappeared beneath the waves in a river run golden.

"Windweaver pluck him from the waters!" exclaimed Nalia. "He can't swim!"

Arandel was crossing close behind. He'd seen the runnel of water hit Belec, startle him, and the next surge that carried him off his saddle. Without hesitation he turned his horse downstream. No longer heading across current, mount and rider were swept rapidly along and closed on the floundering elf. Belec's head emerged; an arm struck out, he sank again—his laboring gasp for air carried above the river's clamor, and Dalin winced as the underwater light showed the elf slam hard into a boulder.

No longer struggling, Belec tumbled downstream like so much submerged flotsam. Arandel was close behind, Torvin and two kinsmen following after but much farther back. In that moment a chance eddy nudged the lightstone loose from wherever it had stuck and that source of illumination, a small sun in its own right, moved abruptly downstream. Lodging briefly here, tumbling rapidly there, the lightsource followed the men in the river— then caught up in some strong current, it moved even with them and past.

The white water of the downstream rapids glowed incandescent with its passing—and there it lodged, caught for the moment in some underwater nook, resisting the tug of the Ranulf and lighting the river that swept men and horses toward the deadly rocks that captured it.

Sembra and others dashed downstream along the bank, to head off Belec if possible. Slowed by snags and boulder-strewn banks, they could not speed ahead of the man they hoped to rescue. Dalin's feet carried him along with Thengel and the others, unable to help in this crisis, yet unwilling to stand idly by.

Only Arandel was near, but not near enough. The water became rough, a handful of boulders pressaging the field of rocks that created the rapids ahead.

The Silverleaf's fingers were busy at his saddle, doing what Dalin could not discern—until Arandel left his saddle. He spoke a word to the horse that sent the black shoreward, and at the same time the elf struck out into the water, swimming hard for Belec's unmoving form ten bowlengths ahead.

Closer he came, closer. . . . The chop of the water tossed unconscious man and swimmer violently about. Arandel grabbed his fellow in a whole-body hug that submerged them both. Surely they were dead men, Dalin thought, for the river ran unbeatably fast, plunging into underwater rocks and the teeth of deadwood snags. And that is exactly where the current pushed them—until they were brought up sharply at the end of a rope.

It was the rope Arandel had made fast to his saddle, and there ashore his horse, Daile, now pulled against the strain of the line. Sembra reached the black first and took his reins, led him upstream and inland. Towed from the raging Ranulf like fish on a string, Arandel and his burden were dragged ashore.

Exhausted though he must have been from his swim, the Silverleaf waved men off with a sharp word. He rolled Belec facedown, then lifted the unconscious form with hands doubled under the sternum. Water poured out of Belec's mouth. Another heave, more liquid seeped forth. Then Arandel did a thing Dalin thought most ungainly, leaning hard into the elf's back so his chest compressed, then pulling back on his arms 'til his shoulders cleared ground—again he repeated the motion, and again, until Belec convulsed in a paroxysm of wet, retching coughs. Only then did the Silverleaf throw himself to the ground and catch breath from his own exertions.

The rapids growled on, but thwarted of their prey, chance or a river god plucked again at the lightstone. The balefire glare washed through the cascade and tumbled down the riverbed until the light faded past a downstream bend.

"Next time you're so eager to jump off your horse midstream," Arandel rasped, "warn me, so I can let you go your own way."

Belec coughed before he found his voice. "I thought I had a good-enough seat. Then that wave hit me—"

"Ripple, more like. Riding lessons I've offered you, too."

He waved a hand weakly at Arandel. "I don't need lessons—"

"Whenever you're ready, cousins," Nalia said lightly. "I know you want to dash to the seacoast, but taking the land route might be faster after all."

Arandel favored her with a scowl and tossed a pebble in her direction. Belec simply groaned.

They were under way within the quarter-hour, their path lit by torches, with Sembra in the lead.

CHAPTER 20

THE KING'S ROAD was unmistakable even to those who had never set foot on it before. It was wide enough for two freight wagons to pass each other by, a broad, cobbled expanse of highway with a raised crest and gutters to the sides to carry rain and melting snow off the roadbed.

Now, in the dark before dawn, no other travelers were to be seen on this lonely expanse beyond Vaer. Dalin's party headed north on the road, their horses taking up an easy canter on this safe footing.

"Over there"—Sembra pointed north and east into the darkness—"lies a peninsula flanked by the sea. A trail to it intersects the King's Road. Tesvi is a fishing hamlet sheltered in the curve of that headland."

Dalin could not see the peninsula though he heard the ocean crashing at its feet. The sea cliff flanked this strip of road, giving way in a sheer drop to seal-claimed rocks below. The salt tang of the air tickled his nose. He was a dweller in northlands and mountain, and never before had he been in sight or scent of the sea. He heard it now, a distant roar not unlike the wind in the tops of pines. He followed Sembra's lead, as did others, trusting the Finskili man would know what crossroad to follow to Tesvi.

He was not disappointed. There was only the one hamlet along this coast of uninhabitable sea cliffs, and the road to the cove was clearly designated. A marker of gray-weathered granite scored the dirt trail eastward, down the slope of the headland and toward the sea. Sembra reined his horse that way, and the others followed.

Not far along the trail he came to a halt. Short pine trees battled the ocean winds here and grew in twisted, spreading canopies. Tangled brush covered the ground in low, tight growth between them. The trail seemed a cow path, lost in the darkness that cloaked the headland before them.

"We've bought and sold in Tesvi many times before," Sembra said. "The fishermen are up before dawn to launch their boats. If there are Nimmians here in longships, they'll most like be holding fisherfolk hostage to ensure their silence, if they haven't killed them outright. In any case, they'll be mounting a guard. Now I'd say is time to ease forward as if we were stalking the marten in the high forest. Soft and wiley, 'til we see who nests where." He spoke to Torvin. "I'll go with Jan and Segrim to scout this out. No more, 'til we see what's to see. Let us move now; we'll be back by first light."

While Torvin gave him the nod, Arandel stepped forward. "I'm going also."

Sembra frowned and the Silverleaf anticipated his refusal. "No doubt you know how to stalk silently with your kinsmen. I do not know your ways and do not plan to scout with you. This is no time for a newcomer to learn your signals and pacing."

Sembra nodded, glad that his reservations were understood.

"But I have my own way of scouting," Arandel continued, "and so I go alone."

Thengel dipped his head in agreement, and that was all the endorsement Arandel needed. Before the men could muster a protest, the elf vanished into the night. Sembra hesitated, then shrugged and led his fellows down the path to Tesvi Cove.

THE EASTERN SKY lightened to a twilight hue that outlined the headland and hinted at the curve of shoreline below it. From their impromptu hillside camp Dalin looked eastward, the ocean a blanket of restless darkness, the horizon tinged with the faintest hint of pink bleeding into gray. Arandel chose that moment to return, stepping unexpectedly around a bent pine, startling the human who was guarding the trail and who belatedly noticed him within the camp. He squatted by Thengel to give his report; Torvin and Efric joined the gathering.

Arandel cleared a patch of dirt, scratched lines with a twig as he spoke. "Here, the hamlet. Twelve houses, as many families, some guesting sailors from the ships. Fishing boats, here. Farther along, pulled up on shore—two longships. Forty crewmen each, I'd say. They're of the same size as those we traveled here on."

"Crew sleeping aboard?" Thengel asked.

"Three on one, two on the other. Two on guard in the hamlet. They're guarding it no longer." Arandel smiled coldly. "Sixty and some in a shore camp, here." He sketched a circle inland along the beach.

Torvin let out a low whistle between his teeth.

Thengel looked at him sharply. "Is that more than you are prepared to deal with?"

The Eskrin chieftain spoke grimly. "These invaders never set foot on our land with welcome. We'll see them in the sea or dead before we invite them to stay on our shores. Eighty men, though . . . that's many more than the handful we've pursued from upmountain."

Low voices heralded Sembra's return. He and his companions joined the circle, confirmed Arandel's report. "Can't say how many in the shore camp. Too dark for us to count that closely," the woodsman said. "But this we found: they had three men set to guard this headland trail, in case peddlers or a chance visitor should stray down into the cove while their ships are ashore. They were fast asleep—they found Ivar of Tesvi's winter supply of brandy, and the Nimmians shared it out and polished it off. They've been here six days, since the new moon. They're bored with the waiting and nervous about staying on this shore for so long. Sounds like their captains are having a time keeping them in hand. The drinking settled them down this night."

"They're all sleeping heavy in camp, then?" asked Thengel.

"That's what I mean."

"And the guards you found sleeping?"

"They won't be bothering us."

"Torvin," said the elf. "You've fifteen men from Eskrin. How many joined us from Finskili?"

"Seven more."

"Twenty-two, then. With us, twenty-eight."

Sembra spoke with reluctance. "Drunk or not, I think we're not enough to take on two shiploads of Nimmian raiders in direct attack. They fight berserk as often as not, even more gladly when drunk."

"There aren't many of us," Thengel agreed, "but with Belec's spellcraft we should be enough to take them by surprise. We'll sneak into their camp and capture them while they're sleeping."

Belec looked far less convinced than his leader. Torvin was not the only one who looked at the elf incredulously and shook his head.

Sembra spoke bluntly. "That is very good-hearted of you, but a generosity that will not be repaid by the raiders. These people come here for blood and rape and loot. They kill or capture our folk and carry them overseas with them. Think you that when they collect their friends and head homeward they'll leave Tesvi untouched behind them? Hardly. They'll strip the hamlet bare, torch everything to the ground, and steal folk into slavery. They'll not stand by while you walk into camp and put a sword to their throats and ask politely for their surrender, be they ever so hungover. Your plan is too gentle with the enemy."

Thengel shifted uneasily. "It is not honorable to attack sleeping men and kill them."

"It is not asking for a fair fight when you take on a force that outnumbers you nearly four to one to begin with," Torvin replied. "We must even the odds."

"And we must do it quickly," Arandel added. "Soon there will be too much light to shelter stealthy movement." He was right; pink and yellow streaked the eastern sky, and the far horizon glowed with a band of blue. The sky overhead was dark velvet, but lightening rapidly. Now Dalin looked downslope and could make out the shadowy hulls of longships pulled up on the beach.

"Here is what I say," the Silverleaf spoke again. "We must burn the ships. Then, even if we must retreat from superior numbers, the murderers we follow cannot flee across the sea, and we'll have another chance at them later."

Nods greeted his proposal. "Swift now like the hawk, Torvin, your two stealthiest men take one ship; Nalia comes with me to the other. We slit the throats of those who sleep there. They are a token guard, easily handled. Let us follow the headland ridge, then down the slope to come on them unawares. Two more follow behind us to each vessel: they carry torches and, as soon as we signal from the decks, come aboard and set fires. Set two, three archers to watch the hamlet—they can pick off any raiders who come out of the houses to investigate the disturbance.

"Let the rest of your men fall upon the camp from the village side, Sembra. Kill who you can as they sleep, and keep them distracted from us. When the longships are burning well, we'll take the camp from the opposite side. They have a tent or two, but most sleep under open sky. Easy pickings for your bowmen, or men moving silently with knife in hand."

Torvin nodded grimly. "A sound plan. Agreed."

Arandel regarded the Truthsayer's apprentice. "Dalin. You and Belec bring cold torches and follow us. When we wave from the deck, come on board and kindle your flames."

Torvin's folk were astir with similar orders. The directive took Dalin off-guard. He had envisioned himself confronting Hanno Runemaster with armed men by his side—not clambering up a ship's side in the gray light of dawn to set fire to it. But Arandel's plan made sense, and Dalin would do what he could.

Men and elves scattered down the headland. Thengel came to his feet and heaved a sigh. The dwarf by his side studied his expression.

"They are right, you know," Hagar growled. "You cannot cross a battlefield square off, against odds like this."

Thengel shrugged. "I don't like throat slitting in the dark. It's not right."

"No, it is not," agreed Hagar. "But sometimes it is necessary. You may have to do the necessary a time or two more before in your hands you have the Panoply."

"I hope not," said the Guardian of the Silverthorn. Then he turned his feet downhill to join the men who would attack the Nimmian camp.

THE LONGSHIPS WERE narrow and lengthy, shallow of keel, resting at a gentle list on the rocky beach just at the high tide mark.

Dalin wondered why anyone would want to be standing guard on that cockeyed deck in the cold when they could be snug by a fire in the beach camp. *Ah, but if my only way home were a ship on a hostile coast, I would order a guard on it, too. At the very least, to protect against mischief from a villager. At worst, to guard against . . . well. What we're about. The attack of an enemy.*

He reassured himself with a touch of the warm censer hanging at his belt. The filigreed iron ball hung from a chain and held an ember packed in ashes. He had it on loan from Efric's kinsman, the one who had shared his aleskin. Open the hinged top, feed it a little tinder, and a flame would blossom—a quicker and more reliable method of lighting a torch than relying on a flurry of sparks from flint and steel, fearing the noise would carry, risking that sparks would not catch when needed. . . . He shifted his two torches to his other hand. Belec carried two more, surely sufficient to fire the hull a stone's throw before them.

Planks braced on oars on the lowest side of the ship showed how Nimmian crewmen came and went on the grounded vessel. Arandel and Nalia had crept silently up that bowing pathway and disappeared over the rail unto the shadowy deck. Dalin's eye wandered past the ship to the shore beyond. He watched low breakers roll in from the sea, washing ashore in a swirl of foam—a fascinating variety of waves, and the blanket of water that stretched far beyond. . . .

Belec nudged him. Nalia had reappeared at the rail and was gesturing to them with a broad wave of her arm.

The sun was touching the eastern sky as Dalin hurried up the gangway, feeling naked and revealed as the first rays of light struck the beach. He was grateful to be on the far side of the ship away from the Nimmian camp and possibly observant eyes.

He bounded the last step off the plank and over the rail, knees flexing with the impact of his landing. He bent forward a bit to keep his balance—and the motion brought his eyes directly in line with a puddle of blood. Sticky red leaked from a prone figure, a cloaked and bearded man sprawled on the deck near an oarsman's seat.

Dalin straightened hastily and bumped into Belec behind him. He collected himself with an effort. Nalia caught his eye, but neither amusement nor scorn showed there. She ignored his discomfort and gestured below decks where raised planking revealed a small cargo hold.

"Down there, both of you," she said softly. "Burn the cargo, and the crossbeams where decking meets hull. That's a good place to start. The caulking pitch should catch quickly. Mind you work away from the fire you set. Don't get yourselves trapped down there."

Dalin mumbled an acknowledgment and turned his back to the gruesome scene he had glimpsed on the deck.

And what did you think it meant, that someone would be killed while dozing on an uneventful watch? he asked himself. *Did you think to see no blood?*

He'd seen no gore when Granmar had been killed, and the Truthsayer's body was lost to the treacherous crags at the base of Kodanit's Spire. As a huntsman he had seen and caused death to living creatures, but killing his dinner was one thing. He had never before seen a dead man lying in his own blood.

His stomach gave a heave. He sat on the edge of the storage hold and, to distract himself, pulled the censer from his belt. He concentrated on feeding tinder to the ember within, blowing the flame alive, sharing fire with Belec. Soon one torch lit another, and the fackles burned smoky and hot. Into the hold he dropped, wedging one torch between cargo bale and a rib of the hull—there it would burn until the wood around it burned just as merrily and nothing could put it out. With his remaining torch he fired bales and casks, caught the resin alight that sealed the planking of the hull, held flame to the edge of the deck where tarred rope was coiled and planks laid carelessly atop it. . . .

It was not an incendiary glee that Dalin felt but a workmanlike factuality about his task, a place to hide his thoughts from the dead man overhead. It was a chore, like any other, like charring wooden stakes to order before they were made into spears. Belec laid about less methodically, and the Truthsayer's apprentice was oblivious to his companion's work until thick smoke caused him to look around.

The ship was afire and it was time to leave the hold.

Nalia gave them a hand up. At the prow, where a dragon's neck curved proud above the sand, Arandel stood braced against the tilt of the deck with bow in hand. He shot an arrow as Dalin watched. A figure dropped in the beach camp, and the youth observed the melee there dispassionately. The Nimmians had awakened to blood and mayhem, caught in their blankets and sleeping furs and cloaks. Many were struck down where they lay; others struggled to their feet and put about them with a vengeance, with sword or battle-ax or whatever was to hand.

The raiders noticed the smoke coming from their ships. Some had broken off from combat to run out upon the strand—but Arandel's arrows picked them off and two bearded men lay facedown on the rocky beach between longships and camp.

Another mass of fighters gathered in camp. As Sembra had remarked, the Nimmians fought berserk as often as not, and now that wild battlelust was directed at saving their ships from the enemies who threatened them. Never mind that it was already too late; smoke poured from the hold behind Dalin and tongues of flame leaped high. Perhaps the Nimmians did not see, or did not care. They were enraged and now they needed a target. The few interlopers who denied them their ships became that target.

Thirteen men turned their backs on the skirmish in the camp and charged the burning dragonships. Belec joined Arandel in the prow, taking his bow from his back and mirroring the archer's stance. Their blood kinship was unmistakable in that moment: they resembled each other, wore similar travel-worn leathers much like Dalin's own; each wore his long hair tied back at nape of neck and leaned into this bow at just such an angle. . . . Dalin had the impression of brothers, fighting without the need for words, so well they knew each other's intent.

Fight in unison they did, but the complex links of Nimmian chain mail trapped their missiles and lessened the damage they inflicted. Some shots missed; others injured but did not drop a target. Two men went to the ground—three, as supporting arrow fire came from the neighboring ship and Torvin's men there. But still the Nimmians came on.

"They're good," Nalia said of her cousins in an aside. "I'm better. I think I should join in."

The charging mass of men was thinned by the arrow fire, but nine yet dashed toward the ships. Nalia joined the pair at the bow. Dalin had grown so used to seeing these outlanders with bows strung across their backs—but never held in hand and used—that he thought nothing of what they had carried until the weapons came to hand and death flew in turn. Nalia's bow seemed no different from the others, wood laminated with layers of bone. Her stance was if anything more casual, yet her arrows flew with amazing accuracy. Here a throat, there an eye, everyone she pointed an arrow at fell dead on the strand a heartbeat later.

Two of Torvin's men jumped to the beach, swords at the ready to deal with any who made it past the barrage of withering arrow fire. Fire-heated wood popped and snapped, and a part of the deck of the other ship gave way in an explosion of sparks and high-jumping flame. The rest of Torvin's men left that vessel as well. With its immolation the berserkers turned their attention solely to the remaining vessel. As the Turakemi woodsmen engaged with some of the howling attackers, Nalia and her cousins continued to drop the charging berserkers.

Dalin shifted uncomfortably from foot to foot, then looked down at the smoking wood beneath him. The deck had become unbearably hot. He moved forward and to one side—and tripped over the legs of an unmoving body. The second guard, slain by Nalia or Arandel.

Dalin jumped back, unwilling to advance past the corpse yet reluctant to lose sight of the fight before the ship.

Suddenly an arm took him around the neck, yanked him backward nearly off his feet. "Ahhgg!" he yelped in consternation. The scent of alcohol and sweat and campfire smoke clogged his nostrils; his fingers clutched reflexively at the hairy arm across his throat as a man's voice growled curses in his ear. He saw the flash of a knife blade out of the corner of his eye.

Nalia spun about in the prow of the ship, arrow nocked and drawn and poised to fire. No sooner did she face his way than she loosed.

An arrow sped towards Dalin's head so fast he saw only a point and then nothing at all. He felt a burning sensation alongside his neck at the same moment that a *thunk* reverberated through his body—no. Through the body behind him. Arm slacked and knife tumbled to the ground as a gurgling sounded in his ear.

Dalin staggered but kept his feet. He whirled around, cold chills sweeping over him. The Nimmian who had darted up the gangplank and grabbed him from behind had toppled over dead. Nalia's arrow stood from the hollow of his throat.

A warm trickle of blood seeped down the side of Dalin's neck. He wiped at it with one hand. A cut stung there. It was just a nick, from the touch of his attacker's blade or Nalia's arrow he did not know. Did not want to know.

The deck was ablaze now. Nalia nudged her cousins and motioned Dalin to join them. The gangway could no longer be reached, and the beach was a short drop below the prow. The elves made it and Dalin followed. He tripped as he landed, sprawled on the gravel—saw more slaughtered Nimmians on the shale before him, the gray-and-white fletching of these elvish arrows proclaiming who had ended these raiders' lives.

Mixed feelings warred inside the Truthsayer's apprentice. He wiped his neck once more, trying to ignore the sting there and the smear of blood upon his hand.

TESVI FISHERMEN CAME cautiously out of their stone-and-driftwood huts. No Nimmian remained standing to terrorize them. Children imitated their parents, spitting on corpses and marveling over death wounds while Torvin's folk busied themselves with their own. Four dead, seven wounded at Nimmian hands, and those to be tended before anything else.

Dalin trudged near the bodies of the Turakemi laid out near the raiders' camp. He recognized one young face there, that of the friendly woodsman who had loaned his censer for carrying embers. Dalin clutched the chain of the iron globe at his belt, and hurried on past.

He gravitated to Thengel's party, stood near as the elves debated their next course of action. His attention wandered and he watched Torvin's folk looting corpses, comparing prizes, and laughing over their victory. Then one by one the dead were taken and thrown into the fires of the burning longships. The vessels would burn for a long while yet; the hulls were not yet consumed by flame, though the decks were gone. No hotter pyre could be built with driftwood from the beach. Dalin knew the danger of abandoning the dead without a proper funeral—sprits could walk the earth restlessly, haunting the living, or a neglected corpse seek its killer. Not common events, these, but certainly enough tales were told of the risks. With a few words said to ease the soul of the dead to Ruhnkeil, the remains were consigned to the flames—grand pyres marking death of ship and sailor alike. More ceremony was taken with the Turakemi dead, but they, too, were put in the fire, with prayers for their peaceful rest.

Dalin noticed then the dark smoke that rose from the two burning ships, twin columns spreading in the offshore breeze, curling low along the headland . . . and it was exactly that smoke that was the subject of argument beside him.

"Now you've a beacon set that will warn the Nimmians away," Hagar complained. "They come to find their way home, see the smoke they will. Taking caution, they spy us out, and come never closer to this place. How, then, will we find them?"

"We had no choice about the ships," Arandel snapped. "If we failed to defeat the raiders, we would have left them all a way back across the sea. It was too much to risk."

"It is done now, and no use debating it," Nalia said.

"No, but this fire, or the smoke from it, will surely be visible from the King's Road," Thengel spoke sternly. "How do you suggest we find our bearers of stolen goods, then?"

That question caught Dalin's attention. He stepped closer to the group at his elbow.

"They are not here yet," Arandel replied, "but we know they are on their way. I say let us lay a trap for them and lay in wait on the road."

Hagar snorted. "Were I them, I'd send one scout ahead to investigate the smoke. We will be wasting our trap on just a scout. We need to seek them out."

"Not if we ambush them farther south, where the smoke is not yet visible."

Thengel raised both hands to still the debate. "Let us do both," he said decisively. "I'll ask Torvin to join us in concealment along the road, out of sight of this ruination we've left. Then you can scout about as you please, Arandel. They must be traveling this way; that much is certain."

"And how will you know them?" asked Nalia. "Dalin is the one who knows their faces. He must go with Arandel."

The Silverleaf regarded the youth without enthusiasm. "I need no human's assistance."

Dalin did not care if he scouted or not, but the disdain in the elf's voice bothered him. "And will you be knowing a runemaster at a glance, then?" he asked. "Of all the Turakemi you may see on the road or near it?"

The Silverleaf took that in silence, then shrugged one shoulder noncommittally. "Come if you like. Keep up if you can."

CHAPTER 21

HANNO LED THE Nimmians out of the hills, across country, and due east to the coast. Forested slopes rolled in gentle folds to the sea cliffs there, obscuring a long view of the coast. It was just coming midmorning as they rode out of a gulley and up onto the King's Road. They looked where Hanno pointed.

The headland and the cutoff to Tesvi Cove were in sight.

So, too, were the smoking, burned-out hulks of longships on the shore of the peninsula.

Joro sat his horse stone-still for a moment, then whirled about and spurred back to the gulley. "Off-road!" he ordered. "Now!"

The others followed as quickly as they could. A short ride carried them into the concealment of a copse of trees. Joro's horse minced in short sideways steps, reading his rider's tension. The others reined in and gathered round. None dared dismount in this moment of discovered disaster.

"We've been found out," said Berin.

"Not necessarily." Joro spoke sharply. "Ulf and his crews were found out."

"And if they talked?" asked Aral. "Or if we're hunted?"

Joro held up a hand to hush the warrior. It was already clear to him how this must be handled. Indeed, he had rehearsed plans for unforeseen contingencies, and the chance that they might be stranded—from weather, from discovery, whatever—was a possibility he had already considered.

"We'll find out if we're sought. I say, one person stealthily into Tesvi. Scout out guards, if there are any. And question someone about what has happened there."

With one accord, eyes fell upon Rudic. The archer gave a half-bow from his saddle. "So, we acknowledge how sly and quiet I can be, how persuasive in conversation?" He chuckled, dismounting. "I bow to your superior judgment."

"Judge this, Greycloak," Joro said. "Who was here; where they are now; are we sought. Return quickly. If they're in the area we're in growing danger the longer we wait."

"Consider it done." He took bow to hand, wrapped his cloak about himself, and stepped between birch trees, vanishing from sight.

Joro slipped to the ground. "Kaylis, scout to the north. I'll scout south. Aral, stay here with Hanno and Berin, and keep our mounts safe. I want everyone silent as mice, 'til we know that we're alone and unobserved."

Yellowbeard rested a hand on Redeemer's hilt. "I'll kill whoever strays near."

Joro brought himself up short. "No. This is a time to sit quietly and let Turakemi pass you by unseen. Keeping the horses quiet will be enough of a challenge. Do not invite more by seeking a fight."

"I'll fight if I must."

Joro calculated his next words carefully. "Of course you will. I would expect nothing less. But everyone's safety depends right now on you keeping yourselves hidden and silent until all scouts return to report. I know I can count on you for that."

Aral's eyes narrowed. The flattery was not lost on him, but he saw the necessity of the moment. He inclined his head in acknowledgment, and Joro felt satisfaction. Let the man think he was uniquely responsible for something. That was the trick to leading him along. At least, it would do for now. . . .

Kaylis and Joro went their ways into the woods. Aral and his companions settled to await their return.

ARANDEL HIKED FAR south with Dalin in tow, flanking the King's Road, taking care to observe who traveled there or who might be camped by the roadside. The Silverleaf traveled always just fast enough that the youth could never quite catch up with him. He stayed several steps behind, following in the elf's wake like a puppy dog.

Arandel ignored Dalin's presence until they passed through a patch of woods where old pine needles and dry twigs scattered the ground in a carpet. An ordinary step on such cover would crackle and snap and announce every footfall, Dalin knew. Arandel passed silent as a cloud over the minor obstacle—and the Truthsayer's apprentice knew from his own woodscraft skills just how to step so that his passage, too, was unmarked by noise or disarranged ground cover.

At the edge of the clearing, Arandel paused and looked behind him. Saw Dalin close, and raised one eyebrow. The elf continued on, wordless, stopping now and then to observe the road or sneak close to travelers who made pause to break their fast. Finally he led them up a small ravine, to drink from the clear water of a secluded stream.

"I am thinking," he mused softly, "that our murderers and thieves may not be traveling this road." He stared to the west, up into the low wooded hills that rose above the King's Road. "I am wondering if perhaps they have been flanking this route of travel, as have we."

Dalin studied the hills as well. "Why would they do that? They don't know they're pursued."

Arandel cocked his head. "We don't know what they know. But I would be avoiding local travelers if I knew I were in a hostile land. We have seen how welcome Nimmians are, here." He quirked a smile. "Indeed—my companions and I experience that ourselves when we say we come from Nimm, Caerlian being within its borders, you see, although a territory unto itself. We have learned to mention only Caerlian, here, in our introductions."

"Hm." Dalin filled his water flask from the stream. "It was your idea to ambush them on the road. Now you think they are off the road."

"I own no crystal ball, Dalin Truthsayer. Can you foretell where the runemaster is at this moment?"

Dalin shook his head.

"Neither can I. I can only plan as best I can. If they come up the road, Torvin's ambush is ready for them. If they cut along the hills, you and I must find them before they pass us by and elude us. It is that simple."

"Simple."

"Yes." The elf came to his feet. "I think . . . we loop back along that line of hills. Look for tracks, if anyone has traveled that way."

"I know how to track," Dalin said.

"Good. Then you will be of assistance and we can broaden our sweep. At least you do not walk with the clumsy-footed crashing of a man."

Dalin considered that, and other things he had heard from the elf. "You don't like humans very much, do you?" he asked.

Arandel looked back over his shoulder, his green eyes studying the youth coolly. "I like you well enough, Truthsayer's apprentice. Now—let us seek a trail."

He ascended the ravine, and Dalin followed after.

"HAVE YOU LOST your senses?" Hanno challenged flatly. "There are twenty-two of them! I don't care how many are wounded. There are only six of us. How can you possibly hope to kill them all and have us remain unharmed?"

Yet even as he objected, he recalled the murderous frost that Kaylis directed with a word, the deadly attacks of the fighters in this group, the glow of power around the sword Aral carried. . . .

And these mountain men who lay in ambush knew that he, Hanno, traveled with these outlanders. He was suspect to them—and that he could not permit.

"With your aid, Runemaster, we'll be rid of these tracking hounds once and for all, and we can travel in peace."

Hanno knew that was coming. With his aid indeed. "What do you want me to do?"

Joro smiled nonchalantly. "Whatever you can do. What spell have you mastered that would be most helpful, would you say?"

Hanno gritted his teeth. Spellmastery. Pfaw. He spat in the dirt and reined his temper in.

"I do not do 'spells,'" he said to the cocky Nimmian. "I craft runes. I summon effects invoked by esoteric symbols whose mysteries you clearly do not grasp."

Joro spread his hands. "Pardon my ignorance. What effects can you apply that might help us?"

Hanno had a sour look on his face. The words were sarcastic, but the tone was innocent. This man was infuriating.

"I have no battle runes, nothing that affects a broad area or large number of people."

"Ah."

"But I have something better."

"That is?"

"A rune of celebration."

"How is that better?"

A slow smile spread across the runemaster's face. "Do you worship Ardruna in your land?"

"Many do."

"As do we. Midsummer is nearly upon us. At that time, we honor the Earth Mother's abundance. It is a time to celebrate joyful things. To encourage fertility."

"Yes?"

"There is a rune reserved for such occasions, called Celebration. It affects many at once; under its influence people feel intoxicated. Gleeful. Amorous, even. Giving way with abandon to the slightest impulse."

"My, my," said Kaylis. "Such decadence."

Hanno ignored her inference. "It is used only for holy celebrations."

"I'm sure," Joro remarked dryly. "What would the effect be on the warparty that awaits us?"

Hanno sighed. "I've never seen a warparty under such an influence. But they will be besotted in various ways; that much I'm sure of. You'll want to stand well clear of the road until the rune has worked its magic."

"Well then. A Celebration it is."

CHAPTER 22

THENGEL SAT WITH his back to a wind-warped pine, separated from the road by a small stand of birch. He scanned the empty cobbles of the highway, visible in segments beyond the white peeling bark of slender tree trunks.

Hagar sat nearby nursing a watchful silence. Thengel was content to share the quiet and the watch; an hour passed, and then another. An elderly peddler bent beneath a heavy pack labored slowly by. In another while, a man dressed in dark brocade rode past, an aristocrat followed by his single mounted servant; later, a man driving a creaking wagonload of preserved fish. All traveled unchallenged, of no interest to the many warriors who lurked behind bush and tree.

Hagar finally broke the silence. "Do you think the smoke has betrayed us?" he asked in a hoarse whisper.

Thengel did not answer right away. "I don't know," he finally answered. "We're out of sight of the headland, here."

A minute passed. The dwarf hissed again. "We would not in doubt be sitting here if we had laid a trap for them at the longships. Course, we would need longships whole on shore to carry that off with—"

"What are you talking about, Hagar?"

"Other ways with this problem we could have dealt."

"No use going on about that now. We're here, and things are as they are."

"They would be different if you had not lost control of events, Thengel, my overtall friend."

Thengel sat upright, stung. "How have I lost control of things?"

"Feh. You are not planning ahead. You let Arandel step in and direct the action. Or others." Hagar jerked a thumb over his shoulders. "Torvin. Sembra. Whoever has a plan in the moment."

"I'm good at strategy." The elf sounded injured.

Hagar growled in his throat, "What kind of strategy?"

"Battles, cavalry charges, archery from horseback, skirmishing—"

"Pffft. Military maneuvers. There is much more to the world than horse-fighters facing one another in battle. Or Guardians of the Silverthorn fighting gorska and their karzdag allies. That is your training, Thengel. Open warfare. You need to learn how to plan for . . . for all these other things." He waved a broad hand in the air. "How to deal with a fishing hamlet. How to lay an ambush. How to take on superior odds in sneaky ways."

Thengel frowned. "I haven't needed to before."

"It shows. Look you. When we took on Esk'kek and slew the emerald dragon . . . how did you plan that? Warfare that was not."

Thengel thought back to the events that had delayed their travels through the jarldom of Kalajok some months before. "I just . . . thought ahead. Used common sense."

"Considered the ways your opponent might respond and planned for those, yes?" Hagar knew he was right. He had been there as well. "Do it now, Thengel. Do not wait for events to force your decisions. You sound unprepared for command, so Arandel steps in with his ready ideas. He is quick to act, but he is also very hasty. Just because he can toss a plan out quickly does not mean he has thought it all through. You seem to think that is your job. So do it."

Thengel considered what he heard. Hagar was high in rank among the Schoinevrik dwarves; how high he did not know, but the dwarf was no stranger to leadership, that was clear, and his advice had been helpful in the past.

"You're saying I seem uncertain?" the elf asked.

"Yes. Uncertain. Not sure what is the best course. Ask opinions if you must—that is a good idea—but then the final decision *you* should be making. And remember, you might need to do the necessary, distasteful, though it may be."

Thengel shook his head. "Not if it's dishonorable I won't."

"Suit yourself. You will have a harder time of it."

"Then so I will. But you're right; I should be leading. I am the natural leader of our troop."

"Are you? Why you are thinking so?"

"Why . . . why . . . ," he sputtered, "I'm a Guardian of the Thorn!"

"So?"

"So? I'm oath-sworn to keep Caerlian safe. To do what I can with body and sword and honor to defend the holy grove, to keep gorska out of our borders. . . . You know!"

"I know your reputation. And Arandel thinks himself specially chosen also."

Thengel laughed. "He's a Silverleaf! He ranges the woods and feeds the people and caretakes the forest. . . . He is not charged with the defense of Caerlian as a territory. I am. In Carelian my rank is greater than his."

"You are not in Carelian now, and you each see yourselves uniquely equipped to lead. You have more military training. He has more woods-wise ways. And he is a wonderful scout."

"But . . ." Thengel couldn't explain it, but he knew Hagar was wrong. To be a Guardian of the Silverthorn was to be one of the last defenders of an ancient tradition and homeland. He traced his roots to the honored warrior ways of fallen Arilethne. No Silverleaf could say the same. And it was Thengel who had gotten them all into this, journeying so far from home, seeking against all odds what might finally turn the tide of battle against the gorska. . . . It was Thengel who would get them out of this again, and safely back home with the keys to victory in hand. He had sworn it to himself and to the sacred Melicanthus, the Silverthorn that was the living heart of Caerlian's magic, that he was sworn to protect.

"Hey!"

A shout of astonishment rang in the air. The sound that came after was one they both recognized: the meaty *kerthunk* of a blade chopping into flesh. One electrified glance passed between them, then Hagar and Thengel were on their feet and running north, to aid Efric's men posted by their side.

They ran to where ambushers were stationed, but total chaos greeted them. Some men staggered upon the roadway, wandering in a daze; one lolled against a tree, seemingly drunk. One lay dead in the brush. Beyond him, an Eskrin man approached a stranger, arms open and hands weaponless. The stranger was a fellow with short brown beard and long mustaches; he wore a green-and-gray surcoat with a badge of a golden flaming sword over his heart. Blood dripped from the broadsword in his two-handed grip.

"—no need to fight," the Turakemi was saying to him in friendly, slurred words. "You can put that down—"

A thrust took the woodsman through the gullet and came out again with a twist. He fell to the ground clutching his entrails. The swordsman saw Thengel and Hagar closing with him, weapons in hand—and seemed startled by their presence. "Joro!" he called over his shoulder, and struck a defensive stance as the pair came on.

From across the road an arrow flew to skewer the man who lolled against the tree trunk. A second shaft, then two more struck down those who wandered the sunny cobblestones of the highway. Where there had been five Turakemi on guard here now there were five dead men, and Thengel wondered how the rest of the woodsmen fared.

Another man joined the surcoated swordsman, a fighter of moderate height and wiry build, shoulder-length dark brown hair visible behind the edge of his nondescript shield. A broad grin showed his white teeth; he seemed amused by the moment, or glad to see his opponents.

"So much of you for a spell to affect," he said, closing with Thengel, "is that why you're not bemused? No matter—you're all the more to whittle down to size."

Thengel's sword had leaped to his hand during his charge toward the sounds of danger. He squared off now against this talkative fellow, sparing a glance to the woods beyond to see if Torvin's folk held their ground or if they had all been taken by surprise. . . .

But surprise. The ambushers had been ambushed. And whose plan had it been, to lie in wait here?

Then there was no time to think, as the combatants exchanged a flurry of sword blows. Thengel saw he was better, but the man's shield would slow him down. It took different tactics to work around that kind of defensive device, and the man called Joro was very good with his shield, using it to nudge the elf's blade to one side and create openings for his own powerful slashes. He wore some kind of leathern battle harness over his shirt, shoulder plates and breast piece giving him added protection, but Thengel saw that if he could get just one good thrust in, he could spear this man and put a quick end to their duel. He wanted to move on, to see who else needed help. The two swordsmen before him were an irritating delay.

Hagar engaged with the other of those irritations, swinging with forceful but slow blows from the heavy, long-hafted hammer he carried at his belt. His opponent dodged Hagar's attacks but was unable to land a telling strike on him, for the dwarf wore his favored scale mail, and strike after strike was turned by the sturdy armor. A wild grin was upon Hagar's face, too, as he recognized that he was virtually impervious to attack by his modestly skilled enemy. Sooner or later he'd land a blow that would crush something vital . . . just as soon as the fellow quit hopping about so spryly.

Abruptly the surcoated man turned tail and ran, legs pumping hard, darting back through the trees and around a double-trunked pine. Hagar hollered and started after him—but the fellow had gone only far enough to put some distance between him and the dwarf. He halted, spun about, took a breath or two as Hagar charged on. Then he made an empty-handed gesture that looked like the flourish of a sword, held his palm out toward Hagar, and shouted, *"Rusne!"*

The command charged the air with power. Hagar's legs gave out in mid-stride. His momentum carried him forward, and he crashed to the forest floor, unable to catch himself with his arms. He lay there perfectly motionless.

The disaster that befell Thengel's friend happened in sight over his antagonist's shoulder. As much as he'd like to finish this man off, he could not leave Hagar defenseless on the ground. Thengel circled with his opponent, then ran in the dwarf's direction, planning to defend his friend until he could come to his senses, or however long was necessary.

He did not see the look of relief on Joro's face as he disengaged. Joro and Berin fell back across the roadway, leaving Thengel in a fierce guarding stance over the body of his companion. He looked about, then looked about again. Was there anyone in hiding? Was anyone sneaking up on him? Were there any Turakemi who could rally to his side or help with Hagar?

No, on all counts. And what had happened to Nalia and Belec, who had been guarding the road opposite his own position? No knowing.

He looked down to see the blackest scowl on Hagar's face he'd ever seen. To his surprise the dwarf was awake and conscious. "Why don't you get up?" Thengel asked.

"May Balin Doomfire your brains in brine soak and serve the treats at my wedding feast!" the dwarf cursed. "Not a damned muscle can I move!"

"Your mouth works fine," Thengel muttered. His eyes on the other side of the road, he debated for a moment the wisdom of pursuing his attackers. They were, no doubt, the Nimmians they'd sought so long. But no, not with Hagar down and who knows who else dead or injured. . . . First things first.

Thengel helped the dwarf sit up and leaned him against a tree. Hagar slumped there like a rag doll, unable to control his major limbs. Paralysis had touched him, and the elf squatted beside him, worried.

"Are you all right?"

"I'm alive."

"I should look around, see what happened to everyone. But I don't want to leave you in danger."

"Think it through, Thengel," Hagar gritted at him.

"Danger's probably past, already. I need to see who else I can help."

"Exactly. So do it."

Thengel squeezed the dwarf's arm in reassurance, then left to assess the damage they had suffered.

Hagar closed his eyes and took a labored breath. He had watched it happen, but he had not felt Thengel's touch upon his arm.

HANNO USED HIS ax to dispatch bedazzled freeholders like rabbits at slaughter time, losing track of the Nimmians who spread through the woods ahead of him. Working south along the road, he soon ran out of targets. Joro's people were silent and vicious in their elimination of their pursuers. The runemaster brought up the rear, trailing behind Kaylis and Aral as they slew their befuddled enemies.

With so many Turakemi in a daze, he was amazed to see one figure—no, two—move aggressively against the Nimmians before him: a man and a woman with the same sloe eyes and narrow features as Kaylis. Elves, it seemed, and untouched by the euphoric effects of the Celebration rune. What were they doing with these upcountry woodsmen? He wondered that as he saw the man point at Aral's feet, a string of foreign syllables tripping off his tongue.

In a heartbeat the undergrowth writhed to life, stretching in tendrils and quick-twining lengths to grab at the feet and limbs of the Nimmians who walked there. Root and twig clutched Kaylis, securing her in a leafy grip; Hanno halted his own forward progress at the edge of the eerily animate growth. But plant life remained dormant under Aral's feet, for he was protected by the power of Redeemer, bloodstained and brandished in his grip. He ran to engage the unarmored pair before him.

"Damn you, Aral!" Kaylis snapped at her companion. "Get me out of this!"

The warrior continued his charge. He would not turn his back on the enemy that confronted him. The woman before him held a short bow in her grip; she raised and bent it as he came on. Before he could close, she let fly an arrow, followed by another.

He caught one on the edge of his hide-covered shield just before his throat. His triumphant grin was wiped off his face by the second shaft. It sank into his collarbone just at the edge of his chain mail hauberk, and he blanched white with shock and surprise, staggering to a halt.

The runemaster saw the woman nock again while the man beside her also took bow to hand. Hanno had had no time on this constant march to craft more useful runes, and there was little he could do in combat against archery fire. He took a step back, then another, ready to retreat.

It was then that Kaylis rattled off an invocation, her contained rage making it sound more like a curse than a spell. She flung her arm out with a final imprecation—and a deafening crack of thunder split the clear sky overhead.

A lightning bolt followed, searing the tree behind the archers. Bark flew in a charred explosion; the female archer threw wide her arms and dropped to the ground.

Still Kaylis chanted magic. Dark clouds formed from nowhere, and an icy downpour flooded from the heavens. Thick sheets of rain drenched

Hanno where he stood. Aral staggered back to where Kaylis alternately called and cursed him. When he stood close, bespelled sword in hand, the undergrowth stopped its unnatural movement, and she was freed from its embrace. Together they turned their back on the chaos they had created and half-ran, half-staggered into the woods.

"Out of here, now!" Kaylis barked to the runemaster. He glanced behind. One archer on the ground, another stunned and half-drowned in the torrent that assaulted his position. Now would be the time to finish them off. Hanno's steps slowed—then a tall warrior pushed through the brush, ran to the side of the injured with his sword in his hand.

Yet another elf, and too hale a swordhand to tempt the runemaster. Hanno hurried after his fleeing comrades while the fighter was distracted behind him.

A short distance away, the sky was clear. They found their tethered horses, helped the wounded Aral into his saddle. Joro, Rudic, and Berin extracted themselves from the scene of the ambush as well. As the last of the cloudburst battered the lightning-blasted tree, Hanno whipped his horse along behind the outlanders and they all rode for the western hills.

CHAPTER 23

DALIN AND ARANDEL followed the crest of the inland hills. They had seen no tracks of interest and were heading back to the road when the rush of galloping horses carried to them on the wind.

A moment later they saw six riders cross a nearby slope, galloping between copses, across a brushy clearing, up and over the hillcrest and gone to the west.

Dalin clutched Arandel's arm. "It's them!"

"Go." The Silverleaf pointed to the road. "Spy out what happened on the highway. I follow the horsemen."

"Afoot?"

"Stay by the road. I'll find you." Arandel turned his back and loped uphill. Dalin watched him go until he was out of sight, then sighed.

He crept cautiously downhill, not knowing what to expect. There fled the Nimmians, obviously escaped from the trap they had so carefully laid. Would Torvin's men follow?

Soon enough, Dalin saw that they would not. The sight numbed him: bodies sprawled where they had died, pierced by arrows, hacked by blades, one with a skull crushed by someone's stave. There beneath a tree lay Torvin; Dalin noted the expression of stunned surprise on the dead man's face. The freeholder and his folk had died without a fight, without so much as an attempt at self-defense, for their weapons were still sheathed. Dalin began to search for elvish bodies, too, wondering what he would do if he were all alone.

He found Thengel and Belec tending to Nalia, propped against the roots of a lightning-charred pine. The force of the bolt had flowed partially through her body and stunned her when it hit. A long, narrow burn traced its way down her left shoulder and back and down her left leg. The heel of her left boot was charred, the fabric of her clothing seared. Except for the moderate burn, she was unharmed.

She met Dalin's look with a dazed half-smile. "It could only be Alistana Windweaver," she said. "She is the Stormbringer. She must be watching over me."

Dalin had heard of people surviving lightning strikes, though only when Heimek Mountain Lord in his guise of Weathermaster chose to favor someone. That must account for Nalia's incredible good luck, or perhaps her foreign god really did tread Tura-kem while she was here. The tree yet steamed behind her where the bolt had burned it, in spite of the rain that had followed.

Someone lumbered slowly through the underbrush to join them: Hagar, movement returning to his leaden limbs, his awkwardness diminishing slowly the more he moved his body. A dark look was upon his face, and he sat unheedingly atop damp pine needles so he could rest against the tree that sheltered Nalia.

Thengel regarded his tattered crew and then spoke to Dalin. "We met your Nimmians, it seems. I'm not sure who got the best of that encounter."

"They did not." Dalin inclined his head toward the nearest of Torvin's men.

"No. They did not. Where is Arandel?"

"Trailing the runemaster and his friends."

"Good. Then we shall follow."

Belec had raised Nalia's shirt to examine the burn down her side. He dropped the charred cloth as he spoke. "She needs a salve on this, and rest. And so, I think, does Hagar."

"We can't do it here," Thengel said. "Look around." He waved at the highway where men lay dead on the cobblestones, at the woods that sheltered more corpses. "When one wayfarer notices, the alarm will carry. We will be the ones questioned about this, and detained. Or hunted. We don't have time for either."

"We can't leave Torvin and his people here, like so much carrion!" exclaimed Dalin.

"I fear we have no choice," Thengel said. "Do you wish to create a burial party? Tidy up the woodlands? Clean the road of blood? Then you linger while travelers can ask what you are about. Meanwhile, the runemaster flees with his friends and the Truthsayer's robe. Is that what you wish?"

It was a tough question. Thengel nodded at the youth's silence. "I do not like it either, Dalin Truthsayer, but I think . . . it is the necessary thing to do." He glanced at Hagar. "You can travel?"

"If I must. Yes."

"You must. Come then. If we lose the runemaster now, we lose the Robe as well. Let us make tracks after our enemies. Arandel can find us on the way."

Dalin tore his eyes from a body half-caught in a thicket, one arm thrown out, hand empty of weapon. "The dead. . . ."

"We'll send word to their kinfolk and silver to Tesvi to pay for a proper funeral. But we cannot stay here now. We dare not."

Dalin ducked his head, disturbed. He had been forced to leave Granmar behind, lost in the jagged rocks of the Spires, but had said more than enough prayers for the rest of his granduncle's spirit in these days. The idea of abandoning men who had helped him, the risk of leaving the dead long enough for their restless spirits to haunt this stretch of road . . . it was not something he wanted to be part of.

"You'll send to Tesvi first stop we make?" he persisted.

Thengel nodded solemnly. "I swear it."

With that Dalin had to be satisfied. When they rode he brought up the rear, unable to stay, reluctant to go.

JORO HALTED IN a secluded hollow by a wooded valley. A brook fed into a stream there, the bosom of land at their fork covered with grass and wildflowers, edged with birch and thickets of hazelnut for shade. They pulled Aral from his saddle, laid him down on soft leaf loam. Berin knelt over his companion to examine his wound.

Kaylis stared at the stub of the narrow shaft that Aral had broken off as he rode. "Who were those people?" she demanded of no one.

"Who shot Aral?" Rudic inquired. He had not witnessed the fray, and there had been no time to talk on the road.

"Elves," said Hanno. "They were unaffected by the rune magic."

"Elves, yes," agreed Kaylis. "A Nimmian clan, I'd guess. They had the look of *calianestu*."

"And a dwarf with them as well," ventured Joro. "But no matter where they are from: they rode with the men who followed us from Eskrin. They seek us, and they remain alive behind us."

"What would you have us do?" Kaylis asked. "Return and kill them before we journey on?"

Joro remembered a sword fight where a lengthy blade and a slender giant's overlong reach taxed his shield work to the fullest. Not his favorite way to fight, and not necessary to court. "I don't want to linger here, now we're stranded in this gods-forsaken land." Joro caught the runemaster's eye. "That's where you come in. Swiftest done is, we vanish into the country and leave this trouble far behind us."

"Easily accomplished," grunted Hanno.

"Yet we must find a ship that will carry us to Nimm."

Hanno puffed out his cheeks. "Most difficult. None will carry you."

"We'll pay well."

"It's not the money. None will journey to Nimm by sea, none along this whole coast. It's asking a man to go where the coastal trade will turn on him like dogs on a bone, if raiders let him even catch sight of shore."

"Surely there are smugglers."

"A few, here and there. I don't know how to find them. And if I did, they'd as likely take your money and dump you in the sea midcrossing as go at your bidding where you like." The runemaster sucked a tooth thoughtfully. "Except in Etjorvi."

"What's in Etjorvi?"

"There are some ships that sail to Nimm, sanctioned traders traveling under the King's flag by treaty with the Duchy of Nimm. They ply only from Etjorvi to Nimm-on-Witholl, with escort of longships each way, from each country."

"Ah. The Green Ships, yes?" So-called for the color of the banner of safe passage they flew. "A two-year-old treaty, if I recall correctly." He did; it was the kind of knowledge a Nightrunner filed against future need.

"So I have heard," Hanno said. "I am traveling to Etjorvi at any rate. Come with me. Once there, I will secure you passage on the next Green Ship to Nimm."

Joro gave the runemaster a calculating look. "Are you so certain you can do that?"

Hanno lifted his chin proudly. "I once advised the King, and I will again. I have the connections. Soon I will have the open authority. You'll have passage home as soon as I can arrange for it. Some people owe me favors."

"We won't be waiting weeks," Joro warned. "Not with the unknown behind us like we've left on the King's Road."

"You won't be waiting weeks. As soon as we're there I'll have you lodged in Eritanos House like the Koribee traders you have posed as in the past. I'll have you on the next possible ship."

"Koribee traders again." Joro grinned. "How appropriate. Very well, then. To Etjorvi we go."

He stood, went to look over Berin's shoulder. "How fares our pincushion?"

The priest looked up. "He'll be well enough in a while." Berin had pulled the arrow and cleaned the wound. "I'm asking Tornor's blessings upon him. . . . It's best for a body to heal naturally, but sometimes there is no time to do that, and further one's duty as well. If you'll leave us, now, so I can pray?"

Joro bowed and retreated with the others to the far side of the meadow. Berin did not seem to be doing anything in particular, simply kneeling by Aral's side, his hand cupped over the wound, his lips moving now and then in murmured supplication. The priest bowed his head and seemed sunk in thought, and stayed that way for long minutes. It was far different than the oath-binding ceremony that he had conducted in the god's temple, the Denkorvik of Vikkar Tornor, with much ritual and formal prayer. Now it seemed he only sat in thought beside the injured warrior.

Rudic nudged Joro and pointed. A rose-yellow light glowed around the priest's hand where it rested on Aral's collarbone and neck. The aura suffused the air around the men and then faded gradually away. Berin removed his hand and shifted to a cross-legged position, a half-smile upon his face.

Yellowbeard sat up. Where his wound had been a pink scar remained. He followed his priest in a prayer of thanksgiving to Vikkar Tornor, a quiet ritual Joro left them to on their own. He was not a religious man. Neither, he knew, was Rudic, and Kaylis kept to herself whatever beliefs her people and the Collegium Magisterium had left to her. Yet the touch of a god was nothing to be scoffed at, and at times like this Joro almost wished he trusted so easily to a priest's channeled power.

But it was better, he had found, to trust in himself.

Arandel could not follow Joro's line of thinking, but from his hiding place behind hazelnut shrubs he had heard enough of Etjorvi to know their plans. Marking this place for when he would return with his companions, he slipped off downstream while priest and warrior engaged in prayer.

CHAPTER 24

A SALVE AND Belec's supplication to Onderye Bowmaster eased Nalia's injuries, though the remaining discomfort left her sitting gingerly in her saddle.

Dalin could not see himself riding double with her, jostling the woman with every rough patch of ground they crossed. He looked to the Turakemi horses for a mount he could ride on his own.

He found a likely one, a well-fed cream-yellow mare from Finskili, gentle and hopefully as surefooted as her fellows. He rested his hand on her cheek, wondering for a moment what to call her, for surely she had a name and would respond to it. It was not possible for him to treat a creature as a dumb beast, with a naming of no account: certainly not one that he asked to carry him and be forgiving of his un-skill at riding.

He closed his eyes for a moment and reached out to the mare with his senses. It was the same ability he used to commune with a tree or talk to a mouse, a receptivity to what the other being conveyed about itself. . . .

This horse felt the absence of her owner, her regular rider, and sensed the lack of his presence, the energy she was accustomed to. What name that steading man may once have called her was nothing Dalin could grasp.

"What do you want to be called, eh?" he murmured near her ear.

She was not a fiery beast, that was easily felt; she would rather be grazing in a sunny field right now than toiling over the countryside beneath a rider. Dalin smiled. Like many people he knew, this horse enjoyed her food. And yet she waited, only, for a human to ask something of her, to give her a chance to work in partnership. She was, indeed, very willing to please her rider and help when the need arose. . . .

He settled on a name. Rufslaenit, he would call her: helper-in-need.

With a trade offering of sweetbark to the spirit of her dead owner, Dalin took the reins. He had learned at least how to keep a seat on horseback, and that riding double. Now was time to learn the rest on his own, with the help of Rufslaenit.

Hagar followed his example and caught the reins of a free horse. He did not pause to talk to the creature, to learn anything about it, but occupied himself in a businesslike manner adjusting stirrups. "Are you sure you should do that?" Dalin asked, so used to seeing the dwarf ride behind Thengel on his massive charger.

"The same I could be asking you," Hagar replied. "I rode a mule to your mountains, until one night wolves took it. That is when we quit hobbling our beasts to graze and began to tether them close to camp."

"Oh."

"A mule I will ride when far-travels must be done. A horse I will ride if I have no choice."

"What's a mule?" Dalin asked.

"A cross between a horse and a donkey. Have you no donkeys here?"

Dalin shook his head.

"Surefooted, they are. Mules are that, and stronger, too. Best thing for a dwarf, if he must ride."

Dalin pondered that, wondering what it was like to live in a land that held different creatures than he was used to. It would be exciting to come across the unexpected in the woods—

A picture of Torvin's body fallen in a woodland thicket came to mind, and his excitement faded. And a pool of blood upon a wooden deck . . . and how a knife must feel in the hand when it slit a human throat, just like blooding a deer, perhaps. . . .

He mounted and rode beside the dwarf, troubled in mind and heart.

"How do you do it, Hagar?" he finally asked. "Don't you hate yourself, after?"

Brown eyes regarded him from under bushy brows. "After riding a mule?"

Dalin blushed. "The killing, I mean. I came after these men because they murdered Granmar. I want them punished for it. And their theft—I want the Robe back. All the rest of this, though. . . . I don't want to kill people. And here are more people dead than . . . well. Between the longships and the road, almost as many as live in Nevi. It isn't necessary. Is it?"

Hagar chewed a lip. A long while passed before he answered.

"I have killed few men in my life, Dalin. Each time in self-defense. I have killed other creatures, though, who threatened me or would harm people I cared for. It is never easy.

"This, that you have seen . . . this I cannot explain. There is more to this than you are knowing. It is not because of Granmar's death that more death happens. It is not that simple."

Dalin heard but did not understand. What was Hagar trying to tell him? "What more is there to know?" he asked. "What's difficult about the fact that Turakemi kill Nimmians and Nimmians kill Turakemi?"

Hagar shook his head. "That is not what this is about at all."

"It's what I've seen."

The dwarf nodded. "That is so. And I wish I had an explanation for you. But I do not."

He seemed to become tongue-tied then and a moment later clucked to his horse and rode ahead. Dalin studied Hagar's back. It wasn't that the dwarf *could* not tell him more. He *would* not tell him more.

He knew in his bones that was only because Hagar chose not to. Curiosity blossomed in him in that moment, and he resolved to discover, after all, what "this" was all about.

ARANDEL MET THEM in a clearing. They dismounted for a break, to share what he had learned and plan strategy.

"We can follow them, yes," he said in answer to Thengel's question. "And catch them easily enough, if we push on rapidly. This country takes tracks better than the rocky high mountains. I say we stalk them in their camp tonight, unawares, take them by surprise."

"Like the longship crews?" Thengel considered. "No. They're not drunk, and they know they left us behind them. There's no telling if we'll have surprise or not, and they're likely to scout their back-trail. And they're powerful in unexpected ways, with at least two adepts among them. I'd not have a lightning bolt greet me at the edge of their camp. Or in the middle of our own."

"That spell that felled Hagar, that took command of his muscles . . ." Belec shook his head. "That could be divinely inspired. I have heard of such, among some human mystery schools."

"Arcane or divine, it matters not. Some of them are casters of spells."

"As are some of us," remarked Arandel. "If we wait 'til they reach Etjorvi, they'll be among friends and assistance. At least, the runemaster will."

"Can we not wait until they pass through a town," asked Dalin, "and report them to the Justiciar? A charge of murder is enough for a magistrate to detain anyone."

"We cannot tell what route they'll take or how long they may abide in any town," Thengel replied. "By time we make our charges, they are as likely to be gone cross-country again. In the capital we know right where they are to be found: Eritanos House, which hosts foreign traders."

"Why rely on human justice?" the Silverleaf persisted. "We can waylay them in the wilderness and keep this business between us. If the authorities become involved, we have no more control of the situation."

"Who says authorities will be involved in Etjorvi? We have friends there also."

Arandel snorted. "Follow behind if you must. I think you're missing a good chance on the road."

"We'll deal with them in Etjorvi," Thengel said with finality.

The Silverleaf was not quite ready to give up the argument. "The longer we follow, the more chance we'll be detected. Stray smoke from a cook fire, a glimpse of our horses across a valley, one who scouts back-trail well—many things could betray our presence. It is best if just one scouts along who is skilled in such things—"

"Like yourself," supplied Thengel.

"—and the rest follow farther behind."

The tall elf's lips turned down. "I don't like being far behind and out of sight of what my quarry is doing."

"The runemaster scouts behind them at times," Dalin pointed out. "That's why you found me bound on the mountain. He caught me trailing them." He started at a sudden recollection. "And he appeared out of thin air. One moment he wasn't there; the next he was."

"Invisibility?" Nalia asked.

"I know nothing of that." He shrugged. "I thought he posed as rock or tree, then dropped the guise, as I can do."

That put concern on many faces. "I like this less the more I learn," worried Thengel. "No, it's best to await them at their destination. It would be far safer than trailing and risking putting them on their guard. Or having one of us come to harm."

"Yet we risk losing them by not following them," Belec said. "What if they change their plans? Or become delayed? And us lurking near the traders' house for an arrival that will never come. . . ."

"We could attack them unawares and have this over with." Arandel endorsed his old plan.

"Enough of that." Irritation tinged Thengel's voice. "If they spy us out or we fail in a surprise attack, they're alerted and we're likely hurt. No telling where they'd vanish to then. No. Safest is, we let them move on. We'll outnumber them in the city and can assure they'll have no place to run."

Dalin looked around quizzically. "Five of you outnumber six of them?"

A smile touched the edge of Thengel's lips, but Belec replied directly. "We've companions awaiting us in the city, and we have friends in the King's Hand to call upon should we need them. We can outnumber the Nimmians easily, once we're there."

The King's Hand? That was a term even Dalin knew in his wilderness isolation: the Hounds of Hammankarl, the elite guard of select warriors who carried out special duties for the Selkie King. His opinion of the outlanders shifted in that moment, and he wondered with renewed fervor why they had sought the Truthsayer in the first place.

"There's a nice inn across from Eritanos House," Nalia ventured. "The Golden Lamb. We could watch the comings and goings very well from there."

The Guardian of the Thorn was silent for a bit, nudging a rock with his foot, then looked around the circle of his companions. "Belec's right. If we go ahead, we risk losing them. And Arandel's right also: if we trail them, we risk alerting and losing them. So we shall divide our risks.

"Arandel, have your fun, and follow as slyly as ever you tracked a karzdag back home. The rest of us will go on to Etjorvi. We still have a message stone left, do we not, Hagar?"

"One."

"Good. Keep the stone with you, Silverleaf, and if we need to talk, use it. So we will know if their path changes or you have come into grave difficulties—may Onderye guard against it."

The dwarf fished in a pouch around his neck, took out a rough blue stone wrapped in wire and set upon a leather thong. "Uncut sapphire," he said to Dalin's questioning eyes. "Sung to readiness, and ready to sing in return. I wear its mate." One thick finger touched one of several thongs around his neck as he dropped the pouch back down behind his armor.

Sung to readiness . . . and the dwarf had been introduced to him as Hagar Gemsinger. More than a fanciful name, then? Dalin wondered what gemsinging consisted of—but that was yet one more question that would have to wait for later, because in all of this there was one thing that stuck in his craw, and he had to spit out now.

"You won't talk to a magistrate," he interrupted. "You won't waylay them on the road—but you'll take them on in the city where you have friends to help. Why go to all this trouble just to help me?" he asked bluntly, staring directly at Thengel. "*Is* it to help me?"

The Guardian locked eyes with Dalin. "Or is it to help ourselves?" he filled in the rest of the question. "Yes, and yes, Truthsayer's apprentice."

"Why? What's your interest in this? You came too late to talk to Granmar. Surely it's not only your promise to help me bring them to justice that moves you to so much effort."

There. It was said. He licked his lips nervously, but no one refuted him or silenced him. The outlanders became eerily still, regarding him with unhuman quietude. Not an eye blinked. It was left to the Guardian to respond.

He chose his words carefully. "We . . . have our own reasons for interest in what you call the Robe."

"It's mine," Dalin said flatly.

"So it is. And we would help you to recover it. But then—then I would have you learn why we have helped."

"Tell me now."

Thengel shook his head. "It is too much to go into now. And I would have you learn of what nature we are, first, that you can better judge . . . well. What will need to be judged, later."

"I don't understand."

"Nor do I wish to say more at this time." The Guardian studied him through sharp blue eyes. "Help us to help you, Dalin. I promise when it is in your hands again to tell you of our interest . . . and more. Are we agreed?"

Dalin leaned forward where he sat, rubbing his chin with his fingers. Could he trust them? *They haven't given me reason not to. Yet . . .*

"All right," he conceded. "But I don't like secrets."

"We have no secrets," Thengel said, "just things we will not speak of until the time is right."

"Hmph." Dalin ducked his head in grudging agreement, and a look of relief flickered across the tall elf's face. He came to his feet, rising to his full gangling height above the rest, and turned to Arandel.

"Let Bowmaster and Leafwatcher guide your stealth, Silverleaf. You can find us at the Golden Lamb. We're—what? Six days' journey from the city, cross-country?"

Arandel nodded.

"We'll take the highway and be there in three. Let us know when our quarry enters the city. If we don't hear from you by day six, Hagar will use the message stone to contact you."

"Well enough," acknowledged the scout.

"The rest of us—we part ways here. We cut to the King's Road, and then north to Etjorvi."

And so they rode.

CHAPTER 25

Hanno led Joro's people north, into the fertile lowland valleys of the Vorsemya farmlands. They came to where the tumultuous Ranulf descended through the coastal hills, a stone bridge and dike diverting half its flow into stone-lined irrigation canals that fed the broad northern valley, the remainder wending a less raucous path to the sea.

"Work of the Greywatch dwarves," Hanno explained to the marveling outlanders, "contracted by the Jarl of Vorsemya three centuries ago."

They crossed the bridge and cut northwest, past farmlands and pasture, making for the rocky forested slopes of the Heimekvosk. This was the rugged range they had skirted at Eskrin: Heimek's Spine, the legendary resting place of the earth god, Father of Stone.

"The inland paths are traveled only by farmers and folk from small steadings," Hanno explained. "When we reach the Vosk foothills, we'll take to the grazing trails and so pass as unnoticed as we may." The Way stone rested in his belt pouch to ensure that effort, the one rune he knew he must work with and renew in power that very evening.

The runemaster rode with a smile on his face, amused at how obediently the group followed him. As arrogant as the Nimmians were, when it came to taking guidance about his country, they knew to bow to his lead. It was one of the few things he was glad for about this association, besides the chance it gave him to reclaim his rightful place at court.

He had been amazed to recognize the seal of Saroi Sarilos on the introduction Joro had handed him. He had not communicated with the former ambassador of the Koribee Empire since they had come to subtle understandings at court, only to be discovered by Granmar Truthsayer five years agone.

For that challenge and the secret coercion that had forced Hanno into sudden "retirement" Granmar's debt was finally paid.

It must have been a portentous day when Joro sought him out in his home outside Etjorvi, passed on Saroi's regards, spoke their old code phrase of recognition in flawless Koribe. The runemaster looked twice at his visitor: too light of skin to be a Korib, but with the wavy dark brown hair and gold-flecked brown eyes of those bloodlines. His family name, Narialnos, told of his father's origins, but he claimed Nimm as his land of birth. His face was shaven clean, a style that suggested his city breeding. He looked younger than most clansmen of Nimm, with their full beards, but his hair was graying lightly at the temples. Not as young as he seemed, then. A most unusual visitor.

At least the stranger had captured the runemaster's curiosity, and soon the encoded letter in his hand persuaded him to be of assistance.

Saroi's offer to secure Hanno's appointment as Riedskana, High Council-lor, was not empty air, he knew. They were picking up exactly where they had left off scheming years before, when Freggi was named Councillor after his departure from court. These days Hammankarl looked westward, desir-ing to expand settlement into the lands left long-abandoned in the wake of the Kin Wars. To reclaim those territories Tura-kem was eager to gain mili-tary and magical assistance from Koribee. A treaty to that end was on the table now. If the Empire withdrew from negotiations, it would be the end of years of work and high hopes for the future.

He could guess how the ambassadors would play that game: did Ham-mankarl not have a Riedskana they could work with, the treaty would not be signed, and a great deal of other trade would languish as well.

The Selkie King would never let himself be coerced; naturally, the Ko-ribee intrigues would be the most refined and subtle machinations imagin-able. In the end, Hammankarl would see it in his best interests to appoint an experienced adviser well-known to himself—and one also skilled at dealing with the wily Koribi. Hanno had established that reputation long ago. Now he need only put himself before the King and become active at the court again to become the likely choice when the time came for an appointment.

Someone rode up close by his side. It was Kaylis.

"This Eritanos House, where you think we should stay," she said. "How safe are the rooms?"

"How safe?" he echoed blankly, his mind on other things.

"Is this place like an inn, where many come and go? Do doors lock? What guards guests against thievery?"

"Ah. It is safer than an inn, certainly. It was built by the Furriers' League, to host trade with Koribi merchants. Later sponsored by the King himself, as wayhouse for notables as well as wealthy traders. They're persons who travel with valuables and their own personal guard. Doors all lock. There are some enchantments of alarum protecting certain rooms and storage areas. And the

Housemaster keeps a vault; he'll be glad to lock away valuables for you. You are concerned about the Robe?"

"The Tapestry," she corrected, and gave a short nod. Her pinched lips betrayed her unease at his question. None of these folk cared to talk in Hanno's presence about what they had taken from the Truthsayer. She fell back behind him before he could question her further.

The runemaster tugged a long gray-blond mustache in amusement. Did they truly think he would pay no heed to what they were stealing from his country? Did they imagine that he would let them go their way as the price of his Councillorship?

They forgot who had hatched schemes every bit as convoluted as those of Saroi Sarilos. He would delay their departure until he was appointed highest of the King's officials and then take the Robe from them. Or he would have them beset by brigands and let the Robe come into his safekeeping with an appropriate accounting he could pass on to others. He would handle it so not even Koribi agents could see his hand at work, but the Truthsayer's time-honored robe of office would not leave Tura-kem in the hands of thieves. It was far too valuable a token: something he could and would bestow upon a biddable seer, some heir to Granmar's office of his own choosing.

A troubling recollection came to mind in that moment, and his high spirits left him. There was already an heir to Granmar's position, a youth he had half-expected to die on a cold mountainside. Torvin and the upland men had stalked them to the King's Road—and what, exactly, had set Eskrin men on their trail? When they'd met, Torvin had guested the runemaster in all good spirit and helped him on his way.

Hanno could think of only one reason steading men would pursue and attempt to waylay a runemaster. It could only be news of the Truthsayer's death—and just one person could have related that tale. Dalin, the apprentice he had let live.

This was not the time to voice his suspicions, when the Nimmians were in a fever to travel and he was not in a place, yet, to deal with the lot of them. Perhaps the boy had been killed in the ambush, after all—or maybe he'd gone back home to the Spires and was staying out of the runemaster's path. He would stay far away from Hanno all the days of his life, if he knew what was wise.

Yet Hanno knew in his heart the youth must have talked to Torvin, and where one tale was told, many could be told. He could not pretend there was no hazard. When he thought about the ambush on the road behind them and all that it implied, Dalin was clearly his enemy. He considered a skenjis and dismissed it—no telling where the boy was, to direct the ill-wishing his way.

There were other ways, though, to hinder an enemy from afar.

CHAPTER 26

"HOLD, RUFS."

Dalin reined his mare in. Road travel, he found, was vastly easier than the overland trekking that had brought them down from the Crystal Spires. Their pace altered between walk, trot, and short canters, a ground-eating speed that carried them through the trade villages of the Vorsemya valley and left the port town of Bjalinik far behind.

Dalin spent a great deal of time staring at other travelers on the King's Road, most on foot or with carts or wagons, puzzling out what brought people to a point on the highway so far from where their homes must be. He understood the need to range in order to hunt, but otherwise his whole life had been based in Nevi village or Granmar's cavern abode. It was not until now on the King's Road that he comprehended how trade or personal business moved people from one place to another.

He stopped now with his fellows because two wagons caused a roadblock on the highway. One with a modest load of straw pulled by a horse had tried to pass a wagon full of wooden poles creaking behind two oxen. Wheels locked; a few poles tumbled to the roadway and rolled like giant pickupsticks across the cobblestones. The drover stood red-faced, waving his cattle prod, shouting at the driver, who shouted right back.

They were less than a day from Etjorvi, and traffic was heavier than any so far. A stream of travelers and tradesmen edged around the roadblock and the heated exchange. Some stopped to gawk or offer opinions and congested the road further.

Thengel eased past a man pulling a grindstone on a wheeled handcart, found his way to the side of the road. The upset poles lay in a tangle across the small drainage ditch at the highway's edge. Thengel touched his gray with his spurs, jumped the small obstacle in one leap, and was on his way in the grass beside the road.

His companions followed suit, but when Dalin came to the ditch he called Rufslaenit to a halt. His hands were still scraped up from his headlong dive on his first day of riding. Reining her in from a canter he had used too much force; she had tucked her haunches and come to a sudden stop. Not knowing to lean his weight back in the saddle to compensate, he had flown off over her shoulder and lay, more embarrassed than hurt, on the cobbled road.

Now he knew how to rein in from a canter and, through brief derring, a gallop. He had not yet jumped his mare across anything, though, and did not relish the idea of finding yet one more way to unhorse himself in front of many onlookers. He was thinking where he could cross the ditch away from the poles when Nalia came up beside him.

She smiled as if amused by his dilemma. His thoughts on the matter were probably visible on his face, he realized.

"Nudge with your heels, rein her straight ahead, and urge with a sound," she said. "Lean forward a bit as she gathers for her spring, and put your weight in the stirrups so your knees have some give. Straighten as she clears the jump, or the jarring when she lands will pitch you forward. Like this."

She did as she had described, and from a standstill Frelin, her dappled gray, took a few steps, stretched out, and cleared the hindrance.

Dalin licked his lips. He could walk around the obstacle . . . but sooner or later there would be something else he must jump, and he had best get about learning the trick of it. He clucked to Rufs, bumped his heels against her sides. The mare moved, gathered herself, flew lightly over the wood. A heartbeat later he felt the jar of impact and found he had forgotten to straighten up in the saddle. He caught himself from falling by gripping tighter with his legs and clutching at the pommel of his saddle with his free hand.

Nalia's smile broadened. "You'll get it," she encouraged him. "Jump any small thing you can. It's all in the balance."

A second quiet session with Belec and his prayerful attentions had sped her healing, and now she sat at her ease once more. She rode Frelin in perfect balance, poised and cheerful in the warm sun. Her hair was loose down her back and, for once, not tickling Dalin's nose. He smiled to himself. She often talked to him about small things, pointing out a wasp nest on a tree bowl or grouse paused in unmoving alert behind a blackberry bush. She enjoyed the country as much as he did, and it put him more at ease with her than he would have thought possible when he had first clambered awkwardly up behind her saddle. He traded on that rapport now as he rehearsed the question that had been in his mind for days.

"Why is it," he asked as he rode beside her, "that you came to see the Truthsayer?"

There. It was out. An innocent-sounding query, practiced for many long leagues on the King's Road. He was proud of himself. His words sounded perfectly ordinary, he thought. Surely it was not intruding upon Thengel's wish to talk about the Robe later. His question was not about the Robe at all.

It seemed to strike Nalia differently, though. Her casual banter faltered before she picked up the thread of conversation again. "We had business with him," she said.

"You've never mentioned it to me."

"You're not the—well. You're not Granmar."

Dalin pulled himself up in his saddle. "I am the closest thing to a Truthsayer you'll find in all of Tura-kem. You can ask me your questions. I'll see truth for you if I can."

What possessed him to make that claim, he was not sure. Of all people he was the only one who knew anything about a Truthsayer's ways; that much was true. Yet for all that, he was no Truthsayer himself, and now, without one to complete his training, he might never be. Without the Robe he could not even imitate the dignified pose of a seer listening to petitioners, then sinking into trance to see and speak truth before a smoking fire of divination.

Yet somehow he felt his claim was not too presumptuous. He knew things, sensed things, that others did not. He realized that from his talks with tree and stone, and how he sensed Rufslaenit's feelings. It should encourage the elves to open to him, he thought, and might win him what he desired to know. *Tell me your concerns, and like the Truthsayer, I will be your seer.*

At least it would cause them to reveal what brought them to Kodanit's Spire.

Or maybe not. Nalia shook her head to his offer. "We had no questions. Only business to discuss, and that, I'm afraid, died with the Truthsayer."

She rode a bit ahead from him then, distancing herself from the conversation and the other questions that lingered on his lips. Dalin sighed in frustration. Who else could he pry information from? Belec was too reserved, Hagar too unsociable, Thengel affable enough but too close-lipped about their affairs. Arandel did not care to talk to humans, and Nalia evaded his questions.

Perhaps other tactics were called for. He mulled over what might serve him, and had Rufs jump the ditch back onto the road without a second thought.

CHAPTER 27

THE LONG SHADOWS of late afternoon stretched away from the travelers as they crested a hill, following the road down to the banks of the Aelvoss. Before them Etjorvi lay bathed in the soft golden light of the westering sun: the high-walled Old Town to the north of the river, the slate-roofed stone houses in the unwalled New City to the south, beyond them the glittering towers of the White Palace at the edge of the fiord.

Dalin's eyes widened. This was the city Granmar had always promised he would come to know—the seat of the Kings of Tura-kem. Traders to the hinterland told improbable tales of its wonders, yet even skalds praised it in epic song, for Etjorvi was closely tied to the legends of this northern land.

A dispute between gods had led to strife between the men who worshipped them, and so God War had turned to Kin War in Tura-kem's ancient past. Brother fought brother, and generations were slain in hateful vendetta. Over two centuries of feud and rebellion left its scars upon the land until open warfare pitted faction against faction for control of the realm.

With the destruction of the capital, Taehanti, King Hakkon was forced to withdraw to Etjorvi. He strengthened that town and expanded it into a walled city where the Aelvoss flowed into the Dannenborch, Dannen's Sound. Its first burst of growth was accomplished with the fervor and looted riches of wartime. It was left to his grandson, King Haevig, to conclude the Kin-War with the forced expulsion of the leaders of the heretic factions. They and their followers and all who were friendly kin to them traveled in mass exodus to Nimm on the far side of the northern sea. The diaspora happened swiftly; on pain of death did they linger.

They who would become Nimmians left behind them a nation united in worship and lofty principles but stripped of nearly half its population and staggering from the ravages of a protracted civil and religious war. For another two centuries the remnants of power struggled for ascendancy, their visions of the future divisive, no one person able to unite the jarls of Tura-kem and gain their commitment to a common goal or king.

This impasse was broken by the arrival of Prince Graumnir, the fey son of Fris, goddess of the hunt, and Egior, lord of the selkie folk, they who shift shape between man-form and seal. Having grown up among the selkie and come of age with the creatures of the wild, Graumnir was desired by his mother to live with land-dwelling men and learn their ways.

He did as she wished and visited the court at Etjorvi. His divine and magical origin let him cross boundaries between people and factions that were insurmountable to men of lesser stature. He wed Elfrith, descendent of King Hakkon, who but for her sex had the birth rank that entitled her to rule. And so it was Asmund, the son of Graumnir and Elfrith, who became the first Selkie King—so named for his heritage and the traits he inherited from his father.

Asmund's heirs ruled Tura-kem to the present day. They continued the work of their forebears and built on to the city with great care and planning, a showcase for their benign governance. Fine craftsmanship and pride of place marked the architecture of the capital, its major avenues broad and stone-paved, its houses and public buildings tall, narrow, of pristine moun-tain granite roofed with gray slate, windows sheeted with transparent gyp-sum or in some cases expensive thick glass. The more modest shops and dwellings were nevertheless neatly built of doweled wood and fine joinery. Inside were other marvels: water at the turn of a tap, heated floors, smoke-free hearths—Dalin had heard many more unlikely things than that and scarcely knew what to believe or expect in this city of wonders. He rode star-ing about him like a cowherd at his first country fair.

Thengel followed the King's Road into the city; the Truthsayer's appren-tice noticed that they passed no gate, no guards. They rode through out-skirts, by stockpens and inns that catered to drovers and common tradesmen. The fortified walls of old Etjorvi loomed across the Aelvoss, the gray stone height of the Hakkonkalye, Hakkon's Keep, visible from afar. Dalin realized the city had outgrown its bounds long ago, like a steading too full with kins-men; new settlement had been made outside the walls and here where he rode men could come and go as they pleased.

That new settlement had grown with time to be larger than the old city contained behind battlements. They came to a broad crossroads, and there they paused in the flow of wagons and foot traffic. To the north was a bridge fortified with a large barbican serving as a gatehouse. "Tolvar's Gate," Nalia pointed out. To the south a shady tree-lined avenue led to a distant grove— "The Denkorvic of Fris," she added, a place honoring the divine heritage of the first Selkie King. Ahead the avenue curved east and south, leading eventually to the gates of the White Palace, the residence of kings who no longer lived in the small, dark, military confines of the Hakkonkalye.

"And where is the Golden Lamb, that you recommend us to?" Thengel asked Nalia.

"This way," she said, and led toward the Palace, leaving the avenue after a time to enter a square. She skirted a round fountain in the middle, its water gushing from four spouts into the blue tiled basin below, a topmost stream burbling an arm's length into the air before cascading down in a fine, glittering spray.

Dalin stared. He had never heard of such a thing. No trips to the well were needed here: water came rushing at the seeker instead. Servants and serfs with buckets in hand attested to the fountain's utility for residents roundabout.

His name called him back to his departing companions. He followed down a smaller street to a row of houses and gated courtyards. Polished glass shone in the windows, and embroidered banners hung over several doorways. A painted wooden sign depended above one courtyard entrance; Nalia pulled up beneath the symbol of the gold-fleeced lamb depicted there. She motioned to the open gate with one hand while nodding over her shoulder in the direction of the street. Dalin looked where the bolder gesture pointed his gaze.

Across the way was a tall house of quarried stone, its courtyard gate shut, its broad door framed in green-veined marble. On the wall above the lintel hung a banner, a tawny winged lion above three golden disks. Dalin recognized the symbol of the Koribee Empire, for enough tales were told of their trade and their military—that flag flying at the head of their ranks—that even a Nevi hunter knew what a crouching beast with wings on a field of blue must be. The gold disks were a merchant's symbol, perhaps, for this could only be Eritanos House.

Thengel paused by Nalia's side. "Well chosen. We'll get settled, then send a messenger round to gather the others to us here."

"And if the inn is full?" she asked.

"Then room will be made," he said confidently, "or the King's Hand will make the request for us."

The Guardian of the Thorn led the way into the courtyard of the Golden Lamb, his companions close behind.

CHAPTER 28

I<small>T WAS THE</small> dinner hour. Lodgers and local folk filled the tables in the Golden Lamb's common room. Brisk business was done between kitchen tables, and the smooth oak countertop of the short serving bar. The innkeep, Thoralf, was a thin-lipped balding man preoccupied with the bustle in his establishment. He brushed off the elves' inquiry.

"All the front rooms are taken. Best I can give you is the one common room under the attic, over the courtyard. It's all I've got left."

Dalin watched Thengel take the man aside and converse in quiet tones. There were titles mentioned and names the youth did not recognize, and soon the innkeep seemed much friendlier. He bid them wait in the common room for a time and served them tankards of ale while two serving men went upstairs. They came back down after a goodly while, and Thoralf returned to their table.

"You have the entire suite of rooms in the front now, Lord," he said to Thengel with a half-bow. "My girl here will see you up." He left a maid to guide the newcomers two flights up the stone staircase. She let them into a series of four large adjoining chambers, gave the keys to Thengel, and curtsied her way out.

The rooms were clean but in a little disarray. It looked like they had been recently and hastily vacated—as indeed they had. There was a stool away from the wall, covers not snug on the bed, a used towel overlooked on the washbasin table.

Thengel surveyed the rooms with adjoining doors between them: three sleeping chambers, one reception chamber with cushioned benches that could also serve for sleeping. Double-leaved windows opened over the street, giving the perfect view of Eritanos House across the way. Through the trees that overhung its arched gateway the interior of its walled courtyard could also be glimpsed.

The elf put hands on hips and smiled in broad satisfaction. "It will do for now," he proclaimed, "and better than us lodged piecemeal all over the city. Please, settle in."

Dalin clutched his bearskin cloak in one hand, his staff and pack in the other. He looked around, completely lost.

"You'll be wanting to pick a bed," Nalia said over her shoulder as she walked by. "Come." She walked into the second bedchamber, through that into the third. She dropped her pack on a stool, her bedroll on the trunk at the foot of the wide quilt-covered mattress. Dalin shifted from foot to foot uneasily.

"You needn't sleep in here with me," she said, a mischievous gleam in her eye, "unless you're of a mind to."

His cheeks reddened and he shook his head.

"Well then. Where is it you'd prefer to sleep?"

He looked around, clearly ill at ease, and shrugged. He would not meet her eye.

Nalia cocked her head to one side. "What is it, then? What's wrong?"

"I . . ." His face brightened again. "I don't belong here," he said in a rush. "I'd be better in the stable with the horses. There at least I know I can sleep on the hay."

"I don't understand."

"This." He waved the tip of his staff, gesturing around the room. "It's—well—I've never seen such a thing. Such *things*. I sleep on a straw pallet or sleeping furs on the ground. Here you sleep like a jarl in a giant soft bed. I'd fall off in the night and break my neck. All this furniture—I don't know what half of it's for—and yet they leave out simple things like a hearth. How will you make a fire if you need one . . . ?"

His voice trailed off and he hoped Nalia understood his distress. He was out of his depth and feeling it now. The villages and towns along the way were places he had passed through, stopping in the common room of an inn for a hasty meal or dickering for a chicken with a farmer on the high road—none of these things had prepared him for what a city would be like. He was used to life in a small steading, a hunters' settlement, in harsh and simple conditions. Living with Granmar in a cave for years had made Dalin's life even more primitive. And here . . . here everything he laid eyes upon or touched was different. The crowds in the streets, the press of people everywhere . . . even the air was different. It smelled wrong, the scent of too much humanity living too closely in warm weather, of too many odors—of food cooking, the sickly-sweet scent of garbage and horse droppings—the heartbeat of trees diminished, and the stone here so worked by man's hand that it no longer spoke as living rock should do. Inside the Golden Lamb not even the granite blocks of its construction were left to the eye: plaster and paint obscured the walls, and the floor was of wood no more alive than the rock.

What Dalin had at first marveled at, the oddities that caught his eye everywhere, had become too much, too many, inescapable. He jutted his chin to the door that gave unto the hallway. "There," he said, "doors I understand, but locks? Here every door has one. Why? Are city men so little trusted?" He looked to the other wall. "This glass in the windows—a wonder, I'm sure, but it has no life to it, no vibrance, and stops the air." He tapped the floor with the tip of his staff. "And no one in the common room talks to you or greets you—they stared at us like we were stoats strayed to the dinner hearth."

"Did they?" Nalia plucked at the sleeve of her once-white shirt. "Perhaps we look a little stoatish, in this state of road-wear. . . ."

"They could at least return a friendly nod. They look away instead." He shook his head at the rudeness. "And Rufslaenit is far downstairs and across a courtyard, while I'm up here. I'm not even close enough to hear her if she's distressed."

"Your horse will be fine, Dalin. Trust me. You worry too much." She sat in a chair, motioned to him to put his things down. He did and joined her on a nearby stool. She chewed her lip for a bit, regarding him thoughtfully. When she spoke, she abandoned the breezy flippancy she presented to most of the world. Her tone was gentle and warm.

"When I left Caerlian I was very young and had never been among humans before. Your kind live very differently than we, in our *eliafin* of trees and living shelters. I had heard stories but did not really know what to expect. I remember what it was like to notice locks, surprised that humans wanted to cling to their possessions so tightly." She smiled with the memory. "I took it as a personal challenge and spent some years helping men to hold less closely to their belongings.

"I didn't understand their hearts, or man's strange nature. Not that I understand so much better now, but I have seen much more of it: the quick tempers of humans, their furious industry, their terrible impatience, as if you know you are a candle burning out too quickly. . . .

"It took me months to get to the point where a speedy human dinner and the conversation that is engaged in there came to seem . . . normal. If that word can apply. It is what men are accustomed to, at least, and so I became accustomed also to what your folk do and how they live.

"Every people do this differently, Dalin."

He looked at her, his expression doubtful.

"In a way," she said, "it is like you come from a different race and are for the first time visiting humanity. In some wise, I think, that is true—for your background and experiences are very different, are they not, from those of men who dwell in cities or towns? So I think you are like a young *caliane* leaving Caerlian and stumbling for the first time into the realms of man. If it feels like another world that is because it is another world. Different than you are used to, certainly. You must simply accept that and set about learning it like a hunter learns a new terrain."

That was a telling observation, and it struck Dalin as a wise comment. He nodded slowly. She was right, and he could not argue with a bit of it. He wondered how Granmar had learned to fit into such a place as Etjorvi—or any town, for that matter. Had he felt as out of place, as overwhelmed with all that was strange, especially on his first visit?

Probably. But if the Truthsayer had come to terms with the differences here and still found a love for the city and its ways, then Dalin could do no less.

He offered Nalia a half-bow and a clasp of hands before his chest—the gesture of gratitude and respect that was the custom of Nevi folk, an offering to elders and those who shared their wisdom.

"You're right. I have a lot to learn."

"You do. Ask me anything you are curious about. If I don't know the answer, I'll send you to someone who can answer you or tell you how you might discover it for yourself, if I can."

"Thank you. I will."

"Meanwhile . . ." She stood up in sudden resolution. "Let me show you what's of interest here."

Dalin came to his feet. *And just what did I expect?* he asked himself. *Granmar always did call Etjorvi 'different'. All those stories and fables—maybe they aren't all yarns after all. . . .*

"I'm sure I can figure things out on my own," he said, already regretting his outburst of minutes before. He had not wanted to sound like such a pup, and perhaps he was not, really—he just felt so off-balance in his surroundings.

"Nonsense," Nalia said lightly, dismissing his concerns. "You said you couldn't even tell where we'd make a fire. Let's start with that." A few steps put her next to a strange object against the wall of the room, one of the many items Dalin had been puzzling over a short while before. She put her hand on the dark green tiles that completely covered the thing: as tall as Dalin, built like a large chest turned on end, a tube of metal connecting it to the wall, thick flagstones underneath to protect the wood of the floor from its

THE TRUTHSAYER'S APPRENTICE   149

base. On the front a little hatched metal grating and a tiled square with
hinges inset . . .

"A haskran, they call it here," Nalia pronounced. She patted it with one
hand. "A tiled oven. A box built to hold a fire, like a fireplace. That metal
pipe its chimney, venting the smoke. The tiles hold the heat, so that even after the fire goes out the warmth radiates for hours after. It takes a while to
heat thoroughly, but when it does . . ." She beamed. "It's a lovely warmth in
the cold weather. And no smoke. They should have these in Nimm, where
men are so fond of smoking themselves and their homes every time they
want to take the chill off."

Dalin examined the haskran. "I've never heard of such a thing," he said.
"Do they have these everywhere?"

"In the Palace, in better homes, yes. Lesser homes make do with snug
fireplaces or stoves and a good draught. Not the smoking hearths or fire pits
we've seen in the country here."

"How'd they think of it?" he wondered out loud. "Dwarf work?"

Nalia shrugged. "Who knows. Men are inventive, too. And they cook on
raised heaths here, so they don't have to bend over. That was a mannish conception, I'm told."

She moved to the basin table against the far wall. "Now this"—she
demonstrated—"is a water tap. For drinking and washing. The basin has a
drain in it." She pointed. "The same thing is found in a room down the hall,
only larger: there's a tub for bathing, there. Water is heated by the fireplaces
in the kitchen. Now that *is* dwarvish craftsmanship. They designed the piping and laid the waterways underground that supply many buildings with
water." She grinned. "So, because of a king who enjoyed his pleasures and
his deal with Greywatch artisans, you can run water whenever you wish and
have a hot bath. Which"—she wrinkled her nose—"I suggest we all do before we have dinner. It's been too long on the road for us."

That was a thought so unexpected that it took a moment to percolate
through Dalin's brain. A hot bath? Not a cold dip in a stream or water
splashed from a well? He was no stranger to a soak—there was a nice hot
spring at the base of the Middle Spire—and saunas he knew well. Granmar
had improvised that essential chamber in a back alcove of the caves. But a
hot bath, on purpose, for no special occasion? What a luxury. *How pleasant,*
he thought, *to relax like that. Like the hot springs, but much more convenient.* . . .

He grinned. "I shall have to see this bathing room."

"Yes." Nalia quirked a smile in return. "You shall."

She showed him more interior marvels, so many he had to quit thinking
about what he saw and simply take it in, in plain observation. He put his

mind in that open, receptive state and absorbed what he heard like a sponge. No judgment, no reaction, just listening and learning. Here, the lamp that burned oil with a wick so well made it lasted a week at a time. Underfoot, a small tidy rug, woven so that the colored threads portrayed flowers in red and blue and green: the weaving of Etjorvi women, Nalia said, a product sold as far away as Koribee.

Against the wall, a cabinet for holding clothes, with two drawers on smooth-sliding runners—cunning woodwork, far more refined than steading construction done with adze and plane. Near the bed, a writing table, its smooth surface of fine polished wood, the tabletop inclined at a slight angle for ease in scribing. It held pen, quills, ink pots, blotting sand—and paper, not coarse parchment, to write upon. Dalin picked up the quill, examined its sharpened tip.

"Can you write?" Nalia asked.

"I know my runes and some cyphering. Not the Koramnoiye, though. Not yet." He referred to the alphabet descended from the runes and the common tongue that it captured in cursive script.

"But runes are enough for notices and legal documents, and letters in this land, are they not?"

"They are," he agreed, setting the quill back in its rest.

"Clever manling. That is more than I know."

"Do you not know the Koramnoiye?"

"Not that, nor runes. No writing at all, except for the *emloë,* the script of my arcane studies."

It took a moment for that to sink in. "You do not read, then?"

"Nary a word," she said blithely, "except for the *emloë.* I've had no need for it." She shrugged. "I expect I'll learn one day, when it seems useful and I want to."

He considered that. Few of his kinfolk read, either: it was a skill for scholars and scribes and those who studied rune lore. Granmar had impressed upon him, though, how important it was for the Truthsayer to be able to record visions and pass on readings and advice in a way that man's memory could not distort. Reading and its cousin writing were things he had committed to learn the day he'd come to live with his granduncle.

He had thought somehow these elves, so traveled, so wise in the ways of the city, would be lettered like the nobility, or merchants who traded. He was still adjusting his perspective as Nalia took him through other rooms, showed him cupboards to hold his belongings, pointed out the thick featherbeds beneath down-filled coverlets. He tried out one mattress, decided it was even softer than it looked, and flatly refused to sleep in one. It would be like sinking into a bog, he thought, and he would dream of drowning all night long. Best he should sleep instead on the cushioned bank seats of the reception room.

Nalia showed him the water closet, another plumbing wonder, and the bathing room. He started when someone moved unexpectedly beside him, and he spun toward the intruder. It was a young man, tanned, dirt-smudged, his blond hair greasy with days of travel and sweat, his leathers once beige-brown, now dark—

He was confronting himself over a marble-topped toiletry stand.

"A mirror," said Nalia.

Dalin reached out with a tentative finger and touched the surface. His finger contacted the tip of his reflected finger, and he snatched it back hastily. Another marvel, and a startling one. He knew of mirrors—a cousin in Nevi had owned a small hand-held one of polished silver, but kept it so dear she had never shared it or shown it around. Granmar had no need for one. Until this moment, Dalin had never seen himself reflected in anything other than pond water.

How magical it was.

Nalia showed him how to run a bath, then left him on his own. The bath was framed in wood, flagged with mortared stone, the tub a small rectangular pond in this unlikely place, covered with watertight tile and grouting. He took a long time experimenting with water taps, then fumbled with the plug and lost a quarter of the tub's water down the drain before he jammed the stopper hastily back in place. Finally he got into the steaming water, sitting with legs outstretched, and sighed in comfort. Soon he was splashing about, trying the exotic sea sponge, the pumice stone, the brush he found there— he decided that the sponge looked strangest but felt best, and he applied it to good measure with the scented soap he found in a stone jar. He sank beneath the water to rinse his hair—and cursed when he came up, eyes burning. He had cooked more than a batch or two of soap for Granmar, but to be lost in a small pool covered in its suds was a whole new experience for him.

A knock at the door interrupted his pleasures. Belec came in with a bundle in his arms. "For you," he said. "It's well turned out we all must be." He collected Dalin's leathers, stiff and road-stained on the floor. "These will be returned to you later."

"That's all I have to wear!"

"Not now." He patted the stack of garments he had set down. "A loan from Arandel's pack. You're close to a size. They're yours for now. And you'd best hurry; others need in here, too."

Dalin sped himself, pulling the plug, toweling himself off, donning the loan of clothes he'd been given. Green linen trousers gave loosely around his legs; a sleeveless tunic of russet fustian felt light and cool and comfortable.

He strapped on a broad leather belt and still felt a little naked, unadorned by the red-and-white beadwork he wore on all his Clan Nevi clothing. Still. It would do for now. He slicked his wet hair back, forgoing a braid for the while, and left the strange little room with taps and drains and a steamy wall mirror shared by all.

CHAPTER 29

THORALF OVERSAW THEIR service in a private dining room downstairs. Dishes were brought and arrayed on the cloth-covered table before them: steamed cod in oyster sauce, roast stuffed pigeon, slices of boar, a sauté of bacon, peas, and tomatoes, a berry compote, loaves of crusty bread, and red wine rather than ale—it was a feast as good as the Nevi Skan's wedding, Dalin thought, and his stomach grumbled in anticipation.

The Guardian of the Silverthorn thanked their host but did not seem to think the food remarkable. The elves sampled the viands in leisurely manner while Hagar set to in an organized and silent attack. Dalin followed his example; he and the dwarf let the others carry the conversation while they gave dedicated attention to the food.

Thengel poured wine and handed the pitcher on to Belec. "I've been rethinking my idea to summon the others," he said. "It presents some difficulties to our tactical plans."

The cleric nodded agreement. "I've been thinking the same. Once Sembroie knows we're back, she'll want to know where we went, exactly; what we did . . ."

"True." Thengel sipped his wine thoughtfully. "I'd feel beholden to tell what we know of Granmar's death. We'll do that, naturally—at a time of our choosing. But we mustn't speak too soon, or we won't be free to hunt down these brigands. Members of the King's Hand may help us as our friends, but if we engage them formally, they'll have to take official action in turn."

Dalin said nothing, but he listened all the more intently as he studied his plate. As he suspected, they weren't going to report Granmar's murder—they were keeping the authorities out of it completely. Yet they made plans to deal with Joro. Thengel had promised, after all, to help him see justice for Granmar's death. Would this serve him as well? He did not know.

Thengel glanced at the Truthsayer's apprentice and then around the table. "Best, I think, if we avoid contact with the Hounds of Hammankarl for a few days—until we've seen our birds to roost at Eritanos House and had our chance to handle them on our own terms."

"You still want the others to help?" Nalia asked.

The elf nodded. "Ask Cathmar and Valdarius to join us as soon as they can. The adenye, though—in training barracks and page service with the Hounds . . ." He shook his head, clearly having second thoughts. "Sembroie will have to turn a blind eye if they're to join us, or we'll have to make that formal report to the Hand that we're avoiding for now. . . ."

Adenye? Dalin wondered at the affectionate term for youth that he heard. Whom did the elf mean?

"I don't like leaving them there," countered Belec. "If we have to move fast after the thieves or out of Etjorvi, we'll all need to be together. We won't have time to regroup. You should at least alert them to be in readiness to join us at a moment's notice. Or you must resign yourself to leaving them behind, Thengel."

The tall elf shook his head adamantly. "We've had this talk before. I promised them a year of service, and more if they want it. Abandoning them is not possible."

Dalin could no longer pretend to study his plate. Year of service? Adenye? It was Turakemi slang meaning "kids" or "lads" or "the young-sters"—affectionate, diminutive, suggesting a familial relationship. Did Thengel have *children* traveling with him?

"Get word to Katrije," Hagar said between bites. "Have her tell the others."

"She's easiest to reach," agreed Nalia.

"Who are you talking about?" Dalin finally interrupted. Exasperation at being talked around tinged his voice, and his question stopped the conversation cold. The others exchanged looks. It was for Hagar to answer. "We're speaking of Thengel's . . . entourage."

Something akin to a giggle escaped from Belec, and Nalia struggled not to smile. Thengel nursed the offended dignity of one who is used to being ribbed on a topic.

"They are not my 'entourage,'" he corrected. "They are my squires. And my page."

"Every noble fighter should such escort have." Hagar said it with a straight face, and Belec snorted around his wine.

"They're good adenye," Thengel said defensively. "And they've more than proven their worth. We've all seen that."

"We know that," Nalia said soothingly. "And some of us owe our lives to

Udo distracting that dragon . . . but Thengel. Really. You are the most unlikely father figure. . . ."

With that, gales of laughter swept the table, leaving only Dalin untouched. Even Thengel looked amused. He finally took pity on the youth's
ignorance and looked his way.

"We speak of some promising young folk I recruited to aid me in Kalajok, countrymen of yours. I needed a squire. There were two likely persons,
and so I took them both on. I understood then that I was committing to
training them—but then I always expected to have to train anyone in my service. A Guardian of the Thorn has specialized needs, at times."

"I see."

"And then there was a young girl, very young, yet very clever. Seemed
likely enough as a page. . . ."

"Two squires not being enough," muttered Hagar.

"And hence my 'family,' as they call it."

"How long have they been with you?" Dalin asked politely.

"Oh. . . ." Thengel counted in his head, then looked surprised. "Why—
only four months!"

"Seems longer," said Nalia.

"Seems like forever," groused Hagar.

Thengel shot the dwarf a frown and replied to Dalin in a serious voice.
"Four months, more or less. But they have risked their lives beside our own,
and suffered far worse things in this short time than such young people
should ever have to. They're in the caretaking right now of friends in the
King's Hand, being trained and taught in my absence. That is why it is prob-
lematical to contact them at this moment. Yet I owe them much, and so they
are, indeed, my entourage of sworn vassals—and my extended family, of
sorts—for as long as they wish to be."

"Well said," nodded Belec, sobered by this last from Thengel. He raised
his wineglass. "To the adenye."

The others joined him in the toast.

"Tomorrow, then," said Thengel, "we send word to Katrije." He set his
wineglass down. "And the day after, we should be hearing from Arandel.
Then we shall see what we shall see."

CHAPTER 30

"WHERE ARE YOU going, young Truthsayer?" Thengel asked Dalin as he took his staff from the corner.

"Out. To take a look around. . . ." He trailed off as he caught the skeptical look on Thengel's face and the small shake of his head.

Dalin's brows pulled together. "Why not?" he asked.

"Thinking, you are not," Hagar spoke up in his rumbling voice. "A large city it is, and strange to you. You are bumbling around for cutpurses to fleece. You are likely going astray. Worst: your face is on the streets to see, and should our runemaster spy you then surprise we have lost."

"They're far behind us! We don't expect them for two, three days yet. You said so yourself."

Thengel shrugged. "That was an estimate of their time. If they are moving on roads, they are traveling faster. None of us will be wandering the streets until we know precisely where our quarry is. Or we will be moving only for the most urgent and minimal of errands."

Dalin leaned his staff back in the corner. Impatience stirred in him. If the elves stayed holed up in the Golden Lamb, how could they apprehend the runemaster and his cronies?

He swung about to face the Guardian of the Thorn. "How are you going to take them by surprise once they're here?" he demanded. "Are you simply going to walk in on them and arrest them yourselves?"

Thengel caught the fire in the youth's eye and responded coolly. "There is something to be said for such an approach. We've discussed it already." Dalin remembered the late-night murmur of quiet conversation as he had nodded off in the reception chamber and wondered what schemes he was not privy to.

"We can't snatch them out of the trade league's house," said Belec, "or off the streets, for that matter, unless we have legal authority to back us. Otherwise we ask for a fight that will draw unwanted attention and perhaps bring the guard down on us rather than the culprits."

"Yet you've refused to go to the Justiciar."

"Perish the thought," murmured Nalia.

"The details will be taken care of," Thengel said firmly. "I have given you my word that you'll see Granmar's death avenged, and so you shall."

Dalin noted there was no mention made of the Truthsayer's robe. Temper gave his next words a sharp edge. "You mean we sit here cooped up for days until Hanno arrives?"

"In a word: yes." The Guardian held up his long-fingered hand. "And that is an end of it. We've made our plans, and now we follow them through. If you want to be of help, you can join us throwing dice for the watch. The more who take turns, the less wearing it will be for any one of us."

Dalin scowled, but finally ducked his head in agreement. It was better to be part of this than to be excluded from their plans as he had been last night. He got the third watch and before noon settled down in the window bench seat abandoned by Hagar. Across the way were the many-storied stone facades of the various ferenye, the merchant league houses. He leaned an elbow upon the casement and watched the street through the open leaf of the glazed window.

Nalia had left midmorning on the errands the Guardian had delegated to her. Dalin eventually turned his watch over to Thengel and tried to amuse himself with an interminable dice game Hagar played, laughing politely at elvish humor and jokes he did not quite get the point of. Nalia finally returned as the sun crawled toward the west. The youth felt as confined as if he had spent days awaiting a vision in a back hollow of Kodanit's Spire. When the street finally grew shadowed with the slowly encroaching dusk of the northern summer, he was trapped between irritable restlessness and a complete lack of interest in the talk, the company, the endless watch.

How can you stare for hours at a door and gates and try to see who might be who from two stories overhead?

He looked at Hagar, baffled. The dwarf was doing exactly that, perched on the bench seat, his legs thrust solidly before him and crossed at the ankles, arms crossed on chest, staring unblinkingly across the way.

How does he do it?

Unmoving as an oak tree, the dwarf kept steady watch, seemingly unbothered by the tedium of his task.

Dalin yearned to take some kind of action. He paced for a time, until he noticed the others staring at him. He sat down, looking forward to the supper hour, when they would go to the common room—but on this night Thengel had food brought in, and they ate in the same place they had watched from all day. Was there to be no respite? Long shadows had blurred into twilight when Nalia took her turn at the window.

"Dalin," ordered Thengel, "quit pacing."

The youth caught himself midstride, unaware that he had begun again.

"Come here and have some wine with me," the elf invited him to the table. He took up the offer—it was something to do besides wander the rooms half out of his wits with boredom. He picked at the remnants of dinner, not yet cleared away.

Dalin was not certain he cared for the bite of the drink Thengel poured from a fat-bellied pitcher. He preferred simple ale to this rich man's beverage—yet he found the edge of tension that haunted him was dulled after the first goblet was emptied, and he began to relax into banter with his host.

They had finished their second round when a knock came on the door. Belec opened it, and suddenly a jubilation of greeting crowded the air of the room. The elves gathered around someone Dalin could not see over their shoulders, and then they turned and ushered the newcomer into the room.

"Katrije Molinoes," Thengel introduced her. "One of my squires."

Katrije was a girl.

Well, of course she was. But *squire* . . . he'd heard the name last night. Somehow it had not registered that the girl's name would fit a future man at arms. Woman at arms.

He shook his head. It was not the way for Nevi hunters to expect women to track through the woods or to bear arms, unless the steading was actually assaulted. They might shoot bows from the walls defensively when the men were away and wield a wicked knife if they were personally attacked . . . but women in battle? Whether that was a skirmish grown out of cattle raids or the summoning to arms of a jarl, none of it was fit place for a woman. Certainly there were female warriors in the King's service—but they seemed unnatural, something Dalin had never seen, and heard about only in a skald's hero-tales.

That was not the same as a Turakemi girl close to his own age, returning his stare level-eyed. She could be a cousin from some distant northern steading—and this was the girl who had faced a dragon, along with her companions? He found it impossible to believe.

"I'm from Kalajok," she said. "Where are you from?"

Dalin had the distinct feeling he had missed a sentence or two of greeting while his thoughts had raced so loudly in his head. She was not from the north, then; her softer accents spoke of the south, as did the place-name of her clan affiliation.

"Clan Nevi," he said in rote politeness, "at the edge of the Koreis." He was aware that he lacked the beadwork on his clothes that would normally identify him at a glance. As did she, for she was clad in a livery tabard of particolored red and gray. Thengel's colors, he guessed.

She stuck out her hand in the frank clasp that warriors greeted each other with.

He hesitated, then shook her hand, letting go as soon as he possibly could. She looked at him oddly, then sat at the table on the Guardian's other side.

Katrije was near his own age, perhaps a bit older. Her auburn hair fell in softly curling lengths to her shoulders. Her eyes were hazel, and freckles dusted her nose. She was wiry of build and poured the wine with quick, efficient movements.

"How long can you stay?" Thengel asked as Hagar and Belec joined them at table.

"Some hours."

"Good. And Nalia told you—?"

"—that we must be ready to ride as soon as you send word? Yes. I've told Udo and Jaele. We have packs put aside, and we can reach the stables at need. So you've found the Tapestry?"

Dalin's world froze for an instant, then lurched forward again. Conversation hitched awkwardly as Thengel paused, caught off-guard by her unexpected question. "We're on the trail of men who slew the Truthsayer and stole Dalin's inheritance," he covered smoothly, and proceeded to fill Katrije in on recent events.

The young man listened with only half an ear, torn between leaping up in accusation and keeping an iron grip on himself—his temper, his breathing, his expression—in this suddenly stressful moment.

So you've found the Tapestry?

What he called the Robe, they called the Tapestry. All the incongruent bits and pieces of conversation from these last many days came home to him in the space of a heartbeat.

Thengel and his friends had not gone to the Crystal Spires to talk with the Truthsayer. They had gone seeking the Robe. Just as the Nimmians had. And they sought it still.

"Our business died with the Truthsayer," Nalia had claimed—and he had believed her, and her accomplished thief's dissembling. . . .

"So you really bespelled a mouse like that?" Katrije asked.

He brought himself back to the moment with great effort. How to deal with this he did not know, but like one on the stalk, he must not betray himself until he was ready to move exactly as served him best. . . .

"Mouse? Mouse. Um, yes," he stuttered out a response. "Not quite the enchantment I wanted."

"Effective, though. And the glacier? How'd you do that?"

He rubbed his chin. Her questions forced him to pay attention to her, to this conversation.

"Ah, yes." Thengel leaned forward. "That is something that interests me greatly. How is it that you led us across the ice, after all?"

That, he was not prepared to answer. He'd given the glacier experience little thought since their crossing; there hadn't been time to dwell on it. And, truth told, he felt uneasy at the memory, for something strange had happened to him there, something he had not yet made sense of. Nor was he like to share any insights with these outlanders who were using him to get to the Robe.

"I'm not sure, really," he said glibly, offering the simplest truth that came to mind. "I was reaching out like I do, to talk to trees. . . . There's a way the ground feels, when you river-walk in winter—that was what I was trying to sense, to see if the glacier felt that way, too. Then I was walking where the ground felt solid. And kept on. That's all."

Thengel shook his head. "That's not quite all. We saw your footprints."

"My footprints?"

"Yes. They changed. They resembled a creature. A bear, perhaps, or halfway between man and bear."

For the second time in minutes, Dalin felt the world slip out of joint around him. He guarded his reaction closely, and to the face of those assembled he merely shrugged.

"You're a shape-shifter?" Katrije asked brightly.

He lifted and dropped a shoulder again. "I only felt where the ice was solid. Like river-walking. That's all."

"Perhaps you have the blood of a shape-shifter in your family, then, and other-senses of that sort," Belec ventured. "That would account for it."

Dalin kept his mouth shut and made a noncommittal gesture.

"If you've such blood in your line, you are blessed to be so close to animal-spirit," Belec continued. "In Nimm men pervert the gift, all the better to fight and kill with. Some even embrace their animal natures and forget over time how to be human. Here, I understand, things are different. . . ."

That, too, Dalin let pass. Not letting himself be drawn out, the conversation faltered. More wine was poured, and talk shifted elsewhere.

If they thought he did not detect their appraising glances, though, they were mistaken. He drained half his drink in his next swallow and hoped that no one else noticed his hand trembling as he set the goblet down.

Uncle Sigurd was known to be bear-kin. He who had perished to Elsta's grip, with his bounty of winter furs.

And they saw bear-track on the snow behind me. . . .

Most regarded shape-shifting as a gift from the gods. He shook his head to himself. *It's not a gift I want. I only want to be the Truthsayer.*

Dalin helped himself to more wine and kept his own counsel. Talk had shifted to Katrije and her activities. He sat, a silent prisoner of the cama-raderie around him.

The unlikely squire spoke of her training, of horse riding and practice at the pels, of Udo's improvement with the short bow, of a woman named Sem-broie's continuing interest in Thengel.

The elf smiled when he heard this.

"And Valdarius came by again," she concluded. "Midsummer is but a few days hence. We're invited to the royal entertainments for Ardrunafest."

The elves debated whether and when they should attend. Could their presence be officially known by then? Would it be politic to remain absent? Dalin shut his ears, refilled his goblet, and fell into a sulk. Ardrunafest. One of the greatest holidays of the year: high celebration of the Earth Mother's bounty, a time for country bonfires and feasting and all-night revelry. Even he and Granmar had honored the full moon of midsummer in their remote fastness. Now he would miss this celebration, for he would not accompany these thievish outlanders to any festivities at all. Nor, for that matter, would he remain in their company any longer than he must. . . .

Sullen ruminations occupied his thoughts as Katrije began lighting oil lamps around the room. She left the adjoining chambers in darkness so the watch could remain unseen from the street. She sat again at table, and Dalin had just refilled his empty goblet when Nalia stirred sharply in her window seat.

She peered at the street from behind a half-closed window leaf. She spoke softly, so her voice barely carried to them. "And what would you say, my friends, to an elvish woman with long tow-colored hair clad in white doeskin leathers? And her four male companions? And a blond man, gray-ing, with the braid and long mustaches of Turakem?"

Chairs scraped back across the floor, and soon many pairs of eyes were in Nalia's darkened room, spying cautiously upon the shadowed entrance to Eritanos House. A party had dismounted before the courtyard gate, leaving reins in the hands of one of their number. That man, in a cockaded hat, de-manded entrance with the bell chain that hung there. The others filed one af-ter the other up the stone stairs and through the broad door of the House.

Dalin joined them in time to glimpse this procession and saw the one who led the way. The light from within fell full upon his countenance as he entered Eritanos House.

It was Hanno the runemaster.

"They're early!" Dalin blurted, his tone accusatory.

Nalia shushed him from the window. Thengel spoke with low urgency, his own voice touched with consternation. "Like the hawk, they've flown. Where's Arandel?"

All eyes turned to Hagar, who was already pulling the message stone out from beneath his shirt. "Close the windows," he said. "No need to sing for all and sundry on the streets."

They did as he bid. The dwarf fished out the silver-wrapped gem, held the sapphire in his hand, and closed his eyes. A humming started deep in his barrel chest, a tone that reverberated through the floor—and for the first time in this place Dalin felt the stir of life in the stone of the room around them. Hagar's mouth opened a bit; the hum moved up from his chest to a resonance projected from his throat. The dwarf began an atonal melody— something half-musical, half-primal, enough to nearly set one's teeth on edge, nearly. But each time it approached such a pitch it faded again into the lulling, evocative murmur of the deep lower register. . . .

In that wise, Hagar sang to the stone he held. With what effect none could see—but Dalin could feel it, even in his wine-filled state, and it made his skin crawl. Not in horripilation, but with the charge of power flowing in the room. It felt like standing on the side of one of the Spires in heavy weather, when Nalagar Thunderwalker raged across the skies and prepared to throw bolts of lightning. The stones of this building gave their power to and through Hagar Gemsinger, to the focal point of energies that he held in his hands.

The dwarf let the hum fade away, but Dalin sensed the gemstone resonating like a bell struck a hard blow. The force of it was in the ether all around him; could the others not sense it? Nearly he wanted to put his hands over his ears, but it was no sound he could tune out in that manner.

Hagar knew that force was there, also. Cupping the gem in his hands, he spoke to the stone. "Arandel," he said urgently. "Where are you?"

No answer. He repeated the question twice more before there was a response.

"In sight of the King's Road," came the Silverleaf's voice, tinny, thin on the ear, carried from stone to stone. "I lost them, thought to find their trail again—then this cut to the highway. . . ."

"They are here, ahead of you. Join us at the inn."

"Leafwatcher's blight! How can that be? They weren't that far beyond me!"

"Mayhap they obscured their trail well, or got fresh horses. How soon before you reach us?"

"A day. A half-day if I find a post-horse so I can swap mounts at need."

"Find one," interjected Thengel. "We need you here."

There was no reply. The stone had lost its charge as rapidly as a sieve looses water. Dalin felt it as Hagar must have. The dwarf glanced up to Thengel. "I am thinking he heard. At least he knows to hurry."

"Come, then," the Guardian said. "We've things to settle."

Dalin stayed where he was by the window, leaving them to their tense debate at table.

"Sembroie tonight. . . . Cathmar's help . . ."

He did not bother to make sense of their words. *They're not here to watch after your best interests, Granmar,* he thought to the spirit of his granduncle. *Or mine. Only I can do that now.* He regarded the silent edifice of Eritanos House across the way and came to a firm decision. *It's time for me to do what I should have done all along.*

He moved through the darkened chamber to the door, hesitated with his hand on the latch. Thengel gave directives at the table with the sureness of command.

But he doesn't command me, and he never did.

He let himself out of the room.

Only Katrije noticed him leave. She slipped out quietly after and followed a discreet distance behind. Her caution was for naught. In his wine-fuddled state, Dalin never once looked back.

CHAPTER 31

T HIS WAS NO hour to bring formal charges to the Justiciar's office, but the Truthsayer's apprentice had heard mention of a constabulary in this great city. A server in the Lamb's common room told him where to find the nearest guard station of the district watch.

"Have you a problem, sir?" the man asked worriedly.

"No problem," Dalin reassured him, and walked out the door rehearsing the directions he'd been given.

He set off down the lane, counting crossroads in the twilight. The evening was still young by the pace of city life and the streets occupied. He skirted pedestrians and dodged a rider at an intersection as he navigated through the merchant quarter.

Three streets down, the server had said, then one north—north? Toward the Palace, then, its towers shining against the early stars in the darker northern sky. Through a square, past close-shuttered shops, and at the corner of the first alley—there!

The young man spotted an official banner, crossed halberds surmounted with a crown of gold on a field of white. Lamps flanked the door. It opened as he watched and three guardsmen came out onto the street.

They seemed impressive in their authority, their stature speaking more of a class of soldiery than of staid night watchmen. Their armor implied a foreign influence to Dalin's eye, for it was unlike anything he'd ever seen: no chain mail hauberks, here, or the rare scale mail worn by steading chieftains. Instead, the men wore solid plates of metal on their broad chests, strapped snugly over red tunics. Black trousers and boots completed their uniform, with broad swords at their hips. Two carried lanterns. The trio strolled off into the temperate evening, laughing among themselves, yet keeping an observant eye on the deepening shadows about them.

Dalin took a deep breath, mustered his courage, and marched up the steps into the guard station.

A man looked up from a table where he reviewed papers with a companion. He seemed to be an officer, for his garb was richer, finer than that of the ordinary guardsmen. His trousers were of buff linen, his tunic a fine white cotton. The breastplate he wore was burnished to a high shine and detailed in gold. But it was the ordinary watchman beside him who spoke.

"Can I help you?"

Dalin stopped at the edge of their table, weaving slightly on his feet. "I want to report a murder!"

The men before him tensed. "Murder?" The officer spoke now, instead. "Where?"

"At Kodanit's Spire." Dalin waved a hand. "Far away. But the men who did it are here, close by. I saw them a short while ago."

"Kodanit's Spire . . . ?"

"The Truthsayer." That title nudged the guardsmen's memory, Dalin saw. Every Turakemi knew from tales, at least, the title of the hermit seer to kings.

Their next reactions were unlooked for, though. Consternation softened to mild amusement in the men's faces, and the red-uniformed watchman stood. "The Truthsayer, is it? Well now. I'm sure the King will deal with that in due time." He stepped around the table, closing with the intoxicated youth.

Dalin disbelieved his ears. "The King?" he spluttered. "He doesn't know of it! The travel rune quit working and I was going to Vaer, but they found Granmar and killed him for the Robe—"

"Wait." The officer halted the guardsman's motion with a gesture. "You know the Truthsayer's name?"

"He's my granduncle. I'm his . . . I was his apprentice. I'm Truthsayer, now." Dalin drew himself up. "Dalin of Nevi."

"He's drunk," the watchman said. "Let me put him on the streets. Or in the watch-ward."

"Not yet." The officer stood. "The seer's given name is one not widely known, and not usually bandied in taverns."

"The Truthsayer doesn't drink in taverns, either," the guardsman said drolly, "and last I heard he was old enough to shave."

Dalin bridled. "I'm his heir, I told you. The new Truthsayer." He looked to the man in white. "I've had some wine, yes, but I didn't expect to see them when I did. I'm making formal charges. I'd go to the Justiciar, but that it's night, and if they move before morning, we'll have lost them. You must make haste, before they move on, or . . . or others get to them first."

"Others?"

"They have enemies here."

The guardsmen exchanged glances. "This is getting interesting," said the officer. "Sit down, young man, and tell me the particulars."

"You must hurry!"

"We'll hurry soon enough. Efgar, recall some men from the streets and muster a squad for me. I think we'll take a walk, look into this." He gestured to a chair at the table side. "Please," he said to Dalin.

The youth sat and told his story. A brief and garbled version, but with enough names and bare facts to intrigue the officer. Steading chieftains, Nimmian longship raiders dead, an ambush failed—the tale was improbable but held enough possible truth that it warranted investigation. And if the accused indeed had the Truthsayer's robe with them, this case could be the windfall that made a guard captain's reputation.

Horns sounded briefly in the streets and echoed through the stone canyons of the district's buildings. Soon guardsmen trickled in from their rounds until the small station house was crowded with them. Ten were mustered outside under Efgar's command. Five more were added when Dalin adamantly insisted that ten alone could not possibly be enough to handle the fearsome powers of their quarry, should they resist arrest.

The officer walked to their head with Dalin by his side.

"I'm Captain Bjalit," he introduced himself belatedly. "Come identify your culprits for us, young Nevi, and I'll have a talk with them."

"Don't talk with them," the youth insisted. "Arrest them."

"Let's find them, first."

THE DISTANCE TO Eritanos House was covered quickly enough, the tramp of booted feet at his back lifting Dalin's spirits up. He felt accompanied by an invincible force. Well—not invincible, perhaps, and if the Nimmians resisted with magic perhaps not powerful at all. . . .

He chewed his lip and began to think, for the first time, how the outlanders might respond to this unexpected confrontation by the forces of the law.

His first outright misgiving came when Captain Bjalit took the stairs to the trade house entrance alone and exchanged words with the liveried doorman who greeted all arrivals there.

The Truthsayer's avenging apprentice had fancied they would charge in like soldiers storming a stronghold, overturning chests, throwing open doors, searching for the violators of king's law and Granmar's life, and taking no quarter until they succeeded in their mission. Instead, there was a softspoken private conference before the door was held upon for them and they walked in orderly manner into the marble-floored entrance hall.

The foyer gave unto a hall that stretched the length of the building, a grand staircase at its midpoint, with doors at regular intervals along its length. The doorman led them through the first pair of tall double doors on the right, into a long room whose now-curtained windows overlooked the courtyard. The room held round tables and cushioned chairs with high arms and backrests. A large hearth and high decorative mantel punctuated the interior wall, cold now because of the summer weather. Beyond the fireplace, curtains partitioned off the far half of the room, reserved, apparently, for when there were larger numbers of patrons dining here. For the room was clearly for dining and refreshment, with groups of merchants eating and drinking here and there, their supper catered by servants who brought food on silver trays from the kitchen down the hall.

At the table directly before the empty hearth sat Hanno Runemaster and his Nimmian cronies, helping themselves to the repast that had just been set before them.

"There!" Dalin cried out and pointed. "That's them!"

Hanno saw the youth in the same moment. He spoke a word to his fellows; food went untouched as they all turned and stared. Guardsmen advanced on the table as Hanno stood and boldly addressed the captain.

"Sir! I'm glad to see the watch here, and with our escaped weasel in tow."

The strangers at the table made no hostile moves and guardsmen faltered as they heard Hanno speak thus to their commander.

"You would be the runemaster, sir?" asked Captain Bjalit.

"Hanno of Havneis, retired from the King's Privy Council. Perhaps you have heard of me."

"Lord Adviser!" The captain faltered, stopped his men with a gesture. He seemed to halt himself from bowing with an effort.

This was not going right. Dalin stared at Bjalit and saw the man had gone a little pale.

Hanno smiled. "Ah, you *have* heard of me. Excellent. And you are . . . ?"

"Holveg Bjalit, captain of the Ferenye District Watch."

"Bjalit . . . of Bjalinik birth, I think?"

"Yes."

"I know your jarl, Regmar." Hanno nodded, acknowledging personal ties with the guard officer. Dalin sensed the man beside him assessing the runemaster not as a criminal but as one in power, and in favor with his kinlord. He dare not let this go on.

"Don't listen to him," he interrupted. "He's the one I told you about. And those with him. Search their belongings, you'll find the Robe, I tell you!"

Hanno raised an eyebrow at the youth's words but addressed himself to the guard captain. "This is the one you need to hold tightly and put in chains, Captain Bjalit. We sought him for days, but he eluded us. Slaying Granmar like that. . . ." He shook his head. "Unbelievable, if I had not seen it with my own eyes. A boy so untrustworthy that Granmar dismissed him. Who would not go but snuck back like a thief, to murder his mentor and steal the Truthsayer's robe."

Hanno spread his hands expansively. "Only he didn't know we were there that day seeking counsel with my old friend. We were departing when he crept back to the Spire. Glimpsed him skulking about and followed—but not in time to halt his treachery. Pushed Granmar to his death, he did, and tried to make off with the robe of office. He fled for his life when we confronted him, hid like a rat in the woods, there. We recovered the Robe, but not the treacherous snake who killed my friend."

Dalin's jaw dropped. "That's a lie! They're not friends. It didn't happen that way!"

A heavy hand fell on his shoulder. "Maybe we need to talk a little more."

Hanno held out a hand deprecatingly. "See? His greed for the Truthsayer's prestige is so great, he would claim anything to regain the Robe—with that symbol, you know, he could claim to be legitimate heir to Granmar's power. But I know it isn't so."

"I *am* his heir!" Dalin cried. "I *am* the Truthsayer!"

Derisive laughter greeted that claim. Hanno ignored the boy and spoke to the officer. "The King will be grateful that you've caught this murderous whelp. We know he's treacherous, respects no man's rank, and this creature"—he sneered as he pointed at Dalin—"came to you selling his nearly plausible tales. Drunk as usual, I see. Or is that, smell?"

He laughed, and some of the guardsmen chuckled with him. "He always was an accomplished liar, drunk or sober—but this, Captain, is a murderer King Hammankarl himself will want to see executed. Arrest him, and put him where he'll do no harm."

The captain seemed to hesitate, and Hanno clinched it with a final reassurance. "Now that this has fallen into your lap, I'll be happy to give you an official report about the tragedy at the Spires that you can pass on to your superiors. On the morrow."

Dalin felt another guard's hand descend upon his other shoulder—and it was too much to withstand. All day long his need for action had driven him; all night his drinking of wine had influenced his judgment. He did the impetuous thing the instant he was touched. He stomped on Bjalit's instep and ran for it.

He bolted so quickly he was out of their grasp before they realized he was moving. Not so Aral Yellowbeard, though. The Nimmian had watched him warily from first sighting, and the warrior was up out of his seat as Dalin's mad dash carried him past the hearth, heading for the freedom of the unoccupied room beyond—and the doors that led out of it.

The warrior made a grab at him. He dodged, but the move put him close to the nook of the hearth with no room to maneuver. He reversed course, saw guardsmen drawing swords—spun back once more. There, an opening, past their table—

Yellowbeard lunged at him with a blade in hand. Dalin had to hesitate or be run through.

He was out of time as well as floor space. Three guardsmen bore him to his knees before the hearth, twisting his arms until the least bit of struggle threatened to snap his limbs like twigs. He knelt there panting, wide-eyed, adrenaline burning the alcohol out of him too late, too late. . . .

The Nimmian warrior stood smirking before Dalin, grabbed his hair with one hand, and yanked his head back to look him in the eyes. "You killed the Truthsayer." He accused as if he believed it; his voice was full of menace. "Now like moth to flame, you come here to steal what you covet and ruin our good names." He spat in Dalin's face and let his head go. "Let the King's justice put an end to you, like we should have done at the Spires."

Dalin was numb with shock. He did not resist as they pulled him to his feet, dragged him out the door and down the street.

Angry slaps and kicks buffeted him as he was hauled along, punishment for his "drunken insolence"—the tale he had supposedly invented about the Truthsayer's death. He had no idea where he was being taken until they crossed the bridge beyond Tolvar's Gate and the square tower of the Hakkonkalye loomed before him. He was taken within the keep and down spiral stairs to the dungeons below.

A grating was lifted off a hole in the flagstones, and Dalin was half-lowered, half-dropped inside. He fell some distance to the ground and sprawled on cold dirt and stones. The grating was lowered and the clank of chain securing it in place fell on his ears like the blows of the watch captain's hands.

Dalin's head spun. "You're a bold one," Bjalit said through the grate, "I'll give you that. But not very smart. Eh, boys?"

Their laughter was the last thing Dalin heard before he was left alone in the dark.

KATRIJE STUDIED THE Hakkonkalye, grim against the dark velvet sky.

She had followed Dalin through his rovings and knew why he was here now. It was easy to slip into Eritanos House while the doorman was occupied with the watch contingent—and she had seen and heard more than enough from the partitioned side of the dining hall. A quick dodge past the doorman on her way out again, and he never knew what servitor gave him the slip into the night.

Now, though, she had trailed Dalin as far as she could: to the curtain wall that kept out unauthorized visitors to the military keep and the dungeons it housed. She was loath to depart, but dared not loiter in plain sight of the garrison.

She sighed, turned away from the fortress, and made her way down moonlit streets back to the Golden Lamb.

"TAKING THE ROBE to the King!" Aral prowled the confines of their suite and turned on his heel to challenge the runemaster. "What kind of idiot tale is that?"

"It's one that saves our hides, that's what it is!" Hanno flared back at him. "And what would *you* have said in that moment, my fine foreign friend, to explain what Nimmians are doing with the Truthsayer's robe?"

"They didn't know we had it, until you talked."

"With a charge like that from Granmar's apprentice, they would have searched us to investigate. To hold us for questioning. Or rather: hold *you* for questioning. Me, they would not dare touch. As you saw. Is that how you would have it?"

Joro cut off Aral's retort. "Enough. The runemaster is right in that much: it's his former rank and their respect for it that saved our skins tonight." He glared at Hanno nonetheless. "Aral has the right of the other, too—now they know the Robe is here. It's even more urgent that we leave with it before any can question our doings."

Hanno sniffed. "It would not be wise to leave until we know this boy is dead and can tell no further tales. There are others who might listen to his ravings when he is no longer drunk and insists on throwing his master's name about like an invocation. That would set vengeance on your trail and be the end of my own goals."

"Best if he's slain, then," Kaylis said softly.

"That," replied Hanno, "cannot happen without a trial."

She raised an eyebrow. "I don't mean execution for his 'murder.' Accidents befall prisoners in gaol. One could happen to him."

"Maybe so." Hanno chewed his lip. "Let me think on this and discover who's in charge of the Hakkonkalye dungeons. I need to know who we would deal with. There's no point in letting the boy come to trial if we can help it."

CHAPTER 32

"WE NEED TO know more about this arrest and if it has endangered our mission," Thengel snapped. "Belec, off to court and ask Valdarius about this runemaster. Hagar, fetch Cathmar here. Nalia, fade into the shadows on the street and watch Eitanos House, in case our quarry takes flight."

"Double watch is best, in case they separate."

"I'll be downstairs by a window. I'll tail others if need be."

"I have to leave soon," Katrije said. "Sembroie expects me back by curfew."

Thengel rubbed his tired eyes. "I wish you and Udo could join us, but we have no ruse that will serve."

She sighed. "They're pretty strict with squires."

"You like it after all? The training?"

"For now." She considered for a moment. "I'll say my errands today weren't finished and come back tomorrow."

"Do."

Katrije nodded. "And mind you stay far, far back if you tail someone," she told the warrior she served. "You're too easily made out in a crowd, Lord Dereneth."

He smiled at her concern. "Maybe Arandel will be here before it comes to that."

She bid them good night and slipped out the door. As it shut, Thengel pounded his fist on the table in frustration. "If we only knew what they are planning, if we could spy that out! But this is not a camp in the woods where we can come up in easy earshot."

Nalia pushed her long hair back over her shoulder. "I have an idea," she said slyly. "There are some of our number whose faces are not known to the Nimmians. Here's how we can use that to advantage. . . ."

DALIN LAY STUNNED in the dark for a long time, unable to grasp the sudden change in his circumstances. How had it happened? He relived the night's encounter many times in many variations. What could he have said differently? If Hanno had not been present, would the watch have arrested the Nimmians? Looked through their belongings and found the Robe, proving the truth of his claim?

Would they simply take Hanno's word against his own and leave him locked here forever?

He felt more despair than when he had been abandoned on the mountainside: so close to the Robe, here, so close to justice, and now so far, himself accused, made out to be the killer of his granduncle. Unthinkable. Surely they would discover his innocence.

He forced himself to think calmly, carefully. They must, in time, bring him before a Justiciar. There his claim would have to be investigated; otherwise it was only Hanno's word against his . . . and the word of other supposed witnesses.

Surely the King's court would use a truth spell to discover what had happened in the distant wilderness of the Crystal Spires? They could. They must! To investigate the death of the King's seer—no matter how remotely he lived, his absence would be felt by the court. They would need his heir to pick up the Robe and carry on in his place.

That thought heartened him. He sat up off the cold ground, clutching his scraps of dignity to him. If nothing else, that much was true. He had fallen into the trap of feeling he had done something wrong just because many strident voices had laid that claim at his feet. But he knew otherwise, and he knew he had a right to the title of Truthsayer.

He would prevail, and Hanno and the outlanders would yet be brought to justice.

His eyes had slowly become accustomed to the new moon darkness of this dank hole. Distant lamplight from the hall overhead cast a faint glimmer over the grating, that far glow the only illumination in his prison. It was cold, too, and damp, with the seeping chill of a place near water. He clasped his arms around his knees. Arandel's clothing looked fine in civilized warm inns, but it was not as protective as his leathers and he sorely missed the long sleeves of his woodsman's garb right now.

He sat, shivering, eyes seeking to focus on something in the darkness. There was nothing to see in the midnight gloom, but slowly his senses perceived that he was not in a simple pit. He had expected such, like the prison holes used to contain wrongdoers in towns: a well dug deep but dry so that one could only languish at the bottom unless pulled out with a rope. But something in the way the hint of light traveled, or how small sounds carried back to him, suggested more.

"Hello?" he called quietly, for the sake of the words to fill the air. He listened to sound in the room around him. Walls felt close, but rather than a narrow pit he was definitely in a small chamber of some sort.

Not wishing to walk into something—or off the edge of something—he stayed on hands and knees and crawled in the gloom to discover the boundaries of his cell.

Quickly he bumped into a wall where he had been dropped to the floor. A sweep of the hands told him only that it was stone; whether cut or rough he could not tell. Keeping this to his side, he crawled along the floor, a surface fairly smooth but gritty under his hands. The floor was damp and here he could smell water, not just feel its presence in the air. No sound of water flowing, though. It seemed to seep through the stone; there was enough on the floor to make his fingers and palms damp.

He bumped into a second wall in his explorations, and bits of old mortar crumbled down upon him. He jerked back and his head spun with the sudden motion. He held still until his senses righted themselves: he had enough wine left in him to feel it. *Never again,* he vowed. *I'll stick with the ale I know. . . .*

When the room settled down, his hands sought the wall before him to discover if the stones of the wall were loose—but they were not, just in slow decay. He stood to get out of the damp and walked the length of the wall, feeling with his hands. It seemed to be made of small squares of dressed stone, or perhaps rough brick, interrupted in places by what felt like smooth pillars—and then the large rough blocks of the keep's foundation, running back around to frame the small chamber that held him.

He stumbled in one spot as he tripped over something that clattered and crunched beneath his feet. Suspecting what it must be, he nevertheless reached down and felt with his hands. Bones came to his touch, and he dropped them, shuddering. Human bones, no doubt, of some poor wretch dropped here and forgotten, or condemned on purpose to a slow and thirsting death.

Dalin made a circuit of the chamber once, twice more and then sat down where the ground was cold but dry. He began to shiver in earnest and fought the downward spiral of his spirits. He closed his eyes against the bare hint of light that made him want to focus on something. Wrapping arms around knees, he rocked back and forth and began the Song of Waiting, that had warmed him in the caves of the Spire.

Imagining he was sitting at the mouth of Granmar's cave, waiting for his master to call him in to tend a scrying fire, Dalin warmed himself and wandered in his thoughts as time passed by.

CHAPTER 33

Hanno breathed a sigh of relief and studied the stone in his hand. He had spent an hour or two in timeless meditation, fingers working without conscious direction, the chisel-edged stylus and smooth amethyst from his belt pouch put to good use. The sense of power channeled, of unearthly craft in his touch and this thing of his making, lingered about him, persistent now with the invocation that activated the rune stone he held.

The stone was half the size of the last joint of his thumb. He blew the powdered gem dust off it and studied the rune he had inscribed there. *Staje:* Truth. The stylized star on the rune glowed with a luminesence not born of the candles in the room. A star, a thing that shone for all to see, like truth, that did not blind with the glare of the sun but shone in its own undeniable radiance. Something the eye could comfortably regard and see for what it was. Or seem to see.

He had only desired a way to be more earnest, more credible, to persuade those who would listen to him, when the gods led him to insight about this rune. Before that revelation, Hanno had not realized that there was an archetype of Truth that existed in the Unseen World, an archetype that, like all such powers, could be echoed in its resonance within a symbol of power. Hence this rune.

When he had first scribed it on the heels of a vision-dream and held it in his hand, he recognized what it could be for him: a false seeming. For whoever held the rune found it easier to speak the truth—if desired. Yet it was possible, with an effort of will, to speak untruth as well, the falsehoods cleaving of their own accord as closely to verity as possible. Most to his purpose: the speaker was *perceived* to be telling truth—heard believably by men and women, divined as truthful by spellcasters who probed.

Its power for misuse in the wrong hands was clear, and it was a revelation he did not share with other masters of his craft. The Staje rune was his secret, and his alone.

Of its efficacy he had no doubt. The only person he had ever encountered who was not deceived by the rune's aura of truthfulness was the Truthsayer himself. Granmar had seen through Hanno's subterfuges in the past.

And Granmar was no more.

The runemaster glanced to the time candle, counted the rings remaining. It was late, but not too: Hammankarl's court supped late and enjoyed entertainments until midnight. It would be easy to reach the King if he went right now.

He regarded the amethyst rune stone in his hand. Almost as an afterthought he leaned his head back, opened his mouth, and swallowed the stone, chasing it with a goblet of wine from the sideboard. It would not do to somehow be bereft of his runes, those that he carried about his person, and so lose this protection he had created for himself. Carried inside his body for two or three days, its effect would be with him, closer than his own skin. And this would be the time that mattered: when he asserted his news and must be believed. By time the rune effect expired he would have time to create another if needed.

Thus assured, he went to his door and let himself out into the hall.

Rooms in Eritanos House were at a premium at this time of year. His was small, and the Nimmians shared a cramped suite that was all his influence could procure on short notice. He was glad to be across the way from them in this moment. He left unnoticed down the servants' stairs.

His horse he left stabled, lest his presence in the courtyard be noticed from Joro's suite and excite suspicion. It would be easy enough to walk the quarter-mile to the White Palace, and it would give him more time to think.

Everything was changed now, with Dalin's drunken accusations made loudly before a room of merchants and city guardsmen. The Truthsayer murdered. The rumor at least would be all over the city by morning, and Hanno's name mixed in with it. He had no time, now, to arrange for the Robe to come into his hands or for the Nimmians to conveniently vanish. It was time to come up with a new plan. He considered the many ways to present his tidings to King Hammankarl, and walked unhurriedly through darkening streets.

Preoccupied as he was, he had no hope to detect the blonde elvish woman concealed in the nook of a gated courtyard. Where there were people on the street she seemed to be another belated home-goer; in more deserted lanes, she moved deftly from shadow to obscurement, always a safe distance behind the runemaster. And so they went, shadow and lead, through the avenues to the White Palace.

CHAPTER 34

"COURTLY ENOUGH, DO you think?"

Belec spread his arms wide, modeling the cleanest trousers from his pack, a white tunic-shirt, a blue leather doublet over it.

"No," Hagar opined. "But at least you're presentable."

On this night, to win access to the bard Valdarius, it seemed wise to look a little more like one who belonged inside the Palace rather than out of it. As indeed Belec did: guest lodgings on the royal grounds still held some of their belongings and awaited the Caerlian companions whenever they returned to the official view of the King.

It was nearly a month since they had left to find the Truthsayer, though Belec planned to avoid scrutiny this night as much as possible. Find Valdarius and get out before anyone questioned his presence: that was his sole objective. With that in mind, he mounted Nowës, his black-stockinged chestnut, and set off for the Palace.

Intent on his goal, the elf did not notice the lone figure walking past night-shadowed residences along the King's Road. The man on foot noticed him, though, as he drew rein before the gatehouse of the royal residence.

Nightfall came late in far northern summers. The gloaming had not yet reached full darkness in the city, but it did not exist at all before the palace gates. It was never night there, for daylight emanated from the stones of the guard station and along the broad facade of the ceremonial portal. It was the showy indulgence of dweomer, a permanent light spell creating the brilliance of noon before the palace.

Belec halted on bright cobblestones as an officer came forward to speak with him. The runemaster studied his well-lit countenance from the twilight edge of the gate plaza. He saw the guard examine the elf's pass, then wave halberdiers aside and let the rider enter into the palace grounds.

Hanno's eyes narrowed. He never forgot a face. Nor would he soon forget this one from a roadside ambush days before, and a spell-casting that had ensnarled Kaylis in grasping shrubbery. The runemaster's footsteps slowed. If he had lingered, after all, to kill that one, whom would he have slain? He would never have known. But here, at the gate, were men who could tell him. And would.

"Former" might describe his state of abandoned office, but the authority of a Lord Adviser was yet a part of Hanno's demeanor. He adjusted his attitude and his carriage and strode to the gatehouse determined to mend his ignorance.

BELEC RODE PATHWAYS of crushed gravel past the reflecting lake and the artfully landscaped ground before the White Palace. The residence loomed beyond, its white walls, sparkling glass windows, and high turreted towers shown to best advantage by carefully placed spells of illumination. The residence of the Selkie Kings was the grandest in all of Tura-kem, as much a showcase for lavish display as for pleasure and living. It was visible always to onlooking eyes from the city and shone across the misty waters of the cold Dannenborch to the northeast.

A visit to the stables, a stroll through a side entrance, and Belec was in the Palace. He walked with an air of confidence, and no one questioned his progress as he sought the banquet hall. There he ensconced himself in a curtained side gallery. He was undisturbed by passing servitors, for the meal was far enough along that the parade of dishes between kitchens and table had diminished to a trickle. Only pages moved about the hall now, pouring mead and wine, while pantlers with trays of marzipan and confections of hazelnut cream presented this last of delights to the King's guests.

He studied the assemblage from his concealment, looking from place to place to see where he might find the bard. There was no doubt in his mind that somewhere here, close to titled folk, good food, and the chance to hold forth, the man was to be found. Yet there were many faces to survey, for perhaps a hundred folk dined with the King this evening, though that was but a moderate gathering by Hammankarl's style and the numbers the hall could accommodate.

That chamber was long and broad, flanked with columns of white marble, its flagstones of marble veined with yellow and orange striations. The patterning of the floor and the line of columns drew his eye to the pillars behind the high table, hung with the royal colors of white and yellow, in the center the golden eagle banner of Tura-kem.

The eagle's spread wings were the backdrop embracing Hammankarl II, descendant of selkies and divinity: a lithe, handsome man in his midthirties, untried by war, but with diplomatic skills and an ambitious vision for his kingdom, the most ancient of human lands in northern Koristan. He was of moderate height and slender build, his hair the rich brown of seal fur, his eyes intense dark pools that overlooked little. Vestigial webbing lay between his fingers; Belec wondered how else his selkie heritage had touched him, for to the eye Hammankarl seemed the same kind of man as any. He was clean-shaven but for long mustaches worn to the edge of his jaw, in the manner of his countrymen. Smile lines marked his face, and only the furrow between his brows hinted where the worries of the crown would leave their mark in future years.

The King was popular with his people and the man well liked by those who knew him. He was mercurial of mood but focused of intent, well intentioned, neither naive nor overbearing in the exercise of his office. He sat now, smiling, sharing a joke with his Queen, wheat-blonde Elfried of fair mien, the well-lettered daughter of the Jarl of Vorsemye. She, soft-spoken complement to her husband, but one who offered private counsel and, it was said, had it heeded.

With the royalty at the dais sat the highest nobles of the land: the Lord of the Exchequer, the Speaker, the Steward, and their wives. Close by sat other notables: the several Lords Adviser, temple Elders, a young runemaster, the elvish mage and court physician Nehvros Ulemos, and Captain-General Molstroe, commander of the King's Hand—

Belec sighed. Half the high table would know his face, it seemed, were he glimpsed. He made sure his curtain peephole was small and surveyed the tables again.

He was wondering if Valdarius was even present in the room when laughter and applause drew his attention to dwarves tumbling in the center of the hall. Or no, not stone-kin, they: they were short, misshapen humans, clad in particolor, clowning an elaborate wordless skit with many pratfalls.

They performed in the center of the U between banquet tables and dais, where another light spell of limited effect cast a diffuse glow to highlight performers. They concluded their charade and were rewarded with a shower of marzipan and a scattering of coin.

They scrambled to collect their bounty and left with a pretense of a slapstick scuffle between them. Belec had looked the room over twice and was beginning to despair of finding Val among the crowd—if he was even here, this night—when a herald's short trumpeted fanfare brought a semblance of quiet to the room.

The herald's announcement carried to every ear. "Your Majesties, Lords and Ladies, Good Sirs and Gentlemen: by pleasure of His Majesty, King Hammankarl the Second, the Eldur bard Valdarius performs for us!"

Through the high, broad entrance doors Valdarius walked into the hall. He strode square-shouldered, clad in green velvet finery, with his lute in the crook of his arm. There was something in his manner of presentation that drew every eye to him, and the room was quiet by time he halted between the tables. He bowed deeply to the King and Queen, gave a flourish of acknowledgment to the noble and well-born onlookers, then grasped his lute properly and began to sing.

Now and then Belec had heard an Eldur sing, when one of those bards traveled through Caerlian. Such skalds were either elves or of elvish descent, as was half-blooded Valdarius; each one trained for years in the Eldur traditions of old Arilethne. Their songs conveyed tales and legend, homage or scorn: never lighthearted minstrelsy or music to dance by, but serious works. Eldur remembered the days-long sagas, the Law chants, the dream-time lays that were half-song, half-enchantment. They were keepers of lore and oral tradition, recorders and retellers of events and history that they had witnessed.

As Valdarius did here, even though introduced as a "performer" at the King's command. Belec heard the first of his words with disbelieving recognition: of Ess'kek and the Dragon-Slayers he sang. The elf shook his head. This was a tale he knew all too well, a tune and lyrics written on the road here from Kalajok. Belec had thought it an amusement to pass the time, the verses improbable, the story exaggerated. Hagar claimed the bard composed it "to overblow our reputations so he can eat free at noblemen's tables."

Belec had not thought it of the bard—until now, as he recognized his own name mentioned in verse and blushed to hear it. Val's fine tenor filled the room to counterpoint on his lute, his intonation a melodic chant halfway between recitation and song. At least he had the good grace to reserve this kind of performance for times when his companions were not present. Except that one *was,* this night, unbeknownst to the bard. . . .

The song seemed interminable, its exaggerations for dramatic effect, no doubt, but the cleric had never seen himself as "white-browed, stern-eyed Belec, of Onderye's Chosen, soft-spoke, bold-stroke, aid to Arandel."

Aid to Arandel? His cousin didn't need to hear *this* paen any too quickly. . . .

And then there was that part about "Ess'kek, emerald-skinned serpent"—the dragon had been of greenish cast, yes, but hardly "emerald." More a tawdry, mold-eaten color, with worn scales . . . nothing that "glittered like a thousand spearpoints in the sun."

Bards and their "poetic license."

I should be grateful, he mused, *that he hasn't turned this into a drinking song.*

Thankfully, such common music was beneath an Elduin bard. Folk of that tradition were highly honored and in Nimm had trained human skalds in the refinements and nuances of their craft. Of course, in that contentious land, bards were honored as neutral go-betweens, relayers of messages unaltered as well as news and epic sagas. A bard sat in hallowed neutrality in any hall or freehold and was a valued counselor in dispute and mediation.

There was no such tradition in Tura-kem, where runemasters came the closest to being the neutral advisers honored for their learning and lore. Bards were given a different weight here entirely, presumed to be simple musicians and minstrels. Many were, though Valdarius was of a different breed, as all who heard him could tell. He had a unique gift. To judge by the rapt attention of his audience, he would not be lacking for meals at the royal table anytime soon.

In due course his recital came to an end and applause flooded the hall. He had presented only a brief portion of a composition Belec knew went on for hours, in typical Elduin fashion. Perhaps Valdarius was doling it out in judicious bits, to keep the King intrigued.

Just as well we've returned now, Belec thought, *before Hammankarl makes him a permanent part of his household.*

He left his alcove and followed the gallery along, seeking out a pantler. A quiet request to the servant and a silver piece as tip left the man bowing and returning to the dining hall. His yellow-and-russet livery was easy to track through the congregation of pages and squires, servitors and the well-born. When Valdarius was finished taking his bows, the pantler said a word in his ear. The bard smiled excuses to those who would have him join them at table and followed the servant into the gallery.

The elf greeted Valdarius from the semiprivacy of another alcove.

"Belec!" the bard exclaimed, his voice carrying far enough to make his comrade wince.

"Shhh!" He motioned. "I'm not here!"

"Ah, but you are!" Val grinned widely as he embraced the other, slapping him companionably on the back. "Come with me; I've just sung about you and the rest. The King will be pleased that you're back—"

Belec stopped him with a hand on his arm. "Things are afoot, Val. We need your help. Now. Tonight."

"Oh?"

"Indeed."

Belec filled him in on events in hurried, terse words. Val's demeanor changed from jovial, to thoughtful, to serious. "If you've fallen afoul of Hanno of Havneis, you have problems," he said soberly. "I can tell you something about him, all right." He chewed his lip, nudged the curtain aside, and glanced back into the dining hall. "I don't know that I can leave 'til the feasting is done. You should go back without me and I'll follow as soon as I—"

"Blood and ashes!" Belec interrupted him with a curse and a start. "That's him!"

He pointed through the curtain gap. Hanno Runemaster stood where Valdarius had but minutes before, making obeisance to the King, a look of distress upon his face.

"Hanno?" Hammankarl acknowledged him. "You have always been welcome at our table, but it has been all too long since you have graced us with your company. And now you join us most . . . unexpectedly?"

Obliquely the King's words addressed the runemaster's late intrusion and his visible look of distress. It was, apparently, exactly the opening the runemaster was hoping for.

"Majesty, I bear terrible news, and wanted to bring it to you instantly. I have just returned from a long journey to the Crystal Spires."

A murmur swept the tables, and conversation died as he took a breath. "Your Truthsayer is dead. Murdered."

Voices raised in sudden clamor. Hammankarl's abruptly raised hand forced quiet.

"What do you tell us?" His voice had the flat tone of one momentarily beyond emotional reaction. "Who would murder the Truthsayer? How do you know?"

"A dastard deed, Majesty, that I had the blessing—or curse—to be witness to."

Hanno launched into his tale, a recital not unlike what he had said to Captain Bjalit a short while before. He held the room's attention with all the skill of an accomplished orator. Indeed, every runemaster was a storyteller and conveyer of oral history—like Valdarius, but in this land, never mistaken as an entertainer. Their word was taken as fact.

Here, before the King and his guests, Hanno spoke with dire conviction. The resonance of truth was in his words. The room believed, and so did Hammankarl.

"I don't like this," breathed Valdarius, and then fell quiet for the last of Hanno's words to be heard.

"And, Sire, I have learned just this night who some of these accomplices were, complicit with the roguish apprentice. His allies, no doubt, in his thievery, if not his murder. For they did their best to stop me from carrying this tale to you, and would have killed me, too, had I not evaded their ambuscade. One has come here tonight."

The King sat forward. "Of whom do you speak?"

"Of folk I hear have insinuated themselves into your good graces, my liege. Perhaps they have done good elsewhere—but here they plan only havoc and betrayal. I speak of these elves you have lately welcomed from Caerlian. They who style themselves, I believe, Guardians of the Thorn? Call them, rather, would-be thieves of the Robe."

Hammankarl's face went white.

The blood drained from Belec's face, as well.

Valdarius flushed hot and plucked at his companion's arm. "Come! We must away!"

"What—?" The cleric was stunned with the enormity of what he had just heard.

"Talk later. Go now."

"He believed it. . . !" He jerked his chin toward where the King sat.

"It's true, isn't it?" Valdarius locked eyes with his companion. "That's what we're here for. However Hanno divined it."

Belec was rooted to the spot, trying to make sense of the furor that had erupted in the dining hall. Valdarius grabbed the elf's arm, pulled him down the gallery and out through side doors. "Now, while they're sorting this out. We ride."

They looked like any ordinary men going about their business, although walking briskly: a stop by Val's room for a pack he refused to leave behind, mounts collected from the stables, riding at a comfortable pace to the gate-house, waved through without question by the guards. They took the first side lane off the broad King's Road.

Only then, out of sight of guards and palace, did they put spurs to their mounts and race for the Golden Lamb.

CHAPTER 35

Belec's hastily whispered words drove a tight-lipped Thengel from his lookout in the common room. He led the way upstairs, waited until they were behind closed doors, then rounded on the bearers of ill tidings.

"How came this to pass?" he demanded.

The cleric and the bard told what they'd witnessed, their words running over each other's in their urgency to speak.

"And the King has ordered our arrest?"

The two looked at each other and back at the Guardian of the Silverthorn.

"We don't know." Val was the first to reply. "We didn't stay long enough to hear. It didn't seem wise."

Thengel rolled his eyes and began to walk the floor with his long legs. "We know we're accused, cast under suspicion, our mission betrayed. It reeks of misdirection so that Hanno's own actions aren't examined too closely. If he did not have the King's ear, it would not work." He turned to Valdarius. "So how is it that a runemaster who travels the backcountry in questionable company has Hammankarl's ear so readily?"

The bard sat, helped himself to wine. "The King has four Lords Adviser who counsel him, along with the high officers of the realm. One of the advisers is, by tradition, a runemaster. For some years that office was held by Hanno of Havneis." He sipped the wine, make a face, and set the goblet down.

"Five years ago the High Councillor fell ill and died of a fever. It was thought Hanno would be appointed to that vacancy, become the second most powerful man after the King. Before he could be invited to that post, though, he absented himself from the council entirely—to the King's great disappointment. He begged a leave of absence, said he needs must undertake a pilgrimage to the Menhir of Koram in the Frislan, the wilderness beyond Rauvasla. It was of great import to his vocation as Fen Ehrden, runemaster, that he go.

"The King could not deny such a request. He was given leave, and his absence grew lengthy. More than two years he was gone. What had been leave became regarded as retirement. When he finally returned he took up secluded residence outside the city and avoided the affairs of the court. His experience at the menhir, it seemed, had changed him. He no longer had an interest in worldly matters, though this was much to the astonishment of those who had known him before. He was left with the honorary title of Lord Adviser in his 'retirement.'"

Val played with the stem of the goblet, his brows drawn together. "The office of Riedskana is vacant once again, and the King has long hoped for the runemaster to return to his service. It may be that this man is a more formidable opponent than you could have imagined."

Thengel absorbed that in silence. Belec regarded the bard, lounging in his velvet finery. "You know a lot."

"People at court talk a lot. There is little else for most of them to do, and I'm a good listener." He flashed a grin. "If you want to know about the peculiar habits of the Lord Exchequer's mistress, I can tell you about those, too."

"Enough." Thengel's voice was brittle. "We must assume Hammankarl will want us detained. He'll have to find us first, though. You're sure you weren't followed?"

"None had reason to suspect us in our departure," Belec said. "What was known in the great hall was not known by the gate guards."

"How long it will stay like that, though? . . ." Thengel's voice trailed off.

"When the word is out, you won't be safe here." Valdarius stated the obvious. "This is a public inn; your faces are known. You gave your title and name to the innkeep, yes?"

The Guardian nodded.

"You should leave, then. Tonight."

Thengel spread his hands, motioning to the empty chambers around them. "Think about that again, Master Eldur. Hagar, returning yet with Cathmar this night. Arandel bound here by midmorning, I would guess, and Katrije as well. Nalia went trailing the runemaster."

"Nalia? We didn't see her."

The elf shrugged. "I would be surprised if you had. She'll be back sooner or later. In any case: we must bide here until our party is together again. Unless we have no choice."

"Exactly." Valdarius went to a window, peered up and down the night-dark street. "Are there other ways out, if guardsmen come this moment down the lane?"

Thengel frowned. "Perhaps. Belec. Scout about now, and see what you can see. Where the servants' entrances are. The tradesman's entry in the alley. Where the access to the rooftops. You know."

"Better Nalia than me," the cleric murmured unhappily.

Thengel looked down from his height, voice stern. "You're the one who's here," he said.

Val coughed quietly. "If I may . . ."

The Guardian turned a dour eye upon him.

"I have some . . . small skill in reconnoitering buildings, shall we say. Perhaps I'm better suited than Belec. Woodscrafty he is, yes. But I can gauge the best way to a rooftop, if need be."

Thengel appraised the bard. The Eldur had traveled with them for only a handful of months, not much longer than the adenye. The Guardian knew the skills of his comrades from Caerlian, but what resources the bard had to draw upon were not entirely known to him. If Val wanted to volunteer, so be it.

"You look like a courtier," Thengel pointed out. "You'll draw attention."

"Not for long. Give me a few moments."

The bard rummaged through the pack he had brought and changed clothes quickly. His fine green hose remained the same, though now worn with buff tunic and leather belt. Velvet doublet and slashed sleeves disappeared into his rucksack.

"There," he said, running a hand through his hair. The result was a casual look quite different from his courtly grooming. He altered his stance in a subtle manner as well, not slouching, exactly, but no longer wearing the straight-shouldered demeanor of a man of substance and pride. He looked no longer the courtier, but perhaps a gentleman's valet.

Thengel nodded approvingly. "You seem quite . . . man servant–like," he conceded. "Very well. Here—a key to the room. Come and go as you must."

Val accepted it and left with a promise to return soon.

Belec stared thoughtfully at the door that had closed behind him. "That is not exactly the pompous ass I'm used to seeing at court," he said dryly.

"No. Nor the windbag who's plagued us on the road." Thengel sat by the window to keep a wary eye on the street. "There seem to be many persons inside him."

"I hope one of them can do what he claims he can."

"So do I."

CHAPTER 36

THERE WERE THREE gates into the palace grounds: the trade gate, the military gate, and the royal gate for all others who sought admittance. The guard officer at that illuminated portal spoke with everyone who passed through, at the very least to offer a cursory salute and a wave-through, or to interrogate about their purpose, or to deny entry to those unworthy of treading royal ground.

Nalia had a pass akin to Belec's and so was certain of her entrance. She waited until the runemaster had gone on, out of sight of the entrance, then strode across that pool of daylight to the guard station. As the officer approached and took the seal-marked parchment from her hand, she glanced beyond his shoulder into the pleasure gardens. There was the main path to the Palace's front entrance; she had some minutes, she calculated, that she could loiter here and still catch up to her quarry if she were fleet. . . .

A gratuitous compliment, a flirtatious smile, and she had the officer beguiled as he gave her pass back. It was a slow night, and he was not adverse to flirting with a pretty woman, she saw. "You waved my friend through ahead of me just now," she remarked engagingly. "Did he say where he was bound?"

She kept the smile on her face easily enough as she heard that Hanno planned to see the King. The smile became stiff when she heard the title "Lord Adviser." The expression became paper-thin as the guardsman rambled amiably on.

"So curious about the adventurers from Kalajok, he was—he saw one come through here right ahead of him. If I'd known the man's face I would have delayed him myself, to ask about that emerald dragon. . . ."

Pleading the need to catch up with Hanno—a true statement indeed—Nalia disengaged from the guard and entered the grounds. Her skin prickled in that way it always did when humans nearby had begun to notice her movements too closely. She walked as if unaware of the eyes bearing into her back and followed the gravel path as quickly as she could until out of sight of the gate.

Our reputations have grown in our absence, she thought. *A month ago only a handful of people at court knew of us. Now, the gate guards want to stop and swap tales with us! Not good, for the kind of business we're about. . . .*

She lengthened her stride and sought the edge of the path where gravel yielded to shredded bark and soft dirt. Her footsteps thus muffled, she broke into a ground-eating trot until she spotted Hanno ahead of her. Her passage was silent as only a stealth-conscious elf's can be, while the human ahead of her stomped heavy-treaded on the gravel of the path. He surely had not heard her over his own noise, and he never looked back. He made for the broad stone steps to the Palace ahead.

Where more halberdiers stood and all was bright as day.

She slowed to a halt as the runemaster disappeared through doors of gilt and alabaster. It was time to rethink her plan. Hanno suspected something and was discovering far more about them than she felt comfortable with. She must be that much more cautious now that he was alert to their presence.

Her first days as guest in these halls had shown her that the Palace was guarded in strange ways, subtleties far beyond what her novice eye could detect. There was a strange symmetry to the runic carvings around door frames and lintels. There were globes of magical light that glowed in certain halls whenever one walked there, leaving no shadows for skulking about in. Other little signs suggested to her that this place was warded far beyond her meager abilities to detect.

It was a caution to her and came to her again in this moment of indecision. This was no place to attempt magic, lest wardings be triggered. No place to try the more blatant of thievish skills, either. Yet if a thief could not safely prowl in order to spy upon a target, what was the alternative?

She knew the answer as soon as she had asked it of herself: it was not to be thievish at all, but to blend into the ordinary so that she could be hidden in plain sight.

If Hanno sought the King, there was no need for her to trail him closely any longer. Like all who had dined at this court, she knew Hammankarl must be at his late nightly table. If not, his whereabouts would be easy to discover. That fact and the unease she felt at risking recognition led her footsteps to backtrack down a different garden path. She skirted the front of the White Palace and went to the west side of the residence. There she walked unchallenged past stables and kitchen gardens to the laundry.

When staying in the guest quarters she had asked once how her clothing was to be laundered, solicitous for the well-being of the blue silk bodice she wore at court. It was then she had learned of the system of battens and scrubbers, agitators and rinse baffles, and all manner of intricacies dwarf-crafted for Hammankarl's large domestic staff. She had shaken her head in amazement then but was grateful for the knowledge now.

She reached her goal by skirting the service area to the rear of the kitchens, past the maze of pipes extending out of the stonework of the great cooking hearths. Here was the hidden backside of palace engineering: where fireplaces heated pipes, which heated water collected from concealed roof-top cisterns, which fed into piping that supplied much of the Palace with water. It was a more elaborate version of the Golden Lamb's luxurious plumbing—and part of it led directly into the laundry, beyond the kitchens.

In a side court where things were left to dry, Nalia found a maid's dress long enough to brush the toes of her boots. Over went an apron and upon her hair a headcloth of the sort serving women wore to keep their tresses out of the way while they worked. It would conceal her blond locks, provide covering for her distinctive ears, and overhang her brow enough that with head down, her exotic eyes were less noticeable. Not that it was a perfect disguise, but it would guard her against recognition from a casual glance.

The final touch, of course, was to seem to be occupied in a way suitable to her apparent role. No one would look twice at another servant going about her duties. Leaving the laundry, she took a silver tray with goblets on it from a kitchen sideboard. She breathed more comfortably as she passed her first test: scullions ignored her as she left the kitchen and walked the servants' gallery to the royal dining hall.

She had not planned to enter the hall directly, but the furor that came from there drew her to the very edge of that chamber.

Ahead was the high table, and there she saw Hanno on the dais. The runemaster sat beside the King engrossed in urgent conversation. Several lords leaned in to catch what they could, and the Captain-General of the King's Hand stood by Hanno's side to hear the better. Courtiers, nobles, servants even, created a hubbub of excited gossip and speculation.

A page leaving the hall with two empty wine pitchers paused where she stood at the threshold, obviously newly arrived. "Did you hear?" he said. "The Truthsayer's dead. Murdered!"

Her expression of shock and astonishment was real enough. In moments she had the news from the boy. He went off about his duties, and she looked at the high table, the vignette there taking on sinister meaning.

She—her friends—revealed as thieves. The King would want them questioned. Neither King nor runemaster knew where they were to be found, she knew—but Captain General Molstroe knew more than the others and would surely mention it, if he had not already. He had three of their party in custody: Thengel's "entourage," asleep by now in the squires' and pages' barracks of the citadel of the King's Hand.

When the Turakemi realized they had no leads to the adventurers but held some of their party already, Thengel's trainees would become pawns and captives. At best they would be a lever that could be used against their comrades, at worst, they could be victims of interrogation and might actually know something damaging to reveal.

Nalia wracked her brain trying to recall what had ever been said to the adenye, if anything, about the real reasons for Caerlian elves and their comrades to be abroad. Nothing precise had been revealed, she thought—but surely they had inklings. Or perhaps Thengel had confided in them in some moment of weak-headedness. . . .

No matter. Udo's angered scream at the striking dragon had given her the precious seconds she had needed, some months ago, to scramble clear of its attack. Katrije had suffered sorely at the hands of enemies, refusing to betray the elves' whereabouts. Jaele was just a child, who to her mind should not be in such hazard to begin with, but the young page served loyally and cheerfully nonetheless. They were all indebted to the adenye, and she could not let them become tools to be abused or used against them.

To judge by the expression on Molstroe's face—calculating, grim—she had not much time to lose.

CHAPTER 37

Nalia slipped out of the Palace as neatly as she had infiltrated it. Her guest resident status permitted her use of a mount. Securing a horse from the stables, she unknowingly retraced Belec's route to the palace gate. Where her comrades had passed but a short time before, she turned the other way and cantered east, hooves echoing, bound for the Street of Shields and the citadel of the Hounds of Hammankarl.

The Street of Shields ended in a broad unpaved square that provided a training ground and parade field for the King's war band. At the far side was a fortified complex of keep, barracks, and stables: headquarters for the elite 200 who served their master as loyally as the war mastiffs that gave them their nickname.

They were a hand-picked cadre with special authority and unusual skills, training together, living together, serving together at the King's command. They believed their service to the Selkie King was a noble calling, one demanding military discipline, high standards, and a nearly fanatic dedication to duty.

Nalia judged them naive in their commitment and too ready to trust those they believed shared the same values. As they had come to trust the Caerlian elves in the jarldom of Kalajok. She hoped that judgement was correct, for she was about to play upon that misplaced faith with calculated intent.

She dismounted beneath the wall-draped banner of the Hand, a gold-bronze running dog upon a field of white, and walked to the iron-bound door beside the barred gates. Gathering a breath, she lifted the great bronze knocker in the shape of a snarling dog's head and let it fall booming upon its backplate.

A peepwindow opened in response to the summons. Her name had little effect on the guard within.

"Sorry," he said. "No one enters at this hour but on official business. Come back tomorrow."

"This is official," she persisted. "Let me speak with Sembroie Kinlayik."

He hesitated. "It's late."

"She'll see me."

Nalia's confident tone had its hoped-for effect. "Wait," he said, and the window closed.

Nalia rehearsed what she would say to this woman, considered what she knew of her character, her gullibilities. She was a balyaden, a battle leader, in the King's Hand, recently promoted in the wake of her distinguished duty in the south. That was where the elvish companions had first crossed paths with Hammankarl's war band and worked together for a time in the jarl's service.

Sembroie was battle-proven, hardheaded, bold. Nalia thought she had no striking foibles except for a naive good faith in others. The elf nodded to herself. That one would serve well enough at this juncture.

The door opened then, and she looked up—and up—into the face of the white-surcoated woman standing there.

Sembroie was of striking stature, broad shouldered, square-jawed, blue-eyed—like one of the Kerias, Udo had insisted, the divine warrior maidens who took perished souls from battlefields and escorted them to the Death Crone's judgment in Ruhnkeil. Like most Turakemi women, she was blonde and fair; unlike most, she stood as tall as a tall man—only a head shorter than Thengel and one of the few willing to stand toe to toe with the Guardian of the Thorn and challenge him directly. Thengel had come to respect her, an accomplished warrior in her own right, and then come to flirt with her. . . .

They both have too many principles for their own good, Nalia thought. *No wonder they like each other so well.*

It had been Sembroie's idea to take in the adenye in their master's absence. "They need training," she'd said. "We have it to offer promising youths." The Guardian had been quick to agree, not willing to risk their young necks in the backwoods so soon after their travails in the south. But that arrangement had been a temporary one—and now Nalia announced their return.

"Sembroie! Greetings. We're back this very night."

"Welcome! It's good to see you." The commander motioned Nalia within, told the guard to see to her horse. "And your journey? What news?"

Nalia kept her smile pleasantly neutral. "It went well enough," she said, waving a hand to forestall further questions, "but I'm not to tell you any more. That's for Thengel to do, he said. And it's at his request that I'm here. He'd like the adenye to join him now."

"Now?" Sembroie looked surprised.

"This hour. He missed them sorely and wants to see them."

"It's irregular." She shook her head. "It's late to disturb them. If he must see them, he should come here tomorrow."

"And so he will"—Nalia nodded—"tomorrow. But now in the moment of his return—it just doesn't feel complete without Udo, Katrije, Jaele. . . . They've been with us through everything else. I'm to take them back with me."

Sembroie frowned, and Nalia rushed on brightly. "Just for the night. We're celebrating, and Thengel insists on it. We'll have them back tomorrow, my oath on it."

As the nonsense rushed off her tongue, she winced slightly inside. She did not spin falsehoods as readily as she simply omitted facts, and she had never yet had cause to lie to Sembroie. *Except for those dice games . . .* , she amended. But the commander took her at her word.

"If nothing else will do then . . . very well. I'll come with you."

Nalia's heart sank. "Oh, no. Thengel doesn't want to see you yet."

The warrior stiffened.

"No, no," Nalia corrected herself in a rush. "It's not like that." She lowered her voice conspiratorialy. "He's vain, you know, wants to look his best, wash the road dust off—and wants to see you someplace with privacy. It's crowded with us right now, and the children will be there. . . ." She shrugged. "You know. There are better places and times for a reunion." She winked.

Sembroie softened and finally nodded. "Tell him I'll make time for him tomorrow. When he brings the adenye back. We've a trial joust tomorrow they can't miss, in the afternoon."

"We'll have them back in due time," Nalia affirmed with a false smile.

Due time. Whatever that might be. I doubt it will be tomorrow.

ON SEMBROIE'S AUTHORITY the squires were awakened and a drowsy Jaele bundled from her bed. They were sincerely startled to see Nalia, for they did not expect her to come to them after making plans clandestinely with Katrije. They took their cue from her, though, and said nothing but empty pleasantries where others could hear.

Their mounts were collected from the stables as they dressed and took their already-assembled packs. They followed Nalia into the inner courtyard, ready to leave in short order.

"You're taking packs?" The warrior noticed as they mounted near the gate.

Nalia played it off. "Thengel. Standing orders." Her tone was slightly mocking. "You know how he is. So proper. They'd be in trouble did they not travel with road kits. It's the sort of thing he'll inspect, for form's sake."

Her mild disparagement of military behavior prodded Sembroie to Thengel's defense. "It's good to have such habits," she said seriously. "They serve a purpose."

Nalia shrugged, letting it go, but smiled inside. What might have caused suspicion suddenly made sense to Sembroie, thinking to defend Thengel's alleged demands on his squires.

Nalia raised a hand in farewell as a guard opened the gate. "We're off then."

"Where are you staying?" Sembroie asked.

"The Redbird, in Old Town. They have large rooms." She winked. "And good dice games."

Sembroie shook her head. "Give everyone my regards," she said. "See you tomorrow."

"Tomorrow."

When a rider came from the White Palace within the hour, Sembroie cursed in ways that caused the messenger's ears to burn and awed every warrior within earshot. Then she marshaled four squads of the Hounds and mounted her Turani palomino before the horse troops.

"You and you." She pointed to the first and second squads. "Rouse the watch and cover the roads out of the city. If they haven't already fled, we might yet catch them. The rest of you ride with me to the Redbird." Her anger was gone and cold steel touched her voice in its place. "I doubt they're there, but it's where we'll start. And then it'll be a door-by-door search of every inn, tavern, and hostel in the city, until we find them, and arrest them all.

"And when we *do* find them—and I swear by Gunnar Strongarm that we will—Thengel and Nalia are mine."

Eyes glinting, she reined her horse about and led her band into the streets of Etjorvi.

CHAPTER 38

THE PREEMPTORY DOUBLE rap on the door bore Hagar's unmistakable signature. Thengel was there in one stride.

"I'm glad you're back." He stood aside for the dwarf. "Cathmar. Welcome." He nodded to the cowled figure who followed behind.

The latter nodded in return, the motion translating to the barest dip of the dark blue hood pulled far over his face, and raised a hand in silent greeting to Belec, on watch at the window. Cathmar followed the Guardian's outstretched arm to a chair and there put off the cloak and hood that he wore. One crooked hand brushed silver-white hair back from a haggard face. Thengel schooled his expression and met the scholar-mage's amber eyes with a level gaze.

It was the rest of the elf's visage that Thengel avoided looking at.

Cathmar was disfigured in a way that no elf ever expected to be: victim of the *ailemar,* also called Sarvin's Blight, a rare wasting disease that destroyed flesh much like leprosy melted a human's. A people naturally free from most illnesses, those few that struck elves seemed to take a greater toll. Such at least was the price paid by Cathmar of Tren.

"You seem better." Thengel noted that though the other's movements were languid and slow, he no longer wheezed when he breathed and seemed to move without pain, at long last.

Cathmar blinked drooping eyelids and touched fingers to his face where tip of nose had flattened into nostrils and knob of chin no longer aligned with jaw. "I catch eyes for the wrong reasons, now," he said dryly, "but the progress of the *ailemar* has halted. Thanks to Nehvros and his medicinals from the Underrealms."

Thengel nodded. Cathmar's sole reason for journeying to Etjorvi had been the rumor that his countryman Master Nehvros—the King's elvish physician and mage—owned a copy of Gorvian's Treatise, and from those pages might know the secret of curatives forgotten since elves ruled Arilethne. The rumors had been correct. Cathmar sat here now in far better health than Thengel had ever known him.

The Guardian thought that perhaps the treatment offered by Nehvros might restore muscle form and function as well, but it was not so. Cathmar had been convalesing for the last month in the home of friends of the physician, yet he had an aura of exhaustion about him, and the marks of his illness were indelibly upon him. On a night like this, when he did not wish to attract undue attention, Thengel understood the choice of a hooded cloak, unseasonable though such a garment might be.

"I'm sorry to disturb your peace," he apologized, "and that so late at night—but we no longer have the luxury of time. Grave difficulties are upon us." Thengel outlined Hanno's accusations made to the King and the danger of arrest that must be imminent.

"I've been giving this a great deal of thought," the tall elf said, sparing a pointed look at Hagar. "Thinking it through, very carefully. My conclusions are these."

He numbered points on his fingers. "First: we need a safe haven. Someplace to stay where we're not known, not in danger of arrest, yet which leaves us free to move about as we need.

"Second: we need to continue to watch the Nimmians—we haven't followed them half the length of Tura-kem to lose them and the Tapestry now.

"Third: we must create an opportunity to take the relic from them, and we mustn't be overlong about it. They are surely as anxious to leave this land as we are. If the authorities hunt us, we'll have even less freedom to get to them. And right now, it seems they're unassailable. Eritanos House is magically warded against theft and assault, I hear, and we can hardly camp on their doorstep waiting for them to come out."

He paused, frowning at that prospect, collecting his thoughts.

"What about Dalin?" Hagar rumbled.

Thengel's frown deepened. "Hm. Well . . ."

"Why is he a concern?" Cathmar asked dispassionately.

Hagar sniffed. "He did not need to come with us. But we promised help and he did, and now a price for it he has paid." His bushy brows lowered. "Leave him, we could. Forget about him, we could. But then we are forgetting one other thing, too."

"And that is . . . ?"

"He is the only one who knows how to use the Robe." Hagar looked to Thengel. "Maybe you are never needing to use these relics. But maybe one day you do."

Thengel bit his lip. That thought had already crossed his mind. "We could get help . . . ask a sage, a scholar, someone learned in these matters. . . ."

Cathmar made an indecipherable noise. "You could be asking for years. If the boy knows how to use the Tapestry's power, then he does indeed have a value. You would be foolish to throw him away."

"I had not planned to throw him away," Thengel said with a touch of self-righteousness. "I just hadn't decided what to do about him yet. That is a fourth point, then: we must get Dalin out of prison, so he can help us once we have the relic."

The Guardian paused. *And if he doesn't want to help . . .?* It was the obvious question, but no one bothered to make the observation. *Just as well. I'm not ready to debate that one yet.*

"And finally"—he clasped all fingers together in a one-handed grip— "we need to know about *them*." He jabbed a finger toward the window and the building across the way. "We have too many questions. We need answers and we need them now. Who *are* those people? Why have they taken the Tapestry? What do we face, in this enemy? Is it safe to turn our backs on them after we have what we came for, or must we . . . must we . . ."

"Put them out of the picture?" Cathmar said bluntly.

Thengel hesitated. "I don't want to kill anyone arbitrarily. We could have them arrested, instead. . . ."

"If they will hound and hunt us in turn, we cannot risk it," Hagar said shortly. "We cannot be guarding our backs every step of the way. Too much depends on this. Or so you say."

The Guardian of the Silverthorn sobered with that remark. "So I say, Hagar." He looked at Cathmar. "There you have it. Will you help us?"

Cathmar sat in silence, shifting his eyes from the Guardian, to the tabletop, to a burning lamp wick. He stared at the flame for a time, ravaged face impassive. Thengel could guess, though, what considerations weighed on his mind.

The elf was not a kinsman from Caerlian. There was no bond of blood or common loyalty to bind him to their cause. He was a learned philosopher, a mystic and adept from Tren to the south. Their paths had crossed, their road to Etjorvi lay together. . . . It was by chance that he had learned the basics of Thengel's quest in Tura-kem. It had seemed of no import to him at the time—he a frail fellow too preoccupied with the threat of imminent death to become much involved with the adventurers he had fallen in with.

And yet his help, occasional though it had been, had been timely. Severely limited in his ability to travel, they had in turn seen him safe to Etjorvi before he was too far gone for hope of recovery. They were not friends, exactly, but they had been of mutual assistance and now . . . now there was a bond of some sort between them. When others would have found it just as easy to leave the stricken elf behind, Thengel had conquered his revulsion and fear of contagion and rendered aid. For no reason but that it was the right thing to do and the fact that Cathmar was an elf far from home, as was he.

The subtleties of energy return were not lost on the philosopher. He let his breath out in a sigh and nodded. "I'll help."

Was it because he felt kindly toward the Guardian's party? Or because he felt obligation, was discharging a debt? The warrior could not tell, and the adept did not say. Thengel responded to his words alone and offered a half-bow from his seat. "We're grateful. I know something of what you can do and appreciate your aid."

Cathmar acknowledged the compliment with a dip of his chin. "I can't help you with a place to hide. The other things, though . . . yes. Insofar as I am able."

Thengel smiled. "We have a proposal, then. Something Nalia suggested earlier." He sketched a plan of action that dealt with one of their problems, and Cathmar nodded.

"For that she is right. Valdarius is best suited to help me."

"When would you want to do this?"

The disfigured face grimaced. "After another week in bed, and after Arandel is back. But given the King's sudden interest in you . . . I think right now is best."

"Now? Tonight?"

"Yes. As soon as the bard returns."

That Cathmar would plunge right in was welcome, if a little disconcerting. "Well then." Thengel glanced around. "Let me make a little preparation for your work." He went to a wardrobe, rummaged through the cabinet, and pulled out a neat bundle of thin rope. He dropped the coiled line on the table and set a knife beside it.

"When you return," he said, "we'll be ready for you."

A bemused Cathmar surveyed the equipment on the tabletop. "Don't bother," he said. "Those kinds of preparations won't be necessary. Here's what you can do instead. . . ."

CHAPTER 39

THE RUNEMASTER'S STARTLING news interrupted the regular progress of the dinner court, nearly at an end when Hanno made his appearance. The King ordered more wine and recalled musicians dismissed earlier. Courtiers, minor nobility, the well-to-do put their heads together in gossiping circles around the hall. The King was engrossed in similar discussion at the high table, a shadowed look upon his face.

"I notice Valdarius is nowhere to be found, either." His eyes scanned the hall. "He must have heard your announcement and fled that very instant."

"No doubt, Sire," Hanno agreed. "Our loss. But with the Hounds seeking him and his cronies, they'll be brought to heel soon enough."

Captain-General Molstroe nodded slightly at the compliment but continued to fulminate in silence. He had been no less taken in than the King.

An expression halfway between distress and indignation touched Hammankarl's features. "I can't believe I've nursed a snake at my breast like this. The Jarl of Kalajok praised them highly. Regarded them heroes! I honored them in my court, took them into my household, gave them aid. . . ."

The runemaster was conciliatory. "They're accomplished at lulling people into opening their doors and hearts to them. It's what that wretch did with Granmar as well. No wonder they're working together. They've probably been plotting this for months." He poured wine for the King before refreshing his own cup. "I was the unlooked-for arrival they did not expect. That I took the Robe into safekeeping can only have ruined their plans."

"I suppose you're right, Lord Adviser."

"When will you bring this murderous whelp to trial, Majesty?"

"Soon."

"In the next few days?"

Hammankarl quirked a smile. "Anxious to see Granmar's death avenged, are you? I thought you and he were not such very good friends."

Color tinged Hanno's cheeks and he ducked his head. That was unexpected, that the King had sensed the tenor of his relationship with the Truthsayer. "We had our differences," he admitted. "But we had lately reconciled them, also. He was going to speak to you of this when next he was at court."

"Ah." Hammakarl nodded. "You always were a good mediator of troubles between people. I've needed that skill here badly."

"Thank you, Sire." He let that linger a moment, pointedly ignoring the discomforted rustlings of the two Lords Adviser seated within earshot. Then he returned to his real interest. "And the apprentice?"

"After Ardrunafest," the King replied. "He can sit until then. Once the holiday is past we can give this our undivided attention. And will. I am exercising liege-right and conducting this trial myself."

Nobles sitting nearby murmured surprise at the King's announcement. Hanno took it more in stride.

"Thank you, Sire," he said.

"Why thank me?"

"This demands that justice be served, and I'm pleased to see it will be handled by you and not an ordinary justiciar. I'm anxious to see the outcome of it, that is all."

Anxious in ways I won't be explaining to you, Hammankarl. . . .

The midsummer festival took place in three days' time. The King could hold trial on his whim thereafter, but that left at least several days in which to arrange for the boy to be killed while folk were preoccupied with festivities.

There was no way, of course, that Hanno could risk letting Dalin stand before the King, to be examined with magic, if need be. Many persons in this court could apply a truth spell to the proceedings; it was nearly a certainty that it would happen. The runemaster, of course, would be prepared with another Staje rune—but if they should bespell Dalin and find that *he* told truth as well, how, then, to reconcile that two stories diametrically opposed were both completely truthful?

It could be reconciled, of course, and Dalin's testimony would be damning to Hanno. This was not an area that could withstand any closer probing. No. It was best not to put anything to the test. Let the boy perish in his prison—that would be the best way. For that matter: when these outlanders who had attempted an ambush were finally caught they, too, must be put out of the way neatly, for their tales would bear a truth-probing no more than Dalin's.

Just this night Hanno learned that Bjorg Palstro was the garrison commander in charge of the dungeons of Hakkonkalye. Now there was a man whose reputation Hanno knew, if not the man personally: a hard, quietly ambitious soldier and one who toadied to rank.

There was a lever to use, and if anyone could manipulate it, the rune-master could.

He smiled to himself and enjoyed the byplay at the table. The King went back and forth between righteous anger and disbelief that he could be so cozened. Captain-General Molstroe kept his own counsel but had a thunderous look about him. The Lord Exchequer had only the most polite natterings to say to Hanno, while Wulfram, the runemaster who sat as Lord Adviser, regarded the older man with a mixture of awe and leery regard. As well he might.

The lords and officials at high table were doing a delicate dance around Hanno, his unexpected return to court upsetting the balance of power here. He stayed comfortably by the King's side, proximity to power being, in this instance, nearly as good as the power itself. That would come soon enough. Already he was laying the groundwork for his true advent: somehow in the confusion he ended up sitting at Hammankarl's right hand. Convenience of the moment? Royal favor? Precursor of things to come? Let the onlookers wonder. Hanno smiled to himself to see that, understanding of it or not, they heeded the dynamic and gave him respect and a wide berth.

People who recognized the signal of a return to favor were careful to call him Lord Adviser this night, not runemaster. He kept a look of cultivated concern and gravity on his face but smiled joyously inside.

A few more days and the Truthsayer's apprentice would be a menace no more. The King would take care of the bothersome elves. Now it remained only to deal with the Nimmians and secure the Robe for himself. With or without the help of Koribee interests, he would be prepared to broker power as he once had and soon would again.

CHAPTER 40

NALIA AND HER youthful retinue arrived at the Golden Lamb as Cathmar prepared to leave it. Thengel's protests died on his lips as she explained the ominous scene at the King's table and the logic that had prompted her irrevocable action. Others agreed with her thinking, and Valdarius, returned from his rounds, seconded Thengel's heartfelt wish: they needed a safer refuge, out of reach of the law.

"I have a place in mind that might serve, for a time," the bard said. "Be ready and we'll leave as soon as Cathmar and I are done with this task."

Conversation was put on hold while the companions worked on hurried packing, preparations for flight, and getting the adenye sorted out.

"We won't be long," Cathmar cautioned them, "and remember: when we return—absolute silence in these rooms. There must be no distractions." Thengel acknowledged him with a wave, and the pair left the chaos gladly behind.

Shortly they walked up the lamplit steps of Eritanos House, and the liveried doorman opened to their knock.

"Sir?"

Valdarius resembled a valet in his casual clothes, and so the doorman spoke to the hooded figure before him.

"We have a message from Hanno Runemaster," Cathmar said quietly, with a small sideways gesture of his hand.

The motion was a key, a focal point for his concentration, to direct the energy he poured out in that moment. The mind control arts of the Luithwë philosophers yielded effects that some deemed magical, but he knew were not. It was merely the manipulation of the energy field that imbued every creature, every object, embodied in the physical world. In the Overworld,

Cathmar's acute perceptions sensed the shape of this man's psyche and nudged it just *so*, with predictable effect.

"A message." The doorman nodded agreeably.

"My friend here will deliver it to his friends."

"Certainly, sir." The servant stepped clear, let them enter.

"Where are Hanno's friends?" Cathmar asked casually, to another small gesture concealed by the edge of his cloak.

The doorman pointed to the stairs. "First floor up, to your right. The Glassblower's Suite," he said. "Look for the glassblower's horn and bulb on a plaque by the door."

It was midnight and the halls were deserted. Valdarius took the steps two at a time. A hall sconce held a single light-spelled stone giving off a modest glow; by its light he found the room with the glassblower's plaque.

He settled himself with a deep breath and knocked.

The persons within were not asleep, for the door opened momentarily. A man Val's own height confronted him, human, with short curly brown beard and longish mustaches, wavy auburn-touched hair, wearing a green-and-gray surcoat over casual tunic and trousers. The man drew himself up in formal manner when he saw Val. "Yes?"

"Pardon for the disturbance, sir." The bard ducked his head submissively. "I come with a messenger from the runemaster. He awaits you downstairs."

The man looked a little startled. "Hanno? I thought he was here." He glanced across the hall.

Val shook his head. "He's at the Palace. We have something for you downstairs."

The man looked curious. "What is it?"

"I couldn't say, sir. It's a box for you."

"Bring it up here, then."

"It's not large, sir, but you must leave us your mark for it—downstairs. The doorman won't let us past."

The man snorted, then looked over his shoulder. "Messenger from Hanno. I'll be right back."

He stepped outside the door and followed Val downstairs. He saw hooded Cathmar standing by the doorman's station inside the entrance.

"Yes? You've something for me?"

"You might say that," the adept replied softly. He took his hand out from under his cloak as if presenting a package, but it was another key gesture for focus. In that moment he sensed the armored areas of this man's mind—and its distinctive places of vulnerability.

"You'd like to come with us," he said.

The man studied him for a moment, then spoke thoughtfully. "I'd like to come with you."

A soft murmur. "You have a lot to talk to us about."

"I have a lot to talk to you about." He scratched his cheek. "But . . . my friends will wonder. . . ."

"Your friends won't worry. You have plenty of time."

"I have plenty of time." He nodded. "I'll come with you."

He followed Val placidly out the door. Cathmar loitered, smiled at the doorman. "You've had a quiet night. No one came through here."

"Quiet night." The servant nodded. His eyelids dipped closed in the semidrowse of one who waits with nothing to do.

Cathmar pulled the door softly shut behind him. It would not do to disturb the night doorman at his work.

They returned with their beguiled captive, walking the long way round the block to the service alley so as not to be seen by guests of the inn. They made their way thence to the reception chamber of the elves' suite of rooms. Thengel had readied that chamber as the adept desired him to: two lamps were lit, with the wicks turned low to an intimate, comforting level of light. In the shadows beyond the end of the room, the door to Nalia's sleep chamber was cracked open. Beyond it she and Hagar sat, ears cocked to monitor the conversation. Belec remained on watch at the window, but in earshot of the talk as well.

What refreshments remained in these rooms had been collected at this table: a quarter of a soft goat's cheese, crusty bread, a bowl of gooseberries, a half-pitcher of wine. The Guardian of the Thorn waited here, his lanky height folded into manageable length in one chair. As Cathmar had instructed him, he neither stood nor spoke when they entered the room but made a gently welcoming gesture to the table.

"Stay nonthreatening, sociable. Soft-spoken. Speak little," Cathmar had warned, *"and make no intimidating movements. Don't even stand—your height is unexpected, might feel threatening to some. Let me lead the conversation. If there is something you need to know, ask it briefly, and I will handle things after that."*

His cautions were well heeded—and necessary. Thengel regarded the man led into the room, and a muscle twitched in his jaw. It was the Nimmian who had run from Hagar at the roadside ambush, then felled the dwarf with a word of power.

There was no time now to warn of this man's deadly spell-casting abilities—but if Cathmar's influence should slip, and the man rebel against this subtle control. . . .?

Thengel reassured himself of the location of the angular silverthorn dagger at his hip, symbol of dedication and weapon in one, from the holy melicanthus of Caerlian. It was, as always, within easy reach should he need it.

He watched the man warily as he sat—a human of mature years, neither young nor old, a little soft of body, with thoughtful dark eyes. Or was that merely a dazed expression? He seemed like one just awakened from a dream or deep thought, preoccupied, not fully attentive to the moment, and speaking from a place of distraction. He sat uncertainly in a chair, glancing about the room as if he thought, perhaps, that he should be elsewhere.

In silence Thengel poured wine, offered food, as Cathmar began introductions. As if this were an ordinary meeting between friends. And so the pretense would continue, as long as it could be sustained, the adept had assured him, for the subject of this kind of beguilement would be neutrally cooperative as long as nothing happened to set him on his guard.

"And who are you, friend?" Cathmar asked, his question flowing naturally.

"Berin Oathkeeper," the man replied, "second curate of the Denkorvic of Vikkar Tornor in Nimm-on-Witholl, hallowed be his name." He replied with a singsong to his rote answer, the long practice of ritual tinging his words.

Now Thengel recognized the nature of the surcoat the man wore: but for its lack of a holy symbol, its colors were those of the Tornor sect. A way, no doubt, for the cleric to wear the uniform of his faith even in this hostile land without overtly proclaiming his Nimmian origin.

Thengel and Valdarius exchanged glances. This man followed the demigod of oaths and loyalty. That a cleric of Tornor was engaged in murder and thievery struck them as more than a little odd, although that temple was closely affiliated with the ruling house of Nimm and so, some thought, had come to support many unseemly acts through the years. . . .

Cathmar, in somewhat more ignorance than they, asked a question to remedy it. "What brings a man of Vikkar Tornor to Tura-kem? This is far from home for you to wander."

Berin sipped the wine Val had scorned earlier. "The quest. We cleave to the Great Oath. I'm here to see my lord the Duke's will done."

"Great oath? That is why you are styled Oathkeeper?"

The man nodded. "None can turn aside from the vows: not me, not my friends."

Thengel leaned forward. "What have you vowed to do?" he asked softly.

Berin blinked at him, distracted, it seemed, by this change in conversational voices.

Cathmar spoke with a preternatural focus. "I'm sure your cause is just."

The man seemed riveted by the philosopher's personal energy and looked to Cathmar as if he could see into the shadows of his hood. "It is."

"What is that cause?"

"We seek the Panoply of the Loregiver for the Duke of Nimm."

Valdarius and Thengel both let out startled exclamations. A strangled outcry came as well from behind Nalia's cracked-open door. Cathmar shot an angry glance at the Guardian, who controlled himself with an effort.

Berin glanced restlessly around the room. His face was troubled, like that of a man on the verge of remembering something unpleasant. "Be calm." Cathmar's voice was soothing, gentle. "There's nothing to be concerned about here."

Except your quest! Thengel thought, and nearly bit his tongue to keep from speaking disruptively.

"What is the Panoply?" the mage asked Berin.

"The carpet, the cup, and the brazier," he replied. "Together they rule a land. Any land."

"The Duke of Nimm rules a land. Why does he want these things?"

Berin shrugged noncommittally. "It is not for me to question the wishes of the Denkorvic or of the Duke of Nimm. I don't know."

"Do you speculate. . . .?" The question quiet, a confidence shared in the half-dark.

The cleric toyed with a mustache, and a thoughtful look came over his face. "The Duke is . . . not a well man. It's hard for him to control the clans. There is rebellion. The Panoply would put him in undisputed control of Nimm. Of *all* Nimm."

Thengel suppressed a snort. Duke Arn of Nimm was known to be mad, or the next thing to it. He ruled with caprice and ill judgment interspersed with moments of great insight and brilliance—but those moments of clarity grew fewer and fewer with each passing year. The real power behind the throne was Galan Vikkarnor, his warlord nephew and chief of Clan Terbal. There was more than rebellion in Nimm: there was open civil war, with loyalist clans warring against those who had finally rejected the rule of an insufferable madman. Torn with strife, the clans were unable to unite to combat the gorska and their karzdag allies who were overrunning the Nimmian and elvish woodlands in the southeast.

At the point of that incursion: Caerlian. And the cure for that incursion: the Panoply of the Loregiver. But what these Nimmians knew of the relics and what Thengel's companions knew of the relics seemed, now, to be two different things. The Guardian leaned into the conversation.

"The Tapestry—um, the carpet you mention. The weaving. Does the Duke know how to use this thing?"

Berin focused his eyes on Thengel with an apparent effort. "I don't ask. The Collegium Magisterium aids him in things magical. They will know or find out. That is enough."

Valdarius let out a breath, nearly a whistle between his teeth, but refrained from words. The philosopher gestured again, drew Berin Oathkeeper's attention.

"What are you doing with the weaving now?"

"We take the carpet to Nimm. Aral and Kaylis arrange for a ship in the morning. We're not waiting for the runemaster to help us."

"Who are your friends?" Cathmar asked. "We don't know them."

"Joro Narialnos, called Swifthand; Rudic Greycloak, both of the Nightrunner's League. Myself. Kaylis Rutherin, *derenesta,* from the Collegium—a Mistress of Elements, she is. And Aral Terilnor, called Yellowbeard, a war leader of Clan Terbal." He took a swallow of wine and looked at Thengel. "And who am I speaking with? We haven't met . . . but you look familiar."

Thengel swallowed. Familiar because they had fought each other on a woodside trail. That was not a memory he wanted to prompt in this fuddled man's mind. The elf glanced to Cathmar, who diverted Berin smoothly.

"Thengel is elvish, as is your friend Kaylis, yes? Perhaps that is why he looks familiar." It was mere obfuscation but sufficient to distract the man's train of thought.

Cathmar tried to distract a little further. "Where is the Tapestry now?"

"In safekeeping."

"What kind of safekeeping?"

"It's safe."

"Locked away?"

"You might say that. It's not where Hanno can get to it." Berin smiled, amused at some private thought.

This line of questioning was going nowhere. The adept changed it slightly. "What about Hanno?" he inquired.

"He wants the weaving for himself; we're sure of it. He must suspect its power, since we came all this way for it. We'll be gone before he can stop us, though. In the morning."

"Where are you going?"

"I already told you." Tornor's priest sounded a little petulant. "Nimm. As soon as they find a ship we're leaving, just like that. Not waiting. Don't trust the runemaster. . . . It's not safe to stay here."

He busied himself with food then, absentmindedly nibbling off the plate before him. A scratch from Hagar's door drew their attention. In a moment Valdarius was there, and then came back to whisper to the elves at table. "Our friend is missed across the way. Two of them are on the street now, looking for him."

Cathmar turned to Berin. "It's nice to nap after a meal, isn't it?" he said casually.

The cleric nodded and yawned, then yawned again.

"You can rest here if you like. You can go home after."

Berin nodded agreeably. Shortly he was snoring on the bench seat, and the three were in whispered conference at the table.

"Like a child he is!" Valdarius observed, astounded. "So trusting."

"Not really. Only if you do nothing to stir suspicions."

"Can't we have him bring us the Robe?" asked Thengel.

"That would stir suspicion."

"He's a priest, protected by his god. Why's he not proof against these magics? Or will he throw them off, suddenly?"

Cathmar quirked a lip. "Those with hard-set beliefs are the easiest misled. Persons who operate from a basis of faith, instead of a basis of know-ingness, they look outside themselves for truth. Those who know themselves and find their truths within cannot be gulled in this way."

Valdarius glanced from the sleeping man to the adept. "We're lucky the elf Kaylis didn't answer my knock. This would be lost on elves and elf-kin. We cannot be charmed like this."

"*Most* elves cannot," corrected Cathmar. "It is a question of what basis you have garnered self-knowledge upon. There are many humans un-touched by this effect as well. I had other methods to try, did this one fail. But humans who are deeply centered within themselves are far fewer in number than among our own kind."

"Your charm has worked, then," said Thengel, chewing a lip. "Why do you not ask him directly to help us? Surely it can be phrased in a benign manner. . . ."

"He'll do nothing directly against his nature or his best interests." Cath-mar shook his head. "Almost anyone will talk, under this influence; even then they'll not betray a confidence they feel affects them immediately. That he spoke of the Panoply tells me that many people know of his quest and what he seeks—he did not regard it as a close-held secret entrusted to him only.

"Notice that he was much more closemouthed about what they have done with the Tapestry of late? That is immediate and affects him now. To push on that point is to risk jarring him from this state of compliance en-tirely." He looked to the sleeping man and back to his companions. "Now I think is a good time to put him on the streets, while we can do so unnoticed."

"Not out the front, surely?" Thengel worried.

"Of course not. The way we came, in the back alley. We can send him wandering. He'll return to the present in a while, dazed, belike, wondering how he got wherever he finds himself."

"He won't recall our conversations?"

Cathmar's lopsided smile widened. "Not when I'm done with him, no. Give me a while."

He sat with the sleeping Berin, hand on the man's forehead. If anything, his snores deepened.

"Amazing," Thengel murmured, watching. "I've never seen magic of this ilk."

"It's not magic," Valdarius replied. "He's a Luithwë adept. A student of metaphysical disciplines."

"Looks like magic to me," the Guardian insisted. "And I've seen him spell-cast."

Val shrugged. "He's old enough, and experienced enough, I wouldn't be surprised if he were a spellcaster in an earlier career. That's not the source of what you see here, though."

"Luithwë? What is that?"

"A mystery school of the *derenestu*. It teaches a sensitivity to energies that imbue the physical sphere and ways to manipulate them at their source, beyond the physical."

"Other spheres of existence." Thengel shook his head. "Like I said. Sounds like magic to me."

Val smiled. "It is rather a different discipline. Much meditation. Much sensitivity to auras and energetics. No ritual or bindings of power."

"Ah! Bindings of power. Reminds me. . . ." Thengel pulled a small velvet bag out of his belt pouch and dumped its contents out onto his palm.

"Those are . . . ?" Val peered closely. Two miniature torcs lay there, twists of bronze coming nearly full circle but only as large as earrings. On one the torc ended in a wrinkled gnomish face, its mouth open wide as if laughing or talking loudly. On the other, the torc ended with a gnomish head in profile, one overlarge and pointed ear showing clearly.

"From the gnomes of Torvisk in Nimm," the tall elf pronounced. "I found them irksome little people, argumentative, uncooperative, constantly chattering. Confused, even. I see why dwarves don't care for them. But they are not lacking in generosity when they feel it is owed. These are a novelty from their matriarch, Agnetha Thistlestump, in thanks for help we rendered once."

He handed the jewelry to Valdarius for closer examination. "It's worn as a ring or an ear cuff. The one with the mouth sends what is heard by its wearer. The one with the ear receives. I'll keep this"—he tapped the listening torc—"and put the other on our sleeping priest. What his oath-friends say in his earshot, we will know."

A smile crept over Val's face. "Clever. Priceless, even." His countenance fell. "And something you'll probably not recover. If they detect it . . . ?"

"We need to know when they move with the Tapestry." Thengel prodded the miniature torc with a finger. "I can think of no other way to do that. We're evenly matched by them—if not overmatched. Two assassins and spies, they count, and a senior mage from the Collegium, an experienced war leader from the Duke's own clan, and this priest entrusted with a Great Oath. . . ."

Thengel sighed. "What do we muster against them? Me, the most junior dedicant of the Holy Grove's force of guardians, the only one who would not be missed during an extended absence." He flashed a deprecating smile. "A dwarf I cannot be rid of since I saved his life. Three cousins—the restless young of our *eliafin*—who followed me for a lark, then found there was no easy way home—and so have thrown in their lot with me, willy-nilly, in spite of themselves. For a cause they know is worthy but may well spell their deaths. And my adenye, largely untried and greatly ignorant." An expression flitted across his face, of wistfulness and guilt. He changed the subject quickly.

"And then there is yourself, one I think the gods pointed my footsteps toward. You have the solution for a problem we all thought could not be solved."

Val spread his hands modestly. "I but recount lore."

"The same lore they seem privy to," Thengel said with a glance at Berin. "Or close to it."

"What I know of the Panoply," said the bard, "comes from the papers of Fingol Fingolnor, which I have kept with me since before we met." He nodded toward the cabinet that held his pack. "Fingol was a sage who once studied at the Collegium. He's the common link, here—or his writings are, at least. Collegium mages and I have no doubt read similar histories, if not identical."

"But for the lore we need to gather now . . ." Thengel studied the sleeping man. "Short of moving in with them, we'll not know what they're up to, and we can no longer stay here to watch their activities. It's worth the loss if these rings keep us informed long enough."

"Let's hope they do."

Thengel hooked the smalled ring on the edge of his ear, its rounded end securing it inside the shell of his near the lobe. He went to Cathmar with the other gnomish treasure.

"I don't know how long it will go unnoticed," the adept said, "but I will suggest to him that he keep it private. It's something he's had a long time and no one's business but his. . . ." He rested his hand again on Berin's forehead and sat in silence for a while, until content with the work he had done. Then he took the sleeping man's left hand. "Easier overlooked on a finger, I think, than on his head, where he is gazed at constantly." In moments the mate to Thengel's ring was in place.

"Now let us free our bird," said the Guardian of the Thorn. "We need to be on our way as well this night."

He looked meaningfully to Valdarius. The Eldur bard nodded. "Whenever you're ready."

They roused Berin, the priest moving like a man half-drunk. Val helped him to his feet, steered him through the door with Cathmar's aid. Through servants' passages they went, out the tradesman's gate, and into the alley behind the courtyard. Cathmar pointed Berin down the narrow lane and to the street beyond.

"Walk," he urged, and pointed down the road.

Tornor's cleric nodded like a sleepwalker and wove off into the night.

"How long . . . ?" Val whispered.

The hooded elf shrugged. "When his rational mind awakens again. He won't remember us."

They turned their back on the alley and reentered the haven they would be departing within the hour.

CHAPTER 41

THE STABLE OF the Golden Lamb, settled for the night, was a warm haven of drowsing horseflesh, trampled straw, the dust of dried hay, and the tang of manure. The hostler slept in the tack room and his stable boys in the hayloft, but for one by the stall gates, curled up under a horse blanket in a pile of straw.

The groom was there by Hostler Olvek's orders, to serve any patrons who should chance to come or go in the night—and on this one occasion, to ignore stray creaks from the courtyard's rear gate. It was ignorance dear purchased with a gold crown and Val's convincing plea for his purported master at the inn. Olvek had winked a sly understanding when he heard a noblewoman's name mentioned and pocketed the crown with the promise of discretion.

It was unexpected, then, when the groom shook him awake, told him the tall gentleman was here for his horses.

"See you to it," Olvek grumbled.

"He wants *all* their mounts, and they won't let me near. They're saddling up themselves."

"What?" The hostler stirred himself from his wool-stuffed pallet and shuffled out to inspect the activity of strangers in his stable.

"Here now," he said. "What's this?"

The gates to four large box stalls were open, the gentle murmur of voices and the restless shifting of animals coming from within. A gray warhorse stood tethered in the aisle, saddle pad and blanket on his back. His owner, the lanky elf, emerged from a stall at that moment bearing his heavy saddle in his arms.

"You . . . you're taking your horses?" Olvek half-asked, half-challenged.

The warrior put the saddle upon the charger's back, then turned to the hostler. "Yes. That is allowed even at this late hour, is it not?"

A blonde woman and the servitor who had tipped Olvek for his discretion earlier came out of other stalls leading more horses. He noticed packs and bedrolls by the gates where the groom slept. Guests were welcome to their own mounts, of course, but so late and handling their own tack . . . It wasn't ordinary.

"Here. My boys will give you a hand—"

"No." The warrior turned back to his horse, busied himself with girth and cinch. "We like this done just so. We'll do it ourselves, thanks."

"Leaving us, are you?" His eyes darted to the packs again, a glance not lost on the elf.

"We've taken rooms here for a week. We have something urgent to tend to this night, though."

"Ah." Olvek stood, uncertain. He could not push his help upon well-born guests when that help was refused, but neither was he comfortable giving them free run of the stable.

"That will be all, hostler." The warrior dismissed him over the charger's broad back. "Thanks for your assistance. I'll mention it to Thoralf."

The invocation of the innkeeper's name was strangely reassuring. At least these people were not leaving in the middle of the night without paying, for even Olvek in his courtyard isolation had heard of this lord who had rented the front suite of rooms for an exorbitant price and paid the full amount in advance. He and his retinue could certainly take their mounts whenever they wished. That much less work for the boys, with a full stable at the moment. . . .

"Very well then, sir. Call if I can help you with anything." He walked back to his bed and cautioned the groom in an undertone. "Keep an eye out that they don't help themselves to tack not their own."

The boy nodded and went back to his place by the gates, where he could watch the readying of the horses.

When the hostler's door closed and the groom was out of earshot, Hagar paused by Thengel's side. "I told you all this fussing with horses attention to you would draw." His low-pitched grumble was querulous. "It is risking, to take them, and not even keep them where we are going."

Thengel kneed Turon's big barrel ribs until the Caerlian gray gave an exhalation and he could pull the cinch that last bit tighter. "Our names are known and we will surely be sought, if we are not already. If the King's men come here, would you have them find our unattended horses and take them from us, so?"

"Feh. More horses you can buy, when needed."

Thengel shook his head. "Not of these bloodlines. Not of this quality and training. None that we know so well. These are our *friends,* Hagar. Would you have it that I left *you* somewhere because you became inconvenient?"

The dwarf snorted. "I cannot be replaced at any livery stable."

"Neither can our four-legged friends," Thengel said adamantly. "We'll see them safe at the same time we safeguard ourselves. Where we'll have them to use later and can get them at need. Are you ready to go?"

Hagar squinted sourly at the shaggy Finskili horse he had come to inherit. "Ready enough."

CHAPTER 42

"BESPELLED, DO YOU think?" Rudic addressed no one in particular. "Or drugged? I can't tell."

He leaned over Berin, the cleric's expression that of a dreamer just rousing from sleep. But he had not yet awakened fully, though Aral and Rudic had found him on the streets and dragged him back to their rooms some while before.

Yellowbeard snorted in exasperation, grabbed Berin by the front of his surcoat, and shook him like a dog with a bone. "Come to, man!" he barked, raising his hand to strike the unresisting fellow.

"Aral." Joro's voice was sharp enough to give the warrior pause. "Leave him."

The big man's hand released the cleric as he turned, clench-fisted, toward Joro. "Leave him. And then what? Let him drowse the night away? Telling us nothing of what happened to him? How he got this way? If ever we had a need to know it is now, not later, whenever he awakens from this stupor. If he does. Stupid-drunk I would call him, a raffiq trance if I could smell it on him, but he's not been drinking."

"That's not the way to get answers, here."

"How will you wake him up, Nightrunner?"

Joro ignored the warrior, turned to Kaylis instead. "What say you to our quandary?"

The woman cocked her head to one side, regarding Berin. The cleric sat like one dazed, not fully aware of his surroundings. She moved in front of him, one sidelong glance causing Aral to shift out of her way. Studying the priest, she tied her hair back, hands moving automatically to secure the long tow-white tresses with a leather thong. That done, she knelt, putting herself eye to eye with Berin's vacant stare. Steepling her fingers momentarily, she inclined her head, then looked up with an air of intense concentration about her.

She exhaled and spread her hands apart and forward, as if pushing something away from her, toward Berin.

The air around the priest glowed briefly, no more than intensified lamplight would produce, and then that effect was gone. A frown creased her brow.

"Well?" demanded Aral.

She glanced toward the warrior but addressed her words to Joro.

"He's not bespelled. Or not in any way I've ever seen. There's no dweomer upon him, no arcane craft I can identify. This languor seems, well—natural, if such can be believed."

"Beyond your skill to decipher, is it?" It was Aral, his comment tart.

Kaylis stood with one graceful motion and turned to confront him. "Beyond my knowledge, perhaps." One step put her a handspan from his face. "Beyond my skill, no. When I know what I'm dealing with I have skills aplenty to bend to the task."

Aral's mouth pursed. He seemed torn between retort and reconciliation. Joro saved him the trouble.

"None of this is to the point. Restoring Berin to himself is one thing—our real problem lies elsewhere. Someone came to our very door to lure one of us away. Someone knows we are here and stalks us."

"It won't happen again," growled Aral.

"That it happened once is tragedy enough. We were caught completely unprepared. Who is it with this interest in us? That plots to abduct one of our number and releases him, vacant-eyed, an hour later? Why? What did they learn while the Oathkeeper was in their hands?"

"It could be treachery from the runemaster," Kaylis proposed. "I think that likely."

"But has he had time for such plotting," Joro asked, "making arrangements? I doubt it."

"It could be those who ambushed us," Rudic said slowly. "Those we left alive. The elves. They waylaid us with the upcountry steading men. What if they've not given up their pursuit? No one else has shown especial interest in us, and that is the only enemy we've left alive at our backs."

"Them or the runemaster—we need to know who did this." Aral pushed forward, grabbed the priest by the tunic again. "Tornor damn your stupidity, Oathkeeper. Talk to me, I say!" His hard hand swung out and forward, striking across the priest's cheek. A red mark in the shape of a handprint sprang bright above the line of his beard.

Joro leaped to his feet. "I said leave him be!"

Aral curled a lip. "Who's going to stop me, little man? You?"

Joro was used to the sneer on Aral's face; maybe it was the contempt in his voice that proved too much this time. Now, when they needed to work together, to cooperate and set their minds to this common problem, this would be the typical time for the Clan Terbal warrior to chose his own path and the others be damned—

No more.

With nary a warning to signal his intent, he brushed past Kaylis and was on Aral with a single stride.

His attack took the burly fighter by surprise. Aral faced Berin, not Joro, and the Nightrunner came on him from the right side. Joro planted his right foot behind and just inside the warrior's own at the same moment he put hand to the man's near shoulder. With a smooth twist of his torso he brought his momentum and the full weight of his body to bear against Aral. Shoved suddenly backward, the warrior's weight caught against the obstruction of Joro's leg behind his knee. He overbalanced, staggered with his off foot, and crashed backward, thrown to the floor with Joro atop him.

The takedown was swift, adept, and utterly unexpected. Aral howled in angry surprise. His right arm was under his attacker; he swung his left fist instead, only to gasp in pain. The Nightrunner deflected the blow with one hand; while he rested his weight across Aral's throat with one forearm, his free hand twisted the fighter's wrist and pinched a nerve there.

Yellowbeard's hand went numb as a sharp pain shot up his arm. "Crone take you!" he cursed as he tried to throw Joro off with brute force, heaving his torso up and forward for leverage.

Aral was the bigger man, Joro a slender, wiry counterpart to the fighter. But muscle alone was not going to win this contest, as the warrior soon experienced. For a moment triumph gleamed in his eye—Joro's arm was dislodged from his throat, and he felt the Nightrunner slip to the side. His right arm free again, he elbowed his opponent in the jaw—or tried to. Somehow the lithe man was beside him, too close, nearly under him. Joro's arm was around his neck again, this time from behind, the warrior's jaw held in a surprisingly firm grip, torquing his head up and to the left at an awkward, painful angle. He had to shift his weight to follow that unwanted lead, and in a moment the Nightrunner's leverage twisted him full around. Somehow Aral wound up with his face ground into an expensive Koribi carpet. In a heartbeat Joro's knee was in the small of Aral's back, forearm once again around his sturdy neck, braced in an effective choke hold.

Aral, red-faced, tried to utter a curse, but only a strangled gurgle came out. He tried thrashing about to toss the Nightrunner off his body, but it was a tactic he abandoned after one heave: blood pounded in his ears as red spots danced before his eyes. Reduced suddenly to motionlessness, he panted in swift, shallow breaths as he struggled to stay conscious.

"Now we're going to come to an understanding," gritted Joro. His voice was harsh, his words uttered close to Aral's ear, but biting enough for all in the room to hear.

"There's one man commanding here. *One.*" He emphasized it with a squeeze of his arms. Yellowbeard groaned in response. "We do things my way. There will be no debate. There will be no defiance. There will be obedience to orders." His tone was acid-touched frost. With each sentence he shook the warrior, pressed his choke hold a little tighter until the merest wheeze came from Aral's throat.

"Do I make myself clear?"

He bit off each word and left the warrior for a few more heartbeats straining for breath. Then the clansman jerked his head in what passed for a nod, and Joro released his grip enough that wheeze turned to gurgling gasp of intaken air.

"And Aral?"

A short groan was his answer.

"If you defy me again, I'll kill you."

The assassin's tone left no doubt about his sincerity. Joro held on until Yellowbeard jerked his head again in acknowledgment. Then the Nightrunner released him and stood clear of the prostrate warrior.

A sheen of sweat testified to Joro's recent exertion, but nothing else in his manner let on that he had done anything out of the ordinary. The battle-seasoned veteran he had so handily overcome lay gasping at his feet, and Rudic gave him a knowing half-smile. Greycloak had been right; he had had to speak a language the bully would understand.

"Come," he said collectedly. "Instead of buying passage on a vessel, I think we'll be commandeering a ship in the morning, so we have plans to make between now and then. How's Berin?"

The priest sat blinking, hand to face, exhibiting the first volition they'd seen since they'd found him. The others busied themselves with the Oath-keeper and left Aral to collect himself and his dignity without further comment.

CHAPTER 43

GARRISON COMMANDER BJORG Palstro rode through the late-night, early-morning streets of the city. The near-full moon silvered cobblestones ahead of him, bleaching his Turani gelding to shades of gray, rendering the wine stains on his russet surcoat dark splotches against dark cloth.

He plucked at the still-damp garment and sighed. It reminded him not of the surfeit of the King's banquet table but of a particular conversation there that had caused him to leave, though the words spoken were not so easily put from his mind.

His thoughts were turning that way once again when a party of horsemen drew his eye ahead: white-surcoated Hounds of Hammankarl, well lit by torchlight, making a striking picture aback their palominos. They gathered before the door of an inn along the King's Road, where two of their number had dismounted and were knocking upon the establishment's door. A handful of the watch stood with them as well; they gave Bjorg a curious glance as he rode past on the far side of the avenue, then turned back to their duty before he could raise a hand in greeting. Some miscreant, no doubt, would soon be answering to the King's justice. . . .

The King's justice. That was on Palstro's mind heavily as he rode, scattered thoughts jumping from one thing to another but returning always to that subject. Justice. The King. The Truthsayer's murder. The rogue who had slain the seer and the words Palstro had shared with the retired Lord Adviser this evening. . . .

He had had too much to drink this night to give full mind to this business, and he knew it. A wine-laden slump carried him on toward Hakkon's Keep, thoughts wandering, gold belt signifying balyaden rank fallen askew over his thickening middle. A girth that made him no less a soldier, that:

there was none better with a battle hammer in the entire Hakkonkalye garrison. But when would he ever use those skills in battle? Not ever, under the peace of the Selkie Kings. Garrison commanders got promoted by staying within budget for provisions, by training militia regularly. Not by battlefield prowess, much to his regret. What a gutless life for a man who would not shirk at shedding blood when needful. . . .

And was that not the opportunity the runemaster had offered him tonight? And why he was giving it consideration?

He frowned. Very little of real soldiering was involved in his command of Etjorvi's old military fortress. Arguably the most truly useful of his duties was keeping transgressors of the King's peace off the streets and overseeing their punishment for their crimes.

That had come home to him tonight when the former Lord Adviser sought him out in the King's hall. Bjorg supped there a few times a month, to see and be seen: it would not do to languish, always, in the Hakkonkalye, as invisible to the mighty as night-duty garrison soldiers or the scrapings in the dungeons. Far better for Commander Palstro to make his presence known, now and then, to the powerful—especially to haughty Vernulf, the Lord General, who was always at Hammankarl's court.

Of all nights to sup at the White Palace, Bjorg could not have picked a better one than this.

That Hanno Runemaster had been surprised and pleased to make his acquaintance was evident. That he engaged Bjorg in serious conversation was unexpected and flattering. That was when the balyaden had begun to drink a little too much—there was an unseemly edge of nervousness he had wanted to dull, to not appear out of his element as the runemaster maneuvered him aside to discuss matters of the King's justice.

"If you asked for that ruffian to be arrested, I'm sure he's in the dungeons right now, Lord," Palstro had assured him. "No ill-doer has ever escaped from the Hakkonkalye. We'll keep him secure for you."

"His safekeeping is not my concern," Hanno said frankly, the man's keen blue eyes holding his own. In that moment there was no one nearby, and their words were spoken in a curious zone of privacy. Or so it seemed, for what Bjorg heard next focused him in one of those lingering moments when the world all around recedes and leaves words reverberating in the ears.

"I desire retribution," Hanno had said softly. "Swift. Certain."

"The King's court—"

"Is for ordinary men. This is no ordinary crime. This whelp occupies more living space than the gods wish to grant him."

Palstro blinked uncertainly. "That may be, Lord Adviser. I'm sure his trial—"

"There's no reason to wait. His existence is no longer desired, useful, or necessary. He'll be condemned by the King, without a doubt."

"Lord?" Bjorg did not quite take his meaning.

The runemaster had regarded him blandly, stroking an intricately carved stone that hung like a small medallion from a thong about his neck. "He is a blight to persons in high places. His immediate absence would be marked with gratitude. Long-lasting, rich gratitude."

"Oh. Ah." Suddenly he understood the runemaster's meaning quite clearly, and he heard it with ambivalence. There was opportunity here . . . but it was risky and flew in the face of his duty.

He shook his head, his eyes drawn again to the stone around Hanno's neck. Some kind of runic talisman, it was, though it was hard to distinguish, so intertwined were the patterns and knotwork. . . .

He drank deeply of his wine, a sudden case of nerves shaking his hand, spilling some upon his surcoat. "His Majesty is holding trial after Ardrunafest," he equivocated. "He will of course need someone to try at that court."

Hanno Runemaster smiled dryly. "If She Who Waits has seen fit to work her own justice meanwhile, who can argue with that verdict? No one."

Palstro repressed a shudder. The Death Crone was not one gladly invoked at a banquet, and his left hand made a horn-fingered warding gesture out of the Lord Adviser's sight. Even as he did that, the logic of the runemaster's statement was something he could not deny. When She Who Waits claims one for Ruhnkeil, no one could argue with it.

Might Dalin, once–Truthsayer's apprentice, not be suicidal in his imprisonment? And if his life ended in such wise, might that not satisfy not only the King, who was sure to find him guilty, but also She Who Waits? And the former Lord Adviser as well. Making this happen would not be the action of a gutless man, but one seizing opportunity offered, perhaps, by the gods. . . .

Such were the thoughts that occupied Bjorg's ride back to the keep. Through the gates of that stronghold he went, passed through by guards. Dismounting, he entered the broad stone tower of the central fortress—and there he hesitated.

Before him, the stairs and his quarters above, calling him to bed and much-desired rest.

To the right, the hall that led to the southwest corner tower beneath which the dungeons were situated.

Palstro hesitated, but not for long. He could at least take a look at this murderer, see what he would be taking on if he chose to help the runemaster. If he chose to act in the Crone's name.

He turned his footsteps down the hall to the dungeons, waving guards back to their dice game when they tried to come to attention for their commander. He inspected the watch book, saw the entry of interest—the last one, the only one imprisoned this evening—and proceeded down the hall alone. He had no wish for company on this inspection tour or prying eyes to witness what drew his attention this night.

Down turntable stairs he went to the corridors where prisoners awaited trial, beyond those to cells where the convicted few worthy of imprisonment languished in dank solitude. Most adjudged guilty of crimes paid weregeld or were taken into slavery as serfs; some were whipped publicly or left in the stocks for a time, that humiliation considered sufficient to pay their debt. Those guilty of more heinous crimes—like calculated murder—were beheaded. There were few for whom a languishing retribution was deemed appropriate: violators of women and children, ferenye tradesmen found guilty of fraud or embezzlement, and the occasional heretic who insisted on embracing one of the defiled gods of Nimm. . . .

There were few rapists, embezzlers, or heretics there now, and Bjorg's progress was not observed by those who slept in moldering straw behind thick locked doors. Taking a lamp from a wall niche, he entered the final hall in the subterranean corridors, a featureless passage but for three traps in the floor: oubliettes, where the most reviled of prisoners could be dropped and forgotten. It was a rarely meted punishment under King Hammankarl's rule; the last prisoner so treated was the arsonist a decade agone who had burned down the houses of his enemies, laughing while the innocents who lived in them perished as well. Nowadays the dark holes were more likely to be used to detain disruptive or reviled prisoners or those who had earned the guards' special approbation.

Like the scheming, spiteful apprentice who had slain Tura-kem's royal seer.

He was certainly someone the Crone would have better use for than the living, Bjorg considered. And it would easily be possible to transfer him this night to a smaller cell where he could, say, hang himself by a belt. Or perhaps he might trip and break his neck at the bottom of this rough pit. . . .

Bjorg envisioned the possibilities as he knelt beside the last oubliette. He set the lamp down to fumble with the hasp of the grating and caught a pungent odor that caused him to wrinkle his nose. It was something different from the mold and damp he expected here. Snorting to clear his head, he heaved the grating to one side, where it settled with a scrape and crunch of metal on stone. The black hole yawned before him. Now a strange sound came to his ears and he cocked his head to hear better. A gentle huff, huff from below, like a labored breath, but unseemly loud, he thought, to carry this distance from the pit.

Against the wall nearby was an iron plate to which a chain was attached at three points—a tray that would stay stable as it was lowered into the hole, used to deliver food and water to prisoners, or a slops bucket if the guards felt so kind. He fetched it near, set his lamp on that tray, and lowered it over the edge by its chain. Down into the oubliette it dropped, a handspan at a time, lighting the stones, the wall, the floor. . . . This would give him enough light to see this rogue, maybe awaken him with the brilliance of it. Who could say? If the moment seemed opportune, he would put an end to the prisoner here and now—

Bjorg gasped and his fists clenched on the cold chain. The lowering tray jerked to a halt, swinging, lamplight dancing wildly about the small stone chamber.

A brown bear sat on the ground below, eyes closed, the huff, huff of its oddly rhythmic breathing coming through its half-opened mouth. Bjorg swallowed, squeezed his eyes closed. The rank ursine scent assailed his nostrils, stronger now that he leaned directly over the opening into the prisoner's pit. He opened his eyes again.

The lamplight was more steady.

The bear was still there.

He jerked back from the precarious edge, forced himself to ease his white-knuckled grip on the chain. He pulled the tray and its light hastily upward to the surface of the floor, then knelt on his heels and tugged the grating back over the oubliette.

"I'm drunk," he pronounced, glad for his solitude in this moment. He stood with lamp in hand, its light wavering from the trembling of his grip, and resolutely turned his back on the pit.

I'll look into this in the morning, he promised himself, and made his way to bed.

CHAPTER 44

THE STONE QUAYS of the Jarldock had once been the private reserve of jarls and chieftans—any with galleys or private craft who had cause to maintain residence in the royal city. Over time, lords with ferenye interests had opened their moorage to league shipping. Now warehouses and drayage providers dotted the banks of the Aelvoss where that river flowed into the Dannenborch.

It was there that Valdarius led his friends by winding back streets, to an overpriced but obscure teamsters' stable where they left their mounts. Carrying personal belongings, they walked across the looming landmark bridge into Old Town and thence into the Tanner's Quarter. In that direction, the bard promised them not lodgings but a hiding place where they could not be found.

Katrije and her youthful companions had explored much of Etjorvi in the last month, but no errand or free-time amusement had yet carried them into this old district of the city. They walked single file, preceded by Thengel and followed by Belec, through half-dark alleys filled with stench and clutter. Udo muttered as he picked his awkward way through scrap debris of the leather crafters' trade; Jaele made a rude noise at the stink of used tanning brine in barrels not well sealed.

"Shh," Katrije reprimanded, only to bite down on her own exclamation as she stumbled over a man's legs—the evident part of a derelict passed out in a shop's shadowy rear doorway.

Thengel's warning look was noticed by all the adenye. This was not the way they had hoped to impress their lord and master, their skills supposedly new-honed in recent training he had secured for them. Their further progress was made in sheepish silence.

As they wended closer to the southwestern corner of the old city, Valdarius led them into the dyers' district that hugged the river's edge. There was no wall at this border of Old Etjorvi, where the sheer steep banks and swift current of the Aelvoss made a formidable natural water barrier. A narrow plaza edging the riverbank held dyers' vats and rinse basins, stained colors that showed only as muted hues and grays beneath the pearly moon. Water burbled constantly from a fountain mouth to the west, lifted from the river below by a water-powered screw pump, let to flow through cleverly designed baffles into the artificial ponds and basins that served the dyers' craft. At the eastern end of the plaza the used waters were channeled back into the river. The whole was reminiscent of the laundry courtyards at the king's residence and indeed had been created by dwarves as precursor to that later, more sophisticated work.

At the far western edge of the plaza, past a maze of drying racks where cloth and thread would hang in the daytime sun, an old retaining wall crumbled into ruin at the river's edge. Valdarius paused there, the rush of the Aelvoss making his soft-spoken words difficult to hear.

"Step carefully," he warned. "The stairs here are treacherous in places." With that he put a leg over a broken stone in the wall, stood at the river's brink for a moment, then descended from sight.

An ancient staircase was cut into the limestone of the riverbank, hugging the short cliff face down to the narrow graveled strand at water's edge. It was a place with the look of shallow rinse ponds and laundering rocks where flat, half-submerged stones interrupted the river's swift current. If it had once served that purpose it was long hence, for the screw pump made water readily available at higher ground and the precarious beach had become of little use. The rough strand was a long-neglected cranny, with trees clinging at the base of the embankment and shrubbery threatening to overgrow the narrow spit. The river plucked fiercely at the edges of the gravelly shoal on its wild dash to the fiord beyond Jarldock.

Except for some scattered lights in the New City across the river, they could have been in the wilderness beside some forgotten spate in late flood.

Valdarius led them into the darkness beneath overhanging branches. Here the sharp eyes of the nonhumans let them walk without difficulty, though the adenye tripped and stumbled through the undergrowth. Val searched the riverbank for something as he walked to the cliff face, then farther west.

Suddenly he halted. Others followed suit; Katrije bumped into Jaele in the dark, reaching out a quick hand to steady them both. She strained her eyes to adjust to the lessened moonlight and slowly came to perceive what the others readily saw.

Here among the trees was a tumble of old masonry fallen down around a collapsed lintel, the whole overgrown by crowding vegetation. The ruined doorway gave directly into the limestone riverbank. Val pushed his way past the obstacles and clambered inside, the others following behind.

It had been gloomy enough beneath the overhanging trees; here, inside a dank chamber, it was darker yet, in spite of the moonlight that danced on the white-rippled Aelvoss.

"I need light," the bard said.

Nalia took a lamp from her pack, one of fine workmanship from the Golden Lamb. Night-sighted Thengel scowled at her acquisition. She dismissed his displeasure with a charming smile and soon had the wick burning. The party looked around curiously.

Gravel, dirt, and debris from the crumbling door littered the floor, but beneath the detritus worked stone could be glimpsed. The chamber was framed in dressed stone—a cubbyhole obviously known to locals, for the walls were marked in places with graffiti scribbled in charcoal or gouged out of the stone in the short, straight lines of runic notation. Those walls were obscured by patches of black mold; upon the back wall, though, a pattern could be discerned behind it all. Katrije struggled to make it out in the flickering light.

Spots, they seemed to her, or dots, many dots, of differing colors, their shapes and hues obscured by defacement and the ravages of dampness. It almost made a picture of some sort. . . .

"A waterfall!" Jaele chirped. "Look. It's a waterfall." She slipped easily between larger people, ran a small hand over a series of tile pieces pressed into grouting on the wall. She was right: taken in their entirety, they tricked the eye into perceiving a picture formed of many points of color. The image she had touched was, indeed, a waterfall. With the eye reoriented, one perceived a woman sitting at its base, in the loose robe and green curling hair traditionally associated with a nymph. Around her feet, a motif of water lilies and minnows. It was unlike any art, any structure, visible in modern Tura-kem. Not even the White Palace featured architecture of such intricate and painstaking design.

"What in the world is this?" Thengel asked in wonder.

Valdarius studied the wall with satisfaction before answering. "An entrance to a forbidden place," he said slowly. "And a forgotten one." He reached out tentatively to a minnow beneath the nymph's feet, a pattern composed of numerous mosaic tiles, each the size of a thumbnail. He sought the one fragment that made the fish's eye and pressed it.

It sank a fingertip's depth into the wall and stayed there.

A small smile of self-congratulations broke out upon his face. "Study this with me, then," he spoke to no one and everyone. "You may need to gain entrance here again. If the records are correct, this is how."

He pressed other stones in the artwork in a precise order: the center of the blossom of a blue horned lily, another minnow by the nymph's hand, the darkest point on the darkest stone at the base of the waterfall's cascade—

A grinding filled the chamber, and one of the natural joins in the wall framing the mosaic section yawned with sudden blackness. A stone panel swiveled on an end point, revealing darkness beyond.

Nalia was first at the gap, shining her lamp within. Light showed an ascending tunnel driving into the limestone bedrock that supported the city.

The bard stood behind her, looking bemusedly along the passage. Thengel's hand reached out, turned him about by the shoulder. "What is this place," he demanded, "where you would have us take refuge?"

"A shrine of Seidrun," Val answered distractedly. "One of the Forbidden Gods, here."

Udo inhaled sharply and sketched a warding sign in the air. Katrije tensed as cold chills ran down her spine, and Jaele reached out for the security of her hand. Oblivious to these reactions, Valdarius took the lamp from Nalia and stepped into the tunnel, wholly expecting the others to follow.

When they did not, he turned back to face them. "What?" he asked a bit querulously. "We need safe shelter. It lies this way."

His companions remained in the ruined antechamber, dumbfounded for the moment. Even the elves of Caerlian were awe-touched by what Val had said, while the adenye native to this land stood rooted with goose bumps on their skin and no little trepidation.

Seidrun was one of the several defiled gods of Tura-kem. Her worship might be commonplace across the Sea of Lan Loros, but in the land of her ancient origin it was a grave heresy.

The elves from the east, the dwarf from Schoinevrik, knew of the deities the men of Nimm intertwined their affairs with. Who could not, when so much was done by humans in the loudly proclaimed names of their gods? They understood, too, the ill will that prevailed between the two countries and the ancient reasons for it. Their reaction at the threshold of the shrine of Seidrun was born of surprise and respect for an ancient power, they who understood ancient powers in ways different than humans ever did.

Katrije and her native-born companions had a different reaction. One more immediate, more visceral.

"We can't," Udo blurted. "We're not. . . . It's not . . ." Unable to articulate the taboo of a lifetime of upbringing, he stuttered to a halt, shaking his head.

Thengel looked over his shoulder to regard his squire. Just turned fifteen, a year older than Katrije, the youth nevertheless had the growth of a man on him, his height not yet filled out with muscle, his gangling body coltish and often uncoordinated. But he stood now, back straight, jaw jutting, adamant at the same time he was clearly uncomfortable.

"Can't?" Thengel asked, "or won't?"

Udo swallowed. "It's not allowed, to visit the old places. They're destroyed, when they're found. This place shouldn't be here. It should have been torn down, long ago."

"But it wasn't," Valdarius said, stepping out of the passage and back into the antechamber. "The shrine was once a refuge on the crest of this hill; it fell into ruin when Etjorvi was destroyed in the God War. The town—and later, city—built atop those ruins. The shrine buried beneath it all, and this hidden entrance made during the Kin Wars." Val shrugged eloquently. "They knew it was here, those chieftains and jarls who battled each other then. They chose to ignore it, to let it stand."

"How do you know that?" Katrije demanded.

"I read it in the old records in the King's library. He gave me free rein there. I found what we desired to know about the Tapestry, how it came here . . . and other things. Tidbits of historical interest." He gestured with the lamp. "Like this."

When Udo did not respond to that, Thengel touched his squire upon the arm. "Are you saying you refuse to enter this place?" The Guardian of the Silverthorn spoke gently, but his eyes were stern.

The young man shrugged and his face colored more red than his strawberry-blond hair. He was unable to refuse the noble warrior to whom he had sworn service, yet was unwilling to defy the convention he had been raised to.

Katrije came to his defense in a voice only half-filled with conviction. "It's not done. It's heresy. None of us would willingly spend a night here."

"Are you that devout?" Hagar asked dryly. "Noticed that, I had not."

Katrije's eyes narrowed. When she had most needed help in her life her prayers had gone unanswered. This wasn't about how much faith she put in gods, and well he should know it. She bristled, but Val spoke up brightly before she could retort.

"Heresy! Is *that* your concern, then?" He smiled smugly. "You're not violating the law here."

Jaele frowned. "But you said—"

Val grinned down at her with his "Listen-to-what-I-know" look upon his face. "Do you know what Seidrun respresents?" he asked rhetorically. Jaele bit her lip, but Udo spoke in irritation.

"She was Lan Loros's consort," he said. "A petty, jealous goddess who drowned travelers in ponds and set nymphs to lure the unsuspecting to false river crossings—"

Val barked out a laugh. "That may be what you are told here, but that is hardly the truth of it. The patron of small waters, she is. Lakes, rivers, springs, and ponds—and the consort of the sea god still. Seidrun is kindly by nature and aids travelers and persons who are lost. In Nimm there are forest shrines and little way stations dedicated to her in out-of-the-way places. You used to have them here, too, in places travelers might pass. . . ." Val waved his free arm. "In this place that was once only a village, they built a shrine dedicated to her. Around hot springs and baths and healing waters—"

"So?" Katrije interrupted. "Why should we risk staying here?"

Val gave her a sour look. "You never have shown much respect for learning."

"Her question is mine as well," Cathmar interjected in his dry rasp. "Why should they risk staying here? Given the nature of this place."

Val sighed, a much-put-upon sound. "This was declared a safe haven by royal decree long, long ago. That decree still stands. The place itself is a sanctuary. Legal, not religious."

Katrije let out a breath she did not realize she'd been holding. "Even though it's dedicated to a Forbidden One?"

Val shrugged. "The decree was never rescinded. The shrine is a legal sanctuary from pursuit and persecution as long as you stand within its boundaries. As we do, here." He smirked. "That should be good enough even for you!"

He turned on his heel with that pronouncement and headed into the passage beyond the secret panel.

The others hesitated a moment longer, then followed Nalia's lead as she moved in the bard's footsteps.

Belec sighed. "Now *that*," he said to Thengel, "is the ass I remember."

The Guardian grunted acknowledgment, then ushered his young servitors into the passage and followed behind.

CHAPTER 45

OLD ETJORVI was built upon a hill that rose from open fields and pastures, with Hakkon's Keep upon its highest point overlooking the Dannenborch. The tunnel they followed drove long and straight to that point in the northeast, an uphill slope all the way. It was cut out of the solid bedrock beneath the city, with the look of a miner's excavation in its straightforward simplicity. It was cold and damp; the walls were rough, the ground littered with scattered rock that had probably lain undisturbed for centuries.

Katrije glanced back over her shoulder. Blackness ate the tunnel behind them and cloaked whatever might lie ahead of them. They seemed trapped in an endless passage, nine comrades walking in the center of a flickering globe of light, only the irregular stone changing to suggest progress.

After a long while, the unexpected crunch of gravel underfoot drew the eye downward. Worked stone appeared beneath their feet, the first suggestion that they had arrived somewhere. Though where that "somewhere" might be . . .

Abruptly the walls changed, passing a line, apparently, where the fine construction of the shrine had given way to the workmanlike drive direct to the river entrance. The rough-cut passage they were in leveled off into a corridor of dressed stone walls and vault-arched ceiling. A handspan-wide band of mosaic bordered the top of the walls: a pattern of stylized minnows picked out in tiny colored tiles, visible for the length of the hall.

Onward they went, along passages in much worse repair, or perhaps that much more fragile, than the plain stone egress tunnel had been. Val led them up a short flight of stairs, over flagstones of cracked marble, past fluted pillars framing doorways that opened into rubble-choked chambers. Katrije looked more closely into one they passed, seeing massive cut stones and large square timbers dropped from above as if a giant had punched his fist through a ceiling and brought all down in a jumble.

She looked at the arched vaulting over her head and shuddered. Above that was—what? Dirt? Stone? The foundations of other buildings, and all of Etjorvi on top of that? She was suddenly conscious that they were in a small part of a lost villa, its buildings ruined, their remains covered over, the whole forgotten and built upon. The weight of an entire massive city was there, overhead.

She felt her heart race with the realization, and her nostrils widened as she struggled to get enough air. Pressing in, these walls were, and what if something gave right now, if a hidden timber cracked beneath the strain, and stone collapsed . . . ? This was not like the Underrealms where caverns and chambers existed amid stone, meant to endure, always, in stone. This was like being trapped in a bubble in amber, able to move for a little while, the freedom deluding, the amber ever-present. And perhaps like a fly the life would be squeezed out of her. . . .

It was then that they had to hunch down, to crawl and crouch through a half-collapsed hallway. She had never thought of herself as claustrophic until now, and she followed the others driven by sheer willpower alone.

"Don't bump anything!" she hissed to Udo as his shoulder scraped a stone. "You'll kill us all."

Hagar's gruff voice from behind startled her. "Not to worry," he said. "A stable ruin, it is. The rubble, interlocked; the basic structures, sound."

She did not spare breath to reply, but his words were reassuring and the remainder of her progress somewhat the easier for them. Still, she was grateful when they emerged into a spacious chamber and could stand upright once more. They came to their feet, knocking dust and grit off knees and sniffing warm, damp air.

Val waved an arm at the room before them. "I give you the Asla Shrine of Seidrun," he said grandly.

They had come through the main entrance into a rectangular gallery. Flecks of crystal gleamed in the white fluted pillars that marched the length of the chamber to left and right. Behind them, doors opened into lesser rooms. This site had surely once been outdoors, for opposite the entrance a rough outcropping of natural, weathered rock protruded waist-high from the marble-flagged floor. At its base a steaming spring bubbled forth and flowed through a natural rock-strewn channel into a small pond in the center of the room.

Later the place had been enclosed by a courtyard, eventually roofed over and developed into the spa and healing retreat it had become. The pond was surrounded by an embankment of dressed stone at a height comfortable to sit upon, with a lip that gave gently into the waters of the pond.

That pool steamed gently and the room was humid. "A warm spring discovered by Asla," Val explained pedantically. "She had a vision here and became a convert to Seidrun, tending the healing waters until her death. She was considered a holy woman by adherents. When they had worshipers here."

He set the lamp down at the edge of the pond, its waters oddly dark in hue. "Take a bath if you like. It's supposed to have curative powers."

"Like a steambath it is in here," muttered Hagar.

"It's not that clinging." Cathmar countered. "Pleasant, I find it."

"And no doubt," said Val, "good for your lungs. I'd recommend a soak."

Katrije found his comment jarring. "That's sacrilegious," she said curtly. Val raised an eyebrow.

She persisted stubbornly. "It's not a tub. If it was so special to S—to her, well, the water spirits who remain might take it amiss if you just . . . you know. . . ."

"Just step in for a bath?" Cathmar looked to the bard. "Valdarius? What say you, from your readings in the King's histories? Is this likely to be a place where secular use will offend?"

"Well." He chewed a lip. "It's always polite to thank whatever deity is associated with a holy place. I would do the same here. No need for special measures, though."

Belec coughed politely. "I would say that thanks are essential and possibly an offering, to appease any sense of trespass. We are not, after all, here for the goddess's worship *or* healing powers. Respect for our surroundings would be in order."

Val shrugged. "I defer to your wisdom in such things, Keeper of the Path."

Katrije heard Belec's verdict with mixed feelings. Thengel had explained to the adenye about their need to disappear from sight and so their sudden remove to this peculiar sanctuary. She wondered, if their whereabouts became know, if they would all become anathema just as Seidrun's worshipers had. And now Belec thought to appease the goddess . . . but surely an elvish thanks-prayer was not sacrilege to the gods of Tura-kem? And in this precarious place—regardless of Hagar's assurances—there was no point to inviting divine wrath. It was unsettling enough to walk these forgotten halls beneath the city, without risking the anger of whatever Seidrun-energies lingered here.

Katrije bit down on any further protests about sacrilege and heresy and left the cleric to his own.

Belec pulled a small pouch from his kit and Hagar, a lantern from his. While the priest busied himself at the rocky spring with herbs and candles, Hagar enlisted the adenye to scout through side rooms and make sleeping arrangements away from the damp pondside.

The smaller chambers were of indeterminate purpose. Most were empty, though one had two waist-high tables and another had clearly been an apothecary. Shelves there still held jars of medicinal herbs, the names of contents painted on in archaic runic script. Old bedding in one chamber suggested that more than one ancient worshiper had taken refuge here in centuries agone, but otherwise the rooms were long disused and emptied of anything that might help identify their purpose.

Katrije picked a chamber to sleep in that suited her and soon tucked groggy-eyed Jaele into a quickly made bed in that same room. Udo set up Thengel's sleeping space while others handled their own.

His modest ceremony complete, Belec wandered by the Guardian of the Thorn where he sat at the edge of the water. He waited until the tall elf looked questioningly at him.

"Arandel," he said. A statement.

Thengel nodded. "I know. I've been thinking of him, too."

"He'll head for the Golden Lamb. And if we're sought . . ."

"I know. We need someone to watch for him, to bring him to us."

Belec shook his head. "Our faces are known. It's too dangerous to wait on the streets for him, and it would be folly to return to the inn now that we're sought." He blew air through pursed lips. "Perhaps we can leave him a message. . . ."

"I'll go." Udo, done with Thengel's kit, had joined them, overheard their words.

The Guardian looked at the scrawny youth. A plain face: unlined, high-browed, narrow-jawed. But distinctively Udo. "Your face is known also," he said.

"Not half as well as yours. You stand out, but I'm like any Turakemi. Only the Hounds will recognize me at a glance, and them I can avoid. I'd have to be blind not to see them coming." He smiled.

Valdarius, seeing the conference, came to join the discussion. "Excellent idea," he agreed. "Udo can pose as a servant or a clerk and haunt the streets near the Lamb. Sooner or later Arandel will arrive, and he will only be traveling the one way, from the King's Road. Wait, spot him, keep him away from the inn, and bring him to us. Easily done."

Thengel looked skeptical, but Udo nodded enthusiastically. "If any ask why I loiter, I'll say I'm waiting for my master to finish business with the ferenye. That can take all day, I've heard. It's that simple."

"And if things are not that simple?" asked Belec.

"I don't know that we have a choice," said Val lightly. "Arandel is on his way to the very place we've left. We cannot let him blunder there. Someone must intercept him, and Udo seems the likely choice."

Thengel grunted. "I hate to agree, but I agree. Everyone on the watch must have a lookout for our descriptions, and humans at least will pass much longer in the streets than any of the rest of us. And a boy will be less noticed than a girl."

He gave his squire the nod. "Go you and sleep now," he ordered. "No telling when Arandel will be here, but he cannot fly, horse-bound as he is, so you can get a few hours of rest before you need to be on watch. Be out there at dawn, in case he's found relay horses. Though he may not arrive 'til mid-morning or later. You could have hours to wait. Do it safely. Udo."

The young man ducked his head. "You can count on me, Sir." He flashed a grin and went to seek his bedroll.

Thengel heaved a sigh. "Sending children to do my work for me. I feel terribly old right now."

Belec shrugged. "Everyone chooses their own path. No choice is unworthy."

Thengel quirked a lip. Comforting enough to Onderye's Keeper of the Path, no doubt, but he found it difficult to apply such lofty philosophy when it came down to the flesh and blood that relied on him for protection. . . .

Katrije joined them, sat beside Thengel on the pond embankment. "Jaele's asleep. And Hagar's snoring in your room, next to ours. I hope he doesn't wake her up."

Thengel smiled; Valdarius snickered quietly. Katrije looked sharply at the bard. "She needs her sleep."

"As do we all, I'm thinking." Thengel stretched and yawned.

Katrije cast an uneasy eye at the vaulted ceiling. "Hagar said it was safe here. Dwarf-sense, I suppose. But I'm going to have a hard time sleeping knowing all Old Town is right over our heads."

"We must be right near the center of it," Belec mused.

"More like at the base of Hakkonkalye," Val said. "Part of the wall beyond there"—he pointed to a northeastern pillar—"is part of the subfoundation of Hakkon's war keep. Of course, it was mostly earth-buried by time that warlord claimed Etjorvi for his own. His architect, Segir Halfnose, decided to build on ruins instead of clearing new ground because they didn't have—"

"Wait; wait!" Thengel waved a hand urgently to stop Val's lecture. "You mean, if we wanted to get to Dalin, and he's in the dungeon—?"

"Then he's somewhere just beyond those pillared walls. Yes." Valdarius smiled. "I was going to mention that. Between Hagar's stone magic and Cath-mar's little surprises, I suppose you can win through to him readily enough. You will be quite out of sight of whatever guard they have. You can grab your Truthsayer at your leisure, and when Udo reunites us with Arandel we can then decide how to wrest the Tapestry from those thieves." Valdarius offered a flourish and a bow. "You're welcome."

"Pompous—" muttered Belec.

Thengel shot him a glance that stilled his tongue.

"I suppose," Thengel addressed the bard, "that you also have an easy way to stop Joro's band from marching on board a ship first thing in the morning and sailing away with the relic?"

"No," Valdarius said lightly. "No ideas at all. I have to leave *you* something to do, now don't I, Thengel?" He turned and walked away before the warrior could do more than work his mouth.

"Ass." Belec finished his sentence.

Thengel punched him in the arm. "Go wake Hagar," he said excitedly. "We have foundation stones to look at."

Belec stood. "And maybe Jaele will get a little more sleep, poor kid."

Rubbing his arm, he went to find the dwarf.

CHAPTER 46

THE COMFORT-CHANT died to a hum in Dalin's throat and then trailed into silence as meditative stillness fell over him. Half-entranced, he tried to go outside himself, to shift into that place where he was *more* than his physical shell. To become a lattice transparent to the many discomforts around him: calm of body, calm of thought, calm of emotion—

What if they kill me? his mind interjected.

He reacted to that in his gut, and hot tears of fear and frustration welled beneath his eyelids. He did his best to redirect wayward thoughts from such doomsaying but succeeded only in falling into a gloomy reverie. Granmar was not around to grump at him and show him a better way to do things. His distant family knew nothing of his plight; they must think he was safe with the Truthsayer. He had no one near who cared about him, no real friends. The elves had only been using him, and now he was accused by a powerful man who had his own ill-doings to cover up. . . .

Don't dwell on those things.

Not permitting his mood to continue its downward spiral, he also could not find anything uplifting in his situation. His body felt calm, but somewhere deep inside he clamped down hard on an urge to take action, on the need to *do* something. It was an urge he could not act out, powerless as he was in this prison. His emotions were no calmer, underlaid with a frisson of tension that sat upon his shoulders and wrapped him like a heavy blanket. His thoughts were disjointed and would not stay in line, wandering instead into unruly dream segments and stray memories. Yet shying away, always, from the dilemma of his situation, one that his thinking mind believed it should have a solution to but did not. . . .

In this strange tangle of calmness and urgency, of focus and wandering attention, Dalin passed time in a blur in his desolate cell.

He heard a jarring noise once, twice, somewhere overhead, but it did not really register, and he did not so much as open his eyes to look about.

Later, much later, another misfit thing tugged at his attention. It was a sensation he would have shrugged off or ignored, but it persisted, grew stronger. He felt something *shift* nearby, and that demanded his conscious attention. Something was abruptly different in his surroundings and close enough to alarm a deeply dozing part of himself.

His eyes flickered open and for a moment he sat in disorientation. He felt heavy, ponderous, not wanting to move his limbs, his breath huffing from his mouth, and that persistent feeling that had niggled him into wakefulness:

The stones had changed.

He had not communed with the stonework of this cell, no more than his initial touch and explorations had permitted, but now there was something he could not ignore—something vibrant and yet stressed . . . *tortured*, almost, about the rock nearby.

He came fully awake and sat forward, the feeling of weight and mass slipping away from him in the darkness. He strained to see a visual counterpart of what he so clearly felt in his bones.

The rock was more alive than before and *moving* in a way stone never did unless compelled. Perhaps his vision had become a little more accustomed to the darkness, for he had a sense of where the rear wall was, the one of dressed stones and pillars that flanked a side of his cell. It was there that things felt so very different.

He uncrossed his legs, muscles aching with long inactivity, and came up on one knee. He peered toward the sensation of living stone. It was nothing he could see with his physical eye but something he perceived just as clearly as when trees in a forest spoke to him.

Aaaaaaaaaahhhh.

It was a primal groan that felt like boulders grinding together, heard more in his head than his ear. But unmistakable.

And then a sound his physical ear detected; a sqooshing slurp, like a pour of mud down a slide face. Startled, he came to his feet, adrenaline punching him fully alert.

Something stirred by the far wall, something black upon black that oozed forward with the sucking sound of muck disturbed. . . .

"Ah!" he yelped, disconcerted, and scrambled back in unthinking reaction.

Something thick and moist plopped to the ground around the moving shape, and the smell of boggy earth came to his nostrils. He groped automatically for the dagger he no longer carried, taken by the watch—

"Dalin? Where are you?" the muck-monster hissed at him.

He let out a breath as if gut-punched. How had it known his name?

It did not come closer, nor did it grow. More plopping sounds, more wet-earth scent.

"Come on!"

It was a voice he knew, tinged with impatience. "This way won't stay open forever, you know."

He could not believe his ears. "What . . . ?"

"It's me. Katrije. If you want out of here, come on!"

He could barely collect himself. From deep meditation, the scrambling from a monster, to this—

He shuffled forward in the dark, toward the darker spot ahead of him. His foot trod mire-soft ground the same moment her muddy hand touched his arm.

"Here." She tugged him closer to the wall. "Sit down. On the ground. That's right. Now—right ahead of you is this mud puddle . . . it's like a bog."

She told truth; his feet had already found the clinging cold wetness of it.

"If you hold your breath, you can go through and up the other side, all right? It's narrow, not wide. You'll have to scrunch down. Go headfirst."

"What?" he asked again, stupid with disbelief.

Katrije sighed in exasperation. "Look. This is the ground beneath the wall, bespelled. The wall straddles it. Cathmar holds the stones in place, while Hagar keeps this bog here. So: you go down here, forward a few feet, then stand up on the other side. Simple, yes?"

When he did not answer, her voice became sharp. "If I can tolerate this slime, you can, too." She moved as she spoke, stepping back into the muck and, from the changing level of her voice, promptly sinking down a ways into the ooze. "Come on. You don't want to be in this stuff when it turns back into stone."

She found his hand in the dark, tugged him forward. As the sense of her words sank in, Dalin shook off the surprise that had paralyzed him. He followed her lead and slid into the mire, waist-deep before his feet found solid bottom.

Clinging, cold, grainy slush soaked him to the skin quickly. He shuddered.

"I'll go first," Katrije said. "This is a narrow passage under the wall. You're broader in the shoulders than me; if you get stuck I can grab your hand, and there's help on the other side to pull you through. I know you're bigger than I am, but I hope not *too* much bigger, or you'll never make it through." On that reassuring note she let go his hand and waded closer to the wall. "It's pretty disgusting, though. I'd hold my nose if I were you, and make sure you keep your eyes closed."

The next moment she lowered herself beneath the mud that closed over her head with a soft sucking sound.

He felt the goop shift around his body, the entire mass quaking with her motion, and then he was alone.

He shuddered again. The texture of the muck was unnatural; this was hardly a pond to go swimming in. . . .

He hesitated until he remembered her caution to him: soon this would turn to stone again. He had a vision of the ground solidifying around him, crushing him, maybe, or trapping him underground without air—

Before his imagination could give him further reason not to, he pushed forward, took three deep breaths, then dropped beneath the surface.

It took all his effort of will to do it. It felt more like pudding than mud. It coated his face with pressure and cold grit, creeping into nostrils he had forgotten to plug and flowing with intrusive fingers into his ears. It plastered his hair and oozed through to chill every root on his head, it seemed. Then he was pushing forward with his legs, groping ahead with hands and arms, feeling the side of the narrow pool he was in. His feet slipped on the bottom, and he scrambled to push and pull himself along. He started to come up and bumped his head against stone.

I'm right under the wall.

Right under the wall! Solid rock overhead, no air to be had. . . .

Don't panic! he lectured himself sternly. *You're halfway there. . . .*

He hadn't taken in enough air, it seemed, and suddenly his lungs wanted nothing more than the suicidal action of inhaling. He pressed his lips more tightly shut and squinched his eyes harder as he pushed on through the mire, a guiding hand on the stonework overhead giving some leverage. He scraped against rock at the side of the channel to his right and squeezed past more of it on his left—a narrow channel, indeed, beneath this wall. No doubt so the weight of the stone overhead was less likely to collapse into the bog—

Anxious to get out of there, lungs aching as he groped blindly forward, his hand suddenly flailed into open air.

He was clear of the wall. A hand gripped his own, and then he was breaking the surface on the other side.

"Pffawww!" Gasping for air, he shook his head free of the clinging ooze. He swiped at filth-covered eyes and clogged nose.

"Here." Katrije pressed a cloth into his hands, something to wipe his face clear with.

He snorted horselike into it, then banged at the side of his head to shake muck out of his ears. Another swab at his eyes, and he blinked them open.

And stood in the mire, gawking at his rescuers.

The bunch of them clustered in the corner of a short hall, one wall of which formed the backside of his prison cell. "See?" A fellow in green hose and buff tunic motioned broadly with the lamp in his hands. "There's nothing like an Eldur memory for maps! I told you it must be here!" He spoke triumphantly in precise enunciation. His gently slanted eyes suggested elf blood, but Dalin did not recognize him.

Dalin knew Thengel, though, and the tall elf replied to the other, "We're grateful for Hagar's speech with stones also, to know where along here Dalin was to be found. But thank you for your guidance, Val."

The way Thengel said that Dalin could not tell if he was sincere or was merely placating the lamp-bearer. From the expression on his face, neither could Val.

Hagar ignored them both and crooked a finger at Dalin. "Out of there, if you do not want to stay there forever. Soon this will be mud no longer."

The young man hastened to get out of the boggy hole, clambering to solid ground by Katrije, as unrecognizable in her coating of muck as he must be.

Another stranger sat against the opposite wall, an elf with a pale, misshapen face and long silvery white hair. He sighed in a rasping dry voice, "That wall will hold 'til the ground is solid again. I need to rest, though."

The others turned to him solicitously, forgetting Dalin for the moment. Thengel helped the sickly one to his feet and, accompanied by the lamp-bearer, started off down the corridor.

"Let us return," Hagar said to the two young people. "Your misadventures later we can discuss, Dalin. You need to get cleaned up first, and we have no shortage of water to do it with."

He turned to follow his companions.

Katrije remained by Dalin's side. "Welcome back," she said. She smiled, a clear spot breaking through her silt-smeared face, and that the cleanest part of her from head to toe.

Gone from near-despair to a most unexpected rescue, his feelings spiraled into giddy relief. And Katrije, his most unlikely rescuer. She stood, bedraggled and filthy beyond belief, and he realized he must look exactly the same. From the expression on her dirty face she found his appearance amusing as well: no doubt every bit the muck-monster he had taken her to be.

A smile tugged at his lips, and she stifled a snicker. Then they burst out laughing together.

All of a sudden the mired ground nearby changed consistency, the moisture sucking out of it with a curious aspiration. They stepped hurriedly away and looked behind them. The surface dried in seconds, then metamorphosed back into the solid rock it had been. They edged nervously away from that spot.

The transformation marred the flagstones that paved the floor—but on the other side of the wall, in his lately abandoned cell, Dalin suspected the evidence of Hagar's magic would blend right into the rest of the rough ground here. It would not be evident to his captors how he had escaped.

His grin widened. Somehow he found that thought highly amusing.

Walking with Katrije and chuckling still, he followed the others down the lamp-lit hall.

CHAPTER 47

KATRIJE TOLD DALIN of their destination as they backtracked through passages and crawl spaces of the underground ruins. When Dalin did not seem to recognize the goddess's name, Katrije prompted him in a nervous undertone. "A Forbidden One," she muttered. "Valdarius is a learned bard. He says it's a legal sanctuary here. Still . . ."

The pair exchanged uneasy looks. Dalin did not know the names of the Defiled Gods, long shunned in remote Nevi, but of the Kin Wars and heretics he had certainly heard. He learned in a few minutes all Katrije had recently discovered about the goddess of small waters and travelers' refuge. When they emerged into the chamber of the warm spring, it was evident that the elves assumed they would simply bathe in the pool to get clean of the grime that besmeared them.

That thought brought the pair up short at the edge of Seidrun's water.

Belec noted their unease as they stood staring at the dark pond. He came over to them.

"It's no sacrilege," he said reassuringly. "The water spirits here are happy to serve a greater purpose, and they've been long unvisited. Go on in."

Dalin looked from Onderye's priest to the gently steaming water before him. But for the stonework built up around it, it seemed to be a warm spring like many others Dalin knew in Nevi and near Kodanit's Spire. He glanced to the rocky outcropping where water burbled forth, the place where Belec had appeased whatever divinity was here with an offering of dried flowers and the lingering scent of incense in the air.

Mire oozed uncomfortably between Dalin's toes, and he gave in to temptation. "Fris be with us," he murmured, hoping the goddess of the hunt and wilderness places would have some influence at a natural spring, no matter who had once blessed it. With that he sat on the embankment and began to ease out of the muck-soaked garments that clung to him.

Katrije followed suit a little more hesitantly. The young Turakemi studiedly ignored each other as they stripped and eased into the warm water, pulling their clothes in after to rinse them clean as well.

The silt they rinsed off clouded the pond for a while, then flowed visibly away, drawn by the slow current that fed the underground drainage of the pool. With clothes clean and hair and skin free of muck, they began to relax in the warmth of the water.

"Nothing to it," Dalin said, glancing over to his companion. "It's just a warm spring like any other."

As Katrije slung wet auburn locks back from her face, he averted his eyes—it was not unusual for unrelated persons to dip naked together in natural springs, but it was not done to stare. Yet curiosity drew his eyes sideways to her again. She was boyishly slender of build but for a slight swelling of hip—and her breasts were most assuredly those of a young woman, something he could not quite cover with a hand if he reached out. . . .

The brazen thought made him blush, and he turned away so she would not notice. He rested his hands on the lip of the embankment where he had placed his borrowed clothes and forced his attention elsewhere.

The stonework was clearly man's afterthought, like all this great hall that surrounded the pond. The bed of the pool seemed natural enough, silt and fine gravel beneath his toes, and he looked in vain for some obvious sign of a Forbidden One's existence in this refuge. *Is our presence welcome here?* he wondered uneasily. Might they accidentally give offense, incur unwanted attention from a thing once divine, now cast out and shunned? And who knew how those supernatural energies might manifest themselves . . . ? Belec's assurances were fine, but he was the cleric of a foreign god, and how attuned could he be to forces native to Tura-kem?

While Katrije splashed behind Dalin, he closed his eyes and sent his consciousness questing into the stone.

He did not know what he expected to find. He sought only to touch the energies around him, as he did in the forest or alpine peaks, getting a feel for the temperament of his surroundings. And this was difficult—he did not have a ready rapport with the worked stone of man's constructions. He remembered how lifeless the quarried rock of the inn had felt to him, until Hagar Gemsinger touched it with his dwarfish magic, causing rock to sing back to him in turn. . . .

The stone beneath Dalin's hands felt something like that, he noticed. It was curiously vibrant, as if imbued with some strange life of its own. His eyes squeezed tighter shut. Was that the mark of divine presence here? Had long-scorned Seidrun been so powerful that her blessings continued to enfuse the space with this, this . . . near-consciousness? If stone could talk . . . if it could think, surely it would feel like this.

It was the strangest near-communion with earth-matter that Dalin had ever experienced. He struggled to grasp what he was sensing. Had Hagar noted this as well? Or was it something only a Turakemi could perceive in native stone? Surely the others would have noticed by now. . . .

Or perhaps not, he corrected himself. He had come to realize since he left the Crystal Spires that communion with stone and tree, water and ice, was not a talent shared by everyone. Not by anyone he'd met so far, in fact, except the dwarf to some limited extent. And that thought spurred Dalin to a sudden realization.

Granmar never read stone or trees directly himself, either. He never really taught me how! I discovered how on my own, after he said I could, and I believed I could, and then he asked me to talk to them. . . .

There was something of great significance here, if only he could grasp it. He remembered still exactly how it had begun: starting with the hearth stones at the scrying fire.

That was when his granduncle had first regarded him with that bushy-browed scowl that he came later to see as shrewdly appraising, not fiercely intimidating. He was newly arrived at Kodanit's Spire, building the first of many fires to come in the rock pit reserved for divination, trance work, and chanting. The first stone he had laid his hand to he had dropped like one scalded. So charged it was! Its power burned as if the stone were still hot from a fire, long-cold though it had lain.

"What is it, boy?" the Truthsayer had snapped.

"Nothing, Skan." He had called him then the honorific for wise elders, not yet Truthsayer or Master to the twelve-year-old from Nevi and "Granduncle" too familial to say to this gruff stranger.

Dalin had put his hand back to the rock, prepared this time for the charge it bore. He wasn't sure what it communicated to him; nothing, probably, except that it had absorbed the concentrated energy of decades of power workings. The next fire stone he touched held the same energy, and the next. Each one content to be part of this circle, basking, as it were, in the sunlight glow of power, the fire they would contain a mere shadow in comparison to the supernatural blaze that warmed them.

"They like it here, Skan," he had offered with a small smile as he set the last of the fire-pit rocks in order.

"What?" Granmar barked.

He faltered. "The stones. Like it here." He pointed.

"You know that, do you?" the Truthsayer asked sharply, pale blue eyes snapping a challenge.

Dalin shrank a bit from the old man's fierceness, but he knew what he knew. "Yes," he affirmed.

"Humph," the Truthsayer grunted. "Build a fire," he said, "with that wood there."

Wood already by the fireside, fetched by the old seer some days before. The boy picked through the wood, tossing one piece, then two and three, aside. He laid the fire foundation from what remained.

"Why do you not use those?" Granmar asked.

"Mold rot," Dalin answered simply, speaking of the bark infection that trapped moisture and turned the pith of the wood to a substance like sponge. It would burn, but not well, and smoky at that.

"How can you tell?" Granmar glowered now at one of the discarded lengths of wood, a piece of a branch that seemed whole enough, weathered on the ends, collected from deadwood off the forest floor.

Dalin's methodical work halted. He opened his mouth and then shut it, picked up a piece of the wood in his hand, and studied it in turn. How *did* he know? The branch *looked* sound enough. It had the heft of ordinary wood. It smelled normal. It just *felt* wrong. That was how he knew what wood to collect for his father's fire. How it felt.

Granmar took the stick from the boy's grip, pried at the bark with a broken, dirty thumbnail.

The bark flaked away in large scales, revealing a greenish spongy material underneath where pith should be.

The Truthsayer grunted and tossed the wood aside. "You're going to be talking to trees, boy," he declared.

And by trial and error and self-taught experiment, sometime over the next year or two Dalin had come to do exactly that.

Granmar was quick to capitalize on it: now his apprentice could return with only the best moss for kindling, find just the right wood, discover the correct bark or pith or the nature of the tree it came from. All skills most useful for the shamanistic practices of a recluse who could rarely be bothered to climb down from the obsidian spire he called home.

Those were abilities Dalin had come to take for granted. He assumed Granmar could do the same, if he ever ventured out of his cave—but the elderly hermit had rarely left except to travel to Etjorvi via rune magic to answer the King's summons. And only once or twice a year did such a summons come.

246   DEBORAH CHRISTIAN

Maybe he never had the ability I have, Dalin considered for the first time. Now that he thought about it, he had never seen Granmar commune with stone or tree, not once.

In that instant it had dawned on him that perhaps he had a unique talent. It came so naturally, and yet it seemed unlike anything others did.

The thought caused him to sit down in the water, relaxing into its warmth that came up to his chin. He rested there, cradled by heat, thinking with his eyes closed, until he was overcome with drowsiness and all he could keep in mind was bed.

CHAPTER 48

THE MINIATURE BAND Thengel wore clasped on his ear worked exactly as the gnomes had said it would. In muted volume he heard what transpired at Berin's location as if he stood there himself. Earlier he had listened with distracted amusement as the Nimmians squabbled among themselves. When he lay down in his bedding he knew that the band of thieves would be off to the waterfront in the morning.

The tall elf fell asleep with that concern in his mind, doing his best to tune out not only Hagar's snores but also the muffled sleep sounds of the Nimmians across the city. Joro faced the same dilemma he did: how to get his people out of Tura-kem. He tossed restlessly through the night, dreaming of tall-prowed dragon ships upon the Sea of Lan Loros.

Weeks before, guested by the King and trading on good reputations hard-won in Kalajok, Thengel had trusted that they would conclude their business with the Truthsayer quietly and depart in the good graces of their host. In one stroke Hanno Runemaster had changed that, cast them under dire suspicion. Hammankarl might not be one to condemn the outlanders out of hand, but he could not possibly be willing to provide them transportation home for the asking—something that had seemed a real possibility but short weeks agone. Now he suspected them of treachery, and Thengel knew their activities, if investigated, would look unexplainably suspicious.

When the Nimmians stirred in the morning—waking Thengel in turn—the Guardian of the Silverthorn did not yet have any answers to his problems. A glance to the corner of the room showed that Udo was gone already. He sighed. It had been far too long a night with far too little sleep in it, and they were not yet done with the doing.

He nudged Hagar and called to Katrije to rouse the others. It was time to ready themselves to counter the Oath-sworn who worked for the Duke of

Nimm. A way home still needed to be found, but first: the Tapestry, and those who would abscond with it.

KATRIJE SHOOK DALIN awake. He swam slowly out of dreams in which stones and trees grew faces and talked to him out of mouths misshapen like Cathmar's. He shook off lethargy with difficulty, taking forever, it seemed, to fumble through his meager pack, which the elves had brought along when they fled the Golden Lamb. Gratefully he dressed in his clean Nevi leathers and followed Thengel's impatient squire to the gallery where her companions sat, sharing out a meager breakfast of trail rations from their packs.

Dalin joined them uneasily, certain they regarded him with distrust—and Hagar, he noticed, certainly turned a sharply assessing gaze upon him. Best to mend his fences for now, he thought, while surrounded by these maybe-enemies, maybe-friends. And better to know what they were up to than to be ignorant. Last night he had not wasted breath in accusations about their designs on the Truthsayer's robe, and no one had been wakeful enough to challenge him about his sneaking out and fetching the watch. Surely it was on their minds. But other things seemed more pressing in this moment, and an uneasy peace prevailed among them all.

Dalin sat beside Katrije in the circle. Thengel seemed to be collecting his thoughts, sitting with his head cocked as if hearing something whispered in the air. The Truthsayer's apprentice sat quietly, nodding his thanks for the oatcake Katrije handed him. He leaned on one hand nibbling at the hard biscuit while Thengel spoke.

"Joro's people will be leaving today," the Guardian began. "We should intercept them before they're on a ship. . . ." He spoke in a stilted manner, as if listening to someone else while he talked.

Well, this is a good place to hear voices, Dalin thought. *The stones are nearly shouting at me, I swear.* The flagstones beneath him veritably hummed with energy, and his palm on the ground felt the sensation through the flagging.

"Before they leave Eritanos House—"

Dalin listened to Thengel's hesitant ramblings with half an ear as he set down his journeybread and rested both hands on the floor.

What are you saying? he wondered. He listened. Tired, his breathing still held the rhythms of sleep patterns. Gently in, gently out . . . little muscle tension in his body. He tuned out the elf's droning.

What is there to know? he asked the stones drowsily, open to anything he might sense. He glanced at the dwarf. Did Hagar not feel this? But the dwarf listened attentively to his friend.

". . . to the docks today . . ." the Guardian of the Thorn was saying.

Dalin concentrated a little harder. The ground beneath him said nothing.

". . . we'll waylay them if we must . . ."

I'm open, Dalin thought more insistently. But nothing was coming through to him, and he heaved a sigh.

". . . Dalin already promised."

His name spoken in Nalia's feminine timbre drew his attention. "What's that?" He blinked at her.

"That you promised to show us how the Robe works. After we get it back for you."

The look on her face was pleasant, nearly smiling, her tone of voice quite ordinary.

With a chill that set the small hairs standing on his skin, Dalin knew in his gut that she lied.

It was not true: they were *not* getting the Robe back for him. If he ever had any doubt—and he had had many in his hours of soul-searching and second-guessing in his prison cell—they were dispelled in that heartbeat. He knew, as certainly as he knew his name, that Nalia did not speak the truth. What she had just said was a falsehood, and he *knew* it.

The stones beneath his hands hummed with energy just the same as before. Was his sudden perception because of his attempted communion with stone? Yet the rock felt no different. That knowingness had not come from the ground beneath him, but from the pit of his stomach. He pressed his lips together.

Nalia frowned slightly and he realized he was staring. "You *did* agree to show us how the Robe is used, yes?" She tried to prompt him out of his silence.

He licked his lips. "Not exactly." He considered what to say. What was safe to say. "I told you I'm the only one who knows how to use the Robe."

At that untruth—that he could use the Robe—his gut gave another twinge. He knew he told a lie when he said that, but his body responded just as strongly as it had to Nalia's falsehood. He took his hands off the flagstones and rubbed them together. What was happening to him?

"We are curious to understand the role of the Truthsayer," Thengel said diplomatically, drawing attention away from Nalia and her questions. "That is all. But that is something we can talk about later, after we've recovered your inheritance."

And at that Dalin felt peculiar. Thengel did not lie, exactly. His words and sentiments were true. But there was more he left unsaid—

And how he knew that in his gut, Dalin was also at a loss to explain.

The Guardian of the Thorn shifted the focus of the conversation adeptly.

"It seems they wish to march on board a likely ship, take it over, and sail forthwith. We'll need to be close behind them, stop them before they get there—"

Katrije interrupted him with a giggle. "No, no." She shook her head. "They won't be going anywhere. Not today."

Thengel looked at her sharply. "How so?"

Katrije, sitting by Dalin's side, grinned and leaned forward. "Ardrunafest," she said confidently. "No sailing is permitted during the three days of the festival. Lan Loros is a jealous god, they say, and not until he is appeased can any vessels safely leave Etjorvi, where Ardruna is so especially honored at this time of year. No ship will put out; most won't even be manned in harbor during this time."

A chorus of surprise greeted her words. She nodded firmly. "I heard it from the Hounds. Right, Jaele?"

Her diminutive witness nodded silent agreement; then Valdarius snapped his fingers. "Ah. Ardrunafest celebrates the Earth Mother, and the Sea Father is jealous. He's not appeased until King Hammankarl renews his bond with the sea in the annual Selkie ceremony. A stricture not observed everywhere but here, where the King lives—she's right. For the next three days our thieves are going nowhere." He grinned and made a seated half-bow as if he were personally responsible for this travel limitation during high holy season.

Thengel ignored the bard's self-satisfied tone. "This might work to our advantage," he said thoughtfully, "for Joro and his cohorts are unaware of this holiday. They hope to find some way to leave today. When they go, they'll be taking the Tapestry with them. . . ."

He and the others discussed options, but Dalin suddenly found he was listening to the conversation with very different ears. He tuned out much of the substance of their words and listened rather for the intent that lay behind them. He sat, palms on floor, and monitored that conversation with the gut reactions of his stomach. After a time he found it did not matter where his hands were placed. There was a knack of listening he was beginning to grasp—something akin to communion with tree or stone and yet subtly different.

It was a new way to hear what was said, indeed. And much more enlightening than the elfish plans that were filling his ears. . . .

CHAPTER 49

COMMANDER PALSTRO SLEPT restlessly, the pounding of his head waking him earlier than he wanted. He had no woman with him this night, no one to tend him with grumbled prompting but for the enlisted orderly down the hall, and that was not the kind of ministration he was in the mood for. He finally left his lonely bed with a growl and a kick at the tangled bedcovers. Dousing his head in the washbasin, he blinked sleep from his eyes and took the time to shave all but his long mustaches. It would not do to look to his men like he had just come in from a night of carousing. If only his evening had been that much fun . . .

He shook his head at wine-induced hallucinations, put on a clean gamebeson and uniform surcoat, and turned his footsteps toward the dungeon.

"You, you," he ordered two of the guards, "with me. We're transferring a prisoner. I want him in one of the small cells, handy for interrogation."

Handy for a suicide's girdle was more like it, but his excuse would stand. He'd given it a great deal of thought, and spent every waking interval in his uneasy night considering ways to make a prisoner's death seem natural, accidental, or a suicide. Such things happened now and then. Not often. Not intentionally, either, under his command. Until now.

Bjorg swallowed his unease at the prospect. After all, who would know? Only the Death Crone and the Lord Adviser. A grateful, indebted Lord Adviser.

And the prisoner, but he would not be telling tales.

The guards accompanied their commander to the farthest oubliette and lifted the grating handily out of the way. No strange noises or scents greeted them, and Bjorg breathed a secret sigh of relief. The soldiers had brought a ladder-pole with them, a length of wood notched with toe- and handholds, set with a crosspiece at the top to brace it against the ground. Together they lowered the cumbersome pole into the oubliette, saw it braced secure for climbing.

"Come, you," one guard leaned over the dark pit and barked at the prisoner. "Up with you, now. You're coming out of there."

Silence greeted his order. They waited.

"Don't make us come get you," he said threateningly. "You'll regret it."

Still no answer. The guards exchanged looks.

"Put the lamp down there," Bjorg ordered tersely. "Let's see what corner he's in." Maybe the fellow had done him a favor, tripped in the dark and really broken his neck. Bjorg motioned to the metal tray and chain he had used but hours before and put the memory of what it had illuminated from his mind. He stood, lips pursed, while one guard lowered the light into the deep cell.

The other knelt at the brink of the pit and craned his neck to locate the prisoner. He paused, then moved around to peer from the other side.

He cleared his throat and looked up to his commander. "Sir? There's no one in there."

"What?! Impossible! I saw—" Bjorg cut himself off abruptly and dropped to his knees. He stared into the oubliette in disbelief. And stared again.

Last night, a bear. This morning, nothing at all. He paled. He ordered a guard down to be certain and the other to check the other two pits. In case there was a mistake. . . .

The only mistake was that the prisoner was gone. While the guards confirmed the obvious, Bjorg closed his eyes against the throbbing in his skull. Someone would have to tell the King.

And the Lord Adviser.

CHAPTER 50

"Break fast with me," Hammankarl had invited his former Lord Adviser at the close of the banquet. "There are things I would speak of with you privately in the morning."

"Gladly, Sire." Hanno accepted royal hospitality and slept that night in the White Palace. He gave brief consideration to the outlanders he had left behind in Eritanos House, then dismissed them from his thoughts. They were a problem that could wait while he discovered what the King's interest in him was.

The Selkie King's chambers were at the rear of the Palace, overlooking a broad landscaped greensward, a narrow strip of rocky beach, the seal rocks, and the islet called Ship Rock in the fiord beyond. Hanno followed the servant who escorted him to breakfast only because it was expected of him to do so. Hanno knew these rooms well enough in spite of his long absence from them—the privy hall, the King's antechambers, the Queen's quarters. There, this new thing the runemaster had heard of, a royal nursery for the one-year old Einar, infant heir to the throne. And beyond, the light, eastern-facing chamber used as the King's morning room.

The servant announced Hanno into a room with white-painted walls and gilded decorative panels, windows of startlingly clear glass, the large panes assembled into frames as large as a man and opening like doors directly onto a breezy balcony. Hammankarl stood by the far windows; the runemaster paused just inside the doorway to make his obeisance, as deep a bow as he had offered in the banquet hall the night before.

The King waved him to the white-clothed table set before the open balcony windows. "Enough of that, old friend," he said. "When we're in private, that has never been necessary between us."

Hanno inclined his head in gratitude. "Your Majesty is gracious," he said, taking a seat at the King's gesture. The table was spread with boiled eggs and soft, creamy cheese, fresh baked rolls, smoked salmon and capers, tiny pickled squab eggs, ruby red plums and green-striped gooseberries, a jar of gingered fruit compote. The hot Istanian beverage they called *kaif* steamed in a silver pot warmed with its own chafing flame, and he sniffed its tangy aroma appreciatively. "Now *that* I have not tasted since last I attended Council here," he said.

"It has been far too long," Hammankarl replied, and poured kaif for the runemaster with his own hand.

That sign of royal favor was not lost on Hanno, and he relaxed a little more. The King seemed intent on putting him at his ease, on making him welcome.

"Warden's Light." Hanno raised his delicate porcelain bowl in both hands and made the toast that spoke in praise of enduring things: duty. Relationships. Friendships.

Hammankarl raised his bowl in kind, the short webbing between his fingers evident in the morning sun that streamed in over the balcony. Hanno's gaze met liquid brown eyes as they toasted and drank to each other. He wondered for a moment if he ever truly understood this man of mixed heritage, so human at times and by turns so thoroughly Other. As always, he had only his own humanity and personality to rely upon in their interactions. As he had found himself doing last night, he quickly fell back upon the genially shrewd comportment that seemed to serve him best when dealing with the King of Tura-kem.

He waited until his host filled his plate and then served himself from the delectables before them. "I'm sorry that it is such a tragic circumstance that bring us together again, Sire."

Hammankarl dipped his chin. "As am I. You were a fox among the hens last night, Hanno, with the furor you created. Wulfram was downright discomforted by your presence, did you notice?"

Hanno raised an eyebrow. "Yes, Majesty, I did."

"You know he took your place on the Council." Hammankarl smiled to himself. "Rather self-absorbed, is Wulfram."

"Are you are unhappy with his advice, Sire?" It was the sort of blunt question that Hammankarl had valued from him in the past.

"He has not the perspective you brought to the office. You are the most senior of the runemasters resident in Etjorvi, are you not?"

Hanno nodded. "There is myself. Wulfram. And that youngster, Aedir, not yet Fen Ehrden."

Hammankarl put a slice of salmon atop his roll. "It's been long since I've had truly far sighted advice from a runemaster. At least five years, by my reckoning, since you vacated your appointment." Hanno stiffened at that remark, but the King was intent upon the precise placement of capers on his salmon. "I haven't seen you since your return from Koram's menhir, those years agone," he added casually. "Why is that?" He bit into the bread and fish, looked expectantly at Hanno as he chewed.

The question took the runemaster by surprise. He composed a careful answer between sips of kaif. "You had plenty of capable advisers, Sire." He shrugged. "And I had much work to do after my pilgrimage. Work inspired by Koram," he hastened to add, divine direction being a compulsion even a king could understand.

"So much to do you could not visit? Found no time at all?"

Hanno cursed Granmar once again for how the Truthsayer had stymied his contacts and his ambitions, so many years wasted. He let a look of real regret come over his face, and he knew, with the influence of the Staje rune still upon him, that he would be heard only in the most sincere manner. "It is with my deepest regret that it had to be so, Your Majesty. I was under the guidance of a dream-vision. Koram gave me to learn and see, the studies after to do. . . . I was not permitted further contact with the world. Not for a long time." He thought of Granmar. "Not until . . . certain goals of mine were accomplished."

Hammankarl sounded at least a little appeased. "Did you accomplish what you had hoped you would?" he asked. "You said it was . . . *imperative,* was the word you used at the time."

"It was a productive time," the runemaster said, speaking purest truth. Forced into self-imposed exile, he had used his time at the menhir to fast, to undergo ritual that granted insight from Koram, god of learning, wisdom, and the magic of runes. Runes, created by dwarves, adapted to the use of men, and imbued with the power of esoteric symbology. How much more he had come to understand, in consequence of that time! He had come into unique wisdom in the wilderness of the Frislan. And he had scried several special sigils: the Truth rune among them and the Persuasion rune he wore now on a thong around his neck—though none of that would he be sharing with the King.

He poured more kaif for Hammankarl. "But surely you are not interested in the dry recountings of a runemaster's fasting and dream-quests?"

Hammankarl smiled, for they both knew how little he cared for ascetic disciplines. "My interests are more in this line," he admitted. "When you returned to Etjorvi then, you said you no longer had an interest in affairs of the world. Yet here you are once again at court, albeit as bearer of sad tidings. So I am moved to inquire: do you still feel the same? That matters of royal interest in Tura-kem are of no interest to you personally?"

Hanno busied himself with the dish of squab eggs. "My interests have changed of late, Sire. I find myself inclined once again to share Tura-kem's interests as my own."

"Ah? Now why is that?"

"For one thing, my esoteric studies have come to a conclusion, and I am ready for other pursuits. For another . . . perhaps it is this tragedy with Granmar. It reminds me that some persons have a valuable service to render the Throne, and it is a great loss when they are not around to do so. Or are unwilling to. For whatever reason." He caught the King's eye across the table. "I know I have been of service in the past, and I have not forgotten what esteem you held my humble services in then."

"And if you were to serve the crown more actively—would you want to leave a post again, for these solitary practices that have occupied you in the past?"

Hanno spread his hands. "What can I tell you, Sire? It is not often one comes under such a compulsion as I was under. But once in a lifetime, perhaps. Were I to take office once again I can vow to you in good faith that I would stay with it, as long as I could be of true service to you."

"I'm relieved to hear you say that. Freggi was not my ideal."

"And what is your ideal, Sire?"

Hammankarl's eyes flashed. "Don't be coy, Hanno. You know. He would be as you are. As insightful. As wise. As adept in reconciling different factions. Willing and able to be hard-edged when necessary, yet knowing how to compromise and still come out ahead." He smiled. "I remember how you defused the Koribi demands for tribute when I was new to the throne. What opportunists they can be."

"Indeed, Sire." Hanno smiled at the memory also, but for different reasons. Koribee had not truly expected to wrest tribute from the independent nation of Tura-kem, but their demand had been a lever to bargain for trade concessions. Hanno had given it to them, for a clandestine percentage of ferenye tariffs and great benefit to his own purse. Until Granmar had become suspicious. . . .

Hammankarl pushed his breakfast plate away. "I want to make you Riedskana," he declared. "High Councillor. It's what you should have been instead of Freggi, may he find peace in Ruhnkeil. Here's our chance to rectify an oversight. Will you take the office?"

Hanno let surprise show clearly on his face. He had been hoping the King might work around to this, but to put it so soon, so openly, on the table . . . It was gratifying that their rapport of old still held. Triumph welled within him.

"Sire. I am flattered. But it's something I must consider carefully."

"Surely you've had years to think about it. Don't tell me you've never considered it before . . . ?"

Hanno assumed a sheepish look, and Hammankarl laughed at the rune-master. "I knew it. What's to consider? A quarter-year has passed, and I need a High Councillor still. You must say yes. Don't refuse me again."

Their eyes met before the runemaster nodded once, decisively. "If you insist . . . I would be honored to serve."

"Good man! I'm glad to hear that. It is time, and past time, to see you there." Hammankarl was grinning like a young boy.

"When would you have me begin, Sire?"

"I'll make the announcement at Ardrunafest—the opening ceremonies, I think. Also a fine time for investiture in high office, yes? There will be a ceremony and parade ready-made to honor you. And the Earth Mother as well of course," he hastened to add.

"Of course," Hanno agreed.

"It's settled, then."

"You do me great honor, Your Majesty. I swear I'll serve you well."

He knelt, kissed the royal hand extended to him, and Hammankarl raised him to his feet. "I've needed a good man by my side and to help leaven these endless debates in council. It will be good to have you back again."

Hanno bowed in reply. "I'm honored," he repeated, and was searching for better words when a servant's gentle cough interrupted them.

"Your Majesty," the liveried footman said, "a messenger from Hakkonkalye begs urgent audience. He comes from the garrison commander."

Hammankarl beckoned the man in with a finger. The soldier came to attention, addressed the open windows beyond the King's head.

"Sire: Commander Palstro reports that the Truthsayer's murderer has somehow contrived to escape Hakkon's Keep. The watch has been alerted and is on the lookout for him." He finally forced his eyes to meet the King's. "The commander extends his deepest regrets. The prisoner was completely secure, and he simply . . . vanished. Magic is suspected. This is being investigated as we speak."

Hammankarl's face clouded over. "I thought Hakkonkalye was inescapable."

"So did we, Your Majesty." The officer spoke grimly.

"Magic, you say. Then find Master Nehvros and take him back with you. Tell him it is my desire that he apply all his resources to this investigation."

"Yes, Majesty."

"Immediately."

"Yes, Majesty." The soldier bowed and retreated hastily from the royal presence.

The King turned cold eyes on the runemaster. "The wretch must be guilty, or he wouldn't have run."

"Indeed, Sire."

"Though how he got out of the Keep . . ."

"I've never heard of such a thing."

"Nor I. This is defiance of my will, as well as murder. When he's found, he'll be dealt with accordingly." The King's affable mood was gone completely, replaced by chill resolve in the tone of that Other that Hanno had noted and hoped to avoid.

"As you say, Your Majesty."

The runemaster agreed politely, but he suddenly wanted free of Hammankarl's company. His mind began to race. It would not do for the King's men to find Dalin and have a chance to question him. Less now than ever before.

No, he resolved. *It would not do at all.*

CHAPTER 51

Udo lefyan was just another spindly youth in the ferenye district, one of the many clerks, messengers, and trade apprentices whose business occupied them in the commercial byways of the quarter. His squire's tabard of red and gray had been left behind for this scouting expedition, and he lounged in simple tunic and trousers on the bench outside the King's Crown, two doors down from the Golden Lamb. Now and then he took a turn across the street to stretch his legs before the trade halls, but always he studied passing horsemen, keeping an eye out for Arandel.

Some hours into his watch, he noticed a leggy black horse that slowed near the gate to the Lamb. Mount and rider were dusty and road-worn; they had clearly traveled far and long. One glimpse of long blond hair tied back and a narrow face was sufficient to launch Udo from his bench seat. Between the long-maned Daile and the Silverleaf's distinctive look, the squire knew he had found his quarry.

Darting past slower-moving tradesmen, he reached the gate just in time to intercept Arandel. The black tossed his head, and the elf glared at the person who had dashed in front of his horse. Then recognition flashed across his tired face. "Udo!"

The youth moved closer to the Silverleaf's side. "They're not here," he said in a low-pitched voice, and Arandel leaned down to hear him better. His voice dropped even lower. "We're sought by the authorities. I'm to take you to our hiding place."

Arandel raised an eyebrow. "An interesting tale, I am sure."

"Come away from the inn," Udo urged. "It's the last place they stayed and may be watched."

The elf frowned. "Then you should have caught me farther up the street. Come." He held out an arm, swung the youth up behind him. For all his height, the squire was not yet a heavy burden—though enough of a load to a hard-ridden horse. Arandel reined Daile around. "He's not up for a race, but he'll take us quickly enough through streets." He put heels to the black, and they trotted away from the Golden Lamb.

"Where to?" he asked over his shoulder.

"First a stable," said Udo, "then the hideaway. Turn here." He pointed, and they began the way to Jarlsdock.

CHAPTER 52

THE COMMERCIAL WHARVES were in Old Town, between the fish market and Hakkon's Keep. Stone quays abutted wooden docks that ran out into the cold waters of the Dannenborch. Across the narrow sound was a shipyard and moorage for fishing skiffs, but vessels large enough to trade or sail the distance across the north sea moored here, where their cargos had been welcome since Hakkon first fortified Etjorvi.

If Joro's band hoped to find transport to Nimm, they would have to look there among the trading knarrs and the occasional longship. Those vessels were destined for coastal trade in Tura-kem, or Tren to the southeast, while some intrepid few would venture around northerly Cape Venstil, an ice-bound route with narrow channels passable only at the height of summer.

"What will they try to commandeer, do you think?" Katrije asked Dalin as they walked toward the waterfront.

He followed her through the twisting back ways of Old Town, trusting her city-sense to navigate this strange maze of buildings. "It's impossible to guess," he replied. "I know nothing about ships."

"Hm. Nothing too big, I'd bet. The more crew needed for sailing, the harder it'll be for them to keep control. Don't you think?"

Dalin had no opinion to offer and shrugged in response. Hakkonkalye was much more on his mind in this moment, the square keep tower visible now and then behind rooftops as they walked. He wanted to stay out of close sight of the garrison walls, and hence their circuitous travel to the docks.

Katrije noticed his furtive glances. "Don't worry," she said, intuiting his concern. "You look so different now, the guards wouldn't know you if they bumped right into you. Or the watch."

That thought was unsettling, but her observation was true. He did look different than the night she had met him, that was certain. Comfortable once more in woodsman's leathers, his hair back in a Nevi braid, the Truthsayer's apprentice now looked like a steading clansman come to town, not the well-dressed city drunkard he had appeared on the night of his arrest. Maybe there was anonymity in his change of appearance. He hoped so, for he wanted to move as safely as he could.

His need for action had fit in well enough with Thengel's plans, and that was why Dalin found himself now in the streets of Old Etjorvi. Yellowbeard and Kaylis were on their way to the docks alone, the Guardian had reported—the better to maintain surprise while they scouted ahead for their fellows, who would come to the waterfront later in force. Joro did not know yet of the stricture on sea travel for these three days of Ardrunafest, so his plans were as yet unaltered.

Berin, the unwitting eavesdropper, remained at Eritanos House, and so Thengel would be ignorant of what transpired at the waterfront. He wanted eyes on the street, to discover what ship the Nimmians would target and where they might be waylaid later.

Perhaps Thengel would have chosen someone else to spy for him, but seeing his chance to take personal action, Dalin had insisted on going. "I'm not standing aside while you deal with my inheritance and future as you see fit," he had declared flatly. He half-expected the elves to challenge him on that, to show him the iron fist they had been hiding in their velvet glove— but they did not. The Guardian of the Silverthorn bowed to his adamant stance, and the Truthsayer's apprentice had not had to confront them about their intentions of theft and trickery. Not yet.

"I want to go, too," Katrije had said. "I know the streets best."

Thengel could not argue with that, though he had tried. "I could use a guide," Dalin agreed, his endorsement finally deciding the Guardian. Who, it seemed, wanted someone of his party to escort the young man anyway, when all was said and done.

Dalin had anticipated that. If he could not go alone, he would rather have Katrije along than anyone else. Of them all so far, she was one who had not lied or told untruths in her conversations with him, from what he sensed. Besides. He liked her.

And so the pair left the refuge of their fellows, slipping through the backways of the dyers' courts and Tanners' Quarter, on to the northeastern segment of the old walled city. Emerging from an alley, they positioned themselves halfway between the royal docks at the fortress and the commercial quays. From there, they could watch traffic on Janske Way, the road that circuited the Keep and gave onto the waterfront. Dalin shot uneasy glances toward the grim walls of the old fortress and prison, but he knew he was not recognizable from a distance. With an effort he settled down to watch the passersby with Katrije.

She plucked at his sleeve, and he followed her a few paces away to a street vendor's stall. Clams steamed in a kettle there with wild onion and kelp pods, while strips of chicken marinaded in oil and tarragon grilled on little sticks nearby. The aroma made Dalin's mouth water, and the novelty of the sight stopped him in his tracks.

Katrije, more used to city living, was better prepared for the opportunity of the moment. She reached into her pouch and bought food for them both. In a moment Dalin held four meat-laden sticks between his knuckles while she cradled a small mound of steaming clams on a straw tray.

She looked around them, clearly in search of something; then her face lit up. "Wait," she said hastily, shoving the helping of clams into Dalin's free hand. "I'll be right back."

Before he could protest, she was gone into a nearby chowder house. Several minutes passed, and he began to wonder what he would do with his burden if Aral Yellowbeard should walk down the road in that instant. Before such an apparition could appear, however, Katrije returned. Good Turakemi that she was, she came bearing a leathern jack of ale in hand, a typical breakfast drink and large enough for them to share. "*Now* we're ready," she said, grinning. "Time for real food, not trail rations."

He grinned his thanks to her and followed her to an alley corner where empty shipping barrels were stacked outside the wall of a chandler's shop. They made impromptu seats there, facing Janske Way where all the waterfront traffic passed right before them. They shared the food out atop another barrel and lit into their repast.

"Thanks." He smiled. "I never would have thought of this."

"Oh?" She popped a clamshell wider open with her thumbs, plucked the steaming meat out with the tip of her knife. "You were hungry, weren't you?"

"That's not why." He talked around a piece of chicken already half-devoured. "I mean . . . I've never seen such a thing." He jerked a thumb toward the stand they'd just left.

"Not even along the King's Road, coming here?"

"Not near the few inns we stopped at, no—and elsewhere I didn't notice, we moved so fast along the way. And I don't carry money."

"Do you not have any?"

He snatched a clam from the tray, tossed it between his hands as it cooled to the touch. "Some. A handful of coppers, a few silvers. In my pack. It's not a hunter's habit to carry coin, but Granmar said I ought to take some for my travels."

"Granmar?" Katrije passed him her knife.

"The Truthsayer," he explained. "My granduncle."

"Oh." A strange expression flitted over her face. "I didn't know you were related."

"My mother's mother's brother."

"I'm sorry to hear that," Katrije offered.

He glanced at her, then busied himself intensely with the clam. "I lived with him for three years. He was my only family for the while. Well. Maybe not family, exactly. He was my Master. My teacher."

She swapped ale jack for knife and took another clam. "Are you angry about his death?" she asked quietly.

He looked at her sharply, startled, then moved his gaze to study the flow of passersby. "Angry. Yes. I was. At first I just couldn't believe it, and then I was angry."

"And then you got sad." It was a statement, not a question.

"Yes."

"Have you grieved for him, Dalin?"

He drank from the jack to conceal his expression and only faced her after he had wiped foam from his lip. "Grieve him? Of course I grieve him."

She shook her head and answered her own question. "I don't suppose you've really had time yet. You've been on the move since this happened, in the company of strangers. . . . Don't wait too long, though. Mourn him. Do ritual for him. It's important to honor him properly and really let him go."

He slammed the jack down on the barrelhead, and ale splashed onto the chicken she was about to pick up. "What makes you such an authority on me and my granduncle?" he flared.

She returned his glower evenly. "I lost my parents last year," she said simply. "I know what it's like."

He felt his rage bleed quickly away. "Oh." He handed her a dry chicken strip and took the drenched one himself. "What happened?" he ventured shyly.

"House fire," she said shortly. "In Kalajok. I suspect . . . it was started. On purpose."

"Started?" A fire set to burn people out . . . that was a disturbing new concept to Dalin. "But why?"

Katrije lifted a shoulder and let it drop. "To frighten us? To kill us? My father was a trader of furs—do such people have enemies? I don't know. It was summer. The kitchen hearth was cold. At midnight the whole house was ablaze." She sounded bleak. "I just don't know."

Dalin blinked. Witnessing Granmar's death had been bad enough, but he still had his family in distant Nevi. Katrije had lost more—and must have been at risk herself, if her whole house was engulfed.

"That's terrible."

"So is what happened to the Truthsayer," she said softly. "But you can't let it drive you."

His face clouded over. "What do you mean by that?"

"If you avenge a death, or not, or get justice . . . that's one thing. But how you deal with that death, in your heart, is something else entirely." She looked him square in the eye. "You need to deal with it in your heart, Dalin."

His brows pulled together, but something made him hesitate to voice the retort that came to mind. Was that how she saw inside him? Because she had been bereaved, too, and knew, somehow . . . ?

Granmar's ghost had not come demanding vengeance, that was true. He had come in dreams, though, trying to get Dalin's attention, and Dalin could not listen, or would not. He only saw that moment, the Truthsayer tumbling down the obsidian slopes of Kodanit's Spire, and that vision shut out anything his granduncle's spirit had to say.

I listen to stones and trees and now, it seems, to the guilty consciences of elves. Why do I not listen to Granmar?

A troublesome question, and one he could not answer. He turned his face back to the traffic on Janske Way and shared the rest of his meal with Katrije in silence.

CHAPTER 53

SEMBROIE KINLAYIK RAN her calloused sword hand over the flank of the massive gray warhorse. There was no doubt about it; she knew this beast, Turon, nearly as well as she knew his rider. She patted his neck as the Caerlian charger stamped a hoof in the stall and motes of straw dust swirled in the late-morning sunlight.

In this land of blond people and blond horses, the gray and black and dappled beasts of the Caerlian outlanders had not been impossible to find. Into the mix a chestnut or two, a few brown mountain ponies and mounts from the King's own stables—and there the long-maned, road-weary black stabled but an hour before. She had just missed catching Arandel, she judged by the horse she recognized.

"At least we've found this much of them," she said to her lieutenant, Luell Half-Hand, standing in the aisle of the teamsters' stable. *Thanks,* she thought, *to the stable boys at the Golden Lamb.* They who had slept in the loft and overheard Thengel's words in the night.

"We'll see them safe at the same time we safeguard ourselves. Where we'll have them to use later and can get to them at need."

How very like the Guardian to say that about his horses. A warrior sometimes shy and bumbling, sometimes uncannily shrewd and able. And softhearted; more so, she thought, than a leader dare be. Perhaps it hindered his leadership after all.

It had for certain if he had truly thought to evade her pursuit.

She looked over her shoulder to Luell, a militant cleric of Gunnar Strongarm. Together they had fought beside the Caerlian band in the jarldom of Kalajok. It was to their mutual sorrow that they must bring them to account for their crimes, or at least to account for charges against them. Captain-General Molstroe was certain of their perfidy, but Sembroie did not want to assume Thengel's guilt. She had thought him stalwart. Yet she wrestled down anger every time she thought of Nalia's late-night deceit and agreed that their actions thus far incriminated them far more than the retired Lord Adviser's allegations had. From the look on his face Luell was aggrieved also. Flight. Deceit. The scorning of the friendship and battle-bonds between them. . . .

"Set a double watch," she ordered, "out of uniform. Sooner or later, they'll come back for their horses. And when they do, I want one to tail them and one to summon us."

HANNO SWEPT INTO Eritanos House in a far grander manner than he had left it, escorted by two footmen and a small honor guard of the King's Hand. They had come to retrieve his meager belongings and accompany him on to his home, a modest but comfortable dwelling in the southwest of Etjorvi at the very outskirts of the city. He had begged leave of the King to refresh himself from his travels in the privacy of his own domicile, which Hammankarl had granted. The former Lord Adviser promised to return to the White Palace in ample time to participate in the festival ceremonies and his own investiture as High Councillor.

And so he would—just as soon as his personal business was complete.

He bore an arrogant smile of self-congratulations behind his gray-touched mustaches. He did not bother to hide it as he rapped sharply on the door of the Glassblowers' Suite. Rudic opened the door to him. "Come," he said. "We'd been wondering where you got to."

Hanno smiled openly now, a feral expression, as he stood on the threshold of the suite. Possible responses to Rudic flitted through his mind, quickly assessed and as quickly discarded. *They still think me a hireling, someone at their beck and call. They are about to revise that opinion entirely.*

"I bring distressing news, Joro." His voice rang commandingly, not in the querulous but cooperative tone he had adopted with them in the past. His manner put a frown on the other's face, but he continued regardless. "The Truthsayer's apprentice has escaped."

The man's high brow creased, but he did not look particularly upset by this information. Nor did he press for details, but inclined his head as if to say, "Continue."

Hanno stroked a mustache. "Perhaps the gravity of this situation is lost on you." His words were touched with condescension. "Let me put this in a way you will better appreciate. The man who would kill the boy for us found him vanished instead. Magic is suspected. If Dalin is free and if he talks, then

I fall under suspicion and *you* will not be able to get out of the country. You will probably be arrested yourselves. I want him found before the King's men catch him, and I want him killed."

Joro regarded Hanno cooly. "He really is not our concern."

"I suggest you make him your concern."

"We have what we came for."

"Perhaps not."

Silence joined them at table for a long minute. "What is that meant to imply?" the Nightrunner finally asked.

"Imply? Nothing." Hanno sniffed. "But here are facts you should know. Tomorrow, at the opening of Ardrunafest, the Selkie King will appoint me to be his High Councillor." His smile turned nasty. "If you leave and when you leave is mine to determine. If I am at risk, I do not see the prudence in you departing Tura-kem."

The outlander heard this threat without emotion.

"And the Tapestry?" the runemaster added, shrugging, his biggest threat dropped oh-so-casually into the mix. "Who is to say who should have proper custody of the Truthsayer's robe of office?"

His words hung in the air. The flare of Joro's nostrils was the only sign of reaction provoked. Hanno held his gaze unblinkingly—and it was the Nimmian who looked away first.

"You do not veil your threats very subtly, runemaster." He addressed his words to the far wall.

Hanno chuckled. There was a time for subtlety and a time for plain talk. He smoothed his right palm across the cool tabletop, the blue and black lines of intricate runic tattoos visible on the back of that hand. The more adept one became, the more complex those markings of esoteric rank; since his visit to the menhir, his natural skin was barely visible from knuckles to elbow on that arm. His was not a power they could trifle with, as they were discovering.

He wore the Persuasion rune as always of late, but he owed it to his common sense and experience to know the next right thing to say. They had seen the stick; now let them taste the apple.

"I do not threaten," he said. "I merely state facts. And thoughts of concern. As the Tapestry should be of concern for you. You hope to take it for use elsewhere—and yet one wonders the obvious: do you know how to use it?"

The question, the change of tack, startled the outlander, and Joro looked back at him sharply. "What concern is that of yours?"

Hanno prevented a smile, knowing not to mock the man at this juncture. He kept his voice factual, neutral of charge. "Do you?" he pressed.

Joro regarded him. "We have sources who will know."

A muscle clenched in Hanno's jaw. That might be true, and if so, his greatest leverage was gone. But perhaps . . .

He continued with his strategy. "I urge you to give that more thought," he said with studied casualness. "If your sources are mistaken and cannot help you, then you return to your duke with a prize he cannot employ." He shook his head. "How disappointing that would be, for all of you. I, on the other hand, can show you how to call upon the Robe's power. So you would return with a useful item."

It was a safe-enough promise with the influence of the Staje rune about him—and a blatant lie. But they could not know that. "Thus my proposition: apply your skills to finding Dalin so we can dispose of him." His blue eyes snapped with sudden intensity. "Before the King's men find him and we are all put at risk. Kill him, and I will show you the secrets of the Robe in exchange. I deem that a fair trade."

Joro's eyes narrowed. "You never said that you understood this relic's use before. I find it strangely convenient that you have this sudden knowledge."

Surely that was not true suspicion speaking. With the rune magic around him it could only be the Nimmian's natural caution at work, not outright disbelief. In confidence of that, Hanno met his gaze steadily.

"Did you think I would tell you all I know? Hardly." He quirked a halfsmile. "Sarilos asked me to help you acquire the Robe, not show you how to use it. I've done that much. But I do tell you there are few in Tura-kem with the wisdom or the knowledge to grasp how the Truthsayer worked. I am one of those few. Why do you think the King is so anxious to have me as High Councillor? Surely that is testimony enough.

"That is my offer, and I let it stand." *My ultimatum,* he corrected to himself, meeting Joro's brown-eyed gaze across the table. *For if you will not find Dalin, there's no reason to let you live longer.*

He had already decided that to recover the Robe he would have to have these outlanders killed. There was but one reason to keep them alive now, and that was that they, of all persons, had the skills and the self-interest to ferret out the Truthsayer's apprentice before the boy talked or was found by royal authorities. If they did not comply, there was no reason to risk their continued existence, not with Hanno on the verge of his long-sought appointment. Besides the boy, only these foreigners could convict him with their secrets, should they decide to talk.

Joro regarded the runemaster's confident stance, took in the aura of certainty he wore. The Nimmian finally dipped his chin in acknowledgment. "Very well," he said. "We'll find Dalin for you. And then you'll show us the secrets of the Truthsayer's robe and help us return to Nimm. Agreed?"

"Agreed."

They clasped forearms in a grasp of accord; then Hanno stood.

"Where are you keeping the Robe?" he asked casually.

Joro's gaze flickered to the corner of the room where their packs were ordered, among them the small cedar chest they had stolen the weaving in.

"Good," said Hanno. There was no need to reveal too much of his interest now; let them think they would be keeping their prize—until the time came to wrest it from them. "Guard it well." He stood and Rudic saw him to the door. "We'll be talking again soon."

"I'm sure of it," Joro acknowledged. The two men nodded a wary farewell, and Hanno departed.

The master archer shut the door behind him; then he and Joro locked eyes and, with a mutually shared thought, burst out laughing.

"What's so funny?" interjected Berin. His recitation over beads had long since stopped. "He thinks he can use us. It's plain to see."

"Yes, it is." Joro nodded. "Surprised I agree with you? Don't be. We're using each other. All that is in question is who will get the last laugh and walk away from the game with the Tapestry and their freedom. Or their lives."

"I don't follow." The Oathkeeper looked perplexed.

"It's quite simple. Our plans haven't changed."

"You said we'd find the boy."

"Yes. Said."

"Ah."

"As I say: our plans haven't changed." Joro's hand rested on the pouch at his belt—a little larger than the average coin purse, of cloth patterned with red and black threads in an intricate design of Koribi origin. The soft bulge of it hung heavy, half-concealed by the overhang and folds of his blousy white tunic. "Let him anticipate stealing the Robe from us." He smiled in self-satisfaction. "Marvelous, what security Koribi wizardry can produce, don't you think?" His eyes twinkled slyly.

"Korib—? Ah." Berin remembered small talk from earlier. "The item delivered while I was absent last night."

The Nightrunner nodded. "From the merchant we spoke with after dinner. Yes. Our travel purse is much the lighter for it, but the Tapestry is safely ready for transport."

Berin, appreciating at last how the scheming runemaster would be stymied, chuckled in amusement as well.

CHAPTER 54

Kᴀʏʟɪs ᴀɴᴅ ᴀʀᴀʟ rode from Eritanos House through a nearby plaza and turned onto the King's Road toward Tolvar's Gate. Neither was in the mood to rub elbows with foot-going traffic this day, and they were glad to ride above the press in the city streets. The road was congested, teeming with up-country men and women clad in leather and homespun. People had come in from surrounding villages and steadings this day, it seemed, and thronged amid the confusion of wagons and carts that had come with them. Many wore streamers of green and yellow cloth at arm or hat brim or braided through the harness of horse and oxen.

"Looks like a market day," Kaylis remarked dryly.

"Holy day," Aral noted. "Those are Ardruna's colors."

Kaylis shrugged, disinterested. The goddess of crops and fertility was one of the few honored equally on both sides of the Sea of Lan Loros; no wonder Aral, the devout clansman, would recognize the token. She, an elf who had spent many long years in the sheltered halls of the Collegium Magisterium, was little concerned with religious festivals of human origin. The bustle was a hindrance in her path, nothing more, and she urged her cream-coated Turani into a trot. She pushed past the closest knot of steading men who clogged the roadway, Yellowbeard close behind her on his rangy bay.

Their short burst of speed did not prevail for long. Across the Aelvoss in Old Town the going was slower still. They followed Janske Way around the fortress, but the closer they came to the docks, the more the press of traffic impeded them. They were nudged to the roadside to make way for a wagon coming from the wharves, pulled by oxen and piled high with barrels. Forcing passage beside it came a cumbersome wheeled sledge with a load of cut lumber and split railings.

"Make way!" the sledge driver hollered. "Cargo for the royal presentation stands! Make way, there!"

Aral sidestepped his bay up onto the walk where pedestrians might hope to pass in safety, ignoring the imprecations of disgruntled foot-goers. Kaylis remained on the cobbled street, skirting wagons and easing past a cluster of brawny tanned youths with leather-wrapped braids, their backs to the waterfront, their faces to the city.

Sailors, no doubt. "Everyone's leaving the docks," she observed to Aral. "Why is that?"

Her observation was correct: the vast flow of traffic was away from the wharves and waterfront, into Old Town and New Etjorvi beyond. They were among the few making their way against the flow of drayage and foot traffic, toward the quays.

Aral muttered something under his breath that did not answer her question. She let it go. His mood had been foul since the night before when Joro had faced him down before them all. Long overdue that was, she thought, though she kept that opinion judiciously to herself. It was not a correction calculated to sweeten the warrior's temper.

She dismissed the matter as none of her concern. Her own interactions with Aral were somewhat different, and keeping a hand on that rein was sufficient to entertain her for now.

They broke free of the worst of the congestion where Janske Way widened into the waterfront proper. They rode past the royal docks, marked by the King's golden eagle on white banners, past the customhouse, and on to the public quays near the fish market.

The tang of brine and fish filled the air. Kaylis drew rein and surveyed the wharves before them.

Close by were numerous small trading knarrs, shallow of draft, rounded of belly, perfect for coastal trade—but not apt for the open waters of the Sea of Lan Loros, nor would they likely accommodate horses. It was not essential to take their mounts with them, but the Nimmians did not have funds to waste buying new mounts every time they set foot ashore, so a vessel that could transport animals was Joro's clear preference. That meant the next-larger class of ship would serve them better, and she wheeled half about to regard the long cargo ships by the customs dock.

These were not the dragon ships of raiding fame—the narrow-waisted, shallow-draft vessels of war—but their close cousin: shorter-keeled, broader of beam, deeper of draft, some with two masts for sails and most with fewer oars than the military galleys. Four such hulls were moored beyond the custom house.

She nodded meaningfully in that direction. Aral was sullen this day; he hesitated, as if he were about to debate her choice, then seemed to think better of it. He dismounted along with her and walked out upon the dock.

The ship closest to shore was a beehive of activity, with fifty or sixty men offloading cargo onto waiting wagons. It was the largest galley docked at the moment, a bank of oars twenty to a side testifying to a crew that rivaled a dragon ship's in number. The warrior looked a question at her, and Kaylis shook her head. There were too many here to intimidate with their meager numbers or force to order with her arcane arts, if such should be necessary.

She considered the vessel across the way: double-masted, a shorter bank of oars, but deserted. There was no crew aboard, or if so they were below decks in the cargo hold. An unmanned ship would serve them naught; they passed that one by for the time being. The vessel beyond it was nearly as deserted, with two sailors keeping lazy watch, laughing over jokes as they spliced rope on deck.

The fourth hull looked most promising: single-masted, eight oars to a side, probably manned by no more than twenty men—that could be manageable, should they need to compel obedience. There were seven crewmen visible on deck; from conversation shouted into the hold there were more occupied below.

Mooring lines creaked as the pair walked up the gangplank, Kaylis slightly in the lead. A bearded redhead saw them step on deck and regarded the woman with openmouthed surprise. Without so much as inquiring their business, he leaned over open decking and shouted into the exposed hold for someone. In a moment a larger version of the redhead emerged from below, an older relative, perhaps: a giant of a man with red-blond hair, stripped to the waist, with smears of pine pitch and moss stuck to his brawny forearms. He held a pitch-covered tamping stick in his hand, for he had been caulking something, and looked unhappy with this interruption to his work.

"Aye?" he asked the newcomers, managing to make it sound like a challenge.

Aral bristled and his shoulders squared. Kaylis cut him off by stepping in front of him.

"We're looking for passage," she said, "or we'll hire the whole ship, if needful." *Or steal it from you, if we must.* "Are you the master?"

"I'm the owner, Ragnar Ergrim, and you're aboard the *Gull*. Where is it you want passage to?"

Aware that crew had stopped work and was listening to the exchange, Kaylis came closer to the big man, and her voice dropped so it did not carry beyond his ears.

"We want landfall near Nimm-on-Witholl," she said.

He laughed, a booming sound. "Not possible."

It was a response she expected; she did not let it ruffle her. "Then passage anywhere you dare put ashore across the sea."

"Cannot."

Also not unexpected. "You would sail to Tren, would you not?" she asked. Though that lay to the south and east, not due east as did Nimm's capital. . . .

He nodded.

"How much for passage there?"

He shook his head. "I've no cargo taking me that way."

"Suppose we hired your ship for the voyage. How much?"

Ragnar looked thoughtful. "How many to travel?" He looked from her to Aral, who had moved up beside her.

"Five, and horses."

"Passage alone would be a crown apiece. But as I say, I've no reason to sail there. To hire ship and crew for the voyage? Ten days there. . . ." He shrugged. "Three crowns a day."

"Three—!" Aral sneered. "You're a thief."

Ragnar folded his massive arms on his chest and looked down at Yellowbeard. "I've a crew to pay, stores to lay in, for there and back again. Three a day."

Kaylis's hand on his arm stilled Aral before he could retort. "How much have you got on board already, in the way of provisions?"

Ragnar pursed his lips. "A few days only. We're just in from a run around Cape Venstil. We haven't enough on board to make for Tren."

Kaylis's smile touched her eyes. Tren might be a ten-day voyage, but Nimm-on-Witholl was only three, in the direction of currents and prevailing winds. This ship, commandeered, held enough supplies to sail at once and get there quickly. But let this man believe Tren their destination. They'd get most of their money back once they were at sea and took over the ship.

"How long before you'd be ready to sail?" she asked

He scratched his beard, considering. "Three days."

"We'll pay five crowns a day to leave today."

His eyes sparked with interest, but he shook his head. "Can't."

"I won't pay more," she countered.

"It's not the money," he said regretfully. "No one sails 'til Festival's over." He jerked a thumb over his shoulder toward the sound beyond the harbor.

Kaylis looked in that direction, where steep cliffs and forested slopes rose sharply above the fiord. A crease appeared between her brows. Across the harbor inlet was a long, low-lying line upon the water. Her eyes narrowed, acute elvish sight taking in detail at this long distance.

A line of logs, it seemed, lay in the water, stretching from where the city wall ended to a point beyond the shipyard on the opposite shore of the harbor. She looked back to the man before her. "What is that?"

"The sea gate's up," Ragnar replied. "Log boom. Harbormaster calls it 'testing the harbor defenses,' but they do it only during Festival. If you make port during the midsummer moon, you know you're staying 'til Ardrunafest is over. That's why I said three days. I'll take you then."

Aral scowled at Ragnar as if the log boom were his own invention, but Kaylis walked past the pair to the far railing, studying what she could make out of the bobbing water barricade. Logs, chained together—and she who could summon lightning, was she to be thwarted by a work of wood and chain?

She thought not.

She stared again, this time with her other-sight, looking beyond the physical to the arcane energies in the area. There, a yellow gleam to the city walls spoke of shielding against magical assault. But upon the log boom itself she saw nothing that suggested arcane or religious protections. It did not seem warded.

Ragnar came up behind her, Yellowbeard close on his heels.

"How often has this harbor ever been attacked?" she asked.

Ragnar chuckled. "Never, since Kin Wars' end, and back then they had no sea gate at all. This is a new precaution, introduced thirty years ago when Nimmian raiders threatened this north coast so fiercely."

Kaylis nodded. That would explain what she saw, or rather did not see, in this harbor defense. It was a precaution after the fact, one the Turakemi did not really expect to need, and the cost of magical protections for it was probably too great to justify the constant expense. How long would these logs last in the water, anyway? Or the ordinary metal that bound them? Replacement of sections of it would invalidate whatever spell was placed on the sea gate, and the cost of renewing spells every time a repair was made. . . .

Her mood brightened and she changed the subject. "And what are your men about, today?" she asked the ship's owner. "You seem very busy here, for a crew not planning to sail."

"Ah." He waved the tamping stick in his hand. "Minor repairs. Nothing that hinders our seaworthiness, though," he hastened to add.

"I'm glad to hear that." She smiled at him.

"I want the work done so we're all ashore for the evening fair, tomorrow. Work comes first, though."

She nodded understanding. "You'll be here tomorrow, will you?"

He nodded. "Into the afternoon."

"I'll be back at noon with my friends, then. They'll want to see your ship. See, too, how you'll accommodate our horses. You can do that, yes?"

He dipped his chin. "I'll have to lay in hay and straw. We've some grain on board, but not enough for ten days of voyage."

She smiled winningly at him. "We'll see you later, then," she promised, and took her leave with Aral.

The sulky warrior unloosed his commentary as soon as they were ashore. "Why did you say tomorrow? Joro wants to leave today."

She shrugged. "If they're caulking the ship, best let them do it before we trust to the sea in that hull, don't you think?"

He snorted. "We can't get out of the harbor anyway."

"Oh, I think we may."

He made a rude noise with his mouth. "And if we do? If no one is free to sail for this time, then all eyes will be upon us when we leave. If we're violating some law or decree, do you think there will be no pursuit?"

She looked at him askance, one eyebrow raised slightly. "Think you I cannot send a storm-wind to deal with any who would dare to follow us?"

"Well. That may be so," he conceded. "I still say it's risky, should we even win free of the harbor. The ship won't be properly supplied; we might be followed—we should just take horse and ride for home."

She sighed, wondering how he could not see past the length of his nose on matters of strategy. Or did he argue only because it was Joro's plan they followed?

"How far is Nimm by ship, Aral?"

"Three, four days in fair weather. So?"

"How far by horse?"

He paused. "Longer"

"Much, much longer. Twenty days south to the Tren border, perhaps, if all moves swiftly. Three, four days more along that coast. And then, oh—what? Another twenty-some days north to Nimm-on-Witholl, if we make it through warring clan territories without unexpected trouble. Yes?"

Yellowbeard pressed his lips together and said nothing.

"That's why we took ship here, and why we need to take ship home again. Duke Arn is not willing to wait months to have the Tapestry in his hands. You know that, not if it can be avoided. For that matter . . . as long as a sea route lies open to us, I don't know that the Great Oath will let us comfortably turn aside and take a slower course." That thought was disturbing, and it had not really occurred to her until this moment. Not that they had as yet tried a circuitous route in the execution of their mission. . . .

"If we can't get to sea, we *must* take horse," the Terbal warrior returned single-mindedly to his argument. "They won't drop the sea gate to let this one ship down the Dannenborch."

Kaylis took rein and swung lightly into the saddle of her palomino.

"Don't be so certain of that," she said over her shoulder. "The Turakemi may not do it willingly, but I venture they won't have a choice about it."

Aral gave her a puzzled look. She inclined her head to the north, along the waterfront. "Come with me," she said, and started in that direction.

Past the fish market they rode, past the docks where skiffs and small craft moored, to the far northern tower that fortified the most seaward end of the old city walls. They dismounted and walked to the foot of that bastion. The rocky outcropping that formed the base of the tower also provided the anchor point of the log boom. The sea gate was moored with reinforcing chain and cables, leading to a single wrist-thick chain that connected log after log in a bobbing, wavering line across the harbor. A similar anchor point stayed the far end of the line across the water.

Gulls squalled overhead as Kaylis stood on the rocky shore, observing this deserted corner of Etjorvi's defenses.

"Like I said," Aral began, "there's no way—"

"Hush." She raised a hand, spoke sharply. As she knew he would, Yellowbeard heeded her. She continued to stand and stare, seeing the defenses now with her mundane eye, now with her other-sight. Finally she turned to her companion, a cold smile on her lips that did not touch her eyes.

"What are you looking for?" he dared to ask finally.

"Exactly what I've found," she replied. "Ordinary wood and ordinary chain—as vulnerable to lightning as I could hope. This won't hold us in the harbor when we're ready to leave." She spoke confidently. "Let's tell Joro. I'll need to prepare for this, and for the voyage. As soon as I have, we can sail tomorrow."

They remounted and rode away.

CHAPTER 55

Their departure through the waterfront crowd was as easily observed by Dalin and Katrije as their arrival had been. The woman's long mane of near-white hair was as distinctive as her angled eyes, her snow-white leathers, the mincing palomino she rode; she was not someone easily lost in a crowd, and hers not a face the Truthsayer's apprentice was likely to forget. The stocky yellow-bearded man who accompanied her was equally unforgettable: Dalin shuddered, remembering that rough hand in his hair and the cruel sneer on a face about to spit.

The Nimmians were unaware that they were observed. When they had first walked out along the wharf, the youthful spies crossed the road to lurk by bales and crates stacked near the customhouse. They were lost from sight against the background of fishmongers, sailors, carters—but their quarry was easily watched down the length of the dock.

They followed the Nimmians to the north wall, saw Kaylis reconnoiter the sea gate, and faded once more from sight until they had departed the waterfront entirely.

It was Katrije who thought how to approach the ship the enemy had briefly boarded. "They'll want supplies for a short voyage, yes? So we'll say we've grain, chickens, hardtack, water for sale; do they want to buy any?"

Dalin nodded; it made sense, though it was not what he would have thought to do. He was more guileless than that: he would have asked outright, *"Where did those people want to go and when are you taking them?"* But Katrije thought such directness might excite suspicion or cause the sailors to lie, if they planned to go to Nimm.

I bet I could sense if they were lying, Dalin mused to himself.

He had no chance to test that ability, however, for Katrije's ruse worked quite nicely. Ragnar dismissed her offer, saying he had his own supplier he liked to use, thanks all the same. "But what would you charge for hay and straw? Enough for five horses for ten days to Tren?" She had promised to let him know a price from her father and scampered back the length of the dock to where Dalin awaited her.

"That's the ship all right. They're off to Tren when Festival ends. Or so he thinks."

"We'd best report back."

She agreed, and they rejoined the traffic along crowded Janske Way.

They walked in silence. They had spoken little since their frank words about Granmar and the death of Katrije's family. Each had entertained his or her own quiet thoughts until the Nimmians had appeared, and then they'd been too occupied for idle chatter.

Dalin glanced sidelong at the auburn-haired squire beside him. There was a great deal he'd like to ask her about, but none of it was anything she'd want to tell him, he was certain. How had she come to be with Thengel? Was it because she was orphaned? That touched on bereavement he'd rather leave be for now. He wondered, too, about the dragon he had heard mentioned—but that would lead to her adventures with this strange collection of outlanders she traveled with, and he didn't have the patience to hear about the elves right now.

Were the fortunes of this young woman from Kalajok truly so intertwined with those of the Caerlian adventurers? As Udo's seemed to be, and even the young page, Jaele? A squire owed fealty to his—or her—sworn lord, Dalin knew that much, but when that was as good as a Nimmian. . . .

Do I really want to know her loyalty lies with them? They're trying to steal the Robe from me.

He bit his lip and glanced again at Katrije. She walked beside him in the trousers and tunic of any young man in service, her gender making no difference to the practicality of her garb. She seemed confident and able, and not at all like any modest Turakemi girl he had ever known. His experience being limited mostly to cousins in backwoods Nevi steading, but still. . . .

Is she a willing part of this thievery? He wondered about her goodwill or ill. *She hasn't lied to me yet, that I know. I could ask her. . . .*

He could hint and draw her out with some ploy or another—but why be roundabout? After all: what harm would the truth do? He was the Truthsayer now, was he not? By default, at any rate, and he knew the truth to be a powerful thing. It made people uncomfortable, but it also could not be denied.

They turned into the side streets that would keep them out of sight of the fortress garrison. As they left the press of bodies and listening ears behind on Janske Way, Dalin made up his mind. He swallowed nervously, then interrupted the silence with a bluntness worthy of Granmar himself.

"I know you want the Robe," he blurted. "That Thengel and the others want to take it away from here, back to Nimm with them. But it's mine, and you—they—have no right to. So I want to know: why do they desire it so? They can't even use it."

Katrije's steps faltered and she shot him a look of concern, her lips suddenly tight. She continued walking, tension stiffening her shoulders.

"Well?" he prodded, committed now to this truth-probing. "I don't know what they really plan to do to avenge Granmar's killing for me. That's not their battle, anyway. But this, with the Robe. I want to understand it."

Katrije cleared her throat. "You ask good questions." She glanced toward him, saw his steady eyes on her, blushed, and faced ahead once more. "I can't answer them, Dalin."

"Can't or won't?"

She waved a hand. "Both. Neither. It's not for me to say, what bits and pieces I know of the Guardian's affairs."

"Why?" he challenged. "Are you sworn to secrecy or something?"

She stopped abruptly and faced him. "Secrecy, no. My Master does not have deep, dark secrets, like you are supposing. But I hear things in confidence now and then, and I'm expected to keep them in confidence. They are not my tidbits to gossip."

"So you won't tell me why they're trying to steal the Truthsayer's robe?"

She gave an exasperated sigh and began walking again. "Oh, Dalin. They're not trying to *steal* it. If they could have talked with Granmar—but it was too late for that." She caught herself then, as if she had already said too much.

"What?" he prompted.

The squire shook her head. "I would love to set your heart at ease, truly I would, but I think you must ask these questions of Thengel. Only he can tell you what you want to know."

He let her words rest between them and walked for a bit in silence. He felt unsettled. She was utterly sincere. She really did wish to offer him some comfort, and her honor or her loyalty prevented her.

He wondered how he knew that—then had to smile as the realization came to him. *I'm sensing her like I would a tree. Feeling her energy, just as I listened to the elves, last night. This morning.*

He chuckled to himself. He felt himself doing it, half-unthinking: like straining one's ears to catch a whisper, only it was a straining of the very fiber of his being, an orientation toward the object—or person—of his interest. Listening extra hard, being extra alert, and his gut told him what he needed to know.

Katrije had heard his quiet laughter as they walked. "What's so funny?" she asked.

"Oh," he said cryptically, "my natural reflexes are taking on a life of their own." For it felt a natural part of him, this way of sensing. . . .

"You seem to do just fine with your reflexes," she remarked, glad for the shift in conversation. "From what I hear."

That caused him to do a double take. He'd told no one of his expanded ability to sense things. What was she talking about?

"The elves said you're very good in the woods, for a human." She chatted on a bit nervously. "And your way-finding is wonderful. Mine's not good at all, not in wilderness"—she shook her head—"though I'm rarely lost in a city. And your shape-shifting, like on the glacier—"

"I'm not a shape-shifter!"

"Thengel said your footprints were different." She glanced his way. "Maybe you used animal-sense to cross the ice. . . ."

Thengel? Ah, that table-talk on the night he had met Katrije. The elves had discussed him while he sat wine-hazed, and now he barely recalled the conversation. They had tried questioning him then, too, had they not? About the strange prints he'd left and the trance he'd fallen into that had led them all across the glacier.

He shook his head. It was nothing like Uncle Segrim, though. *That* was shape-shifting. He'd seen it only once, the great brown bear-form of his uncle crossing the foggy taiga far north of Nevi's walls.

"My uncle could do that," he volunteered. "Animal-sense, as you call it. He used to come and go across the Skjelis glacier all the time, until Elsta set a trap for him one afternoon. . . ."

Reluctant to talk about himself, he found it much easier to talk about his uncle. Then his grandfather, the river-walker; his father, the hunter; even Granmar, gruff and reclusive. . . .

Katrije was a good listener. She asked questions that caused him to open up. Then he realized he had been talking for the last many cross-streets and they were already picking their way through alleys in the Tanner's Quarter. He suddenly fell silent and his footsteps slowed.

How did she do that?

That was more talking in one stretch than he had done in years. *In years.*

Of course, Granmar had never been quite as interested in what he'd had to say. . . .

She turned to see why he'd fallen behind. He had come to a stop, and she walked back toward him.

"Sorry," he said, blushing. "I've been babbling like a drunken runemaster during Lost Week."

"Not at all." She reached out, took his hand. "Come on." She tugged him along until he walked beside her again. He held onto her fingers a little longer than necessary—or she held his. They bumped shoulders as they walked; suddenly aware of how close they were, they dropped hands and moved a little apart. He avoided looking at her, and they fell into silence again, this time a companionable warmth between them.

The unexpected closeness was both comforting and awkward. Dalin fell back a little to ease his tension and followed her lead through the narrow alleyways, eyeing her as she walked—boyishly slender and yet softly curving, even beneath the concealment of her masculine garb.

He felt his cheeks redden again.

She was definitely nothing like his cousins in Nevi.

CHAPTER 56

THE DOCKS WERE quiet. Most of Etjorvi gathered in the south of the city, thousands from town and country filling the King's Road and the Wool Market fields for the opening of Ardrunafest.

Ragnar was as eager as any for the food, the drinking, the amusements, the sights that Festival offered But once they were swept up in it, it would surely be the full three days until his brother and crew could be scraped together again. Grouse they might, but the captain's will came first, and it was Ragnar's single-mindedness that held his men occupied at the nearly deserted waterfront. He would see the *Gull* seaworthy before they abandoned her for carousing or trusted their lives to her for a Tren run afterward.

There was not a cloud in sight on this high summer day, and the late-morning sun shone hotly down into the hold of the ship. Ragnar welcomed the direct light, all the better to spot the mars in wood where he'd noted a bore worm infestation while caulking. He tipped more turpentine from the spouted pot in his hand, dousing the wood and the unseen denizens that threatened his livelihood. Bad enough to find them in the hold. His brother Danmar would soon be over the side, swimming in the cool waters of the bay, diving to look for signs of damage in the planking of the hull.

The burly man scowled. There was always the shipyard across the harbor, and a drydock ashore if the worm rot was severe, but that would eat the profits from the Venstil run. No, turpentine was the cheaper fix, if it would serve, if the infestation was small. . . .

"Ragnar!" It was Danmar shouting his name, the wayward brother not yet in the water. The unexpected hail caused him to jerk, to spill turpentine on his bare feet. Fumes from the acrid solvent bit his nose, and he cursed under his breath.

"What?" he shouted back.

"Landsmen."

The ship's owner put his turpentine pot down grumbling and took himself topside to see what this interruption was that Danmar could not handle.

His redheaded brother stepped back as he cleared the hold, gesturing toward the newcomers with an odd expression on his face. Ragnar mirrored that look as he regarded the strange assortment of people that intruded upon his deck.

Most of them were outlanders with the distinctive almond eyes and high cheekbones of elves—a look he recognized from Trenish ports and west-coast trading beyond the Cape. Here, too, was a handful of youths—among them the girl from yesterday—all locals by their looks, with a dwarf bringing up the rear. All wore packs or carried bedrolls; crewmen on deck chuckled, for the collection of them looked like wayward pilgrims gone astray.

Ragnar's sharp eyes returned to the girl. He looked from her to the willow-thin fellow by her side. "I thought you were bringing me a price for hay," he said.

She shrugged. "Here is one who can discuss that with you."

"Your father?" he asked dryly.

A half-smile tugged her lip, but before she could reply her companion took a step closer to Ragnar. He stood so tall even the gigantic seaman had to tilt his head back to meet the elf's blue eyes.

Ragnar's gaze flicked to the burdened landlubbers and back to their spokesman. Their baggage told its own tale. "Not taking passengers," he said curtly. "Sorry."

"We don't wish to voyage," the tall fellow said placatingly. "But I understand you have sold passage to others?"

His fellows were spreading out about the decks, and Ragnar watched them warily. They did not look threatening, but he didn't need lubbers falling into the open hold and he hadn't enough crew on deck to police them. His brows drew down and he returned his gaze to the elf.

"I'm booked to Tren. Maybe. If they show. What can I do for you?" He asked it peremptorily. His tone conveyed not service but a challenge: *What are you doing on board my ship?*

The elf wore a loose white shirt and beige hose and tall dark brown boots. He drew himself up into a formal attitude, putting a forearm across his chest in some kind of salute or polite gesture that Ragnar did not recognize. "I am Thengel na De'reth, sir: Guardian of the Silverthorn of Caerlian, Protector of the Sacred Grove, and I am here to ask your help."

Ragnar crossed his muscular arms upon his chest. "My help?"

"Indeed. It regards those who wish to take passage with you. May I speak with you in private?"

Ragnar assessed this man quickly. He was thin as a reed and surely no threat to the muscular, brawling ship's captain. He rubbed his hand across his face before lingering solvent fumes caused him to wrinkle his nose. He spat and eyed the strangers once again. They did not seem threatening.

"Danmar. Ask our guests to wait by the port rail. I don't want them wandering."

His brother walked to the closest, a slight figure in a blue hooded cloak out of place in this weather, and began to usher the stranger to port. Ragnar returned his attention to Thengel of the lofty title and jabbed a thumb aft. "I'll talk with you. Come. Here's as private as it gets."

He led the way past rowers' benches to the rudder and the helmsman's station. They were back of the open planking that gave into the hold. Crew were still busy below, the tang of solvent and warm pitch wafting from their workspace. Arold and Ulf came topside to back up Danmar, marshaling the landsmen out of harm's way. Ragnar watched their activity with satisfaction, then leaned against the stern rail and turned his attention to his visitor.

"Have your new passengers paid you yet?" Thengel asked.

Ragnar shook his head.

"Nor will they," the elf said confidently. He pulled a pouch from his belt, tossed it to Ragnar. Though small, it was fat and round, and the unexpected weight of it caused the man's hand to dip. "But your assistance, sir, is worth my while. Let me tell you what I request."

Ragnar glanced inside the pouch. Silver. Enough to earn his attention at least. "What are you talking about?" he said to the Guardian of the Thorn.

Thengel squatted and leaned back against the rudder post, wrapping his long arms around his knees. "It starts with your prospective passengers, and what they really plan for you and your ship," he began. "Let me explain."

CHAPTER 57

WITH AN HOUR'S persuasive chat and another pouch of silver, Thengel reached an accommodation with the captain of the *Gull*. No sooner did the two clasp forearms than Thengel beckoned the adenye near and after short discussion dispatched them from the galley. Soon Udo, Katrije, and Jaele were making their way along the Jarldock river frontage.

The teamsters' stables were more crowded than before, with mounts doubled in small stalls and only two scowling stablemen on hand to deal with their business.

The older one was surprised they wanted their horses before their stable time was up. "You've paid through the week," he pointed out.

"I know," replied Udo.

"Can't pay back your money." He frowned. "I'm not authorized—"

"No matter," said the squire. "Keep it on account for us. In case we come back."

"Can't promise to save the space, if you're out of here."

Udo shrugged. "My lord can talk about it with the hostler, if need be."

The stableman grunted, seeming satisfied with that compromise. He and his fellow helped the youths saddle the ten horses that belonged to their party and bade them farewell.

The routine business of handling tack and mounts kept the adenye well occupied for a time. When they departed, the workman who followed them was unnoticed, trailing far behind the party in the empty streets. Nor did they spot the man dressed like a stablehand who slipped out a side door and made for the crowds gathering elsewhere in town.

The man walked hastily down Grove Way, one of the vast throng passing beneath the ash and elm that shaded the avenue with sun-dappled leaves.

The farther he went, the closer the crowd became, as folk gathered for the royal procession that would begin at noon. Where people clogged the roadway thickest, men blocked his path and snarled at his forward progress. Food peddlers and family groups had waited there for hours for the forthcoming parade, overflowing onto the roadway, until such time as the King's vanguard would force them back between the shade trees to make way for the procession. No one gave place willingly to a stranger pushing his way rudely forward.

Yet rudely forward the stablehand pressed. He returned snarls in kind and assumed a stern, angered look. It was intended to warn off persons who would intrude in his path, and it succeeded. His visage darkened by a scowl that was only half-pretense, he forged ever closer to the entrance to Fris's Grove, the holy sanctuary of the goddess in Etjorvi.

The Denkorvic of Fris, high temple of that sect, existed upon a few densely wooded acres far south of Tolvar's Gate. Four dolmen marked the urban woodland as sacred ground, paired pillars of rough weathered granite topped by a crosspiece, one looming at each cardinal point around its borders. Entrance to the refuge lay through the north-facing dolmen, the gateway framed by the rugged stone arch there.

Fris, goddess of hunt and wilderness, forebear of the line of Selkie Kings, was rarely honored within the confines of a building. The entire grove was her temple: blue pine and ash grew thick around its circumference, giving way to copses of birch and hawthorne around a central clearing. There, a carven menhir twice a man's height was site of altar and outdoor sacrifices. A herd of black-tailed, white-coated deer under her special protection roamed freely within the parkland, grazing on salal, mosses, and hazelnut brush, their feed supplemented with grain and hay in the winter. A small building of wooden stave construction housed the few clergy who tended this place; that modest peak-roofed dwelling was the limit of Fris's trappings of power in Etjorvi. The dedicants of the goddess were more inclined to see her manifest in the vibrancy of untouched wilderness than in the confines of a man-built town. The grove of birch, ash, and pine that was her seat of visible power in Tura-kem was mute testament to that attitude.

With the Festival of the Earth Mother at hand, Hammankarl chose this time to make official recognition of his genesis. While the city rendered all due honor to Ardruna, it would not do to slight her sister-daughter Fris, progenitor of the ruling line of Tura-kem. The Selkie King's procession began of necessity in the holy grove of his ancestor, with a formal blessing bestowed by Fris's high priest. The King would ride, then, at the head of an ever-lengthening cavalcade, north beneath the shade trees of Grove Way to

King's Road, and thence to the Wool Market field where Ardruna's cleric awaited him. The chiefest of the Earth Mother's prelates attended as guest for this annual occasion, come all the way from Vorsemye; he would formally invoke and honor the harvest deity at the official commencement of the mid-summer festival.

This routine of obeisance and blessing took place every year, concluded on the third day by the King's renewed bond with the Sea Father and, by association, with the selkie folk who were his ancestors. The pattern was predictable, and it was easy for a lone member of the King's Hand to guess where his senior captains would be found, for the royal war band performed their escort duty more visibly on this day of the year than on most others. The trooper in the distinctive white-and-yellow tabard of the Hounds did not at first recognize his comrade in arms—but a hastily muttered password earned his instant attention and caused him to let the man pass into the ring of guardsmen who kept the grove free of common spectators.

As bystanders muttered complaint at what seemed privileged treatment, the apparent stablehand walked beneath the mossy dolmen and into the holy grounds that hosted the King.

In the central meadow loomed the menhir, beyond it the clerics' stave house—King Hammankarl must be within, preparing himself for public ceremony, for outside the structure clustered dignitaries in a stance of quiet waiting: Lords Adviser, the Lord General, noblemen . . . others whose velvets and brocades proclaimed them highborn.

To the east a body of mounted horsemen flanked the side of the clearing, their war-dog-embroidered banners rustling in the soft breeze. It was easy to recognize among them the senior officers of the King's Hand, and thence the incognito warrior made his way.

He sought Sembroie Kinlayik where she sat her horse in escort formation. His commander recognized him readily, knowing him as one Half-Hand had picked for this special duty. He saluted and rendered his report to the battle-hardened woman in her high saddle. She nodded to him curtly when he was done. "Get you to a horse," she ordered. "You'll lead us back."

She turned to Luell Half-Hand and spoke in louder tones. "They move. I must go. Hold for me here; I lead this arrest myself."

Backing from formation, she snapped quick orders, and two squads of the Hounds broke off to follow her lead. Captain-General Molstroe looked her way sharply; she made a gesture in hand-sign that meant quarry sighted, and he nodded in return. He knew of her contingency plans. She was not sure she cared for the grim smile that crept across his face, but her way was clear to ride. She did, before the King could emerge from his communion in the house of Fris and formality would cause her retreat to look rude and un-seemly.

At the head of her hastily assembled troop, she walked her horse clear of the grove and out to the avenue beyond. Setting in her heels, Sembroie urged the troop on at an easy trot, the road clearing rapidly of foot traffic before the oncoming mass of Hounds.

CHAPTER 58

Dalin waited in the hold of the *Gull*, the sun-warmed space close and pungent with the scent of pitch and turpentine. He shifted uneasily. Overhead, planking lay loosely upon the deck and across the hold—enough to shelter the belly of the ship from casual sight, to hide him and his lurking companions from detection by the Nimmians when they came aboard.

He reached to the knife at his belt, a blade borrowed from Katrije, squeezed its hilt in a sweat-damp palm to reassure himself of its heft. Then the image of a Nimmian raider dead on a ship's deck returned to him, and his fingers fell away from the blade.

I won't use it, he decided. *If I need a weapon, better use something I know.* Something that did not leave throats slit but could take a man just as well out of a fight, sunk into forced slumber for a time. His hand shifted to the staff by his side, his fingers curling firmly around its middle.

Nearby, Belec and Nalia held their bows in comfortable grips, unfidgeting; Hagar sat beyond, his war hammer at rest on one sturdy thigh. Thengel stood at the head of their line, longsword loose in its sheath, his head cocked the better to hear what sounds filtered through the half-planking above. These were the faces of the adventurers already encountered by the Nimmians on the road or, in Dalin's case, in the city. It was wisest for them to stay out of sight until their trap was sprung. Val, Cathmar, and Arandel were on the deck above, working in small groups with Ragnar's seamen so they seemed part of the ordinary crew. The adenye were away from the ship entirely, waiting with the horses in an alley across Janske Way, the same place where Dalin had eaten clams with Katrije only yesterday.

The Truthsayer's apprentice regarded his companions, how at ease they seemed with this waiting, weapons comfortably to hand and ready to use at a moment's notice. "Do you plan on attacking them outright?" Dalin had asked of their battle-ready stance.

Nalia had shrugged. "If they resist, we may not have a choice."

Only Belec had responded to the expression that flitted across Dalin's face. "Best to confront them so firmly that they dare not risk defiance," he elaborated. "We won't be slaying them out of hand, if that's your concern."

It was more than Thengel had said, but it was clear from his disposition of people that the Guardian planned to challenge the Nimmians once they were trapped on deck. Crewmen and Cathmar's magic would block their retreat should they think to flee. One way or another, they would be compelled to hand over what they had stolen from the Truthsayer.

It was that last that had finally won the support of Ragnar: the suggestion that his assistance would halt a despicable crime—that he might even reap a reward for it. Yet Dalin was certain Thengel's party would not be around long enough to praise Ragnar to the authorities. When the elves finally had the Truthsayer's robe in their possession—then everything would change. They would be intent on leaving with their prize. If Dalin did not take flight with them, he would be left begging for his inheritance. If he did go with them, he would be a fugitive in the very land where he should by rights be Truthsayer.

The solution to this is simple, he thought. *They must not end up with Granmar's robe.*

Not sure yet how he could effect his resolution, the youth concentrated on being centered and collected instead. His palms were slick with nervous sweat and his muscles tight, ready to spring into action—but as time passed and the Nimmians did not come aboard, the edge of tension finally wore itself out. He settled into a state of waiting, listening to the creak of the ship at her moorings, casting about with his newfound sensitivity to the energies of intelligent beings. There was nothing new gleaned by this exercise, but it seemed to become easier each time he tried it: there the feeling of stoic calm from Hagar, of impatience from Nalia, of anticipation from Thengel . . .

Then it came, what they had been waiting for. "Ho!" a woman's voice called in greeting, and footsteps transmitted in muffled tones through the deck as hard-heeled boots trod the wood overhead. Ragnar's rumbling baritone answered the newcomers; to Dalin's ears there was a muffled exchange of conversation, though Thengel gave a soft laugh and shook his head as if he followed the talk distinctly. He crooked a finger, and the concealed adventurers came to their feet. The Guardian pulled his sword quietly from its sheath, then set foot to the steep-angled stepladder and advanced three rungs upward on it. He set his free hand against the plank overhead and halted there, head bent and listening, hand and shoulder poised to shove past the obstacle the moment it became needful.

Feet moved on deck and came closer to the hold. "We'll bring the horses aboard," a man's voice said. "We'll want to see how you'll accommodate them. Is your hold large enough?"

The plank scraped of its own accord, nudged by a booted foot on deck.

"Here, now," came Valdarius's voice just fore of the mast. "That won't be of interest to you."

Footsteps moved away from the hold. "Oh?" the man retorted in challenge.

"Now," Thengel hissed to his fellows. He heaved the plank aside and was up on deck a moment after.

By time Dalin stood in the bright sunlight, the Nimmians were surrounded. Sailors pulled hatchets and battle-axes from concealment beneath coils of rope and behind barrels. They stood in a semicircle between the strangers and the gangplank, with Cathmar at readiness by the railing. Arandel stood aft and his cousins fore, with bows aimed at the thieves. Dalin moved to the harbor side of the ship, while Thengel and Ragnar together confronted the small group before them.

But why, Dalin wondered, did the outlanders seem so at ease? Taken by surprise and outnumbered like this, they should at least be discomforted. He quested forth with his other-sense and was disturbed to feel confidence in these rogues. There was consternation and surprise there as well—but beneath it all, a feeling of conviction and unshakable confidence.

There was no time to mention it to Thengel. A brown-haired Nimmian in a white tunic stepped forward. He kept his hands carefully clear of his sword and the double daggers each side of his belt and gave a tight smile down the length of Thengel's sword.

"You, sir, I seem to recall from a woodland ambush. A failed ambush. Trying to rectify your errors, are you?"

The man's cockiness took Thengel visibly aback. "I'd like to know who dogs our footsteps so persistently," he continued. "I don't believe we've had the pleasure. I am Joro Narialnos, trade emissary of Lord Sarilos, former Koribi ambassador to Tura-kem. I have my credentials in my saddlebags." He tilted his head shoreward, where five horses were tethered on the dock. "And you are . . . ?"

He let the question hang on the air, his authoritative words and hand flourished in polite introduction as if this were a court reception. His tone carried quiet disdain and a hint of sarcasm, as if Thengel were present without an invitation.

The elf drew himself up in unthinking response.

"Thengel na De'reth," he proclaimed, "Guardian of the Silverthorn of Caerlian." It sounded like a proud battlefield declaration from his lips, a title meant to cow the enemy before a contest of arms. "I am placing you under arrest. Lay your weapons down, and give over the Truthsayer's robe that you have stolen."

"Ah!" Joro exclaimed. "Is that what this is about?" His eyes flicked from Thengel to Dalin and back again. "You keep company with this murderer and attempt false arrest so suspicion is drawn away from your treacherous young friend here, yes?"

He faced the ship's captain. "What lies have they cozened you with, sir? Do you know that this one"—he stabbed a finger toward Dalin—"is sought even now by the watch for his treacherous assassination of his master, the King's Truthsayer, and his escape from prison?"

Ragnar's mouth opened and he looked uncertainly at Dalin.

"Lies!" Thengel retorted. "Don't heed him, Ragnar. It is as I told you, and the King's court will make sense of this soon enough."

"We are diplomatic envoys," the towheaded woman spoke. "With the reward on that boy's head, you should be arresting him, not us. The Riedskana will be ever so grateful if you do." She drifted toward the seaward railing as she talked, keeping her sloe-eyed gaze on Ragnar. "The watch also seek the boy's accomplices in his escape. You seem to have them all in your grasp right now, Captain, if you can close your hand upon them."

Her white leathers shone in the brilliant sunlight. Unearthly in her elven beauty, she was captivating to look at, with her leisurely movements calculated to draw every eye to her. And yet every fiber of Dalin's body sang alarm. The untruth in these Nimmian words was glaringly evident to him: could no one else hear it? The ill intent virtually sang on the air—but Ragnar actually hesitated, sidled away from Thengel, putting his sailors to his back. With a single motion he had become an onlooker, not a participant certain of who had the right in this affair.

Thengel noted the captain's desertion and hesitated, no doubt sensing the shifting currents of trust and alignment in that critical moment. If only the Nimmians had blustered or reached to their weapons! But they had not, and their cool refutation of charges seemed plausible. If they persuaded the sailors they were in the right, Dalin and his companions would be the ones outnumbered by captain and crew. And Thengel stood there, caught by surprise, letting Granmar's killers spin more lying persuasions. . . .

"Surely," Joro said with a smile, "you don't believe—"

Dalin interrupted. "There's one way to get to the truth of the matter," he spoke loudly over the Nimmian. "Let's have the Truthsayer's robe. That will reveal who speaks truth and who lies."

Joro sneered at him. "And you, a wanted murderer, will use the Robe to divine who is at fault? I think not."

Ragnar's heavy brow furrowed. "Where is the Robe?" he demanded.

"We don't have it." Joro shrugged off the question. "Ask him."

He jerked his chin toward Dalin, and the youth stood rooted to the spot. Eyes turned to him as if he had answers, or lies to conceal them.

In that moment that Dalin fell under scrutiny, Joro rested his hand on his hip, brushing the belt pouch that hung there, and the triumphant glee that flowed from him shocked the youth stock-still. What he sensed was the chortling self-congratulations of someone getting away with a prime deception. Tension, excitement, and razor-sharp focus all drove the feeling straight into Dalin's gut, and his conscious mind as well.

He locked eyes with Joro.

You have the Robe! He noted where the man's hand rested. *In that pouch. Right there.*

How the massive weaving could be in that tiny space did not matter. Surely it was an outlander trick of some sort, some magic of concealment or some such. But he knew—he *knew*—that the Nimmians were here not to look over the ship but to steal it away and take the Truthsayer's robe away with them.

Perhaps his insight showed in his face. Or his intensity fed back through the circuit of peculiar energies connecting them, and Joro intuited something amiss. The man's face darkened and he snapped out a phrase to his companions, an order delivered in Nimmian slang that Dalin did not understand.

The effect was instantaneous.

Yellowbeard was the first to pull his sword, a blaze of cold light radiating from the blade, and Dalin's heart quailed at the sight. The warrior struck at the nearest sailor between him and the dock, and the man collapsed nearly beheaded, blood spewing from the horrible wound between neck and shoulder. All Nimmians but the woman pulled their swords and surged toward the gangplank.

The elves loosed their arrows instantly, three shafts flying at once toward the enemy. But in the next heartbeat the air glowed brilliantly, forcing Dalin to blink, and when his eyes flicked open again the arrows lay on the decking around the outlanders' feet, dropped harmlessly from the air as if they had struck a barrier of some sort.

Dalin saw the triumphant smile on the woman's face and knew that they had.

Sailors and elves threw themselves forward to mob the Nimmians, but the woman's swift-raised hand brought a searing bolt of energy in its wake, dropping five men in one stroke and blasting a chunk of railing out of the charred and smoking deck beyond. Cries and chaos erupted on board the *Gull* as sailors fell back in disorder.

Thengel's charge toward their leader was halted by Yellowbeard's raised sword; Hagar came to his friend's aid while the outlanders forced their way closer to shore and the horses that awaited them there. Joro followed the push of his companions to freedom and safety. In moments he would be out of reach, and the Robe gone with him.

Dalin threw himself after the man, staff in hand, and clubbed the Nimmian from behind with it.

The blow was swift and ill-aimed; it clipped Joro on the side of the head and staggered him to his knees. The deck was in utter confusion: smoking wood, the stench of ozone, some sailors fleeing, some joining the fray with cries of renewed fury, two staggering back with an injured companion, blocking Valdarius and Arandel, who were trying to close with swords. Others backed away from Kaylis, poised to cast another deadly spell. Hagar grunted by Thengel's side, the pair together barely defending against the onslaught of the magical sword and the furious man who wielded it—

And Joro, half-stunned, groping for his sword on the deck nearby.

Dalin twisted to the side, thrust his staff through the woman's legs to distract her and entangle her step. The wood was yanked out of his hands as she stumbled, and then Katrije's knife was in his grip instead. A slice, a jerk, and Joro's pouch came free from his belt. Dalin leaped away, hearing the Nimmian curse him, feeling iron fingers snatching at him, digging into his calf as he scrambled clear of the melee. He dodged a sailor, spun about to slam full into Cathmar, chanting under his breath until that moment that the air was driven from his lungs. "Oh!" the youth exclaimed, and righted the frail fellow with a tug and a pat even as he stumbled to the lip of the gangplank.

"Dalin!" Someone bellowed his name and followed it with a ferocious oath, but he was running down the gangplank and did not pause to look back. An earsplitting crack of lightning tore the air behind him, and this bolt came close—too close; perhaps it was even directed at him. It blew wood splinters from the deck and burned the edge of the gangplank behind his feet. It set the horses into a whinnying, head-tossing panic where they were tethered onshore.

He did not look back once. The Truthsayer's apprentice bolted as fast as he could run, down the wharf, across the quay. His back prickled and any second he expected lightning to spear him to the ground where he stood. The shouts and screams behind him made him think the spellcasters on board the *Gull* had more urgent business to hand than to hunt him down. His pounding footsteps had not slowed the least bit by time his feet hit

Janske Way—there, in the alley across, were the adenye and horses and his trusty mountain pony Rufslaenit, who had carried him here. And now would carry him away.

Intent on his goal, he did not see the banners of the Hounds of Hammankarl. He noticed the troop only when a voice in the forefront shouted, "He's one of them! Stop him!"

He glanced to his left and the sight nearly paralyzed him in midstride. A column of mounted troops, fifty or more, filled the street four abreast at a rapid trot. A rider clad as an ordinary workman pointed right at him. Some horsemen peeled off to the customs docks; others spurred his way. . . .

Then he was across the road and into the alley. "Run!" he screamed to Katrije and the others. "Hounds!"

He found Rufs in the string of horses, tore her reins from Udo's hand. He stuffed the stolen pouch down the front of his shirt as he clambered into the saddle and yanked his horse's head around before his feet had even found the stirrups. Digging in his heels, he urged Rufs to a risky near-canter down the cluttered alley. Behind him the jingle of tack and the sounds of pursuing riders made his back crawl.

Out of the alley, into a crossroad, Rufs scrambled for footing on cobblestones, and he was forced to let her slow her pace. Hoofbeats followed his own and he glanced back—then his eyes widened. Katrije, sticking close by his side. Where were the others? Caught in the alley by the Hounds? Probably. He let her come up beside.

"I need out of town," he panted. "How?"

Katrije glanced harborward, invisible behind intervening buildings, and bit her lip. Her master was there, in trouble—but there was nothing she could do against an entire horsetroop. Still she hesitated.

Dalin read her expression and faced intently ahead. "Then I'll do it without you." He gathered his reins.

"Wait." She kept pace with him easily. "Old Town's all walled in. On the King's Road you can leave the city. You have to make it across the bridge though."

"Show me?"

She ducked her head and moved into the lead.

There, the road to Tolvar's Gate. Several of the King's Hand rode past, trotting toward the waterfront—bringing up the rear of the large troop they had just skirted, it seemed. The pair came out onto the roadway and eased into the press of the crowd upon the bridge. Dalin looked nervously behind and urged his horse next to Katrije. They were slowed to a walk for all the throng in yellow and green around them.

"Festival," the squire gritted, making it sound like a curse. She looked over her shoulder as well and paled. Dalin followed her gaze.

Ten horsemen in yellow and white, coming out of the side street they had just left. Pursuit, close behind, setting hoof even now upon the bridge.

"Hyah!" Dalin shouted urgently to his horse and to the people ahead. "Clear the way! Clear the way!"

People made room faster for the Hounds that followed than for the two young riders ahead of them. The press was thicker by the King's Road, where onlookers packed the street. Banners waved above the crowd far ahead, and strains of music came on the air, barely noted by Dalin over his panicked breathing and the jostle of his own progress. With Katrije's aid he forced a way onto the broad cobbles of the King's Road itself. A barricade of watchmen near the bridge plaza kept people back from the route of the King's parade.

Watchmen. Dalin was past them before he realized his risk. The route out of town was blocked with spectators, the Hounds were crossing the bridge behind, ahead was a patch of clear road, and he made for it unthinkingly. Katrije stuck beside him as the voices of watchmen rose in angry challenge.

Turning his head to left, to right, seeking a way out of this conspicuous openness, but seeing every path blocked, and every spectator staring right at him—Dalin felt himself blush madly.

"Uh-oh," Katrije muttered, and his eyes darted her way. The hand that grabbed Rufslaenit's bridle, forcing her to a halt, came from his off side, caught him completely by surprise. He looked around in time to realize they were in the bridge plaza, where green-and-gold banners waved atop poles carried by heralds and the forerunners of the royal procession. Pipers and drummers let their music die in cacophony as the King's Master Herald halted the intruder who had nearly ridden him down. Watchmen closed in from the sides of the parade route, and then, only then, did Dalin look straight ahead, down the road before him. He sat his horse at eye-level with a brown-haired man in white samite and gold, a simple crown upon his brow. A man whose expression was at once outraged and coldly hostile.

It was the King, five horse lengths distant. And beside him, Hanno Runemaster.

Dalin blanched.

He dismounted as rapidly as Katrije beside him, near falling from his saddle. *I'm doomed,* he thought. Or was that only the voice of fear skittering through him reflexively? For the sight of Hanno in a gold sash of office riding so closely beside the King spurred him to hot impulse. Before the false accusations could fly, before the one who had machinated Granmar's demise could put blame on Dalin—now was his chance, perhaps his only chance, to prove his innocence, to avenge the Truthsayer's death.

No sooner did his foot touch ground than the youth ducked past the grasping hand of the Herald. He dashed forward and went to his knees before the King. "Your Majesty!" he cried as watchmen rushed in, grabbing his arms to restrain him, to drag him away. "I plea your mercy!"

Hammankarl's lifted finger stopped the arrest before it had begun. "My mercy?" he asked, looking down from lofty horseback at the young suppliant before him. A hush fell over the crowd as onlookers strained to hear what transpired.

"Majesty: I am Dalin of Nevi, the Truthsayer's apprentice. *Your* Truthsayer, now, falsely accused of my master's death. I can prove to you that that man"—he flung out his arm, pointing at Hanno—"is responsible for Granmar's death, not I!"

Astonished murmurs ran through the crowd; the King looked grim, and the runemaster's expression darkened.

"No need to ruin your holy day with the blatherings of a desperate murderer, Sire," Hanno said to the King. "He no doubt has some subterfuge in mind. I'll have him imprisoned again, and we can deal with him later—"

"No." Hammankarl cut off his companion. "What is this proof you claim?" he addressed Dalin.

Dalin reached inside his shirt, pulled out the pouch there. If he had read Joro wrong, if he was mistaken, now all was lost. How the Robe could be here he did not know—but he undid the drawstring as if he knew exactly what he was about and opened the pouch of red-and-black Koribi weaving . . . and opened it. And opened it broader still.

The mouth of the pouch yawned far, far wider than the cloth of it should permit. Like a bag it was, suddenly, and then like a wool sack in girth—and within, the white and red and patterned markings of the Truthsayer's robe.

Relief flooded through him. Dalin pulled the Robe from the enchanted pouch, the bag seeming small in his hand but its storage capacious. Out came the cloth, and out, and out some more, until it lay rumpled on the ground at his knees. The Robe, ever pristine in spite of all its handling, the border lined in red and white, the geometric patterns of its body catching the eye, pulling it into circles and meditative musings, far larger than any square-cut cloak a man might wear; three men could be wrapped in this yardage of heavy fabric. . . .

Dalin blinked at the thing before him. Never before had he touched it. But he had seen Granmar use it many a time.

He looked up to King Hammankarl, determination on his face. "You know this cloak of office, Sire. Passed from Truthsayer to Truthsayer. You know that he who wields it can see the truth where others cannot. You know that persons touched by the Truthsayer wearing the Robe are compelled to speak truthfully as well."

He came to his feet, wrapped the Robe around his shoulders, clasped it to his chest. "And now, I will demonstrate to you the truth of the matter."

Brave words.

Foolhardy words.

As he clutched his inheritance to him, he waited for the thrill of power to course through his veins. Or a sensation that was different from what he normally felt. Or an inspiration of words like the crabbed grumblings of the old seer, who had muttered an invocation every time he'd donned the robe. An invocation Dalin had never heard clearly and could not repeat now. . . .

Nothing.

He felt no different. Not wise, not magical; nothing was altered from moments before. He licked his lips and frowned at Hanno. The man frowned back at him, his expression not impossible to read. Leery. Cautious.

Hateful.

Dalin coughed, cleared his throat. He stepped forward, resolved to do as he had seen Granmar do during a truth-reading once. He touched Hanno Runemaster on the arm and felt the man's muscles tense beneath his fingers. "Tell truth now," he said commandingly. "Who killed Granmar at the Crystal Spires?"

And yet there was no rush of power. No compulsion, no clarity flowing around him. Dalin's heart sank. He wore nothing but a heavy tapestry on his shoulders, and his truthsaying here was a sham. As much a sham as Hanno's next words.

"I witnessed the event, when you thought no one could see—"

Falsehood.

"—and it was you, young man. Treacherous viper at your teacher's breast."

Falsehood.

The deceit of the runemaster's words struck Dalin like a punch in the gut. He stood thunderstruck as the red-shirted watchmen grabbed him and the useless Robe fell from his shoulders to the ground. A smirk played across Hanno's lips.

"For this trespass, and your other crimes," the King said, "you shall be confined to Ship Rock, in chains, until I oversee your execution the day after Ardrunafest."

Execution?

"Take him away."

Dalin was dragged from the King's Road on nerveless feet, too shocked to struggle. At a gesture from Hanno, watchmen collected the Robe he left behind. He heard Katrije call his name, once, before she was silenced, and then despair crashed upon him like a wave. His fate and the crowds and the watch that dragged and cuffed him became a blur and a darkness to his senses.

CHAPTER 59

HANNO SUFFERED THE long procession with ill grace. Hammankarl did not speak of Dalin's bizarre interruption to the royal progress, yet it was only a matter of time before these things would come to discussion. The High Councillor dreaded every hoofstep that brought them closer to the end of the day's official duties.

The boy could only have stolen the Truthsayer's robe from Joro. *That fool.* And he had barged into the parade with a squad of Hounds right behind him. *Have the Nimmians run afoul of them, too?*

He looked sidelong at his liege lord. The Selkie King rode comfortably, a seemingly sincere smile upon the royal lips, an upraised hand that greeted the crowd with a reflexive waving gesture. But with his mercurial nature there was no telling what mood or thoughts were brewing behind that public facade.

He stroked the front of his doublet of midnight blue velvet, felt the reassuring weight of the runic talismans that hung from his neck beneath his court clothes. The Persuasion rune was there, and Silence, and a few others that Koram had given him alone to know. The influence of the Staje rune was no longer with him, and he needed some isolated hours to craft another that would make him impervious to a truth-probing. That was now his first imperative. A truth-reading could spell the end of Hanno's ambitions—even now, now that he had finally secured this foremost of offices, his years of scheming and patient waiting could all come to naught. He clenched his tattooed fist around his reins.

I will not allow that to happen, he vowed, *no matter what the cost.*

SHIP ROCK LOOMED two long bowshots beyond Jarlsdock, nearly in the center of Etjorvi's natural harbor. The jagged spit of black sea-washed stone was long and narrow, in dimensions twice the length and breadth of a dragon ship. It had a comparable height as well, its barren rock shelving steeply to a mast-high spindly peak visible from every point onshore.

The watchmen's skiff pulled from the King's Dock behind Hakkonkalye. It made straight for that landmark spire, white-crusted with the nesting residue of generations of terns.

Dalin slumped in the stern of the boat, apathetic and unresisting, with hands bound behind him. He had known nothing of the fate that awaited him, but the guardsmen—resentful of his earlier escape—had taken pains to paint a short and unhappy future for him. "It's a place for traitors and those in special disfavor with the King," the guard sergeant had told him blithely. "You must be special, boy." He chuckled. "Last one confined there perished in a winter freeze, before he could be drawn and quartered."

"Oh," Dalin said listlessly.

"It was the Jarl of Fenvar, right?" A watchman nodded, and the sergeant continued. "Plotted treason against the King, he did. Thought to become his own little princedom on the West Wall, no longer part of Tura-kem. Allied with trolls from the Underrealms. . . . He failed. He died."

"His cousin died, too," the watchman added. "Man tried to rescue him—but the Selkies keep safe what the King puts on Ship Rock. They holed their boat, and he drowned in sight of land. They wouldn't let him ashore on the Rock, and the current dragged him down."

They said it factually, not gloating. Not needing to. Their tales had the effect they were hoping for: Dalin felt nothing beyond utter despair. He nearly envied Granmar his quick end upon the rough slopes of Kodanit's Spire.

When the skiff grated onto the gravelly shore, he stumbled behind his warders through cold seawater and up to a point that, on a ship, would be halfway between mast and bow. Chains were there, set deep into the native stone of the Rock, sailing perpetually shoreward toward Etjorvi. A prisoner confined here could be viewed by passing vessels and the curious anywhere along the city shore. To the south there was a direct view of the White Palace, behind the rocky shoals where seals basked in the sun.

Dalin stared dully in that direction as the sergeant secured an iron shackle around his left ankle. The King could look out his windows at any time and survey the harbor and study his prisoner several bowshots distant in the bay. Exposed to the elements and onlooking eyes, trapped as securely aboard Ship Rock as if in the deepest dungeon—more secure, probably. A head broke water behind the skiff as it departed, and Dalin found himself looking at a seal studying him closely. Or was it a seal? The brow seemed more human, the mouth like that of a man, formed for ready speech—and then the figure submerged beneath the green waves without a splash.

Selkie folk. To guard the Selkie King's prisoner.

Dalin's hand strayed to the iron chain that bound him to the rock, a staple the size of his arm driven deep and securing the links that kept him there. The iron had a sheen of rust on it from weathering, but it was not so exposed that it was weakened in any way. The links were heavy, the shackle rusty but snug. The sun was bright, but the breeze off the water was cool. Dalin wrapped his arms around his legs and huddled into himself on the rough stone. His mind would not work. He could only stare endlessly at the Palace, a blur of white through wind-teared eyes, and rock a little from side to side where he sat forlorn.

CHAPTER 60

"I'M NOT SURE we should be keeping them all here. This is just tempo-rary holding . . . ," Commander Palstro protested unhappily, knowing as he did so that his reservations would be shrugged off by the officer of the King's Hand.

As they were, readily. "We'll sort this out soon enough," Kinlayik said gruffly, and turned her back on the garrison commander. She had no au-thority to dismiss the man ultimately in charge of these prisoners, nor did she command here. But the King's personal war band had special preroga-tives, and she was using them to full advantage now.

On her order, all prisoners had had their hands bound. "Risk of magic," she snapped when Palstro wanted to argue. It was common knowledge that gestures were a necessary element of arcane invocation; without the ability to gesture, a spellcaster's powers would be severely hampered. Unless the mage was so adept that a word of power or a thought would suffice. . . .

The commander paled and hoped there were none such in this group of prisoners. He waved his guardsmen to follow the captain's orders, and she smiled in grim satisfaction.

Now she paced before the holding cells in the first sublevel of the Hakkonkalye, glaring at the suspects before her: Thengel and his people in one cell, Nimmians in the other, separated only by metal bars sunk in floor and ceiling. The two groups of prisoners paid little attention to her but eyed each other warily.

Etjolf, her duty mage, sat nearby, slumped with the exhaustion of the warding spells he had just placed. There were spellcasters here, too many of them, she knew, and their strengths and abilities could only be guessed at. She had already dispatched a runner beseeching Master Nehvros's aid in dealing with this hazard. For now the prisoners seemed worn out from their shipboard conflict, but there was no knowing what forces they yet had in store and might spring on their unsuspecting warders. To prevent the least hazard, even the children were restrained. Sembroie regretted the necessity, but with this bunch it was better safe than sorry. Besides keeping them bound, Hounds with bows stood watch nearby, ready to skewer from a safe distance any who began a chant or lifted a finger suspiciously. It was the best she could do for now. Meanwhile, there were far too many unanswered questions to give her ease.

She halted her pacing and came to a decision. "Bring him." She nodded toward Thengel. "I'll question him myself."

"That's really my duty," Palstro ventured.

Sembroie rounded on the portly commander and stepped into his space to intimidate him with her own statuesque height. "This is business of the King's Hand. What we don't do, you can. I'll tell you what that is, and when." She scowled at Palstor's guardsmen. "Fetch him."

With barely a look at their wavering commander, they ducked their heads and obeyed her order. They opened one cell door, pulled the slender elf from within, and pushed him down the hall after the white-surcoated officer. In a private chamber nearby, she nodded Thengel toward a seat. "Wait outside," she told the guards, and shut the door in their faces. Then she turned on one heel to face her prisoner.

Thengel sat uncomfortably, arms behind his back, his face half-shadowed from the single lamp upon the table. His hair, normally caught back and tied at his neck, was in straggly disarray, and a shallow wound on his shoulder had stained his torn white shirt red. A superficial cut; she'd already confirmed that. He could bleed yet awhile. . . .

He regarded her, his expression indecipherable, and all the anger she had kept leashed since Nalia's defection welled up in that moment. She strode to him, her strong arm swinging out. Hand cracked against cheek, and the elf's head jerked in response.

"How dare you!" she cried, as her hands became fists at her side. "After everything . . . after I trusted . . . you've made me out a liar! You played us all for fools!"

She trembled with her rage and hurt restrained. Thengel was taken aback, but his expression was not that of one about to offer feeble excuses. His look was sober and he wisely did not comment on the tears of anger and frustration that glittered in her eyes.

"It's not like you think."

The blonde warrior looked half away and mastered herself with an effort. She confronted him again. "Like thieves in the night, you've been. Work your way into our good graces. What was all that, that you did in the southland? Accidental heroism? A way to build credentials the King would believe? That I would believe?" She spat. "And then, sneaking and treachery and thievery. Murder, if the High Councillor's charges are true!"

"One of the Nimmians mentioned a High Councillor as well. Who . . . ?"

"Hanno Runemaster, returned from his pilgrimage to the Crystal Spires with charges against *you*, Thengel. And Nalia's abductions to speak truth to them." The edge in her voice was steel.

Thengel's mouth opened, and he blinked in disbelief.

"Oh, no." She waved a finger. "You'll not fool me with that puppy-dog innocence again. I want to know it all, what you're about, what you did with the Truthsayer. What is the depth of your perfidy, warrior whom I once called friend?"

She bit her words off. More than friend. There had been gifts exchanged, soft words spoken, intimacies shared . . . was it only battle companionship? She had thought it something more. But no.

What was this leader of elves really up to in this, her homeland? That remained to be confessed.

She sighed and sat down across the table from him. "I'll have it from you," she said tiredly, "one way or the other. Either talk with me or the Captain-General will put you to the question, and all your friends as well. Better you talk with me. Let's start with Granmar."

"But . . . we did nothing with the Truthsayer!" Thengel stammered in protest.

"So you say."

"It's true! Dalin told us he'd been killed. We tracked the murderers as quickly as possible after that."

She sneered in disbelief. "You're implying you never saw Granmar yourselves?"

"Not implying. Saying. We never met the man."

Her eyes narrowed "You weren't accomplices to his apprentice?"

Thengel huffed indignantly. "Dalin didn't do anything to his master."

"How can you say that? Were you present when he was with his master?"

"No."

She nodded to herself. "Then you don't know what he did for a fact."

"I fail to see why he would kill his master, then leave himself trussed on a mountainside to die, afterward."

Sembroi paused. "What did you say?"

"Arandel found the boy tied and magically blinded. In that desolation he could not have expected anyone to find him, and it is impossible to tie a Gef-fian knot behind one's own back, I'd say."

"Someone left him there?"

"That's what I'm telling you."

"After his master was killed?"

"The boy was badly shaken. We believed his story to be true. We found the trail he'd been following when he was waylaid, tracked the killers to Es-krin Freehold. The steading chief knew them. It was Hanno Runemaster and his friends, whom you're holding now."

Sembroie collapsed back in her chair. "This can't be. The Nimmians claim diplomatic protection; they're envoys contracted by Sarilos. . . ."

"That's as may be." Thengel shrugged. "They're also the ones who killed the King's seer. Dalin witnessed it."

"The runemaster. . . ."

"I don't know what role he played exactly, but aid them he most certainly did. And left the boy to die on the mountainside."

Sembroie sat silent for a long minute. "This doesn't account for your presence at the Spires," she said finally.

"You knew we were off on a journey. You helped me plan it, drew me a rough map!"

"And all the more betrayed I feel for it. You were off on backcountry ex-plorations, you said! You told no one where you were truly destined—and that's all the more reason to suspect your motives. Why to the Truthsayer? What did you want there?"

Thengel's brows pulled together. His teeth worried his lip in that way he had when he was truly uncertain. That, she knew, was no pretense, for she had noted the habit in his unthinking moments.

"I'll tell you," the Guardian of the Thorn said slowly. "It's never been a se-cret, really. We just never found any among your folk who would listen, or who cared, and so it has been a tale not told."

She looked at him expectantly.

"In Caerlian," he began, "we are fighting for our lives. . . ."

She listened attentively, her questions few but pointed. Two hours later she summoned Luell Half-Hand. The cleric of Gunnar Strongarm joined her in the chamber where Thengel still sat, his arms long since unbound.

"You know our charter, studious one." She offered her second in com-mand a half-smile. "Better in the amendments and precedent than I. What say you about an officer's discretionary powers, on assignment?"

"Ma'am?" Luell scratched his chin with his maimed left hand. "I'm not certain I understand."

Sembroie ran a hand across the top of her braided hair. "Discretionary. What latitude have I to dispose of prisoners or suspects, one way or another?"

Luell shook his head. "You have some latitude, but it depends on the circumstances, really. Much must be approved by the Captain-General—"

She cut him off with a sideways slice of her hand. "Not an option. What can *I* do, as commander of a unit?"

Luell looked from her to Thengel and back again, and suspicion crept into his voice. "What exactly are we talking about, here?" he asked leerily.

Sembroie blew air through her lips. "This is the long and short of it. And if ever you had a justiciar's sense of logic splicing I expect you'll use it now. Because we'll be accounting for this to Molstroe all too soon, and probably the King as well."

Then, ignoring Luell's dumbfounded expression, she began to talk.

CHAPTER 61

Joro WATCHED THENGEL being led away for interrogation with silent glee, but it turned soon enough to trepidation. If the elf and his friends were questioned, what could they reveal? Nothing directly incriminating of his people, he thought. As long as the boy was not queried, the only real witness. . . .

And yet, the longer they stayed in custody, the more at risk they became. That the Truthsayer's apprentice would be questioned. That someone would question them next. That their purported doings for Koribee might be investigated—and found nonexistent.

The Hounds that had stormed aboard the *Gull* and broken up their fight were inclined to view them all with hostility. Joro's head ached, not only from Dalin's blow but also from the swipe with the flat of a sword that had subdued him when the war band made the deck. Their plight was not desperate yet, but only if they could win free of this predicament.

How to do that?

The tension between the garrison commander and the Hounds' officer was not lost on him. The woman was imperious and curt and driven by a short temper. Joro noticed the look of resentment the commander shot toward her back when she left with her prisoner.

That was enough of a rift to work with. He hoped so, anyway. It would have to be.

When the commander paced by their cell again, Joro stepped near the bars and cleared his throat. The man paused in his stride, and Joro knew he had his attention.

"Did you find my credentials?" he asked. "They were in my saddlebags."

"Not yet," the commander replied shortly.

"This is an unfortunate misunderstanding," he persisted. "The Koribi ambassador will demand our release." True enough; their letter of introduction to Hanno Runemaster had come also with a letter of authorization to act on Sarilos's behalf in trade transactions. It was an obliging piece of cover fiction from the clandestine ally of the Duke of Nimm and one sure to be honored by Darsius, the current ambassador.

The garrison commander was clearly uninterested. He turned away.

"The High Councillor will be unhappy that we're detained," Joro added.

The man halted in midstride and turned back, an opaque expression on his face. "How do you know of the High Councillor? He was just appointed today. We just heard—while you were being arrested, as a matter of fact."

The Nightrunner kept elation off his face. At last. A name to drop that mattered. "We knew of the appointment before it was public knowledge," he said casually. "We're personal friends of Hanno's. We represent some of his business interests. He'll attest that we were going about our ordinary affairs when these brigands accosted us."

The commander stroked a mustache thoughtfully, looked past Joro's shoulder to the man's companions. The blond-bearded warrior with a bloody cut on his brow, slumped in exhaustion against the wall; the long-haired elvish woman sitting awkwardly with her hands tied and looking mad as a wet cat about it. The short brown-bearded man staring quietly into space, the slender redhead listening to his conversation with their leader. . . .

"The High Councillor knows you?"

"Indeed he does. Very well. Tell him you're holding Joro Narialnos and his escort. He will command our release instantly, I assure you. The longer you keep us, the more upset he'll be when he hears about it, I have no doubt. Ask him."

An unreadable expression came over the commander's face. "I just think I will," he said, and turned his back on the prisoners.

Palstro left the guard chamber with a decisive stride. Friends of the High Councillor? If that was so, this was his chance to repair the damage he'd done by letting the Truthsayer's apprentice escape from Hakkonkalye—however that had happened, for even Master Nehvros's investigations had not revealed the boy's trick. If only he could question the youth. Maybe he would have a chance to do so before the King dealt with his prisoner in other ways. As long as he languished on Ship Rock, however, he was out of reach of Palstro's inquiries, for no one was allowed to talk to a prisoner confined there, on pain of death.

No matter. The Hounds had who they wanted: the elves and their companions, the boy's accomplices. These others had gotten caught up in that sweep by chance. With one stroke he could curry favor with the High Councillor, and win these friends of the Koribi ambassador. If their claim was true—

It must be true, if they expect they can call on the aid of the High Councilor like that.

Joro's confidence was persuasive, enough so to prompt Palstro to take horse and make his way to the Wool Market fields. There he would no doubt find Hanno in the King's court, in the grand review stands. With patience, he should be able to win through for a brief word. A word that would redeem him in the eyes of the powerful and, for that matter, that would snatch a third of Captain Kinlayik's prisoners from her overbearing grip.

Palstro smiled to himself and spurred his horse down Janske Way.

CHAPTER 62

Katrije sat in a corner, Jaele tucked against her side. Her hands were not free to embrace the girl, but she leaned into her, resting her cheek atop the ten-year-old's head. "It's all right," she murmured under her breath. "Thengel will sort it all out, and we'll be out of here in no time."

Jaele sighed and snuggled closer. They were unrelated by birth, but their situation had lent all the adenye a siblinglike relationship. Jaele was the little sister Katrije had never had, she and Udo the older sister and brother the little one lacked. When their master or his companions were otherwise preoccupied, they had only themselves to rely upon, they found. They had become close, in the last many months, far closer than most of their older companions realized. In some ways closer than sibs in a family of birth, for their very survival had turned at times upon how they helped each other.

There was little help to be afforded now, though. Everything was out of their hands, and they could only wait to see what their liege could make of this situation. Sembroie—for a short time a near-parental authority figure in their daily life—did not so much as spare them a glance. It was as if their presence now pained her. Her warriors followed her example, and though the adenye knew these men from their time training in the Hounds' citadel, they had become their warders now and refused to so much as meet their eyes. Katrije sighed in frustration, blowing air from her lips, then blew away Jaele's hair that tickled her nose.

Udo sat on her other side, his bony knee jabbing her thigh because he sat cross-legged. She was trying to get comfortable again when she noticed the elvish woman in the other cell staring at them. The lighting here was dim, meager lamplight shining through the bars from the guardroom, but there was no mistaking the malevolence in the woman's face. Katrije frowned. It was Kaylis, whom she and Dalin had tailed only yesterday.

Katrije looked nervously away.

"I've seen you somewhere, haven't I." It was a statement, not a question, and Katrije was glad for the bars and distance between them. She ignored the question.

"You. Girl. Have we met? Why do I know you?"

Still Katrije ignored her, and resumed her pose of relaxation with Jaele. Only now it was just a pose, and the page was just as tense as Udo had become on her other side.

"Answer me." The woman's voice became steely. A foot grated on the stone near the bars, and someone interposed their body between the woman and the children.

"Leave them alone." Nalia's tone was conversational, but there was an undercurrent in it that Katrije had never heard before. "They don't concern you. We're the ones you should be concerned with."

Bitter laughter came from the opposite cell. "Oh?" Kaylis said. "We should be concerned about . . . what? People who trail others for leagues, not brave enough to deal with them face-to-face, but happy to skulk in the dark behind them? Who spring failed traps, who let their companions die for folly? Who spread lies to justify their thievery attempts?"

Nalia snorted. "That's not the way it was."

The towheaded woman gave a mirthless smile. "To the contrary. That's exactly how it is. You have your own schemes . . . what are they? Why do you hound us? We've done naught to you."

That was a truth, as far as it went, and tense silence came over the twin cells as everyone's attention was drawn to the confrontation.

Nalia bit her lip. She could spin a fabric of believable lies to talk her way out of a bad situation, but countering logic and spite with clear reason was another skill entirely. This was something Valdarius was better suited to address. She glanced his way and shifted her weight uneasily, suddenly unwilling to meet the woman's eyes. Nalia had no ready answer to Kaylis's charges.

"I say you're greedy thieves and skulking assassins," the Nimmian pressed home. "You're nothing we want at our backs. Leave us be, or we'll have to kill you."

"Kaylis," Joro warned with her name. "We've no reason to threaten these folk. Let them pursue what folly they will." His half-smile did not touch his eyes, and his words were clearly for the guards who might overhear. "We have our own business to conduct, and as long as we're left in peace to do it, we have no reason to engage these ruffians at all."

Kaylis opened her mouth.

"At all," he said sharply.

She glowered at him, then turned her narrowed eyes back to Nalia. Her lip curled, and she managed to look down her nose even though seated against the far wall. "Calianestu daru," she sneered with acid scorn.

Daru: a lesser breed, an uneducatable subrace that could barely be trusted to lick the boots of well-born *derenestu*—the adept and wise lineage that had once ruled lost Arilethne.

Katrije's head jerked in astonishment. Her eighth-elvish blood was not visible in her appearance, but her quarter-elvish mother had been from Tren, and that dialect, sprinkled with slang and swearwords, was something she had heard since birth. Kaylis spoke a dialect from some other region, her pronunciation slightly different—the phrase, though, was the same. Never had Katrije heard the word thrown with such vitriol.

Nalia, of the *calianestu* bloodline, heard the insult for the slap in the face it was. As did every other speaker of Elvish in the room.

Nalia stood stock-still, and Kaylis pushed her advantage in the tongue that her leader clearly did not understand. "I smell magic about you, *cuishe.*" Mongrel puppy, she termed her with another loaded insult-word. "Baby magic. Stay out of my way or I'll swat you down like the gadfly you are."

Katrije realized she was holding her breath. There was an aura of power around the towheaded woman and a hard line to her face that said she would stop at nothing to get her way. If she were free to spell-cast in this moment, no telling what havoc she might wreak among them. In spite of the warding the Hounds' mage had woven here, the air crackled with tension and maybe supernatural forces as well.

It was Cathmar who diverted the charge between the two. His soft rebuke in Elvish came from the shadowed corner where he had been resting. "You bluster, child. It makes you sound scared."

He stood and stepped forward into the half-light, to the bars where Nalia stood rooted to the spot. "Arrogance is not the measure of one's power in the world," he said dryly. "We seem to be at odds. You need not aggravate that with spite. It serves nothing."

This was not the kind of response Kaylis expected. She stared at Cathmar for a moment. Katrije, like others viewing the pair, could see they were related. Cathmar's silver-white hair was not a sign of age but a *derenestu* trait, as was the pale tow hair of the woman. His malformed face looked nothing like the woman's fine features, but the glint of their amber eyes was identical, their height and build similar, and very unlike the green-eyed, brown-or-blond-headed elves from Caerlian. . . .

"Who are you?" Kaylis demanded haughtily.

Cathmar cocked his head. "I don't know that we need to be on familiar terms."

She sniffed. "Hide in anonymity if you like, old man. But why do you waste your time with these *darui*?"

He shook his head once. "I could as well ask why you waste your time thieving and slaying hermits. Such things seem beneath an *arvindia* like you. You know the old term for mage? 'Noble worker of arcane arts.' It carries an obligation of behavior with it. Have you lost the nobility in your art, Kaylis?"

He spoke as if he saw right through her. She hesitated to answer and locked eyes with him as she considered a reply—

The moment shattered as the far door was flung open and an escort of Hounds trooped into the room with Master Nehvros in their midst. He wore brown brocade as court finery on this day, a modest pendant of gold and rubies signifying his office as royal physician and mage. The narrow band of worked leather around his brow was the only fashion that indicated his Tren origins; it held back the silvery collar-length hair that revealed his distant kinship with the other adept elves here.

His amber eyes widened in surprise as he recognized the frail prisoner before him.

"Cathmar? Fallen into bad company, are you?"

The older mage regarded the younger somberly and inclined his head in respect. "Nehvros. Things are not as they appear."

"Then let us hope we have it soon rectified. You've taken me from the opening ceremonies. The pagent is the best part of the day."

Joro's eyes narrowed. Clearly the two were acquainted and on friendly terms. This did not bode well for his own interests. . . .

Nehvros fell into conference with Etjolf, who pointed out the wardings; then he studied the area with the unfocused vision of his other-sight. He nodded approval and ordered he be taken to Sembroie. A guard led him down the hall and through a certain door.

As the men moved out of earshot, Joro leaned over to Kaylis. He had not understood the Elvish, but her baiting tone was sufficient to anger him. "Leave our enemies be," he growled in quiet menace. "I don't want them engaged with."

"Why?" she challenged.

"They have no need to learn a thing about us. Not from conversation or an unguarded word. Best solution, then, is to leave them without unguarded words. Do you understand me?"

He said it with an edge in his voice, and after a minute she looked away. "I understand."

"Good," he said, and wary silence returned to the holding cells of Hakkonkalye.

CHAPTER 63

Hammankarl sat at his ease in the afternoon warmth, chatting with courtiers and Queen Elfried about the pagent before them. He smiled upon the children in green and cloth of gold who led it—the offspring of various highborn notables, with banners and symbols of Ardruna's bounty held high. He joked about the unruly lambs that followed in their wake. With everyone else, he offered somber obeisance as Arlan himself blessed the ceremonial sheath of half-ripe barley in the goddess's name.

Not once did he turn to the Councillor's high seat to bring up the unpleasantry from earlier. He seemed, for now, to have forgotten it entirely.

Hanno gradually relaxed in his chair of honor by the King's right hand. *Of course he'll not speak of Dalin's charges here, among so many prying ears and eyes. It will be later, when we are in private together. Perhaps before the feast, or after. . . .*

The pagent was forby, the last of the sheaths of grain and the final stray lamb carried and herded from the field. Now the contests were under way. Steading men occupied themselves with hand axes and log targets in the well-trodden grass before the stand. Soon the ax throwing would have a winner, and the Queen would award a prize. Afterward, the wrestling would begin.

Against that backdrop, a trickle of visitors circulated through the King's canopied reserve, jarls and aristocrats permitted by the Master Herald to approach in ones and twos. They paid their respects and good wishes to the royal couple on this day; before departing, they congratulated the new High Councillor upon his appointment also.

Looking to his left, past the King and Queen, he could see who would be coming next to pay their respects. The ponderous Jarl of Rauvasla wheezed forward now, a florid man who enjoyed the bounty of his rich hunting lands far too well, and the mead they brewed to go with it. His lady wife followed a step behind. Behind them, awaiting their turn, were steading chieftains, jarls' sons, other notables—and among them a russet-surcoated military officer.

Hanno looked again and frowned. Commander Palstro, daring to rub elbows with rather lofty company on this day. Yet his rank as man responsible for the city's defense meant he would not be turned away by the Master Herald. Well. That incompetent would get short shrift when he came near. . . .

Or so the High Councillor planned, until Palstro had paid his respects to the King and Queen, then stopped to bow to the runemaster. He put a foot on the riser up to the Councillor's high chair and leaned slightly forward. "Your friend Joro also sends his greetings," he said, his voice pitched only for Hanno's ears.

The High Councillor froze.

"He's my guest right now," Palstro continued. "Do you wish me to carry word back to him?"

He has Joro in custody.

Hanno kept his face impassive and hoped the King would not glance his way. "I'll be glad to share that horn of ale with you, Commander," he replied, his voice at a normal conversational level. "Wait for me at the brewer's booth behind this stand. . . . I'll be with you in a while. During the wrestling matches, perhaps. Yes?"

"Understood, sir," Palstro replied. He offered a bow and departed in the footsteps of the jarl who had gone before him.

As soon as Elfried was done with the prize awards and the wrestling commenced, Hanno excused himself for a short absence. None of the courtiers wandered the fair freely while in attendance upon the King, although brief visits to the jakes or nearby booths for food or drink were not unusual. Too, Hanno sensed that Hammankarl preferred his High Councillor in particular to be proudly on display by his side as long as they were in public. He was glad he had the Persuasion rune about his person, for after some hesitation the King finally waved his hand in reluctant dismissal. Hanno resisted the urge to bolt and strolled leisurely out of the stands and around to the food booths behind.

Palstro wiped brown foam from his mouth as the runemaster approached. He looked torn between offering a drink and wanting to blurt his news out. Hanno gave him the chance to do neither, but beckoned him with a crooked finger and moved to a spot away from jostling fair-goers.

"Now," the runemaster rounded on the man. "Tell me about Joro."

CHAPTER 64

THE NIGHTRUNNER'S HEAD jerked up as a cell door screeched on iron hinges. Hounds marched into the opposite cell, rousing the elves from their various positions of repose around the cold stone chamber. "Up with you," a sergeant ordered gruffly. "Out. Walk this way." He put a white-gauntleted hand on the youngest girl's arm, lifted her gently to her feet. "Get on, now."

Thengel was not to be seen, but his companions were taken out through the guardroom and up the spiral stairs. Hopefully the elf who led them was broken and bleeding on the rack by now and his cohort destined for a similar fate. . . .

Then the officer of the King's Hand walked past, followed by Nehvros. Who was followed by Thengel.

Unrestrained. Walking like a free man.

Joro was on his feet and next to the bars in a heartbeat. "Where are you going?" he demanded of them all, of Thengel. They barely glanced his way, kept on through the guardroom, and out. "Answer me!" Joro shouted angrily. A guard growled at him, and Joro snarled a Koribi curse in return.

"What's going on?" Berin asked.

"How in the Icy Hells should I know?" he snapped.

His companions fell quiet and did the only thing they could do: continued their waiting in silence.

He had nothing he would say to his cohorts, but speculation ran rife in his head, and he didn't like where his thoughts were leading him. When he finally saw Palstro his heart gave a jump and again he was next to the bars in a bound.

"Well? You found him?"

"Indeed I did." The commander motioned to guards who came forward, opened the door of their cell with a screech that was music to Joro's ears.

"Good!" He was the first to the door, falling eagerly into step with the garrison guards who marshaled around him and his companions. Instead of passing through the guardroom, they turned down the hall and walked farther into the recesses of the fortress. "Where are we going?" he asked.

"You'll see," came the reply.

He didn't like the tone of that response. His steps slowed, and a guard shoved him along. In a few minutes his misgivings were complete. They were in a hall lit by dim, smoky lamps. A series of squat oaken doors bound with iron lined one wall. Palstro stopped by the first of these, opened it with a key from the heavy ring at his belt. The door creaked open. The stench of moldering straw and old human waste wafted out into the hall.

The guards shoved Joro inside.

"Hey!" He spun about. "You can't—!"

"Watch me," Palstro cut him off.

The door slammed shut and the lock turned, sealing Joro into the close chamber in fetid darkness. The only light was the glimmer that came through the crack beneath the door and leaked around the peepwindow that was shut now from the outside.

Something chittered and scurried away from him in the darkness. He threw himself at the door and pounded on it with his bound hands, to no avail. It was like hitting a tree trunk for all the sound carried—and for the hurt it did to his hands. He stopped and flew into a storm of cursing. He ranted until he could think of no other ways to curse Palstro or the runemaster's ancestry, then sank exhausted to his knees in the filthy straw.

SEMBROIE'S TROOP MOUNTED in the bailey of Hakkon's Keep. They surrounded the horses of Thengel's band and kept a watchful eye on the folk so recently arrested. But they were freed now—provisionally—and the Hounds did nothing more than cautiously observe as the elves, the dwarf, and the adenye took saddle and prepared to ride.

Only Thengel seemed reluctant to leave. He stood by his gray Caerlian charger, reins in hand, and argued toe to toe with the blond-braided commander of the war band. Her warriors turned a politely blind eye to the confrontation, but the substance of the dispute was heard by all within earshot.

"How can you do this?" Thengel snapped in angry disbelief. "Master Nehvros's truth-reading is the proof of our innocence; you said so yourself. If we're free, we're free to stay, no?"

"No, you pigheaded simpleton. I'm not *asking* you to go, Thengel. I'm *telling* you how it's going to be. I'm deporting you, and all who came with you. Right now. This instant."

"You can't do that!"

"I can, and I am, and that's an end to it. It is within my rights to rid the realm of imminent danger. I deem you an imminent danger. I'm ridding the realm of you."

"I don't believe what I'm hearing!"

"Believe it. How I justify this to my command is none of your affair. But believe me when I tell you that if you are not gone from here posthaste, you may never leave at all. You've done too much that's clandestine, and you're a ready scapegoat. I'm doing you a favor."

"You're interfering with our lawful business! I won't permit us to be cast out like this!"

"You don't have a say in it. Now, are you going to get on your horse, or are we going to tie you on him like a sack of cabbages? Your choice."

The tall elf stood rigid.

"We've got four hours to make the tide at Vengar Cove, and we need that time for travel." Her tone was sharp. "Mount up, Guardian of the Thorn, or you'll be in bonds for this leg of your journey, and all the rest of it, too. I promise you."

The pair glowered at each other for a long minute. Thengel was the first to look away. Stiff-backed, he stepped to Turon's side, mounted awkwardly. "All our things are aboard Ragnar's ship." He bit the words out.

Sembroie shrugged. "The captain's already crying for damages; if he sees your faces you'll be arrested again." She swung into the saddle. "You can replace your belongings. Be glad that's all you're losing."

She gestured with a hand, and her troop rode out of the fortress, the prisoners under close escort in their midst.

CHAPTER 65

Hanno left his public face at the door of his house along with his small escort of Hounds. For years he had resided without a live-in servant in his well-appointed but modest abode. The recent change in his circumstances had not yet caught up with him; right now he had no one underfoot to spy upon his preparations, and he wanted to keep it that way. The Hounds would find what comfort they could in his small courtyard garden, and the High Councillor would have the privacy his walls afforded him.

The Wool Market fair was still under way and would be into the night, but the King had taken his leave when shadows lengthed toward evening. He and the rest of the court desired sufficient time to prepare for that night's palace feast. If Hanno was quick about it, he would be able to protect himself with another Staje rune before he reappeared for the evening's amusements.

In the corner was a table. One quarter of it served as altar, holding spreadcloth, offerings in harmony with the elements, consecrated candles, and tools of ritual. The rest of the surface was used for rune crafting and ritual work of a broader scale. He took a seat there now, lit a candle with a hurriedly muttered prayer to Koram, and rummaged about in a small lidded box for a virgin stone suitable for his purposes. There were only two amethysts left, he noted. *I must remedy that, if I'm going to be using Staje runes often.* He pulled out the one in better condition, took his set of carving and etching tools from their shelf, and sat in readiness at his worktable. He took a deep breath, set hands palm-flat on the wood, expected the feeling of centeredness to flow through him. The feeling that heralded transition into that place of power in which a rune was crafted under the guidance of the divine.

Yet no exalted vibration entered his body at all. If anything, he felt only exhausted from the worries of the day. The instant he turned his attention that way, he saw why he could not readily fall into a rune-working trance. A critical voice in the back of his head nagged him and condemned his actions and wanted to engage him in frenetic debate over the dangers he faced.

The Nimmians are imprisoned. They were trying to flee with the Robe, clearly, though Dalin somehow snatched it from them. But now they are where they can be truth-read, and put to the question if they won't cooperate. . . .

Hanno had no illusions that they would or could withstand torture—or a well-cast truth spell, for that matter. Someone would break or say just the wrong thing, and then it would be clear to everyone that Hanno Runemaster had helped to eliminate his nemesis, Granmar Truthsayer. Tainted with suspicion of murder, and the certainty of abetting murderers and thieves, Hanno would not be High Councillor for long.

I need them dead. That was the way of it. They knew too much to be left alive. But how to dispose of them believably? Aye, that was the rub. There were too many of them for a suicide to look plausible. *I don't trust Palstro to do the planning of such a thing, either, not after his failure with the boy.*

It was wisest, of course, to keep the Nimmians closely confined for now, and so Hanno had ordered until he could decide how best to dispose of them. Put that way, his problem was simple: he had only to think of a believable reason why all five prisoners would die.

Easier said than done, but it was a conundrum the back of his brain would not let go of. *Very well,* he promised himself. *For now, give me your undivided attention on these delicate carvings.* He twisted the amethyst in the candlelight, envisioning the stylized star that would soon radiate across its surface. *Then, when Staje is properly made and activated—then I promise to give my undivided attention to the problem of the Nimmians, yes?*

Yes.

In accord with himself at last, he was able to still the clamoring worries and concentrate exclusively on the rune of truth. Two hours later he blew the last of the gem dust from his incising tool and smiled at his handiwork. This small rune stone, too, he swallowed down, so that under no circumstance could he be separated from the source of his apparent veracity. He had enough time yet to refresh himself and change for the feast.

And time to consider the fate of the Nimmians.

CHAPTER 66

VENGAR COVE LAY southeast of Etjorvi upon the long peninsula that flanked the Selvien Ulloya, the Selkie Isles. It was a little-traveled place, visited only by fishermen and those tending lobster pots and oyster beds. And it provided occasional moorage in a secure location for certain of Hammankarl's most precious shipping.

The white-and-yellow banners of Sembroies' troop crested the headland and paused there, the late westering sun at their backs. The shadow of the peninsula stretched upon the green waters before them. Offshore, a myriad of islands large and small speckled the seascape like pebbles strewn on billowing silk. Onshore was a small village—Thengel thought immediately of Tesvi Cove and the fishermen there—but here also a long jetty had been built of stone, and from its breakwater shelter a wharf ran out into deeper water.

A dragon ship was moored there and across the wharf from it, a vessel longer and much broader than a ship of war, rigged with double masts and two banks of oars per side.

"The Green Ship," Sembroie remarked to Thengel's questioning look. With that, she led her troop over the crest of the ridge and down to the cove.

Thengel had heard the Green Ship sailed in trade but two or three times a year to Nimm, carrying sanctioned cargos thence and back again. It would not do to have it occupy needed shipping berths as it lay idle for long periods. He saw instantly why it was safe in this alternate moorage: this water must be much broken up into shoals and shallows by the Isles that lay thick along this coast. That terrain and the selkies who lived here must make this one stretch of coast that was safest from intrusion by Nimmian raiders.

For that reason as well, the warship must be moored here. Nimm was open in its overseas raiding, and though Tura-kem responded in kind, this country did not encourage the keeping of military vessels by every small steading chief with a yenning to raid. Instead, the dragon ships of war were subsidized by the King and dispatched only in planned retribution for Nimm's offenses.

There were, no doubt, similar ships hidden up and down the coast. Thengel had heard rumor that they were kept manned and in instant readiness; now he saw for himself that that was so. The Green Ship was clearly inactive, her decks cleared and deserted. On the dragon ship, though, a watch was kept and the vessel seemed in readiness to put out. When the Hounds drew rein dockside, a sailor—or was that warrior?—came forward, a lean man in a stiff leathern jacket that seemed like it could serve as armor, if needed for that purpose. He greeted Sembroie with a salute and listened to her orders. In moments he had dispatched a fellow watchman to the village.

He returned in short order with the ship's commander, a brown-haired stocky man who wore a short beard in addition to the lengthy Turakemi mustaches of fashion. He seemed a land-based warrior ready for a fight, to Thengel's eye, with chain mail shirt worn over padded gambeson and a broadsword at his wide belt. *I should not be surprised,* he thought. *Like the Nimmians, these humans are as ready to fight an enemy to the death as they are to sail their ships. . . .*

"Balyaden." He nodded to Sembroi's rank, comparable to his own.

"Kinlayik," she introduced herself. "And you are Captain Torsjak?"

"I am."

"I have orders for you. Read them now." She presented sealed papers from her dispatch pouch, and he read them right there. Twilight was not so thick that his expression of astonishment could be hidden—but he was also instantly compliant. He saluted the officer of the King's Hand and turned to his crew with a rapid string of orders. More sailor-warriors were summoned from the village, and the ship was soon a hive of activity.

Sembroi turned to her prisoners and regarded Thengel atop his tall warhorse.

"Now I will ask you something I need to know, Guardian. Do I have your oath that you will go quietly as the *Talon* conveys you to Nimm? That you will not try to escape, nor divert the ship, and will not return to these shores without prior permission and safe-conduct from this government?"

He looked down at her, her face stern in the evening shadows. *What earnest single-mindedness of purpose she has.* Even though he could not honor it.

Lying to her never crossed his mind. He simply told her the truth, regretfully.

"I cannot promise you those things. I will not swear to them, or give false oath that I'll abide by those terms. Nor will my companions."

She looked saddened to hear that, but did not ask again. She looked to Luell Half-Hand. "Bind them. And have Captain Torsjak keep them in chains until they're delivered ashore in Nimm."

The elves did not resist. The Hounds were no more rough than necessary and never hesitated until Jaele began to cry.

"It means nothing, *briya*. We'll be free soon enough," Belec assured her softly. "Do as they ask, now."

And though no one commented on it, Thengel was not alone in wondering how much longer they must do as commanded.

CHAPTER 67

H AMMANKARL DRANK, AND ate, and later, danced with his Queen in a swirl of lace and white satin. He did not seek the runemaster out, had been distant all day—in fact, it was beginning to seem as if he were avoiding his High Councillor. Oh, he was congenial enough in the company of others, but except for politenesses the ruler of Tura-kem had nothing, really, to say to his highest adviser.

Hanno began to worry.

At the end of a lively *furevar,* Hammankarl led Elfried from the dance floor. Heading for his seat, he passed by the High Councillor and paused for a moment. Hammankarl's face was flushed with drink and exertion; though he was seldom seen to be in his cups, he was as close to it now as Hanno had ever known him to be.

"How does one best deal with traitors?" he said to the runemaster point-blank.

Hanno started. "Why . . . with death, Majesty. That is the penalty for treason."

"Even so." The Selkie King nodded to himself. He leaned in a little closer. "Do you think I'm being harsh with the Truthsayer's apprentice?"

Hanno licked his lips. Was this a test, or an honest question from a man who regretted his impetuosity?

"He has done wrong, my lord, and must be punished for it."

Hammankarl nodded slowly. "As you say—but then I'll have no Truthsayer." He looked unhappy.

"Nor have you one now, Sire. Just a callow boy who destroyed the only seer you had. But there are other kinds of divination and scrying, you know. You will have me for good advice and rune work, and Master Nehvros for truth-spelling, if needed."

"Ah." The King's face lit up, and he clapped Hanno on the shoulder. "So I will. So I will. We'll talk more, later."

He retired to his seat, still smiling. Hanno kept a smile on his own face as well, though his was mere pretense. Not for the first time did he utter thanks for the rune of truth.

THE NIGHT SKY was clear and starry, the full moon just on the rise and not yet washing the constellations from the heavens with its brightness. Dalin lay on his side in a shallow dent in the rocks, as much of a lee from the harbor breeze as he could discover within the circuit of his chain. He was curled up tight, arms to chest, knees drawn up near chin, in a fruitless effort to keep warm. Not that this was such a harsh circumstance—yet—for in the warmth of summer Ship Rock was temperate during the day. But the waters of the Dannenborch were cold and ice-fed, even at the height of summer, and the breeze off the chop was cold, and now the temperature dropped as the moon mounted into the heavens. He could not move about to keep himself warm, and so he had taken the only alternative, hunkering against the elements and enduring as best he could.

His jaw ached where his muscles clenched against the invasive chill that touched nose and fingers and toes. His Song of Waiting did not seem to warm him anymore or help to pass the desolate hours. Tears had long since dried on his face, and when he blinked his eyes open they felt all cried out and parched by the wind. He looked to the distant White Palace beyond the seal rocks. The royal edifice was full ablaze, with candlelight behind every window and glazed door and torches set to light the grounds, flames flickering in the harbor breeze.

Was it always so festive there? Did they celebrate Ardrunafest there tonight?

No wonder he stared. He would not be seeing another such festival in his lifetime.

He closed his eyes and curled a little tighter around himself. Another splash in the water nearby announced a wave slapping the shore heavily or a seal playing nearby—or a selkie, for during the afternoon the seal-folk had come at intervals to regard him in silent curiosity and go away again, never addressing him, never drawing near enough to hail.

If only I could get free, he wished for the hundredth time. *I could swim ashore, be gone . . . or be drowned by the current. No matter which, this ordeal would be over.*

That's what I want. I want it to be over. I want to be away from here. . . .

He dozed, tossing restlessly in his cold slumber. In his dreams he found that meditative space that had eluded him during all these waking hours, the place where he felt quiet, heavy, centered. In his dream he was in chains also, the shackle biting uncomfortably into his ankle until he stretched his leg and strained, and it loosened. *What a nice dream,* he thought, even while dreaming it.

Dalin's body on the crumbling slope of Ship Rock smiled and stretched, then stretched some more. And then he rolled over. Freely. Out of the radius the chain had confined him in all these many hours.

He sensed it, and his dream bled away into nothingness. He was aware of his leg and twitched his left ankle, expecting to feel the weight of the shackle bearing it down.

He felt nothing. His eyes flicked open and he looked down the length of his body. Then his mouth gaped and an outcry lay stillborn in his throat.

The moonlight washed silver over the form of a brown bear. His form. His feet, his legs. Great furry paunch where flat youthful belly should be. He saw things over the end of a blocky protruding muzzle.

He set one paw to the rock to lever himself up for a better look—or tried to. His hands and arms didn't work quite as they should; they hinged differently—but he came up grunting on one side.

No mistaking that whuff of a bear, exerting himself.

No mistaking that shackle, burst asunder at a rusted hinge joint, either. Forced from his leg by the outsize growth of this bear-form.

He had a bear-form.

Like Uncle Segrim.

The bear that was Dalin quit trying to stand and collapsed back sitting on the rock. It was all sinking in, of a sudden: how this felt, the heaviness of body, the quiet space in his center. . . . How many times had he done this before or come close to it and not known it?

And the more he examined it, the more he questioned that he could be a bear. In a few breaths, the animal shape melted away from him just as swiftly as had his dreams.

Still Dalin sat, mouth agape. He curled his left leg into him—clothing intact, soft boots in one piece, his human form and trappings unmarred by the transformation that clearly affected not only his being, but also that which was about him. Was it an illusion? His hand went to his ankle, clasped it. Free, it was, and the broken shackle lay in plain sight. That much was no illusion at all.

How could it be so? How could he change? A shape-shifter, they said, was one touched by the gods, and those who took bear-form were once specially dear to Fadnor, the were-bear and warrior-hero of ancient times, raised to demigodhood in the God Wars. . . .

But I'm not touched by the divine! I'm just me. Dalin put hands to his head. *This is too much. Too much. . . .*

A splash. The grate of gravel on the shore.

"Brother," came a soft voice.

He looked up. A naked man stood on the shoaling rocks, cold seawater dripping from his well-formed body. His eyes were dark pools, his hair short as fur, his fingers webbed.

Selkie. Shape-shifter, calling him kin.

Dalin gave a little laugh, touched by an edge of hysteria. "Sure," he said. "That's me. Brother shape-shifter."

The Selkie man came closer, sat down nearby so as not to tower over the youth. "You are startled. Why?"

"I can't—I'm not—I don't know!" The futility of denial hit Dalin, and he shook his head. "I didn't know!"

The Selkie cocked his head to one side. "Sorry I am that your folk do not see the gift as readily as we. Your children should be taught to use it."

"We're not." When had Uncle Segrim become a shape-shifter? When had he first taken bear-form? Had it come as rudely to him as to Dalin? He had never been told the tales. It would be something to ask his father, did he ever win back home. . . .

Home. A distant place and an unlikely possibility. "Why do you care?" he asked the Selkie abruptly. "I'm to be executed, says the King. Your kinsman."

"Of course you are, or you would not be on this Rock. And yet . . . I wonder why you are here? You have not the scent of treachery or deceit about you, nor of blood on your hands."

Dalin's eyes widened. "You can tell?"

The man shrugged. "With some. You are more peaceful than most with the bear gift. You've intrigued us since you've been here. So tell me, please: what is it that has brought our cousin's wrath so forcefully down upon your head?"

The Truthsayer's apprentice heaved a sigh. Disbelief and relief washed through him at once: here at last, a friendly ear who seemed inclined to believe him. He told the selkie his story. The shape-shifter sat quietly for a time, looked out over moon-washed waves.

"This may not be just, but I don't know that I can help you. We are pledged to guard what is here, and to keep it here to await our cousin's pleasure."

"I'm condemned for no good reason."

"Hammankarl is temperamental, his judgments sometimes hasty. He means well, though."

"That won't help me after I'm beheaded."

"No." The selkie regarded the youth. "I don't suppose it would." He came to his feet. "I can promise you nothing, bear-kin. But I will talk with my family and see what they think of the matter." He looked down upon the Truthsayer's apprentice. "Your transformation may have been seen. This Rock is exposed and the moonlight bright. Were I you, I would at least leave the shackle around my ankle, so it looks from the Keep as if you are still bound. Unless you wish them to put you in chains suitable for a bear."

Dalin blushed. "No. Thank you. I'll do that."

He was fumbling to replace the sprung restraint when the water splashed once more. The selkie was gone, but he no longer felt so alone.

CHAPTER 68

THE RISING MOON washed the peninsula hills in silvery light as Katrije was shepherded into the hold of the *Talon;* the darkness below decks seemed more abysmal for the contrast. Sailors lit their way with lamps, ushered them past water barrels and coiled rope, past kegs containing ale and crates of vegetables, barrels of salted herring, cages with live chickens and a pig.

The livestock had just been brought on board and was the last thing the captain had been waiting for—fresh fare for a short voyage, no doubt. The chickens clucked, getting settled after their sudden transposition. Katrije and her friends were led past the cages to a cleared area near the bow of the ship. There, against the ribbing of the hull, the sailors made them fast with chains, as if they were cargo to be secured to the massive eyebolts set in the timber. No longer did ropes suffice to keep them prisoner: Captain Torsjak relied on chains, as Sembroi had ordered, binding half of them against the port side, half against the starboard. Worse, yet: a man gagged Valdarius, Cathmar, Nalia, and Belec—every one of their number who could summon divine powers or cast a spell. Thus further impaired from the use of magic, they were not likely to be able to surprise their warders or free themselves from confinement.

A lamp was hung swaying from a deck joist overhead and gave enough illumination that the hapless prisoners could see each other and the sailor who guarded them. He sat atop the pig's cage, obviously settling in for a long watch. A horn hung around his neck from a strap; apparently, he was to sound the alarm if there was any problem with the prisoners. Katrije did not know how there could be. They were shackled securely, and with their magic hindered in this way, what risk could they present? They did not even sit close enough to each other that one could help clandestinely with another's bonds.

Those who could talk had little to say to each other. They sat desultorily as the ship got under way, the creaking of oars on deck and the gentle motion of the hull telling them they were easing out into the waterway. The *Talon* did not pick up speed, though. A voice began to call depth measurements from the bow, and the massive oars pulled very slowly through their locks. Surely they moved ahead no faster than a man could walk. Katrije knew of the Selvian Ulloya and guessed the vessel was creeping through hidden channels in the treacherous broken waters. The *Talon* would work her way with utmost care through the shoals and submerged rocks until reaching open water beyond the vast island maze. Only then would they be fully under way for Nimm.

"This is not how we are supposed to be leaving Tura-kem," Arandel said in Elvish. The sailor ignored them, and the Silverleaf dared continue in a low voice. "Do you have a plan for us to get out of this, Thengel?"

The Guardian closed his eyes and leaned his head back against a rib of the ship. Katrije thought she had seldom seen him look so haggard or bone-weary. His long, slender fingers were intertwined, as comfortable a way as any to hold his hands, which were bound at the wrists. The bloodstain on his shirt had long since dried to a rust brown; it looked like dirt in the dim shifting lamplight.

"I have no plan." He finally spoke with his eyes closed. "Have you?"

Udo and Jaele could not follow any conversation in Elvish. "I don't understand," Udo interrupted in Trade, their common patois. He kept his voice low and faced toward Thengel, away from the sailor. It was not quite a whispered conversation, but one in which his words might not be distinctly overheard. "We could have gotten free on the road, Lord. Why did you have us not fight?"

His exasperation and frustration were plain. The Guardian opened his eyes and regarded his young squire. "In spite of what I've taken you on to train you for, Udo, fighting is not always the right way to further a warrior's endeavors."

"We could have taken them by surprise. Valdarius's song magic, Cathmar's great skill—why not? We're being sent away without accomplishing what you wished!"

"I'm aware of that." Thengel's tone was dry. "Do you think it appropriate for us to attack and fight or perchance kill our friends?"

Udo paused. "Uh . . . no. I suppose not."

"They were doing their duty as they saw fit."

"Yes, but . . . we can't just let ourselves be sent away like this!" he pressed. "Val's papers are lost if we do. And what will you do for the tapestry you lack?"

Thengel leaned his head back again and closed his eyes. "Fingol's treatise. . . ."

"Irreplaceable," noted Arandel.

"Without that," Hagar broke a long and sullen silence, "we cannot find the artifacts."

Valdarius was nodding violently, mumbling sounds of agreement around his gag.

The sound and motion drew the eye of their guard. "Quiet there!" he snapped. "Or you'll all be gagged."

A pall of silence fell over the group.

The leadsman overhead called out the depth, and the *Talon* continued to ease her way forward through the night.

CHAPTER 69

Molstroe woke too early after a night of carousing, but he wanted to attend to his duties before losing himself in the festivities of the day. The Guardian of the Thorn and his party of adventurers had seemed to be worthy warriors in service when the King's Hand first crossed paths with them. It was their reputation and officers like Kinlayik vouching for them that had won the elves entrée to the palace and connections with the court.

He had tacitly approved that entrée upon the southern jarl's recommendation. Indeed, it had been Molstroe who introduced the foreigners to Hammankarl some months before. Betrayed, now. All that trust destroyed.

He began his grooming in a black mood and nicked himself while scraping hastily at his gray-blond whiskers. *I will know the why of it. They've sullied their honor and my own. They will either tell me freely or be interrogated more harshly, but I will hear the reasons for their questionable doings.*

Carefully he applied a little grease to his long mustaches, then donned his gold-embroidered white surcoat and took himself to the Hakkonkalye. He marched into the guardroom, demanded to see the prisoners.

"Which one, sir?" the duty officer inquired.

"I'll start with na De'reth. The tall one," Molstroe replied.

"He's not here, sir."

"What?"

"Balyaden Kinlayik removed him and the others yesterday."

"What?" His voice tightened in anger. "*All* the prisoners?"

"All in service to that elf, yes, sir."

Molstroe spurred hard back to the citadel. He sent out urgent summons for Kinlayik and waited, pacing in his office, until her arrival.

It did not take long. She had been close by, as if she had expected to report to him this morning.

Molstroe kept his rage in check; he trusted his officers and expected them to make good decisions for good reason. Surely there was more to this than the Hakkonkalye guard knew. He would have it from Kinlayik and try not to bite her head off meanwhile. He made himself sit behind his desk, though he gladly left her standing at attention before him.

"You've removed Thengel and his people from prison. Where are they?"

"They—" Her voice cracked on a false note, and she coughed to clear her throat. "They're gone, sir," she blurted guiltily. "Deported to Nimm." She colored bright red with the admission.

In the pause that followed, Molstroe heard absolute silence. The war band was scattered about the city on duty ceremonial and practical, and the citadel lay quiet at this hour. Unearthly quiet, he thought, for he could only hear his angry pulse pounding intrusively in his ears.

"Deported?"

The syllables hung in the air between them.

"Yes, sir." Her eyes bored through the wall behind him.

He could contain himself no longer. He leaped to his feet, his heavy chair flying backward behind him, and leaned forward on his knuckles. "You *deported* them to Nimm?" he shouted. "Are you out of your mind?!"

Her eyes flickered to meet his, and though the furious blush continued to color her face, her voice sounded far more under control than his. "No, sir. I was acting within my discretionary powers."

"I gave you no 'discretionary powers'—" he spluttered.

"To the contrary, sir. You did. The King's Hand did, when I was made balyaden."

A retort was ready on his lips, but he held it in check. She had been promoted after her distinguished service in Kalajok in the spring—after service with Thengel. Did she aid and abet someone that rumor had it was her lover? He nearly asked her. But no: that was for later, for if that was part of her misjudgment also, he'd see her in chains, too.

"Explain yourself. Now."

She cleared her throat again and spoke to the wall in words that sounded rehearsed. "According to my charter of duties, it is incumbent upon me to rid the realm of imminent danger. Na De'reth and his party posed imminent danger to the security of Tura-kem."

He sneered. "Killing the Truthsayer endangers the realm?"

"No, Sir, you don't understand. They didn't kill the Truthsayer, but they did have designs on the Robe. They could not fulfill that quest without endangering how the King is advised and protected by the royal seer—whoever the next one appointed should be. I judged that to be an imminent danger, for they were not to be dissuaded from their goal and were going to persist as long as they were free to do so. That being so, they would have harmed the King and injured Turakemi interests, incidentally or otherwise."

"All a fancy way of saying you've helped your friends escape prison."

She shook her head. "I am not disinterested, Captain-General; I admit that. I had personal association with these people. But that does not affect the fact that I saw no way they could remain in Tura-kem and not endanger the capabilities of the Throne. Therefore, they had to go. 'Ridding the realm of imminent danger.'"

Molstroe shook his head. "You're not making sense."

"It's a long story."

He pulled his chair up and sat in it again. Leaving Sembroie standing, he steepled his fingers. "I have time. Suppose you remedy my ignorance."

"As you wish, Sir."

MOLSTROE FOUND HIS liege lord in the review stands, engrossed in the archery contests that were commencing on the field. He was reluctant to disturb the King with news such as he had, but there was nothing for it. Even though there was nothing to be done about it at this moment, it was not proper to withhold such news until a later hour. And so he interjected himself at Hammankarl's right side, drawing attention away from his queen and engaging the Lord High Councillor's attention as well.

"Majesty—some news. Na De'reth and his people whom we arrested along with Dalin of Nevi do not, in fact, seem to have done any misdeeds regarding the Truthsayer." That got Hammankarl's undivided attention, and Molstroe carried on. "They have been deported to Nimm under military escort: an action taken by an overzealous officer of mine. She is being corrected for that misjudgment, but the damage is done. I would advise Your Majesty that a trial for the boy might be in order after all, since it is clear from the elves' truth-spelled statements that Dalin is unlikely to have been the one to kill Granmar."

A strange expression crossed the King's face, and Hanno seemed to go a little pale. King and Councillor looked at each other simultaneously.

"Hanno?" Hammankarl demanded.

The runemaster shook his head. "I saw what I saw, Majesty. I can't account for these allegations from persons no longer available to be questioned." He shrugged.

Hammankarl frowned at the Captain-General. "This is bothersome. Very. And a bad time for an investigation that would take everyone away from Ardrunafest." He chewed his mustache. "Leave the boy on Ship Rock for now," he decided, "and I'll deal with him when the Festival is over."

"With a trial, Majesty?"

"I don't know. An investigation, at least. Who truth-spelled the Guardian of the Silverthorn?"

"Master Nehvros."

"He didn't mention it. But then, we've all been busy with other matters. . . . Hanno?"

"Yes, Sire?"

"You'll be happy to give deposition in Master Nehvros's presence, will you not?"

"Certainly, Sire. Any time you wish."

"Tonight then, before the feast." He turned his dark eyes on the leader of the King's Hand. "Tell Nehvros to be prepared to serve me."

Molstroe bowed. "As you wish, Your Majesty."

"If that's all, then? Good. Now please move, Molstroe; you're blocking the view, and I have 500 crowns bet on the archer who's up next."

The commander of the Hounds took his leave and began to search the crowd for Master Nehvros.

CHAPTER 70

R AGNAR HELD THE small twist of bronze and rolled it back and forth between his fingers. Spiraling metal curled like an earring, not quite in a closed loop, ending in a comical, distorted minuscule head and an exaggerated ear as the end knob of the ring. Strange workmanship—and poor recompense for the damage done to the *Gull.*

He looked about at the ruins of his ship and spat in anger at the charred planking of the deck. This time yesterday all had been neat and orderly here, ready for another run. Now, a full day later, his fortune and future lay in near-ruination. Half the port railing was gone, big sections blown out of it by the cascading bolts of lightning cast by that mage. The mast was splintered at man-height like a lightning-charred tree, and a stone's toss beyond wood had been ripped right out of deck and upper hull alike, the surrounding timber set afire from the heat of the assault.

Danmar's timely action below decks had squelched the flames, and lucky they were at that. The fresh resin that caulked the planking would have burned the *Gull* to the waterline if it had ignited. She could just as easily have been a smoking hull at this moment, instead of a charred and damaged half-wreck.

Well. Maybe not half-wreck. With the exception of that large chunk gone beside the gangway, the rest of the damage could be repaired—at cost—with only a few days' work. Not so readily fixed was the loss of life. Ulf and Bruvik slaughtered outright by the bearded swordsman, Jurg and Arold burned by lightning, and Arold barely clinging to life last night where he lay tended in the healing hospice of Meliors. And the other injuries minor and major—even Grieg was in sorry wise, blown clear of the deck by the second magical attack, his leg broken from his harsh impact on the wharf. He would have drowned had he dropped in the water, for he could not swim a lick. He was lucky it was only a broken leg he had to deal with. . . .

"No! By Graumnir's fire, none of it's right!" Ragnar raged to no one in particular. Who would pay weregeld for the slain sailors? For they had certainly not died by accident. *I don't owe their families. Those outlanders do!* And who would pay for repairs to the *Gull?* He'd already complained to the King's Hand, and they had nodded somberly but not promised any quick results. How was he to be ready to ship without funds to fix this extraordinary damage?

He glared at the collection of packs and bags in the lee of the mast: the belongings of the elf's group, whom he had permitted so trustingly aboard. His by salvage rights, surely—and there was a supply of gold and silver therein and, even more promising, some gemstones and the odd piece of jewelry that might nearly make this worth his while, if he could find buyers for it all. The rest was trash: personal effects, clothes, useless papers and scribblings in some foreign script. The only reason he had not yet tossed it over the side was because it might have a purpose in bartering for weregeld.

The outlanders who had contracted to sail to Tren were the ones who had damaged the *Gull* and harmed his crew worst. Yet their belongings had all been confiscated when the lot of them were arrested, even that unholy sword that had slain the first Hound to touch it. Yellowbeard had been forced to sheath it for them at sword point, and they'd all been taken away, along with their horses. Thengel's crew, though, had had their belongings out of sight in the hold and so were overlooked by the Hounds.

Oh, he could just keep his booty and call it the spoils of war—but that did not sit quite right with him. The elves had, after all, not given the greatest offense here, nor harmed a one of his seamen, to be quite fair about it. Would they pay damages? If they were honest in turn, they must admit their presence led to the deaths and damage and so they held some responsibility for it. Ragnar preferred to win such concession by negotiation, than delay his travels overlong for a date with the justiciar. *Though I'm willing to see them all before the magistrate if I must, to collect for the damage.*

He frowned at the earring, in a stew about how to proceed. Wait on the Hounds to inform him of an award of damages? File claim with the Justiciar? Sell the elves' belongings and hope to recover a little something on his own? Give them their belongings back in exchange for fair compensation?

As he fretted over his options, his fingers strayed to his ear, removed one of the gold hoops he wore there, and threaded the end of the odd spiral ring through the hole. This had been Thengel's, he knew, for he recalled seeing it on the elf's ear when they had sat long in speech together. Knocked loose during the fight, it must have been. He had found it in a tangle of rope when cleaning up the deck.

To the Justiciar, he finally decided. *That's most fair. I won't wait on the Hounds, but I have a claim against all that fought on board my ship yesterday, and that's what I'll press. . . .*

A sound like a whining mosquito made him shake his head, then pass a hand near his ear. But the sound did not cease and he cocked his head, listening. Like a tiny high-pitched voice, it was. . . .

The sound came from the earring. Ragnar's large fingers strayed to that small ornament, and the sound was muffled. He moved his fingers, and he could hear it again. Ah—a finger over the ring stifled the sound. . . .

The big man blinked in astonishment. Magic. It was something magical.

His fingers worked at his earlobe hastily, getting the oddment out of his flesh before it could have any strange effect on him. Finally the ring was free and in his hands and he squinted closely at it.

An ear in bronze, overlarge and conveying something to be listened to. . . .

He held it up near his ear, gingerly—and heard the tiny voice once more. A picture came to him then of how Thengel had worn the thing: not threaded through a pierced hole in his earlobe, but hooked around the shell of his ear, the tiny ear-shaped knob inside. . . .

Ragnar was reluctant to do that. Instead, he kept the ring in his fingers, but brought it closer to his head and held it within the shell of his ear right next to his ear hole.

". . . great Tornor, in this time of need, look upon us in your mercy and know we tread your righteous path . . ."

He took the thing away and regarded it curiously. The voice was distinct. Not loud enough to hear unless held that closely to the ear, but there was no doubt about what was being said. Who was Tornor?

He held the ring close and listened further.

". . . Oath and following your holy path. Bring us succor that we may continue as your faithful servants, Vikkar Tornor, lord of faith and master of unbending will. . . ."

Ragnar jerked the ring from his ear and nearly cast it across the deck. A prayer to one of the Forbidden Gods, that was! He shivered and clenched his fist around the small token. He looked again at the abandoned bags and glowered at them as if at their owners. Did the Guardian and his folk worship the shunned powers of Tura-kem? What heretical pursuits had brought them on board his ship? Just as well they'd been arrested. . . .

He shifted uneasily. This whole affair was taking on a different face than mere conflict between two parties who had apparently crossed swords before. This was heresy, and Ragnar Erngrim had no interest in being tainted with that—not he who must trust to Lan Loros's goodwill in his far-travels at sea.

He went below decks to his strongbox, dropped the defiled earring into it, and locked it up for safekeeping. Right now he was too busy to deal with this item and what it portended. He had yet to check on Arold and Ulf and the rest of his injured. Danmar was asking around the waterfront to see if any spare planking was to be had for repairs, but probably it would be fruitless: he suspected already not much would be doing until Festival was over.

Ragnar decided to take care of what business he could and then go see a bit of the fair. Come by the ship, maybe take the ring with him later: then he could turn this unsettling discovery over to the authorities somewhere along the way and be rid of it. Later he would file claim with the Justiciar. Someone would be made to pay for the injury to the *Gull*—and the weregeld for his sailors' deaths.

Of that he was certain.

CHAPTER 71

THE BRIEF DEPOSITION took place in a second-floor room not far from the privy council chamber. A scribe attended them along with Nehvros, Captain-General Molstroe, and four guards. Hanno hid his unease with great aplomb. Koram's mantle was upon him, and there was no way that the court mage's simple truth-discernment could overpower the elemental rune magic that flowed to and through him.

He sat comfortably, for all the world like an innocent man fallen wrongly under suspicion, eager to give good evidence to clarify any misunderstandings that might be.

Nehvros lit a blue candle inscribed with magical glyphs. The air around it glowed blue as well. He poured a little of the molten wax upon the back of Hanno's hand; the runemaster winced as the air shimmered with sympthetic radiance around him. If that aura changed, he would be speaking false.

In spite of the protection he had given himself, Hanno's heart raced a little faster as the spell-casting commenced. Then Nehvros put the question to him: "Relate, please, exactly what you saw Dalin do to the Truthsayer."

He kept his story simple. He'd traveled with an escort to seek Granmar's advice about some mystery teachings. In sight of Kodanit's Spire, he had seen the boy push the old man to his death. When they had entered the cavern, he was trying workings with the Robe. Clearly it had been that which he coveted, and the powers that seemed to go with it. The boy evaded them, but Hanno had taken the Robe and returned with it to Etjorvi, to keep it safe from theft. The boy had somehow managed to steal it back. To save himself, he was intent on casting calumny upon the runemaster.

The veracity of his tale was plain to see in the unchanging aura around him. Hammankarl smiled as the scribe finished a hasty transcription. He clasped the runemaster's forearm and seemed vastly reassured.

"I knew I chose well when I chose you. Thank you for bearing with me and adding this information to the official record."

"It is my pleasure to serve you, Your Majesty."

The King nodded. "This affair is becoming more complex than it first appeared. We've learned that na De'reth hoped to win the Truthsayer's robe for his own. No wonder they befriended the boy: it falls to Dalin by rights of inheritance, you see. But we have firm evidence that they played no role in Granmar's death, and your testimony bears that out."

The runemaster's eyebrows crept up his forehead. That was the furthest thing from his intention! Much better to keep the elves under suspicion than have the Nimmians—his "escort"—become suspect.

"Perhaps they had some other involvement that remains unclear to us," he ventured.

"I doubt it," Nehvros remarked casually. "I took the Guardian's statement myself. It was as truthful as your own."

"I see." Hanno inclined his head, conceding the mage's authority in the matter. *As truthful as my own. Indeed.*

"We'll know more after we've interrogated the boy." Hammankarl came to his feet, and the others rose as well. He gestured to the door.

"Now. Let's enjoy the feast."

Hanno nodded cordially to Master Nehvros and passed the elf by, walking with the King to his place at the high table.

Panic had long since left Hanno and cold resolve taken its place. *It's only a matter of time before he questions everyone involved with this. All those who can hurt my interests must be put out of the way immediately.*

He joined in small talk, laughing. He took a course of stuffed squab and laid a slice of pâte beside it. He poured mead for the King with a free hand, but took the smallest drab for himself.

Dalin first. I can get to him easiest—tonight, right after this banquet. And then Joro and his lot. I'll make it look like they fought, like Kaylis slew her fellows with magic, and then the guards slew her. . . . I have a rune or two that will suffice to cause such injury as she does with her spells. . . .

But first, the boy.

CHAPTER 72

I T WAS A talent of the Fen Ehrden, gained at a high level of mastery: knowledge of the *yelitstalje,* the seeming. An adept runemaster could project his second form across space, appearing elsewhere as if physically present there.

The *tak yelitstalje* was its inverse of a sort: the not-seeing, or not-form, as the word also meant. A way by which one moved physically but caused onlooking eyes to avert with a wandering thought or a distracted pause. Under dweomer of the not-seeing one could walk as if invisible. It was not a true gift of incorporeality, and animals were not distracted by it, but creatures capable of imagination and abstract thought—they were the ones led astray by the *tak yelitstalje.*

As more banqueters joined the dance and desserts were heaped on the dining board, Hanno pleaded a delicate stomach and made his excuses. With the aura of Persuasion and Truth about him, his claim was taken seriously; one or two remarked on the Riedskana's pallor and urged their favorite physic on him. Thanking them for their concern, Hanno left the King's hall.

He lost no time cloaking himself in the not-seeing, envisioning that runic sigil vibrant in his mind's eye, permeating his being with its radiance. It was the skill he had employed when scouting his backtrail, when he had first encountered Dalin in the Crystal Spires. The same skill that would see him to his final encounter with the boy.

Unnoted, he took a horse from the stables and passed unobserved through the broad gate of the Palace. Soon he was cutting through side streets toward Jarlsdock. It was easily done, to find a skiff and help himself to it. Rowing out upon the waters of the fiord, he maneuvered the little boat awkwardly across the chop and swell where the Aelvoss current roiled the cold harbor waters.

He kept his course with some little difficulty. He was not a vastly skilled oarsman, though he could row a little boat if he must.

And now I must. There, and back again—merely that.

It was not a great distance, but he took it slowly. His rowing fell into a comfortable pattern of exertion, his breathing became deep and regular, and he applied himself to embodying the aura of the not-seeing. Those who would look aside from the spot of avoidance he created would also not notice his boat, as long as he stayed close to it. The Selkies, even, would be in ignorance of his approach, for they, too, were intelligent and every bit as prone to distraction as humans.

Wrapped in the protective dweomer, Hanno rowed steadily across the sound until the keel of his boat scraped upon the steep, flinty shore of Ship Rock.

He spotted Dalin in the moonlit gloaming, a dark figure huddled against the stone at the end of his prison chain. Hanno drew the skiff up close to that spot on the Rock. The boy looked up at his approach, visibly startled as if he could see the runemaster through his guise of magic. Or perhaps it was the unexpected sound of keel on gravel, for noise was less easily disguised with the not-seeing.

No matter. In moments, what the boy heard would be of no consequence to anyone.

PALSTRO HAD DRUNK rather too much at the King's banquet the night before and hoped he had not made too great a fool of himself with the Under-Steward's wife. Better, he thought, to stay away this evening, give them all a chance to forget her shriek and the slap that had marked his face right there at table. The wench had not even the grace to wait until they were in a side alcove—

He wrestled his temper down and decided never to talk to the woman again. There were others with greater interest in a military man. . . .

He was planning who else might fall victim to his charms on the morrow when a runner from the watch officer brought him strange news. It was a welcome interruption, if an odd one; he stood and followed the runner out the door.

The watch officer came to his feet as his superior entered the room, vacating the desk so Commander Palstro could have a seat. Palstro looked from the officer to the brawny, unkempt seaman before him. The man was not drunk, but he had been drinking—making free of libations at the fairgrounds, no doubt. He had a wayward green-and-yellow streamer tied around his large bicep and caught in the back of his trousers.

Palstro stifled a snort and kept his words businesslike. "You were here after the Hounds yesterday, about damages."

"Aye, sire, I was. Not now, though."

"It's late to be here now, man. You've been very insistent." Palstro turned to the watch officer. "Well?" he demanded. "Charges of heresy, you say?"

"He has a token. Says it came from the Guardian of the Thorn—"

The sailor interrupted, his words slurring lightly when he got excited. "Invocations, prayers, whatever you want to call it," he said. "Hold it to your ear and you can hear it all. Nothing else comes from the thing." He fished in a pouch and pulled forth a twist of bronze. "I listened only long enough to be certain what I was hearing," he avowed hastily, and his voice dropped in volume. "It speaks to a Defiled One . . ." He put the ring in Palstro's outstretched hand. "I don't want anything to do with it. Thought you'd be interested, though. Whoever is listening to this must be a heretic. That elf, Thengel . . . you'll want to ask him about this, I'm sure."

"No doubt."

Ragnar shifted his weight uneasily. "I'd like to talk to him, too, about damages to my ship. Now that I've brought you that, do you think there's a chance I could get a word with him?"

Palstro looked at the man coldly. Rather inept he was, if he'd hoped to bribe his way in to a prisoner in this manner.

"Much as I would like to help you, Captain, I cannot. No one here is permitted visitors under any circumstances."

"Oh." He hesitated. "Can you tell me when he'll be released?"

"I'm not in a position to tell you that." *Not without revealing his absence. And a heretic, at that? Why would an elf be involved with the god-worship of Nimm?*

Curiosity ate at him, and he was anxious to be shed of the sailor so he could examine this trinket. "Your cooperation is noted," he said brusquely. "I'll be sure to pass that on to the Justiciar."

"Well . . ." The big man loitered uncertainly. "I'm making claim against them, you know. All of them that damaged my ship."

"As well you ought, sir. Now, if that's all?"

"Um. Right. Good night, then. Ardruna's bounty on you."

"And on you."

The duty officer was far easier to ignore. It was not until he was in the privacy of his office in the ground floor of the Keep that Commander Palstro gave in to his inquisitiveness. Behind a closed door he held the ring to his ear as Ragnar had described and listened to the words that came from it.

His brows pulled together. A Forbidden God, indeed: Vikkar Tornor, once faithful human warlord, later demigod raised to service of Uric the Just, Nalagar's alienated brother-god in the ancient wars. . . .

And that voice, invoking the deity: it sounded like someone lost in devout prayer, chanting some phrases with the cadence of memorized ritual, others with the free-form hesitation and pauses of ad-libbed piety. . . .

He stared at the ring. In spite of Ragnar's impression, this was not an enchantment that simply poured forth prayers and invocation. Surely he was listening to something happening exactly this moment. The man's voice sounded raspy, tired. Here a statement was broken by a cough, there a pause or a long sigh. And the voice—the voice sounded vaguely familiar.

Alarm coursed through him: where had he heard this voice before? It was not mellifluous enough to be the elf. It was human—and accented.

He held the odd creation again to his ear. ". . . in our hour of need, that we cleave to steadfastness and honor that you may descend among us. I give myself to your embrace, O Lord; take this vessel and use it as your tool . . ."

Accented, yes. The prayers were said in an old Turakemi dialect, if his ear served him well. And on top of that dialect, the overlay of foreign pronunciation. Not very foreign: just clipped tones and shortened vowels. As if this were an old clerical liturgy spoken as Nimmians spoke.

The Nimmians.

He started. One among them was lost in prayer these many hours. One of them was a cleric, earnestly invoking his god.

He bolted from the room and called armed guards to him as he ran.

CHAPTER 73

THERE WAS NO telling what time it was in the dank holes they were locked in. Joro slept to pass the while. There was nothing else that could be done, during these long, slow hours of endless waiting. . . .

When freedom came it was in most unexpected wise. The door to his cell creaked open, and he stirred in the bright light that poured in. Narialnos squinted. *What—?*

Berin stood in the doorway. From somewhere Redeemer had come vibrant to his hand. Yet the oathblade that glowed with a light of its own was outshone by the radiance around the priest of Vikkar Tornor.

"Berin?" the Nightrunner asked, not believing his eyes.

There was more to the cleric than a radiance. His eyes were sparkling green flame, and his portly frame seemed larger, more robust. More than that: there was an aura of presence around him; that was all that it could be called. A deep, resonant voice replied to Joro, and he felt chills shiver across his skin.

"No." The single word reverberated like a bell. "Come."

For a nonpious man, a cynical man, even Joro could not mistake the presence of divinity. It could not be the god manifest—such power would vaporize a human being, surely—but this could be no less than an avatar of Vikkar Tornor. Joro bowed his head in obeisance to the apparition and was glad his bound hands were not free to tremble.

"Come," he was told again. As he stepped past what once was Berin, the avatar reached out with one finger and touched the ropes. They fell from his wrists into the dirty straw. He glanced back, saw his companions in the hall, all freed of their own bonds as well.

The entity led the way down the hall, and the Nimmians, awed, followed silently after.

It was in the broad guard chamber where they'd first been held in open cells that they encountered resistance. Pounding down the spiral stairs, bringing a hurried assemblage of swords at his back, came Commander Palstro—alerted, somehow, to their escape. "Seize them!" he ordered, and the guards charged them.

None recognized the supernatural force among them until the first guard entered the glowing aura a man's length away from Berin. He cried out and fell, unconscious or dead, Joro could not tell which. His comrade, charging close behind, fell as well, and it was only then that the others realized their prisoners were bespelled.

"Archers!" screamed Palstor. "On the double! Archers!"

Berin-that-was looked at the man and raised Redeemer. He angled the sword so that the tip of the blade pointed at the officer. Energy flashed from sword tip to Palstro's chest.

It was not a bolt like lightning nor a beam of light, but something in between that flew in the blink of a eye and caught the commander without defense. He threw up his hands, his sword clattering to the ground, and fell over dead, a black and smoking hole where his chest had been.

The remaining guards cried out in fear and shoved each other aside to escape from the room. The avatar raised Redeemer once again, this time pointing high overhead, and Berin's lids closed upon the eyes of green flame. He stood still for a long minute, then opened his eyes again and lowered the sword.

Upstairs, where there had been screams and the clatter of weapons and orders shouted in chaos, now there was silence. Berin walked up the circular steps to the ground floor of the Keep and through the doors that opened into a courtyard.

Guards lay everywhere, dropped to the ground as if felled by a single stoke from on high—as indeed they had been. But what Joro took for wholesale slaughter became something else the instant he heard one of the prone forms inhale in a stentorian snore.

The avatar caught him studying the men roundabout.

"Not dead?" Joro blurted—then quailed, wondering if this would give offense to the demigod, to have his boon questioned.

Berin's face smiled. "Easier than death," he said in those bell-like tones. "Ah."

Aral stepped closer, a strange combination of cowed obeisance and fear on his face. "What now?"

"Now you leave this place." The burning eyes fixed on Joro, their leader. "Stay out of prisons. I cannot help you often, but this was necessary. Those who are Oath-sworn are bound to me, and I to them as well."

The Nightrunner reacted and caught the avatar's eye in a moment of shared understanding. "Thank you."

In the next instant, the divine presence was gone as if it had never been.

Berin stood blinking, his eyes hazel in the lamplight as they had always been. He looked at Redeemer clutched in his hand and looked around in wonder. "Vikkar . . . ," he sighed.

"Do you remember?" Aral asked eagerly.

"Save it," Joro interrupted. "Let's get out of here before they awaken."

Rudic balked. "My bow."

Kaylis stretched forth her long fingers. "My rings. They were taken from me."

"Rings?" Joro snorted. "We have no time—"

"They are bespelled," she said curtly. "And rare."

"Let us look quickly," Rudic urged. "We are setting ourselves back if we leave without our gear, and horses, too."

Joro conceded the point. "Quickly, then. Berin, how long will these sleep, do you know?"

The cleric looked dazed, shook his head. "An hour? Two? Longer?" He scratched his head with one hand—a hand from which his ring had vanished that he had lately worn. "We have some while, if no one enters the garrison and discovers . . . all this."

"Let's lose no more time, then." Joro reentered the keep, and the search began.

CHAPTER 74

Dalin heard the unmistakable crunch of booted foot on the gravel. He was loath to look that direction, and that reluctance alone warned him that spellcraft was here. That and the fact that every hair stood on his body, an uncomfortable prickling over all.

He forced himself to look the way he did not want to gaze. There. Out of the corner of his eye—

Hanno.

Dalin scrambled to his feet, every nerve crying alarm. The runemaster stopped as well.

"You can see me." There was wonder in his voice, followed by a cynical chuckle. "You'll forgive me if I don't drop the not-seeming. Even if *you* spy me, I would rather others did not."

"What do you want?" Dalin demanded shakily.

The man took a step forward, and the youth one back. His chain dragged over the rock at his feet, following the shackle at his ankle. There now: the more he engaged with the runemaster, the easier it was to set eyes on him. He saw when Hanno stopped, rested his hand on the knife at his belt.

"Do you know who I am now, boy?" His tone was haughty. "Did you get an inkling when you ruined the King's processional and found me in my sash of office? Do you?" he demanded.

Dalin shook his head.

"I am the Riedskana, Hammankarl's highest adviser. I am the second-most powerful man in all of Tura-kem. And you are my greatest liability." He smiled bitterly. "I should have put an end to you when we first met and saved myself all this trouble."

He drew the knife. Dalin saw moonlight shimmer on a dull-surfaced blade patterned with runes, and his blood ran cold.

"You don't need to kill me," he blurted, taking another step uphill.

"You are mistaken. I do, and I will. I won't have you carrying tales about what really happened at Kodanit's Spire. I would be most distraught if the King lost confidence in me because of some fancy you have to tell him."

"Fancy! I didn't imagine what I saw!"

"No matter. You'll be telling it to no other." Hanno started up the gravelly slope toward Dalin.

"You—you can't stab me! They'll know it's murder. You'll be suspect."

Hanno smiled and twisted the blade in the air. "This isn't going to stab you. It is ceremonial, and stone. See how blunt it is? It's going to touch you, that's all—and plummet you into a sleep like death. And while you lie there, I will hold your nose and mouth shut for a time, and let your sleeping body suffocate to death. That's all. You'll be found dead, and no one will know why."

Dalin's eyes were drawn to the brandished blade and the runes on it glowing with the baleful orange of ill-wished magic.

Hanno was past the anchor point of the chain, closing in on him. Dalin bent, batted at the shackle with one frantic hand—and the loosely hinged metal fell open around his foot. He turned and darted across the brow of Ship Rock, the runemaster in close pursuit behind.

Youth and desperation gave the boy the advantage. Probably the man had some spell or rune magic he could use to bring him down, did he stop long enough to think about it. Dalin didn't want him to think about it. He dashed to the far shore as Hanno crested the Rock behind him. He stared at the water dashing against the side of the stoney spit.

Jump, he urged himself. *Now. While you can.*

He hesitated, glanced out over the broad cold-water bay. *I can barely swim in a pond. I'll drown if I try this.*

Pebbles bounded down the slope, knocked free by Hanno's lunging stride, peppering his leg with debris.

I'll be dead if I don't.

He leaped.

He plummeted feet-first into shallow water, banged into rocks, was thrown sideways by the wash of the tide as his head broke the surface. His flailing limbs struck rock—he was trying to push himself farther out into the bay, out into deep water where he had a chance to swim away. If that were even possible. His head dipped beneath the waves and he struggled to tread water, his waterlogged leathers sodden through and threatening to drag him down.

When he struggled up for air, he saw Hanno at the edge of the surf, cursing at him. It was no use: his arms and legs felt leaden, exhausted already, and the weight of his clothes and the cold of the water were conspiring to pull him down. His eyes widened in panic, and the runemaster, seeing his distress, began to laugh, low and quietly.

Then strong hands grasped Dalin by torso and legs, and he was buoyed up enough to catch his breath. "Be still," a familiar voice said next to his ear.

It was the selkie from earlier and beside him a companion, in half-man, half-seal form. "Eat this, bear-kin. It will ease your time with us." The selkie held up a mollusk, its shell popped open. Its pale flesh glistened in the moonlight, raw and unappetizing. Dalin shrank back.

"Eat it." His voice was stern. "We cannot linger. Swallow; do not chew."

Lip curled in disgust, Dalin did as he was told and plucked the mollusk from its shell and swallowed it down. He thought he would heave as the cold, slimy thing oozed over his tongue and down his throat.

Almost instantly, though, he felt different. The water became comfortably warm around him—or was it that he had become inured to the cold?

"Do not fear, now," the selkie said, placing one webbed hand gently on Dalin's head. "You will be able to breathe naturally. Just try it."

They submerged beneath the waves.

Dalin could not help himself. Instant panic came over him, and he knew he was going to drown. The selkies held him down, fought his thrashing limbs as he tried to struggle to the surface, the surface that was drawing farther away as they pulled him deeper into murky moonlit waters. He held his breath as long as he could and then with a cry of anguish gave up the last of his oxygen in great bubbles that billowed out of his mouth. When he could tolerate it no longer, he inhaled, dreading the imminent invasion of his lungs with water.

He took in air, instead.

The selkies laughed at the look on his face, bubbles fleeing their nostrils and mouths as well. He was breathing water. It didn't feel like water; it felt like air, and he could see through it clearly. But all around was the water of Dannen's Sound.

"Magic . . . ?"

"A gift of the Sea Father." Words traveled through the water as if it were air. "The *archich,* created by Lan Loros to help those who journey between land and his realm."

Dalin had no response for that.

He saw other seal-folk under water nearby, but he and his two companions soon left them behind. He relaxed into their grip and let them swim with him at shallow depth through the waters of the fiord.

He didn't care where he was going; he was just glad to be going there alive.

Hanno watched the selkies grab the boy, put something in his mouth, sink with him beneath the waves. Not before they both looked at him full-on, though. In the heat of the chase he'd lost the not-seeming, and he stood there in plain sight for all to see.

He collapsed to his knees in the surf and bowed his head, knuckles clenched white around the rune blade. Rage and panic and something near despair battled in him and, underneath it all, a stark fear of discovery.

Selkies. Kin to Hammankarl. With Dalin.

There was no time to follow that to its logical conclusion. First, he had to get clear of Ship Rock. With a great effort of will he put turmoil aside and disciplined his mind to cloak him once more in the tak yelitstalje. Soon enough he was concealed from onlookers' eyes. With any luck, his brief visibility had not been noted by any but the selkies who'd taken the boy.

Soon he was back in the boat and rowing away from the island.

What to do? he fretted. *What to do?*

Half-formed plans and possibilities chased each other through his mind. The Truthsayer's apprentice was gone, out of his grasp. Surely he would tell his story to the selkies, and they could well tell the King. The seal-folk had very little contact with their human cousin, he knew, but if they chose to talk with him, Hammankarl would believe their word above his own; he was certain of it. For that matter, they had only to say they saw him trespassing on Ship Rock: that alone would put his life in danger, for it was forbidden to all on pain of death.

He would never get his hands on the boy now, and he was at risk the day a selkie chose to talk to Hammankarl. He was in no position to order a manhunt for Dalin; the King would want to know why. As soon as he suspected the least thing or questioned the Nimmians or heard from selkies of his trespass and murder attempt—

It will be me in chains on Ship Rock. . . .

Panic threatened to overtake him, and he quit rowing. He needed time to think. He sat in the boat as it rocked on the waters of the sound, drifting between Ship Rock and the mouth of the Aelvoss.

What can I do? Confess before I am made to confess. Throw myself on the King's mercy. Flee before I am discovered. . . .

Every thought turned his stomach more sour than the last. *Not only to leave but to leave as an outlaw? A hunted man? Never.* His face set in grim lines. *I'll see the King dead first.*

The thought was shocking. "What am I saying?" he murmured out loud, but the idea would not go quietly away. *See the King dead . . .*

If the King died, Hanno Runemaster, the High Councillor, would become Regent in his place. There would be no debate about that succession: it was established policy, long-standing in the realm. The Riedskana ruled at need, until the King's heir came of age.

No. I couldn't possibly . . . He shook his head.

Why not? the calculating part of himself asked. *Yes, Hammankarl's been your friend. But not that good a friend. He's never known you, really. You've presented a face to him, and he's believed it, all along.*

And if he were to die . . . You would be safe from discovery. As for the boy—it will be far easier to deal with him clandestinely as Regent than as Councillor with a King to answer to. And you would be the ruler of Tura-kem in all but royal title for a long, long time to come. Prince Einar is only a year old. . . .

The King? Dead?

It had its advantages.

Hanno began to consider it seriously as he took the oars again. Selkies, close as they dwelled, had no contact with the men of Etjorvi, would not likely be bearing tales up and down the coast. It was only the King who was the weak link, only Hammankarl's suspicions that might bring him down. . . .

This time he pointed the little skiff to the royal docks behind Hakkon-kalye. There were outlanders there that might be of use to him, after all.

CHAPTER 75

THEY HAD RETRIEVED their equipment, or as much of it as mattered, anyway—Kaylis's satchel of vials and ritual items used in magic, her rings and staff, Rudic's fine bow, their weapons. Leaving the keep, stepping over slumbering forms of guards, they found several gates roundabout, all closed, and nothing to suggest which way the stables were to be found.

They went one way round, opened one gate—and found themselves at the lip of a quay fronting the harbor. It was the sea gate, with two skiffs docked and a guard asleep by a mooring post.

"Wrong way," grumbled Aral. "Let's go."

"Joro!" A voice hissed urgently from down the quay.

The group jumped as Hanno appeared out of nowhere, standing near a boat that they had somehow overlooked.

The runemaster approached, eyeing the sleeping guard warily. "You're free?" he asked in hushed tones.

"In a way you would scarcely credit," the Nightrunner said. "And for that matter it must be fated that we find you." He flashed a feral grin. "I think you'll be coming with us."

"What? No."

"Oh, yes. You've been our bane more than our help, Runemaster. You can help us now. We've yet to retrieve the Tapestry. We'll ride free of this land if we must, but we'll have your help before we do so."

His companions followed his lead and surrounded the runemaster as he spoke. To Joro's surprise, the High Councillor did not seem much discomforted by threat of coercion. Hanno brushed a hand through the air. "Don't waste time with this farce. Disaster is upon us all. Only if we work together can we salvage anything for it."

"Your meaning?" Joro demanded.

Hanno looked suspiciously at the slumbering guard and glanced up to the deserted battlements. "We are not overheard?"

Aral barked a laugh. "Speak freely," Joro said. "And quickly. You try my patience."

Hanno glared but spoke bluntly. "We have each had our deceits with the other. The time for that is gone. The King is soon to discover from a source he will not doubt that you slew the Truthsayer and that I aided you. When that happens, we will all be dead."

"Not us," Joro snickered. "We're leaving."

"Without your tapestry?"

"That's what we'll have you for. The boy took it from me. We need to find him."

Hanno shook his head. "He's already been found, and lost again. The Robe was taken from him; it is presently locked away in the King's treasure-house for safekeeping. I have no access to it. No one but the King has. You can try to force me to help you, but unless you're prepared to lay siege to the White Palace, neither you nor I are going to steal away with the Robe."

Joro hesitated. If that were so, only direct intervention by Vikkar Tornor was likely to help them, and it was clear the avatar was not going to come to their aid again anytime soon. . . .

"I see a way to resolve this to our mutual benefit," Hanno continued. "It is quite simple. Kill the King, and I will become Regent. I'll give you the Tapestry. You can be on your way, and I'll be able to halt investigation into this affair. We'll all have what we want."

"Kill the King? Am I hearing you right? I thought you were close to him."

Hanno's lips turned down. "His continuing existence has unhappily become a dire threat to my own. Time is short before too many will know what we've done."

"I see." There was little incredulity in Joro's tone. An experienced assassin was not easily shocked by the prospect of murder to conceal intrigue, no matter how high-placed the victim. To leave Tura-kem with the Tapestry, and with the elimination of Duke Arn's historic antagonist to his credit, would be counted a most laudable coup back in Nimm. His sticking point was the logistics. "It is possible to kill anyone. But we have no time to spend weeks planning this, and then hope you will keep your end of the bargain."

"No need for weeks. Tomorrow, Hammankarl retires to Greenstone, his seaside retreat and summer house a short ride down the coast. There he will undergo the sea-bonding ceremony that renews his ties to Lan Loros. It is a small ceremony, and very private. The only persons attending are myself and a handful of others. Neither the King nor Greenstone is heavily guarded, and I can help you gain entrance. It would be your perfect opportunity."

Joro's eyes narrowed. "And then we're to wait until you as Regent see fit to open the treasure-house before we are recompensed for this task?"

Hanno shook his head. "I can persuade Hammankarl to bring the Tapestry with him. He wishes a new Truthsayer. I will tell him a rune scrying advises he incorporate the Robe into the ceremony of renewal. It will be there with us."

"Can you guarantee that?"

"I can." He said it with flat confidence.

Joro believed him.

"Very well then. We have a deal. The King in exchange for the Tapestry in our hands tomorrow."

"Agreed."

"And, Hanno? If you do not have the Tapestry with you, we'll kill you as well and deal with the treasure-house later. You have my word on it."

The runemaster looked angered by the threat, but he did not retort. Joro nodded to himself. "It is all the more urgent that we leave now, then. We seek the stables."

"I'll show you," Hanno volunteered, and led the way through the sea gate back into Hakkonkalye.

Joro glanced back at a splash in the water, but it was just a seal, playing in the moonlight at the edge of the quay. He turned on his heel and followed the runemaster within.

CHAPTER 76

DALIN SHOOK HIS head in angry frustration. "What do you mean, you won't help the King?" He had been listening to Ervir's equivocations for the last long while, and still the selkie's avoidance made no sense to him.

"It's not that we don't desire to," interjected Ferik, who had brought word of Hanno's scheme. "It is that we *can* not. Are not permitted to."

Dalin grimaced at the man-seal lounging on the edge of the grotto shelf. He was half in, half out of the cold water, right where he'd stopped to babble his discovery to Ervir and the few other selkies who had gathered in this watery hideaway. Dalin guessed they were somewhere under the cliffs of the fiord, beyond the mouth of Etjorvi harbor. Where, exactly, did not matter. It was odd enough to find himself here: where strange algae grew on the walls, brightening the water-echoing chamber with a soft green luminescence. The air smelled of brine and fish and the animal-scent of seals. They had all been perfectly polite to Dalin, who was still bespelled by the effects of the archich mollusk. He was discomforted by the clinging wetness of his leathers but unaffected by the chill of them and wondered in what other ways the tidbit lent him unrecognized protections.

Certainly it did not save him from the prevarication of selkies. Ervir, his rescuer, had seemed helpful until Ferik's news had been tossed among them like a stinking fish. The necessary action was clear to Dalin, but somehow the selkies could not seem to get it through their heads.

"All you need to do is tell him," he tried again. "Warn him what his traitorous Councillor plans. You're saying you can't do that?"

Ferik nodded. "That is exactly what we are telling you. We are not permitted."

"Who forbids it?"

"The Sea Father himself."

Dalin blinked. Lan Loros, lord of the great inland sea, creator of the selkie folk and other denizens of these waters? Surely he would take an interest in his creatures great and small. "Why would he prevent you from warning your kinsman of danger? You already do the King's bidding in guarding Ship Rock. Surely you talk with him?"

The selkies exchanged glances among themselves and studied the rock shelf they sat upon. None seemed eager to meet Dalin's eyes. Finally Ervir spoke. "No, we do not, bear-kin. It is a shameful tale. Men have a partial recounting of it, but the full history we do not share with land-dwellers."

"I'm not an ordinary land-dweller," Dalin ventured. That much was evident, he had to admit even to himself.

Ervir sighed. "No, that is true."

The silence stretched between them as Ferik shifted to man-shape and climbed out of the water, joining the others on the rock. "He has the shape-gift. Maybe he should be told. It is a cautionary tale."

The others spoke among themselves in the tongue of the selkies for a time, with glances at Dalin and not a few head shakes to the contrary. At last Ervir turned back to their guest. "I will tell you, manling. But it is nothing for passing on to others. Do we have your oath on that?"

"Yes."

Ervir sighed and collected his thoughts. "You know of Prince Graumnir?"

"The son of Fris and the lord of the selkies? Of course I've heard stories."

"Perhaps you do not know that selkie families are close, and close-knit with others. There is a wide net of kinship and ties of familial obligation that bind all selkies together. When we meet a person, we are less inclined to ask his name than to ask who his kin-father is, and who the birth-mother, and who the heart-brother. . . . How we connect with one another is very important to us. You understand?"

Dalin thought of his own kinship ties in Nevi. It sounded like the selkies had relationships far more complex, but the principle of it was clear. He nodded and Ervir continued.

"Graumnir came of age among a great extended clan of seal-folk in the Selvien Ulloya. He grew up, naturally, as one more link in this vast kinship web. When he went to land he lived among animal-folk for a time, and then returned to the humans here, who dwell so close to his birth-kin. His absence had been felt like a wound in the heart of those who held him dear. When he was near again, it was only natural that his kinfolk would seek him out, to renew their close bond with Lord Egior's son.

"We expected he would come back to us, you see. No one leaves for long, very rarely for a lifetime. There are now and then those who take a human lover or fall in love with an air-breather and live among the land-dwellers for a while. Eventually the human dies, and the selkie returns home, for we are longer-lived than mankind. When Graumnir refused to re-join us in the Isles, we thought it was something of this nature, that he had attractions that held him for a short time on the land. When his infatuation died, or his love did, he would return to us.

"We did not realize that the Prince felt strong allegiance to the affairs of men, that he had, in effect, taken on his distant human kin-connections in Etjorvi—through the affiliation of his divine mother—as ties as binding as those from under the sea."

The selkies shifted uncomfortably around Dalin. Ervir continued to talk but looked to the ground instead of the youth.

"Graumnir had a half brother, whose name is now shunned. He was the son of Egior and what you would call a 'mistress' from a time before the Selkie Lord had met the goddess Fris. That brother was jealous of the place Graumnir held in his father's affections. When he refused to return to us and stayed in Etjorvi, the brother spoke ill of him.

"Later, Graumnir married Elfrith and sired Asmund, the first of the Selkie Kings. The brother believed that that was sufficient occupation for one selkie's dalliance on land, that Graumnir stayed away yet longer merely to spite our custom and provoke his father. Many selkie folk were active in Graumnir's court at that time and had much to do with human affairs. Their opinions were divided, but many agreed with the brother. They urged Egior's son to leave the air-breathing world. He insisted he was in love with Elfrith, and would stay.

"His brother saw this would keep him a lifelong time away from our realm. He took it upon himself to kill Elfrith, so that Graumnir would no longer have the distraction of a human lover to bind him to the land."

Ervir finally met Dalin's eyes. "Many of our people agreed with this plan, and helped the brother slay Graumnir's love. To their dismay, he did not come home to heal his broken heart and rejoin his family. Instead, he begged the Sea Father to judge this action, and Lan Loros did. We have been forbid-den contact with the Selkie Kings from that day forth. We do not tread on dry land in or near Etjorvi. We do not speak to the King. We are enjoined from mingling in his affairs, directly or indirectly, for it has been judged un-wise for folk of one form to mix overmuch in the affairs of a different breed. We guard Ship Rock, not at the King's behest, but at the order of the Sea Fa-ther, who guards his interests."

The grotto was silent, but for the susurrus of wave on rock.

"I see." Dalin considered what he had heard. "He's called the Selkie King. Does he not have more to do with you than a name?"

"Egior's full-blooded descendants are the lords of the selkie folk. Hammankarl bears his name because he is of selkie descent, not because he rules us."

Dalin pondered that. "Will you not ever be close again to your kinsman?"

"We have tried to show our remorse and goodwill over the years, but forbidden contact as we are, it is difficult to demonstrate that our attitudes have changed. That we would be friends but not try to influence the actions of our kinsman." Ervir sounded sad. "Perhaps that will change one day. If he wishes to rejoin our kin ties, the invitation must come from the Selkie King to us. Thus far, none of his line have seemed anxious for our interference in their lives and loves. We stay away."

"Don't you wish to help him, though? He's in danger."

Ervir shrugged, resigned. "We can neither help nor hinder."

"So you won't help me."

"I can't imagine what we could do to help you. We are already perhaps in difficulties: we have taken you from Ship Rock, and that is forbidden as well."

Ferik coughed. "Maybe not. We are to keep what awaits the King's justice. He won't await justice if he's dead. If we return him when it's safe, all should be well enough."

The other selkies murmured agreement. Dalin didn't like this turn of conversation in the least. Then a bold thought came to him.

Never had they said they did not desire to help the King. It was that they were prevented from doing so. Oath? Divine magic? No matter; they clearly felt constrained. But just as he had developed that knack of sensing feelings around him, Dalin knew that their hearts were good and they were not as uncaring about Hammankarl's fate and endangerment as their words alone made it sound.

"Even if you can't help the King," he ventured, "I can. I want to, before it's too late. Let me get word to him, warn him. Then . . . I'll return to you, and you can put me back on the Rock. You will have kept faith with your orders and not helped the King yourselves. I will."

A stillness came over the gathered selkies; every eye regarded Dalin. It was as if he had suddenly appeared in their midst, taken them by surprise, and they paused in that moment of sudden danger. There was an alertness about them that had not been there a moment before.

"We do not trust men to keep their word," one of the selkies said.

"He is not an ordinary human," Ervir mused. "Feel the essence of him."

"He'll keep his word." It was Ferik, speaking with certainty. His confidence surprised Dalin; maybe it was the animal-nature that let him sense such a thing so unequivocally—in the same way a dog could tell a nice person from an ill-natured one. Ferik's opinion was right, of course: Dalin would keep his word, even if it put him back in danger. It was the only right thing to do, did the selkies help him at their own risk.

And how far might they be willing to risk for him, a fellow shape-shifter?

"I cannot just walk into the Palace and give warning. I'm an escaped prisoner and already disbelieved. Unless you have some way to help sneak me in . . . ?

Ervir shook his head.

"Then I fear that the Nimmians will reach the King before I can warn him."

"A reasonable concern," the selkie said neutrally. "And a likelihood. What would you do about it?"

Dalin chewed his lip. He could not ask for overt help touching on the King. Maybe against his enemies—?

"If I had help, I could stop the Nimmians from reaching the King at Greenstone. Their mission would be betrayed. . . ." Ferik and Ervir shook their heads together, and Dalin's voice trailed off. No. That would indirectly help the King.

What else was there to try? A tactic that had nothing to do directly with the King, *or* the Nimmians. . . .

He looked up sharply. "My elvish friends have sworn to help me find justice for the Truthsayer's death. If they were with me, we could approach the King at Greenstone together. . . ." He did not need to say any more; the hidden logic was obvious to all. He would be about his own business. It was merely incidental that a hazard to the King might present itself at the same time. And Dalin's request had nothing to do with the selkies helping or hindering the King. It had to do with them helping himself.

"We do not ordinarily help men in such a way. . . ."

Dalin sensed Ferik's reluctance "I'm bear-kin. And I vow to return to your custody, after I've put my case before the King."

Ervir's eyes shone brightly, and the Truthsayer's apprentice sensed the subdued excitement in the selkie. "We might come to terms with you on that proposal, brother. There is one problem, though. Your elvish friends are nowhere near."

"I saw them after my arrest. They must be in the Keep."

Ervir shook his head. "They are far out upon the Sea of Lan Loros, on their way to their homeland."

Dalin's heart dropped. He thought he was so clever, thinking of this way to stymie the runemaster, to prove to the King his trustworthiness, to halt a terrible plot—and all of it come to naught if he must try it by himself. Alone, what chance had he against his enemies or to win through to the King?

He looked dejectedly at the damp rock beneath him.

Ferik's seal-bark of laughter made him jump. "Yet knowing where they are, it is easy enough to persuade them to return."

"How?" asked Dalin hopefully.   .

"We are not the faithful children of the Sea Father for nothing, bear-kin." His eyes glistened brightly, and the other selkies laughed at the confusion on Dalin's face. "You will see."

THE *TALON* SAILED out of twilight into star-filled night, the mountainous coast of Tura-kem no longer even a smudge of darkness on the horizon behind her. Her square yellow sail bellied with the prevailing wind, saving her oarsmen from the labor of rowing her ahead. They had labored long and steadily already, seeing her clear of the twisted channels and treacherous currents of the Selvien Ulloya. Once free of that labyrinth of waterways, the *Talon* had raised sail and made steady way across the Sea of Lan Loros, bound for Nimm.

Captain Torsjak stood by his helmsman. The day had been long and uneventful, the prisoners despondent, the seaway clear. He was setting the night watch when the wind died without warning and the sail went slack.

Torsjak scanned the sky. It remained clear, cloudless, and the dark sheet of water before them looked no different than before. He looked aloft. "What ho?" he called to the crow's nest watch.

"Nothing in sight, sir," the sailor called down to him, though he continued to scan the horizon roundabout.

"What do you think, Hafnar?" the captain asked his grizzled helmsman, but that experienced sailor shook his head. Abrupt calm in these waters was unheard of, and they both knew it.

"Sir!" called the lookout. "Something comes!"

The man's arm was flung out, pointing directly aft. All eyes turned to look that way.

Out of the last of the sunset gloaming, a small luminescence came winging. The eye suggested the form of a seagull, but it moved more swiftly than any earthly bird. As it drew near, Trosjak sucked in his breath.

Its form was of light.

The unearthly creature neared the *Talon*. Crew murmured and made warding signs; some uttered prayers to Lan Loros, of whose symbols the gull was one. The apparition circled the ship once, twice—then settled atop the rudder post.

Hafnar abandoned the tiller and scuttled clear. The ship had no steerage anyway: she had lost her headway, and the air was breathlessly still. Torsjak took a step or two back as well and set hand to sword. He was not willing to be chased from his own deck and rightful station by the advent of a spirit-bird, no matter how unearthly. He'd sacrificed to Lan Loros only yesterday, on the full moon—surely the Sea Father would protect him. . . .

The bird of light cocked its head at Torsjak. The man knew something unearthly looked at him out of the infinite black hole where its eye should be. The phantasm's beak opened.

"Return to land, my son," it said.

He heard the voice not in his ears, but in his head. He let go his sword and collapsed to his knees in a gesture of obeisance.

"Now is not the time to take this ship from Tura-kem. Free your prisoners ashore where I will lead you to land."

"I-I . . . ," Torsjak stammered uncertainly. Was this a sending from the Sea Father? Or an apparition, a hoax? He had seen omens and signs of the lord of the sea's presence in his many years at sea, but never had his orders been interfered with, nor had divinity spoken so directly. He was not sure what to believe.

"Believe," said the bird. "You know in your heart." Its head turned and looked landward over its shoulder. "Do you try to proceed, a storm will blow you back. Easier to follow me now. And swifter. I will bring a wind at your back."

Torsjak snapped his mouth shut. If Lan Loros wanted to send a wind counter to the prevailing one to blow him that much more swiftly back to Tura-kem, then the Hound's written orders to him were in this moment so much tinder.

"Aye, Lord," he said, bowing his head.

"Then come about," said the supernatural messenger, "and follow."

The bird of light swept skyward. The tiller post smoked where it had stood. It circled the ship twice more, then led back west, the way they had just come.

A breeze sprang up from the east. "Out oars!" Torsjak yelled at his stupefied crew. "Full about!"

When the dragon ship pointed west, the breeze strengthened into a steady wind and pushed the vessel homeward behind the sending of a god.

CHAPTER 77

THE HEADLAND ROLLED into the ocean in pillows of layered stone, broken and crumbling down and out until the bottom most protrusions formed tidepools and shoals at low tide. One flat spit of stone a bowshot long flanked the tidepools; it pointed eastward like a finger into the great sea, dropping off abruptly into the salt water at its far end.

At sea level that rock was draped with seaweed and algae. On the headland behind the spit, lichenous growth covered the stone in shades of green and gray, fed by the salt spray and the sun and the slowly decaying rock it rooted upon. To the north a cliff face dropped sheer away to the water, where stone once fractured had been battered into the sea by pounding storm surf. To the south the native rock was cut by a watercourse that sheered the edge of the pillow-stone and rushed to the sea, spilling at last through an open eroded mouth into the tumbling backwash of an ocean inlet.

This was Greenstone.

For long years the priests of Lan Loros had come to this spit at low tide and walked out upon it to worship their god. They would halt at the farthest end from land, where they were surrounded by roiling ocean waters, churned to cloudiness in its depths, the spray washing the finger of land even at the lowest of tides. On this point so close to primal elements, they felt themselves, too, close to the Sea Father. It was a spot no more or less magical than any location scoured by wind and sea and wave, but it was hallowed through the custom and tradition of usage. There were other places more sacred to the worship of Lan Loros, but this one, a short ride from the capital, was the one frequented by the Selkie King, and so the one attended on this day by Olvar, High Priest of the Sea Father in Tura-kem.

Overlooking the spit on the highest point of the headland was an unlikely edifice that glittered brightly in the sun. It was the summer house that

Hammankarl's grandfather had caused to be built there, as well as that des-
ignation could fit such an exotic structure. The deserted stretch of
windswept coast had a stark and elemental beauty to it: cliffs and surf and
seagrass swept by the wind just two hours' ride from the city. Incongruously,
the summer house perched on the headland with all the unlikely grace of a
jewel-bright dragonfly: a rambling construct of iron rods painted and gilded
against the weather, closed in by panes of gypsum and glass, and a dome
made of triangular sheets of Koribi crystal. The dome had shattered twice in
torrential winter storms, until its substance was magically protected from the
elements. The whole was a conception of Petronius of Koribee, the poet-
philosopher and architect who later went mad from his experiments with
lead and quicksilver. He died trying to climb the spire atop the Emperor's
palace in his homeland.

Hanno wondered if Petronius had not already been a little touched when
he oversaw construction of the summer house for the King of Tura-kem. It
was impossible for many people to live here, for there was no privacy, no
doors between the chambers: every room opened somehow into one or more
of its neighbors. It was as light and airy within as it looked from the outside.
Concessions to practical needs were found in the separate buildings that
housed the kitchen, the stables, a small lodging for servants and guards, all
built of native stone and blending that much more into the local terrain.

The fanciful building gleamed in the sun and was visible as a bright
point from far at sea. It was kept safe from intrusion by the stone fence flanking its distant inland perimeter, out of sight of the house itself. Anyone who
intruded by climbing over the stone boundary fence would trigger an alarm
spell that alerted gate guards to the intrusion—except for groundskeepers, of
course, who had the password that opened the servants' gate to the north.

It was the same password, Hanno knew, as that used to open the trade
gate at the White Palace. He had not been overzealous in any of his official
functions in these past few days as Riedskana, but phrases of access and entry were one of the things he had insisted the Steward share with him immediately. Not only did it underscore his right as High Councillor to have
access anywhere in the realm, but it was also in his nature to wish to know
such things. Who knew when he might need them for his own comings and
goings?

That he had been able to provide Joro with the password here had
greatly simplified his task this day. Now he watched Olvar out upon the spit
of land, preparing a simple altar upon heaped stones at ocean's edge. He
looked to the sun overhead. It was an hour before noon. Queen Elfried was
overseeing two serving women putting together a light repast in the summer
house, refreshment for after the ritual. Hammankarl was changing his

clothes in a chamber draped for privacy, readying himself for his watery communion with the Sea Father. The King's Hand was nowhere near, the Hounds had been left on guard duty at the roadside gate to the retreat. On this occasion, Hammankarl wished to surround himself only with nature, beautiful surroundings, and pious reflection—not the martial distraction of his war band.

Hanno had known it would be so. It was always so, every year the King performed this ceremony, and he had counted on that when advising Joro when best to make his move. It would not be wise to interrupt the ritual of bonding itself: Hammankarl reaffirmed his divine blood-ties to Lan Loros at that time and thanked the Sea Father for his beneficence in the coastal life of Tura-kem. It would be foolhardy to interrupt such a significant ceremony with the ruling descendent of a god.

Nor was it any wiser to slay the King after the renewal of his bond, for surely then the country's monarch would be that much more strongly under the attention of one of his patron deities.

No. There was only one appropriate time to deal with Hammankarl: before he began this ceremony at all. Before Olvar could invoke the Sea Father and bring the god's attention close to this isolated finger of land, while Hammankarl was distracted by putting himself in an introspective state prior to his commitment ceremony . . . that was the time.

Hanno glanced to the north. No sign of the Nimmians—though if they were doing their job properly, they would not be noticed until the last possible moment. The only persons here were the King and the Queen; Hanno, Rurik—the most senior of the Lords Adviser—and Wulfram Runemaster as witnesses, and a few servants. And Olvar, of course, an elderly man in robes of white and blue-gray, on the finger of land beyond the tidepools.

Within an hour it would be noon, and then the ceremony would begin. Hanno had the Tapestry with him, of course, in the marvelous pouch that had also been taken from Dalin. The lie about it being in the treasure-house was a fabric that had served the moment, to dissuade Joro from taking him hostage. The Robe had been in his possession since the boy's arrest, for he had taken it into "safekeeping" at the first opportunity. He begrudged giving it up—but his own late-night experiments with it had shown that he, like the boy, could evoke no special powers from the weaving. Let them have it. They could kill the King and steal booty—including the Robe—and then be gone. He would not be filling the vacancy of Truthsayer under his Regency anyway.

Finally he could no longer contain his nervousness. The runemaster walked out of the summer house and toward the sea cliff, to watch the spray of surf and billow of wave on the bright sea. To the onlooking eye he seemed composed and lost in meditation; and so he was, as he awaited the outcry of attack behind him.

ON THE STRAND far beneath Hanno's feet, tight in against the cliff face, Dalin crept quietly by. Behind him came Thengel and all the rest, moving stealthily, all bound for the distinctive Greenstone pillow-rock a stone's throw ahead.

Not an hour before, they had joined forces where the *Talon* had beached in gravelly shallows. Dalin was past the point of surprise at something so un-expected after his all-night journey with selkies, the lot of them towed by fast-swimming dolphins through the dark waters of the northern coast.

Captain Torsjak had little to say to his erstwhile prisoners; he seemed anxious to have them off his ship and unchained them and set them ashore so fast they hardly realized the reversal in their fortunes until they saw Dalin. As the elves gathered around him, Ervir and Ferik walked past in man-form and into the surf.

"We wish you well presenting your case to the King," Evir called to Dalin. Then the pair turned to seal-form and swam out into the waves.

"Presenting your case to the King?" Thengel echoed dubiously. He looked from Dalin, to selkies, to the ship that was backing water and edging out to sea once more. "Do you care to offer a word of explanation, or must we guess why our gaoler no longer desires our company?"

Dalin grinned at him, at the others, even more widely at Katrije. "I need your help," he began. "Remember that you promised to help me avenge Granmar's death? Now is your chance—and more."

They talked as they walked along the coast. Ervir had told Dalin the headland's distinctive landmarks and headed for that place now. "But I don't know how much time we have," he explained. "At least we can talk to the king before he begins his ritual."

The opportunity Dalin had orchestrated was not lost on Thengel. Here was their chance to redeem themselves and untangle the knot they'd gotten themselves into. After some grumbled discussion started by a recalcitrant dwarf, the others supported the notion as well. Now the band saw the Greenstone headland and prepared to intrude in the royal sanctuary.

Dalin grimaced at the thought. It was not the way he would like to ap-proach his King, but he was as good as dead if he did not get Hammankarl's ear personally and a chance to set forth the truth. The King had been sorely misled by the traitor he harbored. He must be made to see that, and if the only way to do so was to be forceful about it, well, they would be no more rude than they must be.

"Go softly," Thengel said behind Dalin. "Look. On the spit."

Dalin, intent on the gently shelving green rock ahead of him, glanced out past the tidepools and froze in midstride. An elderly man, hair white and braided back, with strands blown loose in the sea breeze, worked with his back to them. He wore robes of gray-blue and white. What he worked on was hidden from their view. At the far end of the spit he could not possibly hear them crunching across the gravel, but if he turned and looked shoreward, he would be staring right at them.

The youth hissed back over his shoulder, "Let's be swift. If that's the King's priest, he can only be very powerful. We don't want him to notice us."

"My thoughts as well," Thengel agreed.

Dalin picked up the pace and soon set foot on the Greenstone rocks. Clambering up and up, he was torn about where to train his eyes. He had to judge each next step on the sometimes-slippery lichen; he wanted to look out upon the spit but did not dare, lest his attention draw the old man's gaze around. Now and then he glanced up to the headland they were ascending toward, where he saw the top of the high dome glittering in the sun. . . .

And saw a thing that flashed like extra-bright sunlight spearing into his eyes, his ears buffeted by the crack of thunder in the next moment. A sound he remembered too well from Ragnar's ship.

"We're too late!" he cried over his shoulder, and began to sprint.

CHAPTER 78

Hanno had expected sharp-spoken challenges, the sound of swordplay, the cries of frightened women or angry men. Instead he felt a blast of power that made his shoulders tighten up near his ears at the same instant he was blasted with the furious sound of thunder. It was followed by the screams of horses and the rumble of collapsing stone.

Kaylis and her elemental magic.

He cursed and spun about. The Nimmians flanked one side of the translucent-walled residence, and the white-clad woman was foremost among them. She must have spied the King inside through one of the glass panes, thought to drop him instantly and have done with it.

The bolt of lightning had refracted, of course, deflected by the enchantments that protected the building from weather elements and storms. The bolt she had cast had sheered off and gone to ground in the stables among the service buildings.

Kaylis was swearing, too, brandishing her staff as if preparing to call down more lightning.

"No!" Hanno shouted and began to run toward her.

Joro shouted something at her as well. Then he and the others were running past the mage and into the summer house, for the inhabitants had been alerted to their danger now and surprise was lost.

It was a sorry collection within: a few women, a junior runemaster, Rurik, a retired soldier with old warwounds that limited his activity—and the King. They had to get the King.

Hanno realized that his headlong dash would look as if he were coming to help. At no time did he want anyone to see him aiding the enemy, not if it could be avoided. When this was done, there should be at least one witness left who could testify that it was these escaped criminals who had taken vengeance on the King and Hanno had tried fruitlessly, along with the others, to stop them.

He shunned the house where slaughter was about to commence and headed for Kaylis instead.

UP FROM GREENROCK and onto the headland behind him came Dalin, followed by Thengel and all his band. Dalin knew the King was in danger, but in that moment the only person he saw in the open and near was Hanno, running away from him. *Fleeing?* The thought darted through his mind. *Oh, no, you don't. . . . !* And Dalin chased hot on the heels of the runemaster.

HANNO ROUNDED THE edge of the house, came near to Kaylis. He heard her chanting. "No!" he cried, "it's bespelled!" And then he let his momentum carry him into her. He knew that spell-casting could be disrupted by something—or someone—jarring the concentration of the mage. He could not leave it to her whim, whether or not she would obey him: another stray lightning bolt could as well leave *him* dead as any other.

They collided; she staggered to one side and lost the thread of the incantation she had been speaking. *"Daru!"* she cursed, and rounded on him with her staff.

It caught him on the shoulder as he dodged aside and nearly broke his collarbone. The pain dropped him to his knees, but before his fury could ignite he saw what was running toward him.

Dalin. Thengel. A handful of elves. Children and the bard from court and a cloaked figure at Greenstone's edge. The dwarf, pounding straight for the summer house, vanishing through a side entrance as he looked on—

"Koram!" he uttered. This would not do at all. His fingers went to the pouch at his belt and the supply of rune stones he carried there.

DALIN SLOWED. THE runemaster was reaching into his pouch while Kaylis raised her staff and pointed at him with her free hand. A baleful glare was on her face, and she was chanting something.

Stop? Dodge? Hide in the house?

Then he heard the clash of swords carried on the air and the curses of men, fighting. His friends were within, engaging the Nimmians. If they could charge boldly ahead, so could he—

—and do what? Throw his slender self at the older, heavier man? Let the mage blast him with a spell? He did not think the concerns consciously; some deeper part of him knew his hazard, knew he needed to be a greater threat or needed greater protection.

A primal, instinctive part of him knew this.

Without thinking how, without knowing his need in his conscious mind, Dalin changed.

A brown bear hurtled himself upon the runemaster. The transformation took even Kaylis by surprise; she could not move aside fast enough. The bear's charge slammed the runemaster to the ground and barreled into the elf with the force of one shoulder.

Kaylis staggered back and fell to the ground, whatever spell she had been preparing lost in that moment of confusion. The rune stone Hanno clutched in his hand was slapped away by a batting bear paw. The man screamed in pain. The bear bawled in anger.

Kaylis scrambled clear.

CHAPTER 79

OUT UPON THE spit of land, the sounds of chaos and hostile magic came to Olvar's ears. He spun about. A cluster of persons at the top of the Greenstone rocks, a struggle at the edge of the summer house—he was far enough out from shore that he could see a bit of what transpired on the highland.

He was never spry or fast, even in his youth. He could not reach the scene quickly, nor could he see exactly what was wrong—but the High Priest of Lan Loros did not need that luxury, not when danger threatened the Selkie King.

Olvar dropped the clamshell he had been setting on the altar, raised both arms high, palms outstretched, and began a prayer.

JORO KNEW THAT if it came to a fight, Redeemer would carry the day for them. Aral, the best swordsman among them, wielded the holy blade. He struck down one screaming woman servant who came in his way, then cut his way through another. The Queen put herself between him and a curtained chamber where the King prepared himself. How perfect. This was a religious retreat for Hammankarl; he would be weaponless. To Joro's side, two courtiers engaged Berin and Rudic, took wounds, fell back—

And then, somehow, it all went wrong.

The holy aura around Redeemer began to change, going swiftly from illuminating glow to sullen radiance. The Queen retreated as Yellowbeard strode upon her, raising the sword over his shoulder—then his arm twisted suddenly and the warrior gave a pain-strangled cry. His hand opened and he shook his arm, letting the weapon drop from his grip.

The blade glowed cherry red, and the smell of heated metal filled the air. The slate flagstones it fell upon cracked from the furnace heat of the enchanted weapon.

There was no mistaking the hostile magic, but there was no time to do anything about it. New swords had entered the fray: the elves, those hated elves who showed up to thwart him at every turn. They drove Rudic and Berin back. Aral was injured. They had not made it to the King—

—but there, on a side table: the red-and-black pouch Joro had bought from a Koribi merchant. If Hanno had told truth, the Tapestry was within it.

The Nightrunner darted past the side table, grabbed up the pouch, ordered retreat. His people fell back, out the open archways they had entered through, but the elves were in close pursuit and would not leave them be. They fought a retreat, and here came the tallest elf right after him, with angry intent in his eyes. Behind him, a blue-cloaked figure gestured from a doorway.

Thengel hit him with a flurry of hard, fierce blows. The elf sliced him on the ribs and nicked him in the shoulder—this was the one he had kept at bay before only with the aid of a shield, and now Joro had no shield.

The elf batted Joro's sword aside and cut him on the wrist—the wrist of the hand holding the pouch.

The bag dropped from nerveless fingers, and Joro howled in anger. His hand was numb. He wanted to close with his enemy and kill him, but Thengel's longsword and his excessive reach pushed Joro back and back some more. The elf snagged the Koribi pouch off the ground with one quick long-armed swipe. Joro glanced to his comrades.

They were falling back. Berin dropped the broadsword he'd had from Aral, turned his back, and fled.

The others followed suit.

ONLY KATRIJE NOTICED the waterspout at first.

She and the adenye hung back with Valdarius, on Thengel's strict command. She heard the words of a prayer on the wind, saw the priest with arms on high—noticed whitecaps beyond where there had been none moments before. The breeze stiffened; as she watched, spray from the whitecaps got caught up in a circling wind. That wind blew stronger and harder with every passing breath, until water was being sucked up wholesale from the surface of the sea, building a waterspout that twisted and turned and grew rapidly bigger as she watched.

Jawle noticed her staring, tugged Udo's tunic, and pointed. Soon they were all watching the thing the priest of Lan Loros had summoned. No more was it a tiny devilment dancing lightly above the water: it was become a gargantuan swirling monstrosity that towered above the height of the shore cliffs.

The breeze had become a gale-force wind. Hair whipped around Katrije's eyes, and clothes were tugged towards the ravenous wind that fed the waterspout. Then, as they watched, the twisting column of water curved and coiled, leaned shoreward, and dashed toward land.

THENGEL WATCHED THEIR enemies rout before them. While they were looking over their shoulders to see if they were pursued, however, the Guardian saw what they were running toward. "Hold!" he ordered his people, and Arandel and Nalia slowed, and Hagar stopped. Belec gasped for breath beside him.

"A summoning," he panted, one cleric recognizing the work of another.

The waterspout sped toward them as if it would jump the cliff and wreak havoc among them all. The Nimmians ran from the scene of their defeat, not directly toward the hazard, but fighting the winds that wanted to pull them that way, they headed north, paralleling the shore. All five of them fled, stumbling against the gale-force draught that threatened to knock them down and drag them across the ground. Even the elves were hard put to keep their feet, bracing against each other, backing toward the residence behind them where a magical calm reigned against the elements, getting soaked where they stood by the spray cast loose from the storm funnel overhead.

The broad, swirling top of the watery tornado spun faster and faster, wider than the column that supported it. Stones and dirt and clumps of seagrass were sucked fiercely up into it. It battered the edge of the cliff, then dipped low to the ground. The lip of the water funnel scoured the ground along the headland . . . and when it rose again the Nimmians who had been fleeing there were gone.

The elemental wind shifted direction and moved out to sea. Out it went and farther still, diminishing slowly in size until the observers could not tell if it had vanished in the distance or shrunk down to nothing.

The cliff top was bare.

Closer in, a seawater-drenched bear squawled on top of a man.

"I think we'd better have a look," said Thengel.

CHAPTER 80

THEY SAT WITH Hammankarl and Elfried in the palace breakfast chamber. Thengel's party were guests; the man so briefly High Councillor was bound and held under close guard, left kneeling on cold flagstones nearby. Dalin sat to the King's right, where he could look easily from the Selkie King to the runemaster who was his prisoner.

"Nehvros's spell shows that Hanno tells the truth," the King said dryly. "His actions appeared innocent. But his truth and your truth cannot both be correct. You say you have a solution for me?"

"If you'll let me talk with him a bit, Your Majesty," Dalin affirmed, "I think I can discover more than he really wants to tell you."

Hammankarl waved a hand. "Please. Be my guest."

Dalin rubbed his hands through his hair and then leaned forward on his elbows, staring at the runemaster intently. *I can do this,* he reassured himself. *Just like I've been doing it all along. . . .*

"Why does it seem like you speak the truth when you are lying?" he asked.

The runemaster clenched his jaw and said nothing.

"Hanno," interrupted the King, "for the sake of our past friendship I will give you a caution. Answer his questions as you would my own, or we shall ask them again in less pleasant circumstances."

Dalin looked sidelong at Hammarnkarl. Brutal methods of questioning were not the standard in Tura-kem, but like all rulers, somewhere the King had an executioner, and the tools of the trade that went with his profession as well.

Hanno seemed to get the same hint. The runemaster met Dalin's eyes, and the youth cocked his head, listening to the energies that came behind that righteous glower. *He's trying to intimidate me . . .*

Dalin smiled full at the runemaster and felt the man's twinge of consternation. Then he questioned him again.

"Why does it seem like you speak the truth?"

"Because I *am* speaking the truth."

False, Dalin smiled to himself. There. He felt that in his gut.

"Have you done something to yourself magically?" That was more than a logical guess; it was a niggling of intuition.

"Of course not." *False.*

"Would that be rune magic?"

"You're babbling," Hanno sneered.

Hm. Uncertain. "What kind of rune are you using?" That was a blind probe, yet it couldn't hurt to try.

"I'm not using a rune." *False.*

Dalin nodded to himself. "I thought most runes have a short effect. Is that so?"

"For most, yes, that's so." *True.*

Dalin considered what he had just gleaned. It was like a game of twenty questions with yes/no answers, only Hanno had no idea what affirmations he was giving away with his answers. It wasn't hard, once he got the hang of it.

"He is under the effect of rune magic," he confirmed to the King. "It'll wear off soon."

"How can you say that?!" the runemaster protested. He sounded righteously angry, the falsely accused man. Dalin sensed how the others heard that in his voice, as if it were utter truth. Hanno continued in his righteous anger. "A rune effect doesn't linger for days unless you have a rune about your person *[false]* and I have none *[false]*! Sire, why are you listening to this malicious puppy?"

Hammankarl raised an eyebrow to Dalin. "Why *am* I listening to you?"

Dalin thought fast. "Has he been stripped and searched, Majesty? To see if he has anything magical about him?"

"Yes."

Dalin squinted at the runemaster, speaking to the real truth that he sensed behind the man's lies. "Then, is it . . hidden?"

"No," he denied. *False.*

"Where is it?"

"I have nothing on me," the man insisted. *True.*

Hidden Dalin thought, *but not on him. . . .*

"Is it inside you?"

"Of course not! *[False.]* Your Majesty, please. . . !"

Dalin laughed and clapped his hands. "Sire, I do believe he's . . . swallowed it! There is a rune about him, and it's inside him, not on him. I think if you give him a few days' time . . . the truth will come out in the end."

A few snickers greeted that remark, and Jaele giggled outright. But Hammankarl only had eyes for his runemaster, who had gone a pasty shade of white.

"How . . . how did you . . . ?"

"How did I know?" The tiniest smile creased Dalin's lips. "I'm Granmar's heir, now that he's gone."

Hammankarl gestured from his chair. "Speaking of gone"—he gestured to the Hounds who stood guard there—"make this one be gone for now. We'll come back to him in a few days and see what color of truth he tells then."

When the shaken Hanno was taken from the room, the King faced Dalin. "I'll wait, of course, so Nehvros's reading makes it official. From his look and his words, though, I know the truth already. I owe you an apology, Truthsayer. Will you accept it?"

His words sank in slowly; then Dalin stammered before he could answer. "S-sire! No need for apologies! I-I—"

Hammankarl silenced him with a gesture. "We got off on the wrong foot, Dalin Truthsayer, but I hope we can remedy that." He crooked a finger at a guard, who brought forward a red-and-black pouch. "You had this once; it comes back to you again. To judge from your demonstration, you do not need it to perform your office. But it is your inheritance, and it is yours to do with as you will, Truthsayer."

Dalin's eyes moistened. "Thank you, Sire."

Hammankarl gave him a smile. "You must excuse me now. I have business with Olvar and a new ritual to plan for the one I missed. My love?"

He took Elfried's hand and the royal couple left the room. All around the table stood in respect as they departed, then sat again when the Hounds marched off behind the King and Queen.

Dalin looked at the pouch in his hands, and noticed that everyone else at the table was staring at it, too.

"Do you think you'd finally like to tell me why this is so important to you?"

His words caused Thengel to jump guiltily and tear his eyes from the magical bag that held the weaving. He inclined his head. "I will, young Truthsayer. It is a long story, but I will make it short.

"Our homeland is being overrun by creatures, not manlike but intelligent, who are fierce fighters and who outnumber us vastly. These are the gorska and the karzdag. They come and they keep coming. We fight them off, but every year we lose a settlement, or several, and our borders are shrinking, constantly shrinking. Caerlian now is half the size it was four years ago. We cannot hold out much longer. Another two years, perhaps—and we will be gone."

"Why do they want your land?"

"They don't. They want territory, to roam, and we are what they have roamed into. They threaten not only us but also much of southern Nimm, but the clansmen fight among themselves while their house burns down around them." He shrugged. "Their war we cannot fight for them. My interest is in saving Caerlian. To that end, this collector of lore and history, Valdarius, gave me hopeful news."

The bard leaned forward. "These people move into our territory because they are displaced from elsewhere. They come from Nithrais and beyond. They and many other folk are dispossessed and are refugees on the move. All are thrown into chaos by a holy war in Sharzan."

Dalin shrugged. Sharzan. A name he had never heard. "What has this to do with the Robe?"

"You've heard us call it the 'tapestry,'" Thengel resumed. "It was never intended to be a robe but was like a light carpet, you see. The Tapestry, a cup, and a brazier together are relics known as the Panoply of the Loregiver. One who holds all three can rule a land."

"You want this so you can rule a land?"

Valdarius shook his head. "The Panoply is sought in Sharzan, where it originated. That is the cause of the war that rages there, that has caused all this turmoil in neighboring lands. The Sharzani search and raid and annex neighboring lands, because all the while they are on a jihad for the Panoply of the Loregiver—long lost and thought stolen."

Thengel nodded enthusiastically. "We want to return the Panoply to Sharzan and stop the war. That in turn will put an end to this influx of people across our borders. You see?"

Dalin saw the idealism in Thengel's eyes. He saw the hope on the faces of the others. How they could even hope to find the rest of the relics they sought was beyond him, but he had heard the truth in their words and their vision. If good intentions could make the near-impossible happen, then they would succeed. But there was one thing yet that stuck in his craw.

"What did you hope to achieve by journeying to the Truthsayer?" he asked, watching Thengel's reaction very carefully. "If you weren't going to steal the Robe from him, how were you planning to get it? By telling him all this?"

"Exactly that. I was going to tell him this history and then ask him exactly what I ask you now." The Guardian of the Silverthorn paused, swallowed nervously. "Now you know our need for it. May we have the Tapestry?"

Dalin listened to that with all the talent so recently honed in him, and knew truth when he heard it. He breathed a sigh of relief. In that much the elves had had sincere intentions, and he was glad to be certain of it at last.

He regarded the magical pouch in his hands. "I don't need this to tell truth," he admitted. "I can do that by listening within myself and trusting what I hear, what I feel. Too, you helped me, just as you said you would, and you helped the King as well. It's the least I can do for you in return."

He pushed the pouch decisively toward Thengel.

The Guardian took it and gave a seated bow. "Thank you, Truthsayer, for your generosity. We shall honor you in Caerlian."

Katrije's response was far less demure. She leaned over and kissed him unchastely on the lips.

When they left the room, he was still bright red.

EPILOGUE

THENGEL STOOD AT the bow railing of the *Gull* gazing at the silky waters ahead. The early-morning wind had died, and Ragnar was urging his crew to a faster pace at the oars. Thengel appreciated the speed, but he did not fret if it would take them some days longer than planned. At least they were returning with the treasure they had set out to get.

Their leave-taking had been brief. They had waited to see Hanno executed on the New Moon after languishing for a brief time in new chains on Ship Rock. He was given a traitor's cremation in two separate fires, and special priestly magic was done so his angry ghost would not become a troublesome haunt.

He had used that time to good effect with Sembroie, as well. The warrior woman had done what she thought best to spare Thengel and still honor her duty. They had made their amends in private time spent together, and though their paths clearly did not lie together, if he ever returned to Etjorvi he had more than a friend awaiting him there.

That time was used by Dalin and Katrije to good effect also, it seemed—for their parting had been private and tearful, and Katrije now spent her time moping in the hold. Not knowing how to make it better, the Guardian of the Silverthorn had left it alone. He noticed, though, that Nalia spent a deal of time below decks, too.

If Katrije had had less time with the young Truthsayer—but no, they could not have left much earlier, anyway. It was hard enough to find any who would dare the Nimmian shore. Ragnar finally agreed but needed the time to put the *Gull* ship-shape again. The salvage from the Nimmian gear and horses left at Greenstone had paid him for those repairs. The balance of the monies Hammankarl had gifted to Thengel's party for their help thwarting the assassination attempt. They were returning to Caerlian rather better equipped than they had left it. The hold was full of their horses and other supplies, and various generosities from the King.

Rufslaenit, of course, they had left with Dalin, who swore he would not spend all his time inside the city walls. He had bear-folk he wished to become familiar with and selkie friends to visit. The selkies seemed a topic of great concern all of a sudden. Even Olvar, the priest of Lan Loros, had suggested to Hammankarl that it might be time to think of speaking with the seal-folk himself. The spirit-bird that had brought aid to a friend of the selkies and thus resulted in helping the King was not an omen to be ignored.

Hammankarl agreed to think about it, at least, and that, Thengel understood, was a promising development.

Hagar's heavy tread thumped on the decking, interrupting his thoughts as the dwarf joined him at the bow. "I have been through it all again," said his friend. "We do not have it."

Thengel's brows drew together. "It was part of the salvage given us by Hammankarl. You didn't forget to pack it, did you?"

"Mold rot for brains I am having, you think? I think not, overtall one." Hagar's downturned lips were nearly hidden by his unruly mustaches and beard, all overdue for rebraiding. He stared out to sea. "It was bundled with our equipment yesterday morning. Now we are halfway to Nimm, the sword is vanished."

Thengel chewed his lip. "It was bespelled. We could only handle it with Cathmar's tricks."

Hagar grunted. "Glad he chose to come. We can use him for forge work, he heats metal so well."

"Which is not so easily done to a holy sword," Thengel chided, "in the hand of a dedicant."

"No matter now. Tornor's sword is gone."

"As are Tornor's people," the Guardian mused.

"Perhaps," was all Hagar would say.

The pair studied the waters ahead as the sun rose before them.

APPENDIX

A. CHARACTERS

Minor characters are noted in the People appendix (C). Significant persons are noted here.

The Turakemi

> *Dalin*—Truthsayer's apprentice.
> *Hanno*—Runemaster.

The Elvish Party

> *Thengel na De'reth*—Guardian of the Silverthorn, leader of this party by ancient authority of rank. *Calianestu* elf.
> *Arandel na 'Torenth e Mithlond*—Silverleaf and Protector of the forest lands of Caerlian. *Calianestu* elf.
> *Belec Eil'fin*—Keeper of the Path, cleric of Onderye. *Calianestu* elf.
> *Nalia Mithlond*—thief and minor spellcaster. *Calianestu* elf.
> *Hagar Gemsinger*—dwarf from the Schoinevrik clan of Nimm.
> *Cathmar*—Liuthwë philosopher, mystic, and adept from Tren. *Derenestu* elf.
> *Valdarius*—Eldur, a bard trained in the Elduin tradition of Arilethne. Human/elvish parentage.
> *Udo Lefyan*—Turakemi youth in service as squire to Thengel.
> *Katrije Molinoes*—Turakemi girl in service as squire to Thengel.
> *Jaele*—Turakemi girl in service as page to Thengel.

The Nimmian Party

> *Joro "Swifthand" Narialnos*—member of the Nightrunner's League, appointed leader of this party by the Duke of Nimm. Of Nimmian/Koribi parentage.
>
> *Rudic Greycloak*—associate of the Nightrunner's League. Of human/elvish parentage.
>
> *Aral "Yellowbeard" Terilnor*—son of the chief of Clan Terbal, nephew of Nimm's warlord. Human parentage.
>
> *Berin Oathkeeper*—cleric dedicated to the demigod Vikkar Tornor. Human parentage.
>
> *Kaylis Rutherin*—elemental mage from the Collegium Magisterium. Of *derenestu* elvish descent.

B. LANGUAGE

Pronunciation

Turakemi and Nimmian languages share identical rules of pronunciation, although the Nimmian tongue is more clipped and faintly guttural, while Turakemi has longer vowels and is intoned with a mild lilt.

The letter j is pronounced like the letter y in English. Concluding vowels are pronounced, very lightly accented. Vowels are pronounced as follows:

Turakemi—English

a—ah
e—eh
i—ih, ee
o—o
u—u
ae—ay
ae—ay
oe—oy

Plurals are most commonly formed by terminating a word with ñ or ñya.

Titles and Honorifics

Turakemi	English	Meaning
Kronug	King	king

Jarl	Jarl	clan leader, city ruler, regional ruler
Thain	Thain	sept leader or town's ruler
Skana	Lord	general honorific meaning "lord"
Skan	Chieftain	settlement or sept leader; also "wise leader"
Skal	Headman	village elder
Riedskana	High Councillor	"Advice-Chief"; chief adviser and assistant governor to the King
Riedit	Lord Adviser	"Wise councillor"; adviser to the King
Daelbanit	Lord of the Exchequer	"Purse Keeper"; head of treasury and taxes
Balyaden	Commander or captain	"Battle Leader"; senior unit commanding rank

C. PEOPLE

Agnetha Thistlestump—matriarch of the Torvisk gnomes in Nimm.

Arlan—High Priest of Ardruna.

Arn—Duke, erratic and unpredictable ruler of Nimm.

Bjorg Palstro—commander of Etjorvi's garrison troops, especially those manning the fortress of Hakkonkalye.

Dalin of Nevi—young hunter who became apprentice to the Truth-sayer of Tura-kem.

Egior—Lord of the Selkies, who fathered Prince Graumnir and founded the line of Selkie Kings.

Einar—infant prince, one-year-old heir to the Throne of Turakem.

Elfried—Queen of Tura-kem, daughter of the Jarl of Vorsemye.

Ervir—selkie leader.

Esk'kek—green dragon slain by Thengel and his party in Kalajok.

Etjolf—duty mage in Sembroie Kinlayik's unit.

Ferik—selkie scout.

Fingol Fingholnor—a human sage much traveled in western Koristan, who had close ties with Elduin bards. His writings document the history of many obscure items of lore and legend.

Freggi—former High Councillor to the King.

Galan Vikkarnor—warchief of Nimm, chief of Clan Terbal, and nephew to the ruling Duke of Nimm.

Granmar Keljornik—the Truthsayer.

Gruithe—Jarl of Vaer.

Hafnar—helmsman aboard the *Talon*.

Hammankarl II—the Selkie King of Tura-kem.

Hanno of Havneis—runemaster, later adviser to the King.

Hounds of Hammankarl—the elite war band that performs special duties for the King; their official name is the King's Hand.

Ivar of Tesvi—headman of the village in Tesvi Cove.

Jarl of Fenvar—died on Ship Rock for treason.

Luell Half-Hand—second in command to Sembroie Kinlayik.

Molstroe—Captain-General of the King's Hand.

Nehvros Ulemos—royal mage and physician, a *dereneste* from Tren.

Olvar—High Priest of Lan Loros.

Olvek—hostler at the Golden Lamb.

Regmar—Jarl of Bjanlinik.

Sembroie Kinlayik—balyaden and unit commander in the King's Hand; an intimate of Thengel na' Dereth's.

Thoralf—innkeep at the Golden Lamb, where Thengel's party lodges for a time.

Torsjak—captain of the dragon ship *Talon*.

Torvin—headman of Eskrin steading.

Vernulf—Lord General, commander of the seasonal levies that constitute Tura-kem's army.

D. DEITIES

Alistana Windweaver—elvish goddess of weather and elementals.

Ardruna—goddess of earth, fertility, and growth, sister-mother of Fris.

Bragla—Death Crone, "She Who Waits"—keeper of Ruhnkeil, the underworld of the dead, and one who decides when souls are reborn.

Elsta—"Ice Mother"; icy sibling to fertile Ardruna, patron of snow, ice, and frozen wastelands.

Fadnor—were-bear and warrior-hero raised to demigodhood in the God Wars.

Fris—goddess of the hunt and wilderness lands, sister-daughter of Ardruna.

Gunnar Strongarm—demigod of battle.

Heimek—Father of Earth and Winter.

Kerias—divine warrior maidens who take the souls of the battlefield slain and escort them to the Death Crone's judgment in the halls of the dead in Ruhnkeil.

Koram—god of learning, wisdom, and the magic of runes.

Lan Loros—Sea Father; god of the sea and seafarers.

Leafwatcher—nickname for Everil Leafwatcher.

Meliors—god of healing and medicine.

Nalagar Thunderwalker—senior deity of the Turakemi pantheon, whose disputes with his brother Uric began the God Wars that devastated Tura-kem long ago.

Onderye Bowmaster—elvish god of archery, hunting, and providing plenty.

Seidrun—minor goddess, deity of lakes, rivers, and small waters and consort to Lan Loros. Worshipped only in Nimm.

Vikkar Tornor—once faithful human warlord, later demigod raised to service of Uric the Just. Worshipped only in Nimm.

Everil Leafwatcher—guardian and patron god of elvish woods and wildlife.

E. PLACE NAMES

Aelvoss—cold water river that runs through Etjorvi to the sea.

Ardrunalit—"Belly of Ardruna"; the fertile valley farmlands between Etjorvi and Heimik's Spine.

Arilethne—ancient homeland of elves, in the north central region of Koristan.

Avar River—channels' runoff from Eskavar glacier to the coast.

Bjalinik—fishing and trading port south of Etjorvi.

Bjaskoe River—drains to the sea at Vorsemy. Mostly navigable along Vorsemye Valley.

Brautilje—ruins of ancient city, haunted by dark shape-changing magic.

Caerlian—elvish settlement in southern Nimm centered around the holy melicanthus (silverthorn) grove. Name loosely translated means "grove home."

Cape Venstil—northernmost spur of Tura-kem, ice-locked for most of the year but open for passage to trading ships in high summer.

Crystal Spires—*see* Istvalmarye.

Dannenborch—Dannen's sound, the fjord that opens into Etjorvi's natural harbor.

Drakmil—sprawling island continent that begins on the equator south of Koribee and stretches far toward the southern polar continent. Homeland of the *karzdag*.

Ek Fenvar (the Westwall)—fortified escarpment, formed ancient battleline for last defense of the west in the God Wars.

Eskalja River—drains the Frislan through Rauvasla and to the sea at Skolji.

Eskavar—large glacier to the east and south of the Crystal Spires.

Eskrin—freehold near the foot of Eskavar glacier.

Fevrael—river that drains through Posbyalik.

Finskili—hamlet at one of the fords across the Ranulf River. Related to and allied with Eskrin steading.

Frain—village at the edge of Kalajok territory, marks entry to the caverns known as the Tol-Frain.

Frislan ("Fris's Lair")—vast, cold piney woodlands named for the goddess of the hunt and wilderness who is believed to live there.

Geff—a land on the far side of the Koreis, from which all manner of evil comes, a place living under a shadow of darkness. The place in which the Geffian knot originated.

Graumnirvang (Graumnir's Run)—name of the range once paced and patrolled by the hero Graumnir when marshaling the eastern defenses of Tura-kem during the God Wars.

Greenstone—the royal summer retreat on the Etjorvi coast where ceremonies dedicated to Lan Loros are performed.

Greywatch—Esromya, mountain chain to the south, homeland of dwarves in Tura-kem.

Hakkonkalye—Hakkon's Keep, the first great fortification of Etjorvi built by King Hakkon. Predominates the heights of Old Town.

Havneis—northeastern clan territory in Tura-kem.

Heimek's Spine—*see* Heimekvosk.

Heimekvosk (Heimek's Spine)—mountain chain southwest of Etjorvi, said to be the home of Heimek, god of mountains and winter.

Istania—trade partner with Koribee, lies on the southern continent beyond Drakmil.

Istvalmarye (the Crystal Spires)—volcanic peaks that lie at an angle to the Heimekvosk. Eskavar glacier starts in the Spires and abutts the Heimekvosk.

Janusk—inland trade center, transporting goods from the interior to Bjalinik.

Kalajok—southern jarldom and trade city.

Kodanit's Spire—the middle of the three most notable spindly peaks in the Crystal Spires range.

Koribee—far-flung trade and military empire dominating the south-eastern portion of the continent of Koristan. Koribee has broad influence along sea trade routes and on the neighboring island-continent of Drakmil to the south.

Koristan—the broad continent upon which Tura-kem is located; it lies almost completely north of the equator and stretches north of the Arctic Circle.

Nevi—northern clan territory in Tura-kem.

Nimm—the country west of the Sea of Lan Loros, once annexed by the Koribee Empire, now a neglected duchy left largely to home rule. Nimm has strong political ties to empire among the Koribee-favored governing clans and is Tura-kem's historical enemy.

Nimm-on-Witholl—the capital of the duchy of Nimm, located on the Witholl River in the far north of that land.

Posbyalik—port known for weaving, pottery, and handcrafted goods.

Ranulf—river that starts near Kodanit's Spire as a spring, is fed by Eskavar glacier, and flows to the sea at Vaer. Not navigable; rough, cold, and fast.

Rauvasla—cold northern inland trade town of huntsmen and woodsmen.

Sea of Lan Loros—the great sea nearly land-bounded, domain of the god of the sea.

Selvian Ulloya—the Selkie Isles.

Skolji—town that trades with ice tribes.

Taehanit—ruins of the ancient capital destroyed in the God Wars.

Telerian—largest settlement of the dominant Beruithwë clan of *calianestu* in Nimm.

Tesvi Cove—fishing village north of Vaer.

Tol-Frain—caverns that open into the Underrealms, west of Kalajok.

Tren—land at the southeastern border of Tura-kem, flanking the south of the Sea of Lan Loros.

Underrealms—not a specific place but the term for the interconnected network of caverns and civilizations that dwell far underground, beneath the land occupied by men.

Vaer—busy fishing town and shipping center on Vorsemya Bay.

Vengar Cove—secret moorage for official vessels near the Selkie Isles.

Vorhargen ("Greyfast")—dwarvish king's capital in the Greywatch Mountains.

Vorsemya Bay—rich bay named for clan that dominates fishing there and once manned raiding fleets.

Vorsemye—town that was original clan stronghold of the Vorsemya before the God Wars caused migrations. Still popular trade city and port.

Vossa ("great river")—river that connects trade from Janusk with the sea commerce at Bjalinik. Navigable.

F. DICTIONARY

Turakemi–English

[ ] contains plural form where notable

aden [~ye]—kids; lads, laddies; *Kinder;* affectionate familial younger person relationship term.

archich—magical mollusk created by the sea god Lan Loros, bestows the ability for an air-breather to exist comfortably underwater for a time.

askran—oven.

askru e vaes—"fire and light"; common toast or blessing.

denkorvic—tempel, high holy place.

e—and.

ehrden/~ye—Master.

eis—ice, glacier.

ek—the.

esro—gray.

estalje—form, figure, shape, substance.

fen—west; rune.

Fen Ehrden—runemaster. Specific title meaning senior rank of that profession.

ferenye—trade leagues(s).

furevar—a partnered dance performed in sets with a total of four couples, notable for the lively pace of the music it is danced to and the kicks and leaps involved. Based on a popular country dance.

haen—title.

haskran—tile oven, heating stove.

havn—harbor.

hemrik—mountains.

istva—silence, silent.

istval—crystal.

kaif—hot stimulant beverage imported from distant Istania.

kal—keep.

kala—clan-gathering place.

kalye—fortress.

kem—realm.

kennik/l—outcrop of rock surrounded by glacial ice. Place where crevasses form.

Koramnoiye—"Koram lore"; runic notation and writing.

koreis—"great ice"; glaciated areas in the far north of Tura-kem and Nimm, some of which run unbroken into the polar icecap.

mar—peak, spire.

Olmarferen—shipping union; drayer's trade and shipping league.

omye—guard, watch.

ro—dark.

Roishuvaesya—White Palace, residence of the Kings of Tura-kem in Etjorvi.

roja—black.

ruf—help.

Rufslaenit—helper-in-need.

Ruhnkeil—the Underworld of the dead.

selvie/nya—selkies.

skenjis—cursed totem made to ill-wish a victim.

slae—need, urgency.

staje—truth.

Staj'tanit—Truthsayer.

Svaenferen—wool trade union.

tak—not. Also, negation.

tak yelitstalje—"not-seeming"; false invisibility.

tan—speak, say, tell.

tanit—speaker, sayer.

te, eh—in.

tol—behind back of, under, to the rear.

tur—tree.

tura—forest, living woodlands.

ullo [ȳa]—island/s.

uvaes—white.

vaes—light.

var—wall.

vas—ten, multiple of ten.

vass, voss—water.

vosk—spine.

yelitstalje—seeming, projection, form.

Elvish

ailemar—Sarvin's Blight, a rare wasting disease that destroys elvish flesh much like leprosy attacks a human's.

briyu, briya—brother, sister, slang term used to address self or as affectionate diminutive to a friend.

caesca—dry.

caliane [a female ending]—a member of the *calianestu* subrace of elves.

calianestu—along with *derenestu* and *ethlianestu* one of the three dominant subraces of elvenkind in the continent of Koristan.

cuishe—mongrel puppy.

daru—pejorative term, implies subservient station to a *dereneste*.

derenestu—along with *calianestu* and *ethlianestu* one of the three dominant subraces of elvenkind in the continent of Koristan.

Elduin—elvish bards trained in diplomacy, song spells, and epic verse.

eldur—wise. As proper noun, refers to a bard of the Elduin tradition.

elia [ñ]—tree.

eliafin—settlement, housing/homes; literally, "tree-circle."

eliane—grove.

emloë—arcane script for magic studies.

fa—go.

fashe—bind.

gorska—large, sturdy, malicious nonhumans who roam in nomadic war bands.

karzdag—vicious dog-men that hunt in packs; descendants of the *karzdagi* stranded in Drakmil five centuries ago.

linae [š]—soft ankle-high suede boots, moccasinlike.

na—of.

naa—from, related to, usually contracted to *na'*.
neneile—freeze.
ni—off.
rusne—hold still, be motionless.
ye—me.

G. NOTES.

Bear Cub Scurries—one of many hunting postures drawn from animal behaviors or natural surrounds, a common tool used by Nevi hunters and by Dalin of Nevi.

Collegium Magisterium—institution for studies of highly disciplined arcane arts in Nimm, founded by Koribi mages when that country was first annexed.

Geffian knot—complexly woven knot that becomes tighter if struggled against. Extremely difficult to master; impossible for the untrained to untie. A not unusual sort of devilment from the land of Geff.

Gorvian's Treatise—a mystical herbal based on curatives from the Underrealms. It recommends courses of treatment for the rare but pernicious diseases and illnesses to which elves are prone.

Karzdag and *gorska*—sentient but unhuman peoples overrunning the southeastern reaches of Nimm. *Karzdagi* are the descendants of the beast-men chronicled in the memoirs of the sorceress Inya in her biography entitled *Kar Kalim*.

Kodanit—ancient mystic deposited in the Crystal Spires by fateful circumstances. He came bearing the Truthsayer's robe and was the first of that line of seers.

Liuthwē—a school of philosophy that creates mystics adept in metaphysics, both theoretical and practical. Their abilities seem arcane but do not stem from traditional magical disciplines or forces.

Lost Week—Dalin apologizes to Katrije for talking like a drunken runemaster during Lost Week. This period is the "time out of time" in the Koribi calendar, honored by all lands using that annual reckoning. Lost Week adjusts the day count in the annual calendar by inserting a short "week" of a varying number of days. This period comes between the last of the moon-calculated months and the start of the New Year. The veil between spheres is thin during Lost Week; it is a time when supernatural events are common and it is easy to pass between worlds and perform unusual magics.

Multiverse—it is common theological knowledge that the world is composed of seven spheres, the first being the physical sphere, the others extending invisibly through dimensional space beyond. These spheres overlap with an infinite number of others from other dimensions: the result is a complex multiverse of existence in which all things are possible. Esoteric understanding of this multiversal construct is the key to all "supernatural" workings in the world, whether magical, mystical, or divine.